Death in the Age of Steam

Mel Bradshaw

RENDEZVOUS
PRESS

Cover art: Edward Burne-Jones (British, 1833-1898), *Portrait of Caroline Fitzgerald*, 1884, oil on canvas, 32 1/2 x 20 1/2 in. (82.9 x 52.1 cm). Collection/courtesy of the University of Toronto, University of Toronto Art Centre. Photograph: Brenda Dereniuk, Art Gallery of Ontario.

Le Conseil des Arts du Canada depuis 1957 | The Canada Council for the Arts since 1957

Napoleon Publishing acknowledges the support of the Canada Council for our publishing program

We acknowledge the support of the Government of Ontario through the Ontario Media Development Corporation's Ontario Book Initiative

Published by RendezVous Press
a division of Transmedia Enterprises Inc.
Toronto, Ontario, Canada www.rendezvouspress.com

Printed in Canada

08 07 06 05 04 5 4 3 2 1

National Library of Canada Cataloguing in Publication

Bradshaw, Mel, 1947-
Death in the age of steam / Mel Bradshaw.

ISBN 1-894917-00-6

I. Title.

PS8553.R2315D43 2004 C813'.6 C2004-900042-X

For Carol Jackson, with all my love

Strange, and passing strange, that the relation between the two sexes, the passion of love in short, should not be taken into deeper consideration by our teachers and our legislators. People educate and legislate as if there were no such thing in the world; but ask the priest, ask the physician—let *them* reveal the amount of moral and physical results from this one cause. Must love always be discussed in blank verse, as if it were a thing to be played in tragedies or sung in songs—a subject for pretty poems and wicked novels, and had nothing to do with the prosaic current of our every-day existence, our moral welfare and eternal salvation? Must love be ever treated with profaneness, as a mere illusion? or with coarseness, as a mere impulse? or with fear, as a mere disease? or with shame, as a mere weakness? or with levity, as a mere accident? Whereas it is a great mystery and a great necessity, lying at the foundation of human existence, morality, and happiness; mysterious, universal, inevitable as death. Why then should love be treated less seriously than death? It is a serious thing...

—Anna Brownell Jameson,
Winter Studies and Summer Rambles in Canada
(1838)

Prologue: The Departed

Now he had to face her.

A last hymn had been sung. The organ continued playing "Holy, Holy, Holy" at a reflective tempo while the mourners edged into the aisles.

Isaac Harris held back a moment before joining the stream jostling its way to the front of the church to pay its condolences. The young bank cashier exceeded average height by some inches, but not by enough to see the dead man's family over the sea of black bonnets. How did she look? Harris would have liked to have caught at least a glimpse of Theresa before their meeting. Normally impatient of crowds, he was grateful today for their shuffling slowness—grateful even for their distracting aromas of rosewater, sweat, stain remover, insect repellent and hair oil. He had no idea what he was going to say.

He inched forward on feet that felt too big and out of step, all the more awkward because he had had so little experience of funerals. Just last week, his subordinate at the Toronto branch of the Provincial Bank, a gloomy man of riper years, had told him he had "a brow untouched by sorrow"—his good fortune made to sound like a reproach. Harris had been pleased, though. He had reported his accountant's words to Jasper Small, who liked to twit Harris on his long, earnest face.

Even had he been as inured to death as an old undertaker, however, and as well-stocked with platitudes to send sliding off the tongue, Harris would have had to think about whether to come today. He *had* thought, at some length.

It would have been shabby not to come, of course. Since Reform statesman Robert Baldwin had retired, there was no one in public life Harris respected more than William Sheridan. Not only had Sheridan been a Member of Parliament up until his death, but he had held cabinet rank in 1849 when the Great Ministry of Baldwin and Lafontaine had finally established the principle of responsible government. "So decisive has been the Reformers' victory," a eulogist had observed during the service, "that today in 1856 it feels like much more than seven years since Canada put the constitutional issue behind her, once and for all."

Since boyhood, Harris had known Sheridan by reputation, but the link between them was much closer than that. In adult life he had taken him legal work, dined at his table, courted his Theresa. He had seen Sheridan's massive, snowy head nod in approbation of a well-argued point, and seen it tremble with rage at corruption or callousness.

Sheridan had all his life stood up against oligarchy, yet never abandoned his faith in British institutions. He would have nothing to do with the Rebellions of 1837. His weapons had been reason and invective, not pikes and muskets. A passionate but essentially orderly man, and still needed.

Plainly, the place for Harris this Tuesday afternoon was the Church of the Holy Trinity. There were not only his personal feelings of grief and admiration to consider, but also the need for as strong a demonstration of support as possible for the integrity Sheridan had stood for.

On the other hand, if he went, Harris would have to meet Theresa for the first time since her marriage. It had not been easy in a city of a mere forty thousand to avoid her without calling too much attention to the fact. To avoid her at her own father's funeral would be impossible.

He would have to comfort her. Though resolute enough in most emergencies, he could not begin to think how he would manage. The three-year separation would have made them strangers, and bereavement have made her a stranger to herself. Even as mistress of her own separate establishment, she must feel the death as an amputation—for, whatever his public virtues, the deceased had been no less a devoted and adored father. His wife and son having died in Theresa's infancy, William Sheridan had in fact been both parents to his only child. And she had been to him not just daughter but companion.

Harris did not know how to meet her in such circumstances, and yet, rehearsing the circumstances awakened in him the protectiveness that would draw him to her. Her rejected champion, but her champion all the same.

When he reached the south transept, however, Theresa was not there. Henry Crane—florid, portly and imposing—stood alone by the carved stone baptismal font, receiving expressions of sympathy on behalf of the family.

Harris could not help stiffening in the presence of Theresa's husband and was about to introduce himself when the other said, "Isaac, very good of you to come."

"Is Mrs. Crane not here today?"

"She wasn't equal to this, poor woman." Crane dropped his voice, which was marked like Harris's own with the native Canadian flatness. "I must have a word with you. Ride with me to the interment if you're free."

Harris hesitated, but it seemed too odd a request to have been made without compelling reason. "Of course," he said. "I'll wait for you outside."

Harris left the church somewhat dazed. From what one read, death had not struck William Sheridan out of a clear sky. He was known to suffer from recurrent bouts of intestinal inflammation. One such had confined him to his room for the past week, and to this infirmity his physician plausibly enough had attributed his end. It seemed impossible then that Theresa had been prostrated by shock. She had never been susceptible to shocks, nor of a nervous temperament. She was a churchwoman besides and would have been drawn to these obsequies no less by faith than by affection. It followed that she must herself be seriously ill. Whereas a moment ago Harris had dreaded meeting her, he now asked nothing better than the assurance of his own eyes that she was out of harm's way. Perhaps Crane would permit a visit.

Filling the sun-drenched square, choking it almost, stood a hearse like none Harris had seen. It appeared to be a shop window rather than a conveyance of the dead, for its sides were broad sheets of costly plate glass, uncurtained, untinted, and bare of frosting or incised design. Through the glass could be seen a bed of sable carpeting. There the decoratively carved casket would presently lie naked to public admiration like an exhibit at the Crystal Palace. By contrast, the two pair of horses harnessed to it stood swathed in blankets of black velvet, invisible save for their eight black ears. A dozen undertaker's mutes with flowing black silk scarves tied around their top hats kept the curious at a distance from every polished surface of the rolling conservatory. No one could say this degree of ostentation was out of place at the passing of so public a figure, and yet the equipage was more St. James Cathedral than Holy Trinity Church, less Sheridan than Crane.

Harris reflected how hard it was for him to do justice to his former rival. Crane was not just a spender, after all, but a builder. Son of a Kingston hardware merchant, he had from the 1840s built steamboats, starting on the upper Great Lakes where the need was greatest. Although accidents had occurred, one fatal to his then partner, Crane had learned from each turn of events.

He had early championed propellers over paddles, which did poorly in rough water. He would supply either, though, of course, not actually making the boats himself but finding people to fashion them for any taste. You might have called him a steamboat promoter who in the fifties switched naturally to being a railway promoter. Personally or through subcontractors, Henry Crane could lay track, throw up bridges, secure government subsidies—anything you wanted in the railway department, and all in jig time. Nor had he given up on steamboats, which complemented the new lines. Toronto to Collingwood by rail, Collingwood to Chicago by water. He would soon find a way to put trains on steamboats. That would be the ultimate. Across the Detroit River, for example, or from his home town of Kingston to Cape Vincent, New York. It was just a matter of persuading politicians to put money into transportation and to pass laws creating the right atmosphere.

Three years after Harris had last heard Crane expound his ideas, they still sounded prophetic. Like the steam-pump fire engine that would become practicable as soon as the city mains could be made to supply enough water.

Harris had met Crane at William Sheridan's Front Street villa. Sheridan had been in the cabinet at the time, and Crane badly wanted his support for a measure affecting the Ontario, Simcoe and Huron Railway. Sheridan preferred to entertain him than to incur obligations by letting himself be entertained. "Convince me your bill serves the public interest," he said after dinner. Crane tried. Such was Sheridan's prestige that Crane tried on several occasions. He spoke of the public interest. He spoke also, as Harris heard later, of resurveying the line of rail to make it run through Sheridan's York County riding to the benefit of Sheridan's constituents. Sheridan remained courteous, but unpersuaded. So Crane's strategy changed. Such was Sheridan's prestige, after all, that any alliance with him would reflect credit on Crane. Sheridan's daughter, moreover, was a lively and most ornamental young woman. Having come to lobby, he stayed to woo—and, unhappily for Harris, Crane's powers of persuasion didn't fail him twice running.

About some things Harris was hypothesizing, but of Theresa's youthful vitality he could not have been more certain were she standing before him on the stove-hot gravel of Trinity Square. He could visualize her wild with grief. He could not begin to imagine her too overcome to see her Papa to his grave. Never. Crane could say what he liked.

The coffin was at last being carried from the church. Among the pallbearers, Harris recognized a granite-faced former mayor of Toronto, a Superior Court judge, two Reform Members of Parliament, and even one Conservative—as well as Sheridan's young law partner, Jasper Small, whose blank expression suggested that he was numbed by his loss and was there in body only. Crane supported the right rear corner.

There was an awkward moment when, possibly owing to pressure from behind, the forward bearers seemed to lose control of the steering. The ornate casket, which from what he had seen of its finish Harris had supposed to be rosewood, clanged metallically when it touched one of the hearse's steel tires. The onlookers gasped.

Aware of a rustle at his flank, Harris turned to find that a pert, round-faced young woman in a plain but neatly stitched black dress was straining to see past him. Straining perhaps to see Crane, the living son-in-law, rather than the resonant box of Sheridan's remains. Thick, jet-black curls seemed to push the mourning bonnet back off her head. There was something familiar about the avidity of her gaze, the jut of her elbow, the moustache of perspiration above her full upper lip.

"Come in front of me, miss," he suggested, "for a better view."

She did so with noisy thanks. Suddenly he thought he could place her.

"Did I not see you at the Peninsula Hotel on Saturday night?"

"My parents are in service there," she threw back over her shoulder. "But I don't remember you there, sir. You can't have stayed long."

Three evenings ago, Harris had attended a July 12 dance on the far side of the bay, and the service was as assiduous as Orange Toronto could have required. He had indeed left early, however. He had no particular reason to celebrate the rout of Catholics at the Battle of the Boyne. He endured quite as many toasts to "Our Protestant Sovereign" as any freethinker could endure. The best of the evening was standing with a cheroot on the deck of the steam ferry that carried him home across the malodorous harbour and watching the city draw near.

"Not long," he said.

While the young woman returned her full attention to the movements of Henry Crane, Harris lingered with the memory of that ferry crossing—of the last moments before the hammer fell.

Twenty years earlier, when his father had first brought him

here as a boy of eight, Toronto had been a city only in name. No longer York, but still muddy. Still lit by smoky tallow. Twenty years from now, the community might well be choking on the soot from factory chimneys, the first of which were just making their appearance.

But on this summer Saturday in 1856, Toronto was a string of pearls reflected in the still water. Gas jets shone from the docks, from the new Union Station, from the luxurious American Hotel, and from the Georgian-style villas along Front Street, dwellings which for the most part still enjoyed an unobstructed view of the bay. Harris's delight was enhanced by the thought that two of these brightly illuminated residences belonged to Robert Baldwin, although he no longer lived there, and to William Sheridan.

On disembarking from the ferry after the dance, he had found that William Sheridan no longer lived there either. There was black crape on his door.

A cast iron coffin was still a costly rarity—Crane's taste again. Once it was securely stowed, the double glass doors at the back of the hearse were closed upon it, and the funeral procession began forming up. Two attendants wearing black capes and carrying black-dyed ostrich plumes were to walk ahead of Sheridan's remains. From James Street, plumed coaches and fours inched into the crowded square. The dignitaries took their time climbing aboard.

"Get on with it," exclaimed the round-faced woman. Then, aware she had been overheard, she turned to Harris and asked if he could see all right.

"Perfectly."

He too was impatient. Fear for Theresa had powerfully seized upon him. He itched to know also what Crane wanted.

"Were you acquainted with the deceased, miss?" he added, conscious of having answered her rather curtly.

"I did some sewing for him. I knew his daughter better."

"Knew or know?" Harris's interest was now more than polite.

"I made all Mrs. Crane's clothes. Everything she had new in

the past year was stitched by Marion Webster." There was pride in her voice, and she evidently hoped for Harris's commendation, which he had not seen Theresa recently enough to give in any but the most general terms.

"You must do good work then, Miss Webster," he said and mentioned his own name. "Has she ordered mourning wear from you?"

"Not a stitch." The seamstress met his eyes boldly. "Do you think it's true she's in the hospital?"

"Hospital?" Harris repeated in astonishment. "Who says so?"

"Her husband, Mr. Crane. I've seen she's not at home, at least."

"I know nothing about it. Her condition...?"

"Bad, I suppose."

Harris knew of no condition bad enough to warrant placing a woman of Theresa's means in such an institution, but he didn't get to pursue the subject. Just then a red-haired man, dressed rather for a country auction than for a funeral, pushed through the crowd and took Marion Webster by the upper arm. Between the frayed cuff of his coarse-weave jacket and his dirt-caked nails, his thick fingers pressed lightly into the flesh beneath her black bombazine sleeve. Without freeing herself, as she easily might have done, the young woman directed towards him a frosty look, which seemed not to displease him. His hooded eyes twinkled. His warty, oval face broke into a sardonic grin.

"You have something for me," he said. "Let's go where we can talk."

"Miss Webster is favouring *me* with her conversation at present," said Harris, betraying less resentment than he felt—both at the interruption and at the rude handling of the young woman.

"That's all right, Mr. Harris," said Marion Webster. "I'll go with Mr. Vandervoort."

"John Vandervoort, Mr. Harris. Procurement officer for the Garrison. I must speak to Miss Webster concerning the... ah... the new battle colours she is stitching for the Wiltshire Grenadiers."

Harris knew for a fact there was no such regiment at the Toronto Garrison, or for that matter in the British army.

He assessed Vandervoort as muscular enough to cause even a strong girl much annoyance if he chose, but past the height of his vigour. Fond of his comforts. His nose was brightly veined, and a tin flask protruded from a side pocket of his check jacket. Harris saw no reason to cringe before him.

"You're sure, Miss Webster, you don't require assistance?"

"Oh, quite. I'm in no danger. Excuse me."

Vandervoort, his hand now at the back of her waist, ushered Marion Webster out of the square. Powerless to detain her, Harris watched with misgiving until they were lost to view, then made his way to Crane's side.

"So, there you are, Isaac. We're next. That's all right, Oscar." Brisk now as Harris could desire, Crane opened the door to his brougham before the coachman had time to jump down.

Mystery seemed to be piling on mystery. As Harris settled into the plush, pearl-grey upholstery, he wondered why Crane—always so avid for the ear of politicians—should choose on this occasion to send them on ahead in the coaches reserved for the chief mourners and himself ride to the cemetery in his own conveyance with no better company than a bank cashier.

Crane settled into the seat beside Harris and pulled the door shut. The confined space smelled of new leather and of Crane's soap. What was it? Something oriental, Harris thought—sandalwood perhaps.

"It's a warm day for a closed carriage," said Crane, mopping his forehead with a black-bordered handkerchief, "but it gives us a chance to be by ourselves for a bit."

Through the front window, the coachman up on the box could be seen flicking the horse into motion with his reins. Four well-oiled wheels rolled smoothly forward.

"Mrs. Crane is rumoured to be in the General Hospital," said Harris. "I find that hard to believe."

"I really should have thought of something better," Crane replied. "The fact of the matter is she has disappeared."

The word shocked Harris. His entire body seemed to clench. Even the gentle forward motion of the carriage became oppressive, and he would have had the driver stop had they not been in the middle of a funeral procession. Doubly oppressive was the presence of the other man, Theresa's husband. His voice was so even that he might have been making a heartless joke, or merely putting out another lie for public consumption.

Harris forced himself to study Crane's pink, clean-shaven face. It was firmly fleshed, smoothly handsome, dignified, amiable despite small eyes, and otherwise unexpressive. Harris remembered, though, an incident during the funeral service.

Theresa's husband had read from the third chapter of Ecclesiastes. Harris thought of Henry Crane as having a glib tongue and heart, but nothing could have been less glib than his performance on this occasion. From the moment he had stood up, the substantial man of business had shown untypical diffidence. He had moved slowly to the reading desk.

A lamp there had already been lit to supplement the daylight slanting into the church through plain glass windows. The gas flame shone off the pink bald patch in the middle of Crane's head as he inclined it over the Bible. Around the ears, his straight sandy hair was clipped short. This habitual if unfashionable cut appeared in the context almost monkish.

"To every thing there is a season, and a time to every purpose under the heaven." His toneless voice reached to the farthest member of the hushed congregation. "A time to be born—"

Here Crane stopped as if paralyzed. The mourners held their breath. The silence lasted too long to be a mere rhetorical flourish. If Crane had at this moment wiped his eye or sat down or given any other sign of incapacity to continue, Harris would have doubted his sincerity instantly. But the voice at last continued in the same steady key: "—and a time to die." Crane completed the reading without further interruptions, then walked quietly back to to his seat.

Harris thought of that halting reading and wondered what more was behind Crane's show of emotion than had appeared at the time. Again the industrialist seemed hesitant.

"Disappeared?" said Harris, finding his own voice with difficulty. "How can she have?"

"She'll likely turn up safe," said Crane. "What happened is she went for a ride Sunday afternoon and didn't come back."

"She went alone?"

"Yes. I was busy with funeral arrangements, but she said she needed air and exercise. I thought they would do her good considering the heavy blow of her father's death."

"Please continue."

Crane continued, calmly reasonable. "She often rode alone. My wife is an excellent horsewoman—as you know. I was concerned, but didn't overrule her."

"And her horse?" said Harris. "I take it she was riding Spat. Has the animal not found its way home?"

"No, Isaac. Look, I wanted to ask you whether she has communicated with you in any way. *Has she?*" Crane's voice sharpened suddenly, as if he suspected Harris's surprise might be feigned.

"She has not."

"Neither before Sunday nor since?"

"There's been no communication between us," Harris flatly declared, "direct or indirect, since before her marriage."

His hazel-brown eyes becoming even smaller, Crane held Harris's gaze. The question still hung between them.

This was not the Henry Crane who—with never a look behind—had wooed Theresa away from the disastrously diffident Harris. Rolling up Yonge Street past the many crape-hung shop windows, Harris reflected on the change.

He had been quiet and respectful as a suitor, Crane voluble and relentless. Harris had shared recreative and scientific interests with Theresa for years, but it was only when offered the cashier's post that he had felt in a position to contemplate marriage. That happened to be the moment Crane began frequenting William Sheridan's table.

Crane had been both older and newer, fresher and more

seasoned. Harris didn't really believe Crane's money had swayed Theresa, but understood that Crane was all the more dashing for never having to think twice about his means. Harris had three or four investments, but Crane had projects. He made things happen. And he wasn't the least bit reticent around women.

The brougham turned east on Carlton, a residential street. Harris's recollection skirted around the snowy afternoon in Sheridan's Front Street drawing room, when Theresa had innocently told him of her decision. Harris had been unable—had she noticed?—to lift his eyes from one green on yellow arabesque in the Tabriz Persian carpet, a writhing curl that from the intense scrutiny of that half hour in the fading light had become for him the very image of pain. His pain. At no time had he wanted her to suffer.

For her sake, it was to be hoped that Crane loved her more sincerely than appeared, or that he would come to do so. Harris still had his doubts. Whatever the present state of his affections, though, Crane had plainly lost his former confidence regarding Theresa's.

Seeming to read Harris's mind, Crane relaxed his wary squint and glanced away into the leafy green of Allan Park, where two squirrels were chasing each other around the trunk of an oak. Having apparently satisfied himself that Harris had indeed taken no part in his wife's disappearance, Crane would have dismissed him had circumstances permitted. Harris, for his part, was glad they were stuck with each other for the eight or ten more blocks it would take them to reach St. James's Cemetery. He had questions of his own.

"Have there been any ransom demands?"

Crane shook his head.

"Did she take any luggage then—any things she might want if she contemplated being two nights away from home?"

"Nothing as far as we can make out."

Harris wondered if the plural, which rang with such authority, included more than Crane and his domestic staff. "Have you engaged a detective?"

"Detective? No-o." Crane shuddered at the neologism. "It's my wife that's missing. I should set a *detective* to find where pilfered construction materials had got to. No—I had thought she might be with friends and would return in time for the funeral."

"And now?"

A wasp was buzzing against the inside of the front window. Crane seemed not to notice.

"I'll speak to Chief Sherwood this evening about police action," he said. "You'll understand, Isaac, I wanted to spare Mrs. Crane the embarrassment of any public hue and cry, particularly in view of her bereavement."

Hue and cry? That had not been Harris's suggestion—though it might come to that. "Which of her friends have you spoken to?"

"I see you take this matter to heart," said Crane, newly suspicious. "Which friends would *you* speak to?"

"Women she went to school with, I suppose. Guests in your home. People she called on. As I think I've made clear, I'm hardly in a position to know."

Crane squirmed in his seat. His irritation was starting to show.

"Can't you do anything about that bug?" he asked.

Harris lunged at the wasp with his folded handkerchief and missed. Wings whining and clattering, the yellow jacket rose to the upholstered ceiling, dived to the thick-pile burgundy carpet, bounced against the door panels, flew everywhere except out the open side windows to safety, and settled at last on Harris's striped trouser leg, where he caught it up in the linen pad and crushed it.

"Thank you," said Crane.

"Don't mention it."

"I'm uncommonly squeamish about killing things, you know." Crane sounded neither proud nor ashamed of his squeamishness and had more or less recovered his composure.

Whether by accident or design, the wasp hunt had filled the time necessary to bring Crane's carriage up Parliament Street to the cemetery gates. The land beyond them resembled a burial ground less than it did a gently undulating park. Although winding roads and paths had been laid out, there were still few monuments of any size and no chapel.

Up ahead, the hearse could be seen turning left just past an elegant grey granite mausoleum with fluted columns—resting place of a distiller—then climbing towards the squat Sheridan obelisk. William Sheridan had said he wanted it built on a broad base, hard if not impossible for Orange ruffians to push over. He had had the rosy stone brought by horse and waggon from the Credit Valley in the mid-forties, when his wife and son's remains had been moved from the old Anglican graveyard in town.

The procession straggled to a halt. Footmen trailing black scarves folded the steps of the two mourning coaches down to the ground, and the pallbearers emerged blinking into the sunlight. Harris scanned the landscape in case Theresa, having missed the church service, might nonetheless show herself at the interment.

"When last seen," he asked, "was she wearing black?"

Crane's coachman was already holding open the door.

"She had nothing black," Crane replied. "Nothing that she could ride in." He climbed out.

"What colour was her outfit?"

Crane was striding ahead towards the open grave. When Harris caught up, he repeated the question.

"Isaac, I appreciate your having granted me an interview."

"Most welcome. Was she wearing blue?"

"I'm sure your interest is kindly meant."

"Green?"

Crane stopped dead. "Yes, green. Now I appeal to your sense of delicacy to pursue this matter no further." The rail baron's face was pinker than before, his voice stern and commanding. "Assure yourself I shall take every measure appropriate to securing the safe return of *my* wife."

Harris saw the futility of asking further questions. Crane was the deceased's only relative at the funeral, and the rector of Holy Trinity was approaching for a consultation. Before turning to

Dr. Scadding, Crane gave Harris's hand a dismissive shake.

But Harris held Crane's hand firm until he had said, "I should like to be informed of any fresh developments."

A sharp, appraising glance was the only reply he got.

There and then Harris made his decision. He was not about to tailor his sense of delicacy to fit Henry Crane's convenience. Not this time.

PART ONE:
Home District

Chapter One
The Provincial Bank

After the interment, Harris sorted quickly through the afternoon's messages at his desk, then changed into cord breeches and riding boots and made for the Richmond Street livery stable where he boarded his horse. Banshee was a dapple-grey five-year-old with large eyes and lots of stamina. He found her picking at her bedding straw. Not for the first time, he asked if the liveryman was spending enough on feed, but avoided threats to take his business elsewhere. Randall's was the cleanest establishment within walking distance of the bank and had the biggest stalls.

Harris saddled up without waiting for the boy's help. He intended to spend the evening running over what he recalled as Theresa's favourite rides to see if he could find any trace of her—someone who had seen her perhaps, or some physical sign of an accident.

The sun at five o'clock was still three hours high and scorching, the air motionless. Only by cantering through it could he obtain the semblance of a breeze on his damp forehead. Unbothered by the heat, the horse whisked him out to Gooderham and Worts's windmill at the eastern extremity of the Toronto bay, and from there onto the peninsula.

While he rode, he forced himself to put some order into the thoughts and questions spawned by Crane's shockingly cool announcement. Respectably married women had never been known to just disappear from this city. Accident apart, what could have happened to Theresa? Harris began listing possibilities in his head:

1. mental disorder
2. voluntary flight
3. abduction
4.

He left 4 blank for the moment.

The least likely alternative was 1. Harris expected grief to shake Theresa hard, but not to shatter her. She had a history of steadfastness in crises. When a drunken cook had hacked her own thumb off with an eight-inch cleaver, sending the housemaid into hysterics, Theresa had dressed the stump without flinching. More to the point, during an earlier—and to all appearances fatal—bout of William Sheridan's intestinal ailment, she had brushed tears aside to discuss funeral and testamentary arrangements with him. It would surely have taken more than his death to unhinge her reason.

And yet, Harris had to admit, much could have happened to change her in the past three years. If he were to reach any meaningful conclusions, he would have to question someone like her father's partner Jasper about her marriage. This topic he had always avoided.

Suppose—possibility 2—Theresa were hiding from her husband. In that case, Harris didn't want to be too helpful to the official search until he had a better idea of her reasons.

They had to relate to her father's death. That couldn't be a coincidence. Perhaps as he faced eternity William Sheridan had told her something that made continuing her life with Henry Crane impossible. Perhaps some youthful shame that Crane had thought safely buried in the forests of the Northwest had, against all his calculations, come to his father-in-law's knowledge. Alternatively, Theresa might some time ago have decided to leave Crane. She might only have refrained from doing so during her father's lifetime to spare him the scandal—though if she had been able to wait for his death, why not wait two days more for the funeral?

Harris stopped at the Peninsula Hotel, situated on the

narrowest part of the sandy isthmus. Neither staff nor guests could tell him anything of Theresa, and his own observations were nothing to the point. Today in daylight he noticed, as on Saturday night he had not, that a couple more of the low dunes had recently been dug away. New city regulations were not stopping businessmen like Joseph Bloor from helping themselves to this sand for their brick works. One good storm now would wash the hotel out and make the peninsula an island.

Riding on, he approached the hexagonal spire of the Gibraltar Light. Its grey stone glowed warmly in the late afternoon sun. He halted to speak to the keeper, a grizzled bachelor familiar to excursionists for his outlandish costumes, though not yet personally known to Harris. Discovered on his doorstep, Harvey Ingram proved more hospitable than informative.

Sit down, he urged in a drink-slurred burr. Have a dram. He shifted a jug from the other half of the rough bench he occupied. Surely, he knew Susan—he meant Theresa—Crane, by sight at least. He had not seen her Sunday or since. Had she bolted then? What had got into her? While he sounded sincerely anxious, his confusion over her name did little to raise Harris's hopes. He wore a Turkish headdress and bits of military gear in apparent tribute to the recently concluded Crimean campaign—dispensing with any stock or collar, however, as he had no appreciable neck to encircle.

The banker at first declined the invitation on the pretext of making the most of the remaining daylight. Only on his darkened way back to town, after the most thorough examination of every beach and thicket, did the prospect of refreshment tempt him. By then the light was lit atop the eighty-two-foot tower and beckoned him over.

Ingram had walked out onto the sward before the tower door. He did not mark Harris's approach. Hands on hips, the lighthouse keeper was shuffling his feet and from time to time essaying a modest kick or hop. Not falling down, at least, thought Harris.

"I came back, Mr. Ingram," he called out as soon as he was close enough to be confident of being heard.

Ingram spun around.

"Who's that?" he cried in a tone both peremptory and apprehensive, as if he could expect nothing good of any that came back.

"No ghost, I assure you." Harris dismounted and walked forward into the rectangle of lamp light spilling from the tower door. "I thought I'd ask if your offer still stands."

"Ah, you, sir. See anything? No? Fortunate perhaps." Ingram's round eyes, whisker-hidden mouth and short neck gave him a fixed owlish expression, or rather lack of expression, which an alcoholic glaze made even harder to read. "I was just doing a bit of a hornpipe—the solitary man's dance, as they say. Well, let's sit down, and I'll tell you how I expect they'll find this Mrs. Crane of yours."

"You know of someone I might ask?"

"I know men's sins. Now you take the cup. I've only sipped from the one side of it."

The drink made Harris's eyes water. A little went a long way.

"Hear the wisdom of a seasoned campaigner," said his host. He was fingering an epaulet, of which the distinctly unmilitary adornment appeared to consist of gold sleeve-links. "They'll find the lady only as a corpse."

"It's too soon to say that!" Harris exclaimed. "No more, thank you."

"Just a drop." Ingram poured. "I wish no harm to anybody, but there are men it doesn't do to tempt. A beautiful woman riding alone—she's with the angels now."

From the deep melancholy in Ingram's Scottish voice it was clear that this prophecy gave him no pleasure, but its authoritative and unvarying repetition with each application of the jug to his lips ended by driving Harris home to a sleepless bed. He had achieved nothing. He had not even managed to tire himself out.

"She's with the angels now!"

Doubtless solitude and sixpence-a-gallon whisky had made the man morbid. By his own admission, old shipwrecks and unsolved murders also weighed upon his mind. Every allowance made, however, Harris still found his down mattress a bed of thistles.

* * *

Tuesday passed into Wednesday. When he rose at five, the morning was already hot, but he still had to light the Prince of Wales wood stove for coffee.

Harris lived in lavish simplicity. Lavish in that he enjoyed sole occupancy of the cashier's suite on the upper floor of his place of work. The Toronto branch of the Provincial Bank of Canada was Greek revival in style and made of cleanly fitted pale Ohio sandstone—for, although locally produced red brick would have served just as well, people expected more opulence from banks. And the opulence extended to Harris's apartments, which included two damask-hung salons, one large enough to serve as a ballroom. Harris thought the building reckless and admired it. Prudently, however, he dispensed with any domestic staff. It seemed more sociable, as well as better husbandry, to take his dinners at hotels than to keep a cook just for himself, and breakfast he could manage on his own.

While the kettle was heating, he chewed a day-old crust of bread and looked out one of the front windows. Below, at the intersection of Wellington and Bay Streets, the dust lay still and dry. It had not rained, a blessing if Theresa had no shelter. If what Crane said were true, and unless she had been found since they spoke, she had now been away from home three nights. The barking of a watchdog in the yard of the piano manufactory next door reminded Harris of a rumour that a rabid fox was at large in the Humber Valley. What if Theresa...?

Stop, he told himself. He was speculating to no purpose.

As soon as the water was steaming, he shaved and—though it was still early—began to dress for work. He had a branch to run with obligations to a staff of four, to thirty-six major borrowers, each of whom he knew personally, to 297 depositors most of whom he could at least recognize, to unnumbered purchasers of specie and bills of exchange, and through head office to thirteen directors and upwards of thirteen hundred shareholders. He could not in conscience give every waking thought to Theresa. There would have to be a balance.

With barber's scissors he trimmed his side whiskers to just below his ear lobes. Beards and moustaches were becoming fashionable since the war, but not for bank cashiers. Harris's work clothes, mostly black, differed little from what he had worn to the funeral—a morning coat replacing the full-skirted frock coat. And for the office he usually put on a coloured waistcoat, a dark blue watered silk this morning. He tied a matching cravat in a loose bow around the high collar of his white shirt.

What shade, he wondered, was that riding habit she had worn? A muted, vegetable-based green or one of the vivid new chemical dyes?

His toilet made, he carried his coffee down the elliptically spiralling staircase and managed to answer the most pressing of yesterday's correspondence before his staff, all but Septimus Murdock, arrived at eight thirty. The accountant had been instructed to go straight to the docks to meet a shipment of money from head office.

Arrangements had been negotiated with Kingston in ciphered telegrams. Security from theft and punctuality of delivery were Harris's two overlapping concerns. He wanted the notes, coins and bullion in the vault well before the branch opened its doors to the public at ten. As the steamer chosen had been due this morning at seven, this requirement should have posed no problem.

And yet the two-horse, iron-plated van didn't pull up in front of the bank until ten past nine. The police constable engaged as a guard had been late, a winded Septimus Murdock explained as he lowered himself cautiously from his seat between the driver and his boy.

"But where *is* the constable?" asked Harris.

The burly accountant's chin quivered, as did the timid imperial that adorned it. Harris waited for him to speak.

"Isaac, he insisted on being locked inside with what he called the *loot*."

Sure enough, when the padlock was removed from the heavy rear doors, a sharp-featured young man leaped out, pointing his single-shot Enfield carbine in all directions. Handled this way, the short rifle was a sufficient threat to the life of any individual bystander. For the purpose of fending off a raid, however, Harris would have preferred to see a double-barrelled shotgun. While the president of the Provincial Bank liked to repeat that there had never been a daytime bank robbery in North America, Harris knew it was just a matter of time. In tandem with Toronto's prosperity, its crime rate was on the rise.

Constable Devlin, whose school had been the city's docks and alleys, understood the situation perfectly. As a public servant, however, he was not at liberty to say what his understanding of the situation was. It was no part of his job to spread panic. Reaching inside his unbuttoned blue tunic to scratch his chest hair, he did explain—in a tone both knowing and aggrieved—that a shotgun was too heavy to carry about in this heat. Harris smelled no fresh whisky on the constable's breath and noted that at least one of his boots had been recently polished. This was by no means the dregs of the force.

Under Devlin's sporadically watchful eye, it took over an hour to get the money unloaded, counted, recounted and signed for. The bars of precious metal were few and quickly weighed, but the gold coins were the usual jumble of French five-francs, British sovereigns and American eagles, plus the new Canadian pounds and twenty-five-shilling pieces. The silver coins were even worse.

The bulk of the shipment consisted of new banknotes of all denominations. When van and constable had left, Septimus Murdock gave sixteen-year-old bank messenger Dick Ogilvie one of the crisp, clean bills to hold.

"Ever have as much as fifty dollars in your hands, Dicko?" he asked.

Ogilvie admitted this was the first time, but swore it would not be the last. One of the tellers laughed.

"But if this is fifty dollars," said the boy, puzzlement clouding his freckled face, "why does it say, 'The Provincial Bank of Canada, Kingston, promise to pay to bearer on demand twelve pounds, ten shillings currency at their office in Toronto'?"

Murdock snatched back the banknote. "Because, my young friend," he scolded, "that's what fifty dollars is worth—as anyone working in a bank ought to know by now."

Harris pointed out that they were already half an hour late in opening and that it was high time to get some of the new notes into circulation.

Later in the morning, he glanced out his office window and noticed Dick Ogilvie sweeping the back stoop while waiting for other commissions. Harris pulled up the sash and beckoned him over.

"Don't let people make you feel ashamed for asking questions," said the cashier. "I ask a lot myself."

The boy's curly brown hair would have looked very well if he had not tried to plaster it flat with water. "May I ask another then, sir?" he said.

He wanted to know why the bank could not let him keep the fifty-dollar note. It would cost them so little in ink and paper to print a replacement. Harris told him that the gentlemen who owned the bank were putting half a million pounds into it and that the government allowed them to print paper to a face value of no more than three times that amount.

Ogilvie's lips moved soundlessly as he did the arithmetic. "So once they've printed their six million dollars, they can't print any more?"

Harris nodded. "By the time you are cashier, the preponderance of north-south trade under the Reciprocity Treaty will have made pounds and shillings obsolete. We're just fortunate that the States uses yards and feet instead of metres or we should have two systems of linear measurement as well."

"I should like to be cashier." Ogilvie straightened his broadening shoulders inside his short black jacket. "Only when I'm older, I'm supposed to go into business with my dad."

"What business is that, Dick?" Harris was surprised to find he did not know.

"Undertaking—he's quite prominent. He arranged the funeral you attended yesterday, sir. It's just that I can't see myself taking orders for caskets day in day out."

"I suppose that's what your father was doing Sunday afternoon." Harris recollected that *funeral arrangements* had been Crane's excuse for not riding with Theresa.

Again the boy looked puzzled. "Oh no, sir."

Although Murdock had come into the office to announce a visitor, Harris was suddenly unwilling to let Ogilvie go.

"Did Mr. Crane not call on Sunday?" he asked.

"That was Saturday night."

"You saw him then?" Harris was sure Crane had said Sunday. It was too soon to have forgotten.

"Not only that, Mr. Harris. He would not have been received on Sunday. My dad's very strict about the Sabbath."

"To be sure." Harris pulled the window down to within three inches of the sill and took, without really seeing it, the letter of introduction Murdock handed him.

The sight of the president's signature at the bottom of the page brought Harris back to the business at hand. The letter asked him to extend every courtesy to Mr. Joshua Newbiggins, whom he invited in without further delay.

The cashier's office was well-appointed for courteous reception. Oil copies of notable European paintings hung about in gilt frames. Two deeply upholstered armchairs and a matching ottoman faced the cashier's desk, beside which a cabinet held a bottle of vintage port and a box of tea.

Newbiggins drank neither, appearing to derive his principal stimulus from his own conversation. He was short, round, flashily dressed and talkative. He talked about the desirability of new industries now that Toronto was becoming a rail hub. At present an importer of Pennsylvania coal, he proposed setting up an iron works, for which he had already acquired a property on Front Street. Demolished the Georgian villa that had occupied it too.

Harris received his loan application and promised it the promptest possible consideration.

"I believe the president's letter mentioned that I am a substantial shareholder in this bank," said Newbiggins, making no move to leave.

"Yes, indeed."

"You realize, Mr. Harris, Kingston has become a backwater. Routing the Grand Trunk railroad three miles back of the port just nailed the lid on the coffin."

"A hard blow to be sure," said Harris, unable to see where this was leading.

Newbiggins sat back in his armchair and laced his ring-laden fingers over his stomach. "It can't be long before head office moves to Toronto," he said. "You could be head cashier."

Harris owned real estate himself, a few residential properties acquired before the current boom. Their value had already doubled and bid fair to do so again, while their sites better suited any sort of commercial venture than the site Newbiggins had picked out for himself. Harris had, in short, prospects beyond the bank. Meanwhile, he considered himself as well housed and as honourably employed as any man his age in the city. He smiled politely.

"In point of fact," Newbiggins confided, "I plan to discuss the whole question with the officers of the bank in the next few days. It would be a great help to me if you could have your accountant show me the records of your recent loans."

"You had best discuss that with the president, sir. He's kept fully informed."

"My eye might pick up some significant details that his would miss. I know it's somewhat irregular, Mr. Harris, but I should be working very much in your interest."

The spacious office felt suffocatingly close. Through the barely opened window slid smells of dust and horse manure. Up and down Bay Street, carters on their way to and from the docks called to their weary teams.

"Let me be candid," said Harris. His situation was unpleasant, but not difficult. "To be appointed to my present position, I had to post a bond. I have the strongest possible interest in transactions that are regular."

Happily Newbiggins did not persist. His patent leather boots squeaked cheerily as he got up and adjusted his boldly checked jacket.

In the course of the leave-taking, it occurred to Harris that the little man had said *railroad* instead of *railway*. "How do you find life in Canada, Mr. Newbiggins?" he asked affably.

"Very much to my taste. People here aren't as tall as in New York, but they have almost as much culture. Why, the very first week I was in the country, I was able to hear Miss Jenny Lind sing down at the St. Lawrence Hall. What drama she put into Bellini's *Sonnambula!* Were you there?"

Harris nodded. He had been there with Theresa—four years ago, perhaps five, or even six. Time with her had been taken so much for granted. Somehow he assumed Theresa would wait for his elevation to cashier, assumed he had asked her to. He never actually had.

Miss Lind's singing should have swept him into a declaration. If only he had let it! He recalled the soprano's heart-piercing sweetness rather than, like Newbiggins, individual selections. The only detail of the evening to come back to him was that of Theresa at his side—eyes closed, lips parted as she soared with the Swedish nightingale—holding her bracelet of silver medallions to keep it from rattling.

Chapter Two
Law and Order

Harris remained anchored to his desk through the noon hour, interrupting work only for a taste of cold pigeon pie and a glance at the day's papers. In addition to Sheridan's funeral, the disappearance of his daughter was at last being reported. Police were said to be investigating. Harris thought he would stop by the chief's office after four to see what headway was being made.

When Harris and Murdock deposited the ledgers in the vault at closing time, the cashier asked his accountant to be particularly on guard in future against any attempt at unauthorized inspection of them.

Earlier in the afternoon, as every Wednesday afternoon, those of the bank's directors resident in Toronto had met to decide who might borrow from the branch. Harris's duty was simply to present the applications. The Toronto directors murmured approval of Newbiggins's guarantors and granted him his loan—despite doubts as to whether, during its term, construction of Conquest Iron Works could even begin. On his way downtown after work, Harris walked past the Front Street site. As he had suspected, it lay between a church and the villa of an influential alderman. A more promising source of dandelions than of stoves and rails!

East of Yonge Street, Harris approached the busiest part of the Esplanade. There the principal docks and markets clustered, not to mention the principal beggars and eccentrics. At the entrance to the new south St. Lawrence Market, which to spare the public purse was also made to serve as City Hall, sat a vacant-eyed individual with a placard reading, "Veteran of

Waterloo." Harris bent over and placed a sixpence in the hat by his side. The man *might* have lost his legs forty-two years ago to a French cannon ball, or more recently in a Toronto construction accident. The exposed pink stumps were real enough.

The portico under which he sat, like the building as a whole, followed the Italianate fashion as far as could be squared with Protestant parsimony. Inside, a compact entrance hall led straight to the police office. Neither the chief nor his deputy was there. Harris proceeded downstairs to Station No. 1, which because of the slope of the land towards the lake looked out on the courtyard of the fruit and poultry market. The only windows, at the far end of the prisoners' airing room, admitted a dulled but insistent odour of sun-ripened chicken guts.

The near end of the basement housed, on the one hand, the building's central heating apparatus in a closet of its own and, on the other, the policemen's room. Stretching roughly parallel to the west or right wall of the latter, an eight-foot-long table served as a counter. Behind it sat hunched a fair young constable, clinging to an unsteady steel pen and holding the tip of his tongue between his teeth. He did not look up. With painstaking deliberation, he was recording a woman's complaint regarding her neighbour's privy. She wore a bolt of cloth in skirts alone, which vied in splendour with the abundant plumes and ribbons on her hat. She insisted, in a voice both affected and familiar, that she was known to the lawmakers. Harris had more than enough time to look around.

Although the station was not five years old, cracks were already opening in the walls as the building settled into the wet clay and sand of the harbour beach. Some of these fissures had been whitewashed over but not filled. Others had been patched with a conspicuous grey-green paste. From a rack of guns on the west wall, an expensive padlock—one Harris knew to be pick-proof—hung open and useless. As for the pine plank floor, it was swept remarkably clear of dust and littered with cherry pits. Everything was halfway right. The place was fairly cluttered with good intentions.

Presently Constable Devlin with his one polished boot emerged from the farthest lock-up cell. Harris tried to catch his eye. Appearing not to recollect their morning encounter, the constable crossed the airing room to the table and seated himself in front of a pile of fresh cherries. These he placed in his mouth one after another, expelling the pits in the direction of a tin spittoon.

"Hi, Devlin," Harris called with more energy than hope. "Is your sergeant around at all?"

Devlin looked up quizzically, but was spared answering when two other men came clattering down the stairs into the room. One was the melancholic lighthouse keeper from the peninsula. He wore a navy jacket and army trousers. The other was John Vandervoort, yesterday's bogus procurement officer, frowning as if he had just been found out.

The light keeper cleared his throat, presumably to make a formal charge of fraud before the constables. But what was this? A plainly unrepentant Vandervoort clapped him on the back, knocking the breath out of him before he could speak.

"Lock this man up, Devlin," said Vandervoort, shoving his winded companion behind the table. "The charge is smuggling and trafficking in smuggled goods. Morgan, write it up."

"Two Gs or one, inspector?" said the blond constable, turning to a fresh page in his book.

Inspector. Harris wondered if he had heard correctly.

"It ain't smuggling, John." The accused wiped the sweat from his forehead with a shaky hand. "On my word as a seasoned campaigner, we've got this treaty with the States now. A recip— reciprostity treaty."

"You mean, 'reciprocity,'" the female complainant corrected self-importantly. Haughty grey eyes cast icicles from under her hat brim in the light keeper's direction. "Now I really must ask you to wait your turn."

Vandervoort reached inside his frayed check jacket and pulled a six-shooter from his belt. Everyone but the seated constables took a startled step back. Morgan's pen froze in the air with a drop of ink quivering at its tip. Gunfire seemed imminent. As soon as Vandervoort had the weapon out, however, he let it swing by the trigger guard from his thick forefinger.

"Harvey Ingram," he said calmly, "I ask you before witnesses here—Constables Morgan and Devlin—ma'am—ah! Mr. Harris—I ask you whether this item which I purchased from you is grain, coal, timber, pork, or any other product of the earth such as falls under the terms of the Reciprocity Treaty of 1854? Just shake your head now. That's right. You all saw that?"

"I see nothing," pouted the female complainant. "I didn't come here to be a witness to anything." So saying, she decided to postpone her business to a quieter occasion, lifted her copious skirts and swept up the stairs out of sight. No one begged her to stay.

"This is—rather—a manufactured product," Vandervoort continued, thrusting the gun under the lighthouse keeper's nose. "In point of fact, it is a thirty-six calibre Colt Navy revolver made in Hartford, Connecticut, and as such subject to import tariffs under the laws of Canada. Have you any proof that such tariffs have been paid? I didn't think so."

"You'll never make it stick, John," said Ingram in a vague, quite unthreatening voice.

Perhaps he too believed he had friends among the lawmakers. Otherwise, Harris thought, he was unlikely to be found at the Gibraltar Light for some time. Vandervoort was making a convincing case.

"This gun and its fellows didn't come ashore through the port of Toronto where tariffs are levied, did it?" asked the inspector. "Oh, no—no indeed! Instead it was landed Monday night at a signal from your light on the south beach of the peninsula. Why there and then? Precisely to avoid the attentions of Her Majesty's customs office. Think that over while you sit in your cell."

Of course, if Ingram were a criminal, his opinion of Theresa's fate might have to be reconsidered. Perhaps, thought Harris, the lightkeeper had been speaking from something besides drunken morbidity.

"Now, Devlin," the inspector went on, "this gun is evidence, so you're to keep it under lock and key."

"Absolutely, John." Devlin's shifty eyes went hard and serious with understanding of the necessity.

"We'll just let Morgan here copy down the serial number first—40099." Vandervoort laid the pistol on the table and glanced over Morgan's shoulder. "Yes, two Gs. That's it."

Harris continued to follow the proceedings closely, flabbergasted to find that the warty intruder from the funeral—who turned himself out like a dealer in second-rate horse flesh—was a senior policeman. To say that Vandervoort's present briskness contrasted favourably with the previous rhythm of Station No.1 was small praise.

Still, any evidence of official competence boded well for finding Theresa. Although Harris had disliked the man on first acquaintance, he readily presumed on that acquaintance in approaching him.

Vandervoort's willingness to be congratulated on his coup made him more approachable still. The business of the arrest concluded, he invited Harris upstairs, where fresh paint covered the walls, and poultry odours barely penetrated. The inspector had city-wide responsibilities, but no desk of his own, so he made free with the deputy chief's. Sitting on it, he waved Harris into the chair and railed against contraband. A flood of discount revolvers was of course a threat to public peace, but he expected no thanks on that score. What scared the politicians was lost revenue, for without the tariffs they could not subsidize their railways.

"I've saved the public purse ten miles of track," crowed the inspector, "with the help of a certain sharp-eyed miss..."

Harris guessed the seamstress Marion Webster was meant. She was familiar with the peninsula and might have noticed any irregular flashing of the Gibraltar Light used to bring in the smugglers' ship. Why Miss Webster, whose clientele included the Cranes, should confide her suspicions to someone as disrespectful of her person as John Vandervoort was a mystery to Harris, but would have to remain one for now, as he had more urgent inquiries to pursue.

"I came," he said, "to see how the search for Mrs. Crane is progressing."

Vandervoort at first resisted the change of subject. "Railway men in politics—nothing wrong with them. Not a thing. Her father was something more, though. I admired him, which makes me somewhat of an exception on the force—but then, as the only plainclothes detective, I'm an exception most ways. When is the last time you saw her?"

"The first of March, 1853."

"You're amazingly precise."

"I've had no communication with her since. I take it she has not been found."

"Not by me, but then I've had other game to snare. Do you know where she is?"

"No, inspector, I don't. She may be at the mercy of kidnappers or lying hurt in the bush. It's seventy-five hours since, according to her husband, she left home. She may be facing her fourth night without shelter." Harris cleared his throat. He felt the fears he had kept in check all day come crowding back. "It would be some reassurance to know what your department has discovered so far, what steps are being taken."

Vandervoort opened a drawer in the deputy chief's desk, found a half-smoked cigar and lit it. "What steps would you take?" he asked.

"Circulate her likeness and description together with a description of her attire and mount to the railway, steamship and stagecoach offices, as well as to every hotel in and within half a day's ride of Toronto. The Home District, in short. Find out her favourite rides from Mr. Crane. Go over each one inch by inch. Apply to her friends, everyone she saw socially, and every domestic or tradesperson she had business with. Examine her personal effects to determine what she took with her."

Vandervoort's heavy-lidded eyes were for once wide open. "I believe you would," he said. "Do you happen to have a picture of her?"

"Of course not. Surely Mr. Crane can provide you with a daguerreotype from which an engraving might be made. Excuse me, Inspector. I feel I'm talking to a mirror. Every question is turned back on me. While I'm happy to assist you, I should like some answers too."

From the floor below came a murmur of erratic singing, on which some municipal clock broke in with brief authority to sound the hour of five.

"I see you take a great interest in Mr. Crane's wife—but police work has its confidences, Mr. Harris, just like banking. You live alone."

"That's no secret." It was not, however, something Harris had mentioned.

"Do you have anyone in to keep house on a daily basis?"

"A cleaning woman comes on Thursdays. I bring in other help only when I entertain. In the past six days, no one but me has been in the apartment. You're welcome to inspect it."

"Do you know any reason Mrs. Crane might have had to leave her husband?"

"None, but as I say I've had no communication—"

"Yes, yes, since that sad day in '53." After a last mouthful of smoke, Vandervoort flattened the cigar end to the floor with his heel. "You had proposed marriage to her yourself. The sight of another man's ring on her slender finger would have galled you."

In one flash of anger, Harris left his seat and strode to the door. There his brain cleared enough to frame the hypothesis that Vandervoort had agreed to see him from the sole motive of determining whether he and Theresa were adulterers. The policeman's latest crudeness might have been calculated to provoke an unguarded admission, or guilty flight.

"Gin a body kiss a body," the inebriate below kept asking, each time louder, "Need a body cry?"

Harris turned. A sharp rebuke might work with tellers, but he saw no profit here in giving his feelings the run of his tongue. "Your information is faulty, inspector," he said quietly. "I never proposed."

"A great mistake."

Would it, Harris silently wondered, have made a difference? Perhaps he had only spared himself the humiliation of a refusal. She had unnecessarily returned every book of which he had ever made her a present—not love poetry or sentimental novels either, but works of natural science, in which subject she had shown an early and tenacious interest.

"Forgive my impertinence," said Vandervoort. "*Was* her finger slender?"

"Yes."

"How would you describe her otherwise, as of the date named?"

"Five foot four inches tall—nearer eight stone than nine—eyes green, hair chestnut brown." The trick was not to remember the details, but to keep them sufficiently objective. "Creamy, clear complexion."

"Any distinguishing marks?"

Harris hesitated to mention the sweet, dark mole on her neck to the left of the nape, though it had been plainly visible whenever she wore evening dress and her hair was up. Asking himself what Theresa would say settled the matter. She would never have seen the point of withholding such information where a life might be at stake. Harris answered the question.

Vandervoort, who was neither taking nor consulting notes, heard about the mole with a smile. "Go on," he said.

"Mr. Crane must have told you all this."

"What about her nose?"

"Straight and strong."

"Mouth?"

"Of course, she has a mouth. If it helps to know, there's a slight gap between her upper central incisors."

"Have mercy, Mr. Harris. I only got three years of school."

"Front teeth. The mouth itself appears to turn down somewhat at the corners."

"Ah. A discontented expression."

"It doesn't appear so. She's not conventional-looking, but..."

"A beauty for all that."

"By common accord, yes—a radiant, spirited one."

"Impetuous?"

"Impatient at times perhaps," said Harris, "like all of us. Have you any more questions?"

"No," Vandervoort replied. "You're free to go."

Harris stayed. "How many men are assigned to this case?"

"I'm not at liberty—"

"Are *any* policemen devoting their full attention to the search?"

"This I will tell you. We have in this city fifty constables, under the immediate supervision of five sergeants. Each constable has to look after the policing needs of eight hundred citizens. Now depend on it, every man is aware of Mrs. Crane's disappearance and can be counted on to keep his eyes open."

Every Morgan, thought Harris, every Devlin. "And what provision has been made for the possibility that she has already left the city?"

"You can address any further enquiries to Mr. Henry Crane." Vandervoort's grin unravelled. "Now you'll have to excuse me. I'm wanted elsewhere."

"Just a moment. The lighthouse keeper you arrested—yesterday he was positive that Mrs. Crane had been killed. Ask him if he saw her."

"You can't be thinking the contrabandists killed Mrs. Crane?" The inspector opened the door and held it for Harris.

"If she had stumbled on their activities—"

"I *know* my felons, sir. These are businessmen, *not* murderers."

When Vandervoort left the building, Harris went back down to Station No.1 and asked again for the sergeant. Morgan answered evasively. Devlin let slip that the sergeant was under lock and key and not able to be seen, though plainly to be heard.

"All the girls they smile at me," rang out from the farthest lock-up cell, "a comin' through the rye."

Harris escaped onto the scorched yellow dust of the square. The heat beat down on his shoulders and rose through the soles of his shoes. Holding his top hat between the sun and his eyes, he stared down Wellington, Front and Palace Streets and up Nelson to where Jarvis began north of Queen. Vandervoort had vanished, but the Waterloo veteran still sat in the shade of the portico. Perhaps those moist eyes were not as empty as they seemed.

"Two minutes ago a tall, red-haired man in checks came out this door," said Harris as he put another coin in the high shako hat.

"Flemish name—I forget what."

"Did you happen to notice which way he went?"

"He's gone for a glass at the Dog and Duck, same as every day at five." The veteran pointed to a hotel entrance on West Market Square.

Shame on Vandervoort! He was late this afternoon, a disappointment to his friends. But sarcasm would not do. Harris's indignation and anxiety required release in action. He decided against the Dog and Duck and started home to change into clothes he could ride in. The veteran called him back.

"Take that second sixpence of yours," he said. "I ain't a paid spy."

* * *

Banshee was put through her paces, culminating in a three-mile gallop west along the lakeshore. The seven minutes and a half it took her wasn't her best time, but close to it. Harris had bought her for endurance and disposition, not speed.

He stretched in the saddle and wiped his forehead as the horse picked her way through the scrub pine at the mouth of the Humber River. Their approach sent a brown-and-buff wader flying off in a zigzag with a rasping cry. Less easily distracted than the snipe, an osprey continued to hover on beating wings just above the water's surface.

The birds and—more particularly—the variety of wildflowers

had drawn Theresa to the Humber Valley often before her marriage. Harris began to work his way upstream, if not inch by inch then yard by yard. In less than three hours, night would fall.

Where the banks were too spongy to ride, he guided Banshee over the shale and limestone stream bed. He stopped to question fishermen. He dismounted to inspect footprints, bread crusts, paper scraps, and every other sign of human passage.

The vale north of Bâby Point had provided most of the items for Theresa's botanical inventory, so he took extra time to survey this ground on foot. Names he could no longer match to plants ran unbidden through his head—painted cup, viburnum, helleborine.

Suddenly, he heard the leaves rustle behind him. He grabbed a fallen tree branch and spun around just in time to see the retreating red-brown back of a snowshoe hare.

As the shadows lengthened, Harris left the valley. He rode back to Toronto in the dark, making fruitless inquiries at every inn along Dundas Street. During the intervals, he reflected that such random leisure-time excursions stood no chance of leading him to Theresa. He would willingly have left the search to others—to the authorities, to the experts. If only such people existed.

He had prolonged this afternoon's interview with Vandervoort in the continually frustrated hope of receiving some assurance of official diligence or competence. For all his professional discretion, the inspector had revealed that his department lacked any procedure for finding people, that they had as yet no likeness of Theresa, that no one was actively looking for her, that suspicious circumstances were not even to be investigated. Nor was it evident that Crane was making up for police deficiencies. Crane seemed content to throw suspicion on Harris.

The horse trotted on, hoofs as regular as a heartbeat. Farmland was giving way to town. The houses drew closer to the road and to their neighbours. Burghers taking the night air on their stoops could call to each other and to passersby, though gas-fuelled street lamps didn't yet come out this far.

One day Toronto would be well lit and well policed. So much stood to reason. What baffled Harris was the weight of obligation he felt settling upon himself in the meantime. His normally reliable good sense counselled him to flinch, to shrug the burden off, but his pulse was beating louder than such counsels. Harris had never known the imperiousness of his own heart. He was afraid he was about to.

* * *

When he had delivered Banshee to Randall's boy for grooming and made sure her manger was full, he went to look for Jasper Small. At nine p.m., however, Small could not really be expected to be home, still less at his law office. At an oyster bar, more likely, the resort of men of fashion. As it happened, no oyster bar had seen him, nor had his favourite billiard parlours, nor indeed was he to be found in any public establishment that could be reached by closing time.

Back in the cashier's suite, another night passed, slowly. Next day at noon, Harris tried again, walking north of Queen Street on Yonge to the end unit of a short row of Georgian yellow-brick houses.

He had first come here nine years ago in the winter of 1847, before he had been employed by the bank. At his father's instigation, he had been working to establish the York County Millers' Association and had needed advice on a matter of legal incorporation. He had heard that William Sheridan was one of the best lawyers in the province, and by no means the most expensive, but that Sheridan might not be available, as he was devoting more and more of his time to politics.

On that January morning, the first thing the eighteen-year-old Harris had heard when he opened the street door was a cascade of angry abuse.

"If you would make a supreme mental effort, Mr. Small," a deep Irish voice thundered, "you would realize that I have a coach to catch to Montreal. What bloated idea of your own importance could have made you think that I have so much as a second to spare on your flea of a client's libel action?"

Harris had leaped back down the steps, flagged down a horse-drawn omnibus descending Yonge Street, and held it the thirty seconds more it took a chunkily handsome man in his mid-forties to burst into the street. A second, boyish figure, vapour ballooning from his startled mouth, followed as far as the top step. Sheridan was waved a farewell he didn't look back to see with a handful of the papers he had not had time to read.

Returning the salute on his behalf, Harris bundled his quarry aboard the omnibus. Together they rode it to where it turned east along King Street. Then they ran and slid the two remaining blocks to Weller's Stage Office on Front Street. Sheridan already had his ticket to Montreal. Harris took one as far as Pickering, which he judged would give him time and to spare to explain his problem.

As the coach runners skimmed over the frozen roads, Sheridan relaxed inside his furs. He understood what the York Millers wanted and saw no particular difficulty in doing it. He said something about the beauty of the Canadian winter and how much he enjoyed sleighing—not as far as Montreal, to be sure, which was where Parliament happened to be sitting—but in short spurts. Did Harris have a horse and sleigh of his own? No? Then he must take Sheridan's out for a turn sometime, out on the bay, with a team in tandem.

Harris smiled at the extravagance.

"I mean it," the lawyer protested. "You'll see. Life's so full of pleasures, my young friend. I'm a jackass to let my temper get the better of me the way it did back there. It will be the death of me."

"I don't know about that, sir," said Harris, crossing several degrees of intimacy at a bound, "and I don't know much about law—but if the flea of a client had opened that door instead of me, I suppose there might have been another libel suit in the offing."

"Slander, Mr. Harris, for verbal insults. I'd have put nothing so damaging in writing."

The young lawyer Sheridan had left gasping on the doorstep that day later became his partner and Harris's closest friend.

Today Jasper Small was to be found in Sheridan's room rather than his own, ostensibly cleaning up Sheridan's affairs. Letters and documents covered both the open front of the writing desk by the door, and a fully extended gate-leg table in the bay window. A wavy-haired man of roughly Harris's age was moving these papers about without appearing to sort them in any way. Small's fleshy moon of a face and pale grey eyes made him look the dreamer even when delivering an elegantly conclusive argument in court. Whether his present task absorbed him Harris found hard to tell.

"Dine with me, Jasper."

"I can't," said Small. "Oh, hang it, I shall. The Trafalgar House has received a shipment of the most amazing claret."

The firm of Sheridan and Small having a progressive reputation, Jasper felt at liberty to wear a bowler in place of a top hat. His morning coat was impeccably cut and pressed, as were his matching loose trousers. An extra-elaborate tie knot was his only real touch of dandyism.

Harris had no criticism to make of Small, and yet as the two emerged onto the plank sidewalk, he realized he had come expecting too much. While more composed than on his return Wednesday night from the Humber Valley, he felt as tense as a drawn bow. He wanted Small to provide all the answers and reassurances that had so far eluded Harris himself.

"Sorry for your loss," he mumbled, to at least get that out of the way. "There was no chance to speak at the funeral."

Small shook his head as if he could not believe what he was about to say. "I took the old man papers to sign Friday afternoon. He was on the mend. No more pain in the gut, he says. The next day off he pops."

"Oh? You don't think his death was natural?"

Harris had heard no suspicion of this—none, that is, but Septimus Murdock's. And what did the accountant *not* suspect? Belonging to the Roman Catholic minority in a Protestant town could only reinforce the apprehensiveness of his temperament, and his noting the "significant coincidence" of Sheridan's death with the Glorious Twelfth was all the easier for Harris to dismiss in that Murdock had so far refused to be more explicit.

Orangemen did have reason to dislike Sheridan. Although a Protestant Irishman himself, he had joined Robert Baldwin in trying to outlaw the Orange Order back in the days of Governor Metcalfe. Sheridan's rhetoric at the time, moreover, had been far less temperate than Baldwin's. But dislike was one thing, murder another. Besides, this dispute was thirteen years old. Drunken brawls might be a Toronto Orange tradition. Long-nurtured grudges and stealthy vendettas, as far as Harris knew, were not.

Nor did Small appear to have foul play in mind.

"Natural to be sure," he replied. "As natural as quack medicine. I'm just not convinced it resulted inevitably from his illness."

Harris asked who had been Sheridan's physician.

"An old friend," said Small through clenched teeth. "Hell, Chris Hillyard was already old in '23 when Willie Sheridan first came to this country."

"I'm surprised Sheridan never made us acquainted," Harris observed.

"Well, in fact Hillyard did retire for a few years, disappeared to the Indies, and then committed the capital error of coming back. He likely gave Sheridan a purgative thinking it was a sedative."

Such bitterness, not typical of his pleasure-loving friend, Harris attributed to the sudden weight of sole responsibility for the affairs of the partnership. Feeling oppressed, Small required an oppressor—which did not of course mean he was wrong about Hillyard. In any event, Small's frown melted away when a girl with sleeves pushed up to her elbows showed them from the inn door to a white-clothed table and set a bottle of red Bordeaux before them.

The Trafalgar House was a small hotel with an oenophilic owner and an indifferent cook. Harris contented himself with bread and cheese to accompany his glass of wine, while it took Small the rest of the bottle to wash down his portion of boiled beef.

"Could anyone else have killed him?" said Harris as soon as they were alone. "Possibly *not* by accident."

"Whoa, what kind of question is that?" Small took a steadying drink.

"Well—had he received any threats? Did anyone come to the office—I don't know—brandishing a revolver?"

"There were times I came close to brandishing one myself," Small replied. "And he certainly made enemies, but apart from the Orangemen—which is to say, apart from the police, the fire department, the carters, the innkeepers and the politicians—any enemies he made he made into friends again right after. My money stays on the medico. But what's *your* interest, Isaac? Why so keen?"

Harris shrugged stiffly.

"That's what I thought," said Small, wiping his mouth on a corner of his napkin. "Then what's this about threats against her father?"

The two seldom spoke of Theresa, whom Small had courted for eight weeks and Harris for considerably longer—so much longer as to not seem a fit subject for raillery.

After two false starts, Harris explained his belief that Sheridan's death and Theresa's disappearance must be linked. He spoke also of his own researches to date and of his unsatisfactory interviews with Crane and Vandervoort.

Small leaned forward. "You won't take advice on this subject, I know."

"Likely not." Jasper's most recent advice—only half facetious—had been that to circulate the blood and reset his compass what Harris needed was to visit a whorehouse, a good one. Jasper knew just the place. On the whole, Harris found he dreaded Small's advice.

"Let me just say, Isaac, that involving yourself in the search for Theresa can do you no good."

"That's not the—"

"No, listen—"

"She has been missing four days," Harris in turn broke in. "All I want is to know she's safe."

"We all want that," said Small with murderous mildness, "and then again, suppose you desert your bank and kill your horse galloping it all over the continent. I won't speak of the worst outcome—but take the best case. Even if you find her safe and whole, you'll be bringing her home to Henry. Can you swallow that?"

"If she wishes it."

Small studied his friend's face. "Given the state of your feelings for her, you can't be serious."

"Yes, certainly, of course—but Crane is not above suspicion in all this. Why isn't he looking for her himself?"

"Business preoccupations, I would guess."

Harris took this as a further instance of Small's contempt for sentiment. "You be serious, Jasper. Any normally affectionate husband would leave his immense wealth to look after itself for a week."

"Not so immense as all that. Have you not heard?"

Harris had not. He had got in the habit of paying no more attention to Crane's activities than he could help. Crane took his business to the Commercial Bank, and their ways seldom crossed. References to Crane in the press were generally laudatory.

Railways he had built in the southwestern part of the province had, to be sure, suffered mishaps. Bridges had collapsed. Iron rails had split in the severe Canadian winter. Stoves had set fire to passenger coaches with fatal results. Deaths had resulted from the lack of gates at level crossings. By then, however, the customer had always paid and taken delivery of the line. Crane had fulfilled his contract and never seemed to come out the loser, not even in terms of reputation.

But Small knew more than was in the papers.

"He has overreached himself," the lawyer announced authoritatively. "He has committed too much of his personal capital to risky or long-term ventures."

The Kingston to Cape Vincent railway car ferry was a case in point, said Small—who had sat at the same piquet table as the treasurer's daughter. Loading trains on boats was to cost less than bridging the St. Lawrence. Wolfe Island did stand in the path of navigation, but Crane had allegedly taken up shares with both hands on the mistaken assumption that a canal across the obstructing land mass would soon be completed. Such miscues weren't like him. Nevertheless... Untypically, also, he had undertaken railway contracts east of Toronto for shares instead of bonds or cash. That meant higher construction standards and worries about rising costs.

"His shrewdness has deserted him," Small declared, "and—whether cause or effect—he's desperate for funds. There are even rumours that he has touched friends for loans."

"Next you'll be telling me he has lost money at the race track," said Harris. "How long is he supposed to have been feeling the pinch?"

"A year," said Small, "fourteen months. And he never bets on horses—*or* drinks, *or* smokes, *or* swears. So much for the wages of virtue!"

Harris thought back to Tuesday. The exquisite carriage in which Crane had taken them to the graveside was so new that the ship that had brought it from England might still be in the harbour. A bold purchase. And yet the most distinguished mourners had seemed to avoid Crane as they would not have done if he still smelled of success.

"Whatever his difficulties," said Harris, "he should still be more concerned about his wife."

Small smiled like a Buddha. Plainly, he thought Harris biased. Harris was, of course. "Are they happy together?" he asked.

"Like any couple. I rarely see them together."

"When did you last see Theresa?"

"Friday at her father's. She had more or less moved down there from Queen Street East while he was ill. I was sitting in the old boy's room, waiting for him to wake up from a nap, when she came in and shooed me out. She said I could tell the housekeeper to serve tea to her and myself in the parlour. She let me back upstairs later on, but only on condition I not bother her Papa with business. So the papers never did get signed."

"Anything important?" said Harris.

"Everything I do is important, Isaac. My God, I wish we had time for another bottle of this."

Small was mooning over the wine label, ostensibly dreaming of the château where it had been pasted on.

"A new will perhaps?" said Harris.

"Nothing I intend to blab about. Not a will, though. His will is no secret. His daughter gets the villa and its contents. Most everything else, no great hoard, goes to charity. Oh, and I inherit his share of the practice, which at present seems a very mixed blessing."

"But would the estate be large enough to restore Crane's fortunes," asked Harris, "assuming he could get his hands on it?"

"Not nearly." Small pushed back his chair, which the innkeeper's daughter took as a signal to bring the two hats.

Harris ignored his and remained seated. "How did Theresa seem?"

"In the sickroom, quite under control. She knew just how far open she wanted the windows and what covers should be on the bed. When her Papa woke up, she took his temperature with a thermometer, which is more than I've ever heard of Christopher Hillyard's doing."

"And downstairs at tea?"

"Agitated," said Small, evidently choosing a word softer than the one he felt appropriate. "She complained of the stifling heat and of want of air. At one point, she excused herself, and I heard her cross-questioning the housekeeper in a most dogged and ferocious manner such as a judge would hardly let you get away with in court."

"On what subject?"

"Couldn't hear. It just seemed indicative of what state her nerves were in. No wonder they snapped when—you know..."

"That's how you explain her disappearance?" Having ruled out this possibility himself, Harris rose impatiently from the table. "After a calm Sunday dinner, she just ran wild. Well, if she has lost her wits, she can't have hidden herself too cunningly."

"I imagine *someone* has seen her," said Small.

"You can imagine anything you like. If you really want to set your mind at ease, Jasper, you can imagine some Christian soul has taken her in and is plying her with roast goose."

Harris walked Small back to his law office, though he was already likely to be missed at the bank. Irresolution gnawed him. His momentary hesitation before attending Sheridan's funeral was but a love bite to this. In the Holland Landing of his boyhood, there would have been no question. Everyone would have helped beat the bush for the missing woman. Urban cynicism might colour Small's advice, and yet Harris lived in the city now too. If Toronto's neighbours were not to be counted on, it wasn't because they lacked hearts, but because they by and large worked for others and were not masters of their own time. No more was Harris. He would likely have to act alone if at all and turn his life upside down to do it.

And then again, the circumstances remained so clouded—everything from Sheridan's death to the state of Theresa's nerves. If there had been some cry for help, some unmistakable plea, the path ahead would have been plainer.

On the steps where Harris had first heard Sheridan's voice, Small turned.

"She mentioned you, Isaac," he said. "I didn't know whether to tell you."

"Please do."

"She asked did I think enough time had passed that you could regard her now as just a friend."

Pain rippled through Harris's stomach, chest, and throat. "And you answered?"

He knew he had given Small no reason to believe he was over his disappointed love. Time and again Small had introduced him to charming young women that he had danced with for part of an evening and gratefully seen whisked out of his arms by enthusiastic young men. As lately as Saturday, he had danced the polka—which was taking ballrooms by storm, and which Methodists found so lewdly suggestive. For better or worse, Harris was not very open to suggestion, he guessed. He nonetheless would have found it hard to forgive if Small had said anything that might have deterred Theresa from seeking his aid.

"I said, 'Try him.'"

"Good." Harris let out a breath he had scarcely been aware he had been holding.

"I gather she didn't," said Small.

"No. I wish I had known."

"Well, she didn't tell me she was about to vanish."

"Of course not," said Harris gently. "Thanks."

Chapter Three
The Rouge Valley

Well-established habits carried Harris through Thursday afternoon's routine business—interviewing loan applicants, authorizing replacement of a cracked window pane, reprimanding a chronically unpunctual teller, perusing economic reports. Canadian wheat production for 1856 was expected to reach twenty-six million bushels. An impressive figure, probably still on the low side—although the new peace with Russia and the consequent reopening of trade to the east could not but depress the price those Canadian bushels would fetch in England and France. The fat years might well be ending.

Harris found it impossible to care, preoccupied as he was with what act of friendship Theresa had required. He had kept Small standing on his office steps and asked him that question in various ways, but—beyond sympathetic companionship during William Sheridan's indisposition—Small had no ideas at all.

"No," Harris was explaining to a chemistry professor, "our charter prevents us from accepting your house as the principal security for a loan. Do you have any bonds you could pledge? Or is there anyone at all that owes *you* money?"

The squat Yorkshireman replied that the University of Toronto owed him an increase in emolument. As this was a moral rather than a legal obligation, however, Harris could only recommend that the man get whatever influential friends he had to speak for him to his employers. Best wishes and good day.

Then the afternoon mail brought a matter that was far from routine. Out of an envelope addressed to Harris personally fell four of his branch's brand new fifty-dollar notes.

He stared a moment in amazement at the harbour scene

depicted on the backs. A classically draped female figure, spilling bounty from a cornucopia, sat at the water's edge while a train steamed towards her from one side, a ship from the other. Both billowed clouds of smoke, intricately engraved for the discouragement of forgers.

These were not forgeries. They were a bribe, equivalent to an even tenth of the cashier's yearly pay. He pulled from the envelope a letter to the effect that Joshua Newbiggins recognized Isaac Harris's abilities and would work to ensure they received wider recognition.

The absence of a stamp showed the envelope had come by private messenger. Even so, Newbiggins must have stepped lively. The money he had picked up at noon he was already putting to work. Harris had suspected its first use would be as gifts, but the likeliest recipients had seemed the railways that Conquest Iron Works hoped to supply or Conquest's influential Front Street neighbours. Not Harris.

He knew, though, why he had been so honoured. One of his branch's major borrowers was York Foundry, an established manufacturer in Conquest's line. Information the bank held regarding York's costs, suppliers and clients would help Conquest overcome the handicap of a late start.

Harris had been offered bribes before, but so discreetly that he had always been able to decline without either taking or giving offence. Newbiggins's crudeness raised questions about his judgement and, unhappily, about that of the president who had recommended him. Re-enclosing the bills and letter in a fresh envelope, Harris entrusted their return to Dick Ogilvie and instructed his staff to say he was occupied if Mr. Newbiggins should call.

* * *

Thursday evening and every free minute of the next day were spent on the kind of inquiries Harris had outlined to Vandervoort. Neither the ticket agencies nor the city hotels admitted to having seen Theresa. A proper detective job was going to require something Harris had not yet worked out how to get, Crane's cooperation or that of someone in his establishment.

Gatekeepers at Crane's home and office kept offering polite excuses. A personal letter went unanswered. Friday noon Harris did manage to intercept him on King Street. Crane cut him off before Harris could speak.

He had been about to ask what funeral arrangements Crane had made on Sunday. The undertaker denied having seen him. So did the priest and the pallbearers.

Harris got a little further with Dr. Hillyard—who appeared in every respect the dotard Small had represented. The opening of his surgery door late Friday afternoon sent dust balls scurrying. Throughout the interview, the doctor's trembling hands wandered between the buttons of a food-stained waistcoat and a high, scabby forehead bracketed by cobwebs of hair.

He said he had last seen Sheridan alive on Saturday morning. At that time he had administered no medicine. He had left none. He had recommended none. The symptoms of inflammation having subsided, no medicine was indicated.

But the annals of physic were full of unforeseen reverses. Sheridan's demise that very evening was regrettable, but not so surprising as to arouse suspicion. "We are not God, sir." A messenger from Mrs. Crane had reached Hillyard's just before nine p.m. and had been sent on to where he was celebrating the Glorious Twelfth. By nine thirty, he was at Sheridan's villa. There he observed nothing to suggest the death had been anything but natural and, indicating that he would report it as such, took his leave some twenty minutes later.

That was all he would say. Further questions should be put to Mrs. Crane. No, Hillyard had no idea where to find her. Was she not at home? Mr. Crane then.

For Friday evening, Harris had a supper engagement he could not decently get out of. After leaving Hillyard, he found he didn't want to. He craved a few hours' relaxation. Last

Saturday's laughter and polkas seemed to belong to a summer long past.

The MacFarlanes' up on Queen Street West was a household with artistic aspirations. Singing rather than cards accordingly followed the meal. Harris had the voice of a crow but could sight read at the piano well enough to be a useful accompanist. Well enough, but not perfectly. The twelve-year-old daughter of the house broke into such fits of giggles when he hit a wrong note that he began making mistakes deliberately just to provoke her. Elsie's mother was the most provoked, however, and the two clowns were driven from the pianoforte in disgrace.

Elsie took this opportunity to corner Harris and show him her sketch book. Managing the crinoline cage her voluminous dress required was plainly giving her the difficulty of a novice helmsman on a broad-beamed steamer, and Harris barely managed to catch a cherrywood teapoy toppled by her passage.

"The thing I *don't* like about these skirts," she said, patting the wire-supported dome of pink taffeta below her waist, "is you can't sit in armchairs."

"And the thing you *do* like?" Harris took the book from her hands.

"Is you can't be ignored. You must start at the beginning now and not just go flipping through."

A sprightly child but very earnest too, Harris realized as he turned the pages and found one excruciatingly literal drawing after another. The birds seemed to be sketched from a taxidermy shop. The houses might have been of great use to a builder. Then there were parts of a cat that, even in sleep, moved around too much ever to have its portrait completed.

It was high time Harris made an appreciative remark. "You know, Elsie, I like these bits. They leave something to your imagination."

Then he turned the page and saw a cloud of cat, a sketch so furious and unconsidered it might all have been done in five seconds. It wasn't what Harris thought of as artistic. The pencilled swirls better suited a storm at sea than a dozing pet.

He wondered if Elsie, frustrated by her own caution, had swung to the opposite extreme.

"That's not mine," she said.

"Whose is it then?"

"Mrs. Crane's..."

Elsie had Harris's full attention. Here was a connection he had not guessed at.

"She said that unless I was illustrating an anatomy textbook, I should not worry so much about the details. I do like her. Do you think she will be found?"

A quick, false yes would not do. If Elsie's parents had trusted her with news of the disappearance, rather than pretending Theresa was out of town on some cosy visit, then Harris didn't want to spew easy reassurance either. At the same time, he honestly could not imagine living the rest of his life with this mystery unresolved.

"I think she will," he said slowly. "Did you ever sketch her?"

"I surely did." The girl's long face brightened. "Don't skip now. You'll come to it."

"Come on back, Mr. Harris," some one called from the piano. "It seems we can't do without you."

"In a moment," he answered.

Elsie's drawings, still highly detailed, did become looser and livelier. Theresa's portrait was easily the best thing in the book. Affection for the sitter must have helped, on top of which Theresa had given Elsie a pose it would have been hard to make static. Her head was turning as if her attention had just been caught by the glimpse of a person long absent, and her lips were parting as if she were about to speak. The drawing was dated the first of the current month.

"What do you think? Am I improving?" Elsie wanted to know.

"You are indeed. Could I borrow this and make a tracing?"

"I should want it back. Do you really think it's good?"

Harris's musical services were again being called for.

"I do, but remember I'm not an art critic, Elsie, just a banker."

"And a dazzling pianist," she reminded him merrily.

"Plug your ears," he warned her on his way back to the keyboard.

After a sufficiency of Mendelssohn and Schubert, the music party broke up for refreshments. Harris watched his chance to get a word with Elsie's mother, who but for darker eyes and a stronger chin greatly resembled her contemporary the Queen. Kate MacFarlane was for some time occupied ordering staff and guests about in a quick, sharp voice. Her folded fan pointed directions. Harris had never seen her wear anything but tartan—a general fad since the completion of the royal residence at Balmoral. Her timber-baron husband—an older man, very tall and substantial—left to her the duties of general hospitality, while he remained towering in the background in conversation with the comeliest of the young sopranos.

Harris had only recently been introduced to the family, which explained his not knowing of their acquaintance with Theresa. And yet he felt quickly at ease. Mrs. MacFarlane's brusqueness had a way of breaking down reserve.

Speak to her? Certainly. Making sure he had a plate of cakes, she drew him out through French doors onto a vaulted loggia overlooking the garden. Gothic arches added to the picturesque appeal of this villa scaled like a castle. Theresa Crane, said the chatelaine, disliked large gatherings and would have wiggled out of this one even if she had been in town. And what did Harris think had become of her anyway?

He said he intended to find out—but confessed he had lost touch with her. He lacked current information regarding her interests, character and friends.

Mrs. MacFarlane stared out at the shadowy carpet of grass. "That's not a good start," she said softly.

"Do you know any old schoolmates she went on nature rambles with?"

"Not one. She may have mentioned a name or two, but as they married, those friendships seemed to wither..."

"What current friends do you know of?" asked Harris.

"I couldn't see that she had any, or family either apart from her father and husband."

Other guests were coming out to escape the heat of the lamps, but remained beyond earshot.

Harris dropped his voice anyway. "Was there discord between her and Mr. Crane?"

It was too dark to read Mrs. MacFarlane's face. When she didn't speak, he repeated the question.

"I'm not sure I should tell you if I had noticed anything of the sort, but the fact is I didn't."

"How often did you see her?" Perhaps, thought Harris, not often enough to tell.

"Once a week or so. She made quite a friend of Elsie."

Harris said he understood. "And when did you see her last?"

"Sunday morning at church," replied his hostess, "at the Cathedral."

"Two hours at most before her disappearance!" Harris exclaimed. "Did she say anything that casts light on that event?"

"Well, she—her father had died just the night before, remember. You could tell it affected her deeply. You'll want to know when she first came here. I believe it was soon after her marriage. Our husbands had business dealings—to do with ships or trains, I suppose. Isn't it always one or the other? Or telegraphs." The mistress of the house was back in stride, one thought briskly pulling the next. "As for Theresa Crane, she and I shared cultural and charitable interests, though I believe she regarded art as a minor recreation, something to do when your brain is tired. Even botany began to seem frivolous to her. Medicine attracted her more."

"Was she ill?" asked Harris.

"No, indeed. Not that I could see, at least, but she felt for those that suffer. We discussed the institutions Toronto is having to build to cope with its prosperity. The casualties of prosperity, that is. You know the places I mean. The new General Hospital, the Roman Catholic House of Providence, the Lunatic Asylum—"

"There you are, Kate," an elderly lady called from the doorway. "Our carriage is out front, but I couldn't leave without..."

While Mrs. MacFarlane was saying good night to the early leavers, Harris waited to see if there would be an opportunity to resume the interview. Under the circumstances, it was difficult to show even polite interest in other topics. He pretended to inspect the oil paintings that lined the reception room.

"Are you an admirer of Mr. Paul Kane?" Kate MacFarlane was again beside him, pointing out features of an eighteen-by-thirty-inch canvas he had taken in only as tepees and canoes. A Lake Huron encampment, she said. Such and such reclining figure could of course be traced to classical models, but no one who had lived on the upper lakes ever questioned the scene's essential truth.

Crane had lived there once. Harris asked if she could think of anything that might have drawn Theresa in that direction.

"No. Nor in any other. I'm baffled." She glanced around in case she were needed elsewhere. "Look, Mr. Harris, I do approve of your trying to find her. Private initiative is the only way *anything* gets done, but Mr. MacFarlane has just this instant been called away on business, and we still have guests. Why not come back tomorrow? Give me till then and I'll see if I can't think of something useful to tell you."

"I'm sorry," said Harris, "but so much time has passed already. By tomorrow she may have spent six nights in the open."

Kate MacFarlane glared at him. "There's nothing I can do about that."

"No, of course not," he quickly assented. He didn't want to risk losing his one supporter. "What I'm thinking," he added, "is that if I start at dawn and ride in the right direction, perhaps I can make sure it's not seven."

"Briefly then."

"What was her favourite ride?"

"The only one I have heard her mention particularly was the Rouge Valley, but then her husband thought it was too far and forbade her to ride there alone. I suppose that's why it didn't occur to me before. Now—if you want more of my company, Mr. Harris, you'll have to come and meet some young men who have been to New York to hear *Signor* Verdi's latest opera."

Harris left. On the walk home, it started to rain. He tucked Elsie's sketch book inside his tail coat and quickened his pace.

* * *

Three quarters of an hour later, Theresa's face traced onto tissue paper stared up from the writing surface of the secretary desk in Harris's drawing room. The likeness was crude, but still—he felt—more helpful than a description on its own.

He tried to compare this face to the one he remembered. Did she look older because three years had passed or because of some particular experience? Or was it because to a child artist every adult looks old? He couldn't even decide if her face had narrowed or filled out until he realized she had simply changed the style of dressing her hair. While it had been puffed at the crown to either side of the centre part, it now lay flat on top and fell smoothly to where it turned under in a loose roll secured at the nape. That rich, reddish brown roll of hair mere pencil lines had no hope of capturing. It must look glorious, thought Harris.

He turned off the gas and found his way to bed by the glow of the street lamps below his windows. Having already removed his wet clothes, he had only to slip out of a light dressing gown. Stretched on his back with the sheet thrown off, he listened to the rain drumming on the plank sidewalks and to the passage of a couple of pedestrians. Well-spaced, heavy treads accompanied by quick and light. Through the moist air rose the clear tone of a woman's laugh. The double set of footfalls ceased sounding in the mud of Bay Street, then resumed on the far sidewalk and faded away to the west. Harris rolled onto his side and felt, as he had not allowed himself to feel for years, the weight of his loneliness.

Always he had contrived to be busy with work, or with superficial social engagements and exhausting recreations—long rides, billiards, card parties, curling and ice boating in winter, sailing and swimming in summer, hunting in fall. Or, if all else failed, voracious reading with the lights turned up full. He had managed never to lie down till he was too tired to remember. Too tired to miss her.

In the darkened room, he rolled over several times more, dozed, and fell more or less asleep.

He was awake again by dawn but far from certain in which direction to ride. No horsewoman herself, Kate MacFarlane said she had never accompanied Theresa to the Rouge Valley and didn't know which part of it she favoured. The Rouge River rose some twenty miles north of town, but didn't begin to carve out anything Harris believed could be called a valley till it had passed Markham. He decided, without much conviction, to start there and follow the stream south to the lake. This had not been a haunt of Theresa's when Harris had known her. The whole area did seem too remote for a spot of Sunday afternoon exercise, and for a refuge not remote enough.

Pond-sized puddles sprawled over the ungraded dirt streets, but were no longer growing—the rain having tapered off to something between a drizzle and a mist. Harris let it settle on the shoulders of his fustian hunting jacket as he strode towards the livery stable. The oilskin cape he had brought was too hot to wear in anything less than a downpour.

He was presently trotting up Yonge Street, which was surfaced with crushed stone on the Macadam system and cambered to shed the water. North of Yorkville, progress was slower because he had not yet made inquiries at the numerous inns and taverns. Nor, of course, had anyone else.

Harris now had the tracing to show, though he began to doubt its utility when a market gardener at Gallows Hill said he definitely knew the subject—a Negress in her sixties, was she not? Then a Thornhill ostler thought he had seen the lady a week ago. She had been dressed in bright green and riding north, but not on a black palfrey with one white hind foot. Harris turned east and galloped on.

On joining the river, he began asking at mills, which at first were nearly as frequent as the inns on Yonge Street. Sawmills predominated, though the white pine had mostly been logged out. Forward-looking owners were also having their wheels grind corn or card wool. Shrubs and trees of no commercial value still lined the riverbanks, but this was far from wilderness. One surmised that Crane's opposition to Theresa's visits was based on the lengthy absences they entailed rather than on anything sinister or threatening about the valley.

Towards eleven a.m., Harris reached a place in the fourth concession of Scarboro Township where the stream flowed east, sharply south, then sharply west again. Over this peninsula, the homey smell of damp sawdust lay thick as porridge. Picking his way between piles of fresh lumber, he dismounted at the open end of a long frame shed. Inside, the rising and falling blade was tearing through a log so clamorously that—rather than speak—he simply touched the elbow of the older of the two men at the machinery and with an interrogative hoist of his eyebrows gestured to the doorway.

The bearded miller nodded and followed agreeably enough, but once outside responded to every question with a noncommittal grunt. An unproductive morning had its disheartening cap.

But wait—what if the man could not hear, if his saw had ruined his ears? Harris unfolded the portrait.

"Mrs. Crane," said the miller with surprising force. "She used to ride here often. In the concession road and down the valley or up the valley and out the concession."

"Last Sunday?" Harris bellowed.

"She had a black mare, skittish, but a treat to look at. I tried to buy it for my daughter."

"Was Mrs. Crane here last Sunday?"

"Um."

Harris found a stub of pencil in his jacket and wrote the question on a corner of the tissue paper.

"No, like I said. In the spring, she and another lady, but not since May or April." The miller gave the coins in his pocket a wistful, indiscreet rattle of which he was doubtless unaware. "I would have paid sterling too," he said, "no paper money."

Continuing the interview would have been awkward enough even if the man had been willing to acknowledge his deafness. Harris approached the helper.

A young immigrant working to bring his betrothed out from Cork, he became cooperation itself on learning that Mrs. Crane's parents had come from that very county. Of her mount's markings he gave a detailed description. It fit Spat exactly. In declining the miller's offers, Theresa had reportedly said the animal was too old and nervous to change stables. The other lady was remembered as dark and fine-featured. The Irishman had not caught her name, nor had he understood anything the horsewomen said to each other. They seemed not to be speaking English. Not Gaelic either. Neither had been seen for weeks.

Harris accepted a slice of pork pie and a glass of cider for his lunch before pursuing an old settlers' road down the east brink of the river. Thirty-foot cliffs shut out any glimpse of the wheat fields and orchards he knew lay to either side and above him. On occasion he would clamber out of the valley to ask well-rehearsed questions at farm houses. Then he would rejoin the Rouge none the wiser. What kept him going was that no one south of the fourth concession could swear that Theresa had not ridden this way last Sunday.

Afternoon passed into evening. He had just left the last mill on the river when the rain began again, tentative and caressing at first. By the time he thought of his cape, his clothes were soaked through.

The valley grew swampy and desolate in its final mile. Enormous steps carved at one point into the cliffs from top to bottom constituted the only sign of human passage. These Harris recognized as the terraced graves of a long-abandoned Seneca Indian village. They were not a comforting omen. Nearer Lake Ontario, the aggrieved shrieks of gulls began to drown out the patter of raindrops on willow leaves.

Then Harris turned the last bend and found himself facing a wall of earth, a great hand pressed over the river's mouth. This must be the embankment of the Grand Trunk Railway. In fact, a narrow outlet spanned by a trestle had been left for the Rouge water to escape to the lake, but the flow was too great and the river had backed up into a lagoon. Its waters had drowned a frame factory building labelled, "COWAN'S SHIPYARD: 2 & 3 masted schooners built to order."

So, another blind alley. Wet and saddle-sore, Harris concluded that the best place for him now was in front of his own fire with a glass of something warming at his side. First, though, he stopped to mop the water from his face and pull his hat brim lower. Standing a moment in the stirrups, he stretched his legs and redistributed his weight. Before his inattentive eyes, two gulls picked and tore at a long white fish that lay on a patch of sand at the foot of the railway trestle. The G.T.R. wasn't yet accepting passengers or freight west of Brockville, but this section of the line seemed to be complete.

Harris settled back in the saddle, preparing to move on. Which end of that fish, he wondered, was the head and which the tail? No, the head must be missing. That end was ragged and torn.

Wearily he tried again to make sense of what he was seeing. It was long and pale, but it was not a fish. Where the tail fins should have been were fingers.

The inside of his stomach began to twitch. Harris was daring enough in a physical sense and not too squeamish to clean and dress the game he killed, but that was a sportsman's courage—not a soldier's—and he had no practice in dealing with severed human limbs.

Only by ignoring this twitching was he able to urge Banshee forward into the water and across the lagoon's sandy bottom. The scolding gulls hoisted themselves into the air and spiralled tightly over their interrupted meal.

Harris could bear to look at it only in glances. Bone seemed to be exposed below the elbow as well as at the shoulder. His first thought was to stop further pillage by burying the remains, but perhaps the topography should be disturbed as little as possible until seen by official eyes. At the water's edge he dismounted and unrolled his oilskin. As he covered the arm, he glimpsed clinging to it green shreds of cloth and circling the wrist a bracelet of silver medallions. The edges of the cape he weighted down with stones.

He did not believe it was Theresa's arm. There were thousands of miles of green cloth in the world. The bracelet...

Remounting a little queasily, he picked his way up the valley in the fading light. If he could only get away from this place, he should be able to think. The place went with him, however. The barest whiff of something rancid and waxy seemed to have rooted in the back of his throat and to be growing there. His nausea made even Banshee's gentlest gait insupportable.

He got down and vomited. The waxy taste was still there, but he felt steadier—steady enough, at least, to realize that he had no idea where to report his discovery.

The last mill was shut this Saturday evening and empty. In the taverns at the east end of the Kingston Road bridge, advice would flow like stagger juice, but anyone asking for a constable would face insistent questions. Harris accordingly turned west at the bridge, back towards Toronto. A talk with the Rouge Hill toll collector some half a mile later did nothing to deflect him from his course.

The toll booth consisted of a faded, two-storey frame house with a roof that extended north across the highway to a blank supporting wall on the other side. The collector had had enough experience with sneaks and bullies to appreciate the difficulty of finding the police. The nearest lived in Highland Creek, but that was Scarboro and this was Pickering. The Pickering lock-up might as well have been on the moon. You would never get a constable out at night anyway.

Harris continued townwards. The pine-planked surface of the Kingston Road clattered horribly beneath the horse's hoofs—an ear-splitting amplification of the agitation in Harris's breast. He quickly switched over to the dirt shoulder. The panic followed him, merely growing more stealthily in the dark and lonely night.

The remains were not Theresa's. Someone must tell him that. He feared, with a fear approaching a certainty, that no one would.

When he reached Market Square, mad fiddle music was spilling out of taverns and breaking against the austere face of Toronto's dark and all-but empty City Hall. Down in Station No. 1, an unfamiliar constable kept vigil. He denied any knowledge of Inspector John Vandervoort. Harris could try coming back on Monday.

Harris tried the Dog and Duck. The taproom was so dimly lit that the elk and whitetail trophy heads along the wall were mutually indistinguishable. Indeed, gloom seemed to clothe the few women present more effectually than their gowns which, as far as Harris could see when he began moving from table to table, all had buttons undone if not actually missing. Overheard conversations between them and their companions often touched on "going upstairs." Impeded by modesty, but more by the dark, Harris completed his tour of the room without finding his man. He applied to the proprietor.

Vandervoort was known to that individual as a dedicated drinker, though by no means a troublesome one. Indeed, his patronage was an asset at licence-renewal time. This was as candid as Harris could wish, but when he asked about tonight in particular, the bluff hotel-keeper turned smarmy.

"Don't see him, I'm afraid. He'll be sorry to have missed you."

"Where's he live?"

"Couldn't say, sir. I might just get a message to him, though, if it's urgent."

"It's urgent that I see him," said Harris—but he was again assured that a message was the most that could be undertaken.

At the stable of the less furtive-looking hotel next door, Harris left his horse to be watered and fed. Returning to the bank on foot, he changed into dry clothes and wrote a letter detailing the discovery of the arm. He asked the inspector to meet him as soon as possible under the Rouge River G.T.R. trestle, where Harris promised to remain until Sunday noon. He then packed a knapsack for a night in the open. Nagged by doubts as to whether the letter would be received or acted upon, he next proceeded to the Union Station at the foot of York Street and sent the Pickering constable a telegram, a copy of which he added to the envelope for Vandervoort.

Back in the Dog and Duck, a leering fiddler was scraping out "Pop Goes the Weasel." One of the pudgier of the unbuttoned women was using her right index finger and left cheek to sound the pops, more or less on cue, and to show her freedom from constraint. These moist little explosions did nothing to revive Harris's long-dead appetite. Notwithstanding, he providently bought some dark stew of unknown composition to take with him and, dodging the murky dancers, managed to place his sealed envelope in the hotel-keeper's hands.

Once outside, he waited twenty minutes in the shadows across the square on the chance of being able to follow the courier. When none emerged, he rode—teeth gritted—back out King Street towards the Kingston Road.

Memories of the gulls' yellow beaks, a fish with fingers, the smell, the waxy taste pushed against him as he advanced. He saw nothing of the countryside. This time he barely heard Banshee's hoofs hammering upon the plank road. He felt he could not go back there, to the beach beneath the railway trestle—but he had to.

The arm must not be disturbed. This was the one sure beacon in a night of doubt.

Whose arm? Where was the rest? As horse and rider trotted on, the wind of their passage whispered unanswerable questions into Harris's too-willing ear. Whose arm? How severed?

He found himself wondering too who was the fine-featured dark lady, the one that used to ride in the valley with Theresa, the one he had heard of at the mill. A cruel hope tempted him. Perhaps not Theresa, but she...

He rode on, still doubting that he could go back to that shrouded lump of torn and soggy flesh.

He was back.

The rain had stopped, though clouds still hung over the mouth of the Rouge. Frogs and crickets whined and belched into the gloom. Harris bit the glass head off a Promethean match, which exploded into flame. He lit the paraffin candle in the tin lamp he had brought and approached the weighted oilskin. It was just as he had left it.

Chapter Four
Sleeping Rough

Stretched on the sand, he managed to sleep till an overnight steamer clattered eastward down the lake towards Rochester or Kingston. Through the narrow gap in the embankment, he watched the sparks shooting from its twin stacks as it passed. You can incinerate a body or sink it. You can bury it or just leave it lying in the bush. Towards four thirty the sky grew pale behind the railway trestle, whose stark beams at dawn would have made a serviceable gallows.

As soon as it was light enough to collect firewood, Harris heated a cup of water for a shave. His toilet made, he inspected the valley floor and sides right the way round the lagoon. Then he clambered over the new railway embankment to look for signs of digging—a messy, unpromising business. All the earth was freshly turned. Nowhere was any grass disturbed, for none had yet had time to seed and grow. By nine he had finished the landward slope and crossed to the lakeward when from the direction of Pickering a dinghy hove in view. Two men pulled on a pair of oars each while a third, hatless and mostly bald, sat firmly gripping the gunwales in the stern. There was still no breath of wind.

The tall front rower wore red whiskers and faded tweeds, including a tweed cap with a button on the top. Harris climbed down to the sandbar to steady the nose of the boat as it grounded.

"So, Mr. Harris," said Vandervoort, jumping out, "it's plain you don't keep bankers' hours. Are all these footprints yours?"

Harris nodded. "The sand was quite smooth when I arrived. Here is the—here it is—this way."

The inspector followed, crouching at the water's edge to

remove the stones from the oilskin.

"Watch where you put your feet now, Whelan," he cautioned the disembarking second man, whose blue tunic looked as if it had been pulled on over pyjamas. "You don't want to be walking on this."

Once the cover was pulled back, there was no danger of Whelan's walking anywhere in the vicinity.

"I'll have a look around," he announced with the assurance of someone not under Vandervoort's orders, though he seemed willing enough to let the city detective take centre stage.

"Can you just help our scientific friend ashore first?" said Vandervoort. "Ah, French perfume."

Harris clapped a handkerchief over his nose and mouth. This morning, however, he resisted the temptation to look away. In time, it had become possible actually to see the arm around or through the images it conjured up.

Vandervoort followed his gaze. "See anything you recognize?"

It was mostly white or the faintest pink, though mottled with darker patches, and too swollen to give any idea of its living thickness. The bracelet was so tight around it as to seem embedded in the flesh. Harris knelt and studied the four visible oval medallions, each of which depicted in intricate relief a European city. London, Paris, Dublin, Milan.

"I don't know if this is a common pattern," he said with difficulty. "William Sheridan did once buy his daughter something similar. Of course, she could have given it away."

"Could she now? She used to ride here?"

"She and another lady." Harris passed on the description he had got from the Scarboro sawmill. "In any event, you would not expect a woman going for a ride to wear this sort of jewellery."

"Maybe she forgot to take it off," Vandervoort casually suggested.

Theresa had been forgetful in just this way. Furthermore, had she intended to leave home, she would have taken as much of her jewellery as possible, if only to meet her expenses.

Rather than utter either of these two thoughts, Harris turned to ascertain what had become of the "scientific friend" and was surprised to recognize the chemistry professor who had come to the bank three days before. He wore the same old-fashioned green frock coat with full skirts and wide lapels. Even with Whelan's help, he was having trouble leaving the dinghy. He seemed to be trying to climb over one of the thwarts, keep hold of both gunwales and carry a bulky leather case all at the same time.

Once his feet were planted on the sandbar, however, his queasiness left him, and he approached the arm without flinching. Vandervoort asked what he made of it.

"It has been in the water," he said. His mouth formed a firm horizontal between sentences. "You can tell by the odour, quite different from decay on dry land. Oh, hallo, Mr. Harris. Not too long in the water, mind. The formation of adipocere is not far advanced."

"Please, Dr. Lamb," said Vandervoort. "I only went to a country school."

"Come now, that fatty substance you smell that causes the bloating. Then again, the epidermis is mostly washed off, but not entirely. Do you see these patches of outer skin with the hairs still attached? Now compare these to the paler and quite hairless inner skin."

Both Vandervoort and Harris took the hairs on trust.

"Going out on a limb, so to speak, I should say it has been immersed a matter of days, rather than weeks or months. Can't tell much more until I get it back in the laboratory. First, though, it might be useful to take a photograph of it just as it was found."

"Photograph!" said Whelan, whose reconnaissance had not taken him out of earshot.

"Don't worry, constable," said Vandervoort. "We are not going to hang it in your parlour." To Harris he murmured, "Knows his cadavers, this Lamb. Foremost expert in the province and a great help to the department. When he writes his book, New York or Boston will hire him away from us in a trice."

The professor had removed a tripod from his leather case and was settling upon it a camera that resembled a bottle on its side—a rosewood bottle with a square base, cylindrical brass neck and brass cap.

"I'm not going to pose with the thing," said Whelan, "and that's final."

Vandervoort looked as if he would not mind posing, but Lamb didn't ask. He merely laid a foot-rule on the sand in front of the arm to give an idea of scale. He slid a glass plate into the back of the camera then removed the lens cap. Glancing between a pocket watch in his left hand and the shifting clouds above, he exposed the plate for more than five minutes.

Harris meanwhile made more footprints. He tramped about impatiently, not looking at or seeing anything in particular. He was inclined to believe in Lamb, but was at the same time hoping that Lamb would find that he had underestimated the period of the limb's immersion, by even as little as a week. Surely, an expert could go that far wrong without disgrace.

The professor at last removed his photographic plate. When he loaded a second, Vandervoort voiced concern for the public purse. One photograph, he said, would be quite enough. Lamb went ahead anyway, uncovering the lens for twice as long.

Collecting himself somewhat, Harris took this opportunity to show Whelan the tracing of Elsie's sketch. The Pickering constable didn't believe he had ever seen the subject.

"Is it *her* arm then?" he asked.

Harris had no reply.

"Well, whoever the poor lady was, bless her soul, her other parts had better not go turning up in the township of Pickering."

When Harris asked if the lower Rouge were considered a dangerous place, he was harangued about the increase in lawlessness generally, short-sighted paring of police salaries, and the drunken rowdiness of railway crews in particular—although they had last month finally moved on to Darlington. Ending on a more cheerful note, Whelan said that at least the valley was no longer frequented by wolves and bears. "The only beasts today are the two-legged kind."

Leaving Lamb to wrap the arm for transport, Vandervoort ambled over with a cadging gleam in his eye. He looked altogether too comfortable.

"You wouldn't happen to have a cigar, inspector?" Harris inquired dryly.

Vandervoort's face fell. "I was about to ask you the same," he said. "Afraid I smoked the last of Lamb's—but we might try Whelan."

Poor Whelan, who was busy hoisting the dinghy's sail, had not even managed to bring his trousers. Harris said he would sooner hear what the police knew of Mrs. Crane.

"We've been down that road before," said Vandervoort.

"But something must have turned up in the last four days. Look here, Inspector, you seem happy enough to have been told about this find. Let's work together."

Vandervoort shook his head. "I saw it at Sheridan's funeral," he said, "when you tried to protect my informant from me. You're an enterprising sort of man, Isaac Harris—and one that *will* not mind his own business."

"Could you not tell me—?"

"I'll tell you this. I've questioned your lighthouse keeper sober, and I've loosened his tongue with drink. I've turned him upside down and inside out. He knows nothing of any harm Mrs. C. may have come to."

"And did you," Harris pursued, "offer him the inducement of leniency in the matter of the contraband revolvers?"

"That's out of my hands. Ask no more."

Harris saw from a purplish tint suffusing Vandervoort's countenance that he was about to anger the detective. The professor's brains would in any case make for better pickings.

The first breeze in over a week had crept up on the lagoon and was ruffling its surface. Waves from the lake pushed through the gap beneath the trestle. A sharpish gust brought Lamb over.

"I don't like the look of this weather," he said. "I'm a hopeless sailor."

"How are you on a horse?" asked Harris. "You're more than welcome to Banshee."

"So, I qualify for a loan after all," the professor commented mildly.

Harris smiled at the reference, which eluded Vandervoort.

"I don't know, really," Lamb continued, "since your animal hasn't yet made my acquaintance, whether I should feel quite safe without you there as well."

Harris agreed to go with him and set about shortening Banshee's stirrups. Lamb meanwhile stood and watched the loaded dinghy—Whelan working the sheet, Vandervoort at the helm—head into open water. As the wind lifted the professor's coat skirts and sent his grey curls scuttling away from the smooth crown of his head to cluster over his ears, he expressed apprehension that the oilskin package and all his camera equipment would be lost "at sea."

This risk appeared negligible compared to the ghastliness of transporting the limb by land, which it was in any event too late for Harris to propose. He helped the professor into the saddle and mounted behind him, reaching around his thick waist for the reins.

"On the row out," said Lamb, "I managed to lose a perfectly serviceable beaver hat to the lake before there was any wind at all. I don't know how I managed to cross the Atlantic—but, ever since I got off the boat from England, I've felt the great thing about Canada is that it's not an island."

Returning to Toronto consumed the balance of the morning. Banshee was unused to carrying double weight, Lamb uncomfortable with any pace faster than a walk. Harris had a unique chance to question the country's top forensic scientist and took especial care that no sudden movement should result in such an eminent cranium's being dashed open against a rock.

Lamb denied having ever met or seen Theresa. His curiosity and his official responsibilities were what had brought him out on the water so early on the Sabbath, a rather arbitrary day of rest in any case—if Mr. Harris didn't mind his saying so. Not at all, Harris assured him. And Vandervoort? Lamb gathered that Vandervoort had had another case upon which he had been counting to secure advancement, but that that case had somehow fallen through. The inspector accordingly found himself in need of an alternate opportunity to shine.

Harris was interested, and at the same time preoccupied by a more urgent question he was afraid to ask. A pricking at the back of his neck kept making him want to turn around. He couldn't be sure he had searched the valley thoroughly enough. What if, in the bushes just beyond...?

"Professor Lamb," he blurted out, "could the woman whose arm this is still be alive?"

"I'm no physician, but I doubt it. We don't appear to be dealing with a surgical amputation."

Harris saw the green-clad figure pulled roughly from her horse by unknown hands. She twists loose, tries to run, but trips over the long skirt of her riding habit. Thrown flat in the marsh grass, she looks up. The axe arcs high and falls.

It keeps on rising and falling.

"An attacker mad enough to inflict this wound would not have stopped there?" said Harris.

"Even if he had," Lamb replied, "the shock and loss of blood must have been fatal."

So further explorations could wait. The broad, blind expanse of the professor's back was suddenly irksome. Harris ungratefully considered bundling his companion into a stagecoach in order to nurse alone the cooling embers of his hope.

Lamb half turned in the saddle. "You referred to the deceased as a woman," he said. "We can't assume that."

Harris begged his pardon.

"I may not be able to say for sure even after I get a chance to weigh the bones. I'll certainly want to scrutinize those hairs under a microscope."

"How soon can you do all that—all that weighing and scrutinizing?"

"The coroner would normally give me a week to ten days."

"The sleeve and bracelet could be a disguise," Harris admitted without conviction. Ten days was a long time to go on searching in a state of uncertainty.

"Come now," said Lamb. "The dress is female, but we must no more base our conclusions on such externals than you bankers do when you decide to extend credit, or to refuse it."

Still digesting Lamb's revelation, Harris did not rise to this bait.

"Incidentally," the professor added, "I took your good advice."

"Oh?" Harris was starting to wonder who besides Theresa, male or female, had disappeared in recent weeks.

"I approached the Hon. Robert Baldwin. He has agreed to petition the regents of the university to pay me more."

"You couldn't have made a sounder choice," said Harris, remembering his manners. "Not only did Mr. Baldwin's government found the university, but he is the one man in Toronto who never breaks his word."

"Present company excepted, I hope."

"Professor Lamb," Harris pleaded, "could you not hasten or somehow expedite your examination of these remains? So long as any chance remains that Mrs. Crane is still drawing breath, every moment is precious."

The green shoulders under Harris's nose shrugged unencouragingly.

Soon after, the end gable and two-storey verandah of the Half Way House came in view on the right of the plank road. When Banshee and her riders stopped for refreshment, Lamb slid from the saddle unaided.

"The chemistry laboratory," he said, brushing sweat from his straight upper lip, "is at present housed in a far from weatherproof pig shed in behind the Provincial Observatory. Look in on me this evening if you like."

* * *

On reaching the cashier's suite in the early afternoon, Harris moved from room to room like a man who can't remember what comes next. He took a bottle of brandy from the dining room sideboard. He left the bottle in the pantry. He opened wardrobe doors, then instead of hanging up his clothes threw them over chairs. Perplexed by this behaviour, he supposed it had something to do with having passed a night in the open on top of five anxious days. Presently he wandered down the corridor to his bedroom, fell on his bed and slept.

He plunged straight into the deepest slumber and ascended gradually. Anxiety returned before fatigue lifted. Waking took forever. Thrashing about the middle ground, he found himself buffeted by more extreme emotions than blew through either his workaday mind or his dreams. He had schooled himself since entering on a business career, and more particularly in the past three years, to give his feelings play within a range not much wider than the arc of the pendulum in his tall mahogany clock. Now, while the wind outside made noisy sport with an ill-secured shutter, his pendulum swung full circle.

Through 180 degrees, he conceived of Theresa as dead. He walked behind the glass-doored hearse, his gaze fixed on the floral tributes piled on her casket. Panicled dogwood, trailing arbutus... His sobs shook bricks loose from houses of the quick. Even if he never saw her, he couldn't bear the thought of her large, green eyes not turning towards a new sight—her soft lips not parting to utter a fresh thought. Or perhaps behind reason's back, he *had* hoped to see her again, and now he couldn't.

Lost, dead, worse than dead. Butchered. Thoughts of the pain and terror this imaginative young woman must have suffered—his Theresa—made him want to eat glass.

Grief needed no addition, and yet the casket he followed was William Sheridan's too. Tears for each flowed together. Harris mourned a fiery old lion together with a child of energy, grace and light. Fate had dashed what was best in the age, its reforming heart, its questing spirit. The world was left to vermin. Harris fancied he felt them crawling through the mattress beneath him.

At the limit of misery, his spirits would begin to lift. Through the other half circle, someone else had been dismembered. Theresa lived. Amid the clamour of the wind, her footsteps sounded on the stair, her crisp tap at the door—which, try as he might, he could not rise to answer. What if she went away? No, there it was again—tap, *tap*. Now somehow she was inside the door, in the hall, in the room, on the bed. The nape of her neck nestled in his hand. Her smooth cheek pressed against his, and he was breathing the sunny scent of her hair. They were each other's, no one else's. For the first time in all his months of inhabiting the Provincial Bank's string of opulent, empty rooms, he was at home.

Then men with black scarves wrapped around their hats came to lay her in a box.

He kept hoping for something like a thunderclap over Bay Street to wake him fully, but after an hour or two his inner storm simply played itself out. When he sat up, it was still Sunday afternoon. The blue and white porcelain wash stand looked cheerful enough against the yellow wallpaper. He poured water from the pitcher into the basin. He brushed his teeth with Atkinson's Parisian tooth paste. Refreshed and on his feet, he knew the world contained decent people and his bed no bugs to speak of.

While water was heating for his bath, he answered bank correspondence. At the same time, part of him wanted to rush back to the edge of town and scour the landscape in broadening rings until he dropped. Somewhere, in one or more pieces, was the rest of a body.

Efforts to establish an agency of the bank in the city of Hamilton seemed frivolous by comparison. For the first time, Harris considered resignation. He would still have the rents from his real estate holdings in addition to his savings. On the other hand, neither his bank nor its competitors could be counted on to understand. Leaving one employer might foreclose his future with any. He tried believing that, whatever its origin, Vandervoort's new interest in the case made drastic action on his own part unnecessary.

It was a hypothesis, at least.

The moment might still come for a prolonged, out-of-town search. Then Harris would have to decide. In the meantime, there were things he could do in Toronto.

Not all could be done on a Sunday. Harris wanted to ask the undertaker if he had buried William Sheridan with both his arms. From what bank messenger Dick Ogilvie had said Wednesday, there would be no point trying to raise the matter with his father today. The Sabbatarian mood was on the rise. Harris took care to date his letters as of Monday, July 21.

The MacFarlanes, he trusted, would receive him. Bathing and dressing quickly, he managed to reach their Queen Street West villa before the end of the tea hour. The servant showed him through to the garden.

Surrounded by three of her children and a pair of spaniels, Kate MacFarlane sat in the shade of a shrubbery. A viewer with stereoscopic photographs of Niagara Falls was being passed around. These were solemnly pronounced to be arresting and sublime, though the water was a woolly blur.

Harris returned Elsie's sketch book, avoiding mention of his grisly discovery, and asked if anyone knew who Theresa's fine-featured companion might be. A French-speaking lady, he suggested, recalling that the miller's assistant had not been able to understand her.

"*Mademoiselle* Marthe!" Elsie exclaimed. "She was teaching Mrs. Crane French."

"Yes, more of a teacher than a friend," Mrs. MacFarlane briskly concurred. "We don't really know her."

"She came here once. I wanted to sketch her, but there wasn't time."

"Elsie, dear, take the viewer from your brother and show him how to put that stereoscope in properly before he bends it."

No one seemed to know Marthe's family name. Elsie had heard and forgotten it. Her mother suggested that Harris speak to Mr. MacFarlane, who was in his study.

Harris finished his tea before going in. Communicative and

attentive on other subjects, Kate MacFarlane appeared to have cooled towards his search. He asked again about her last glimpse of Theresa. She would not speak of it. As he ambled across the scythe-cut lawn, he wondered what had happened to change her mind.

Above the loggia in the centre of the garden façade rose a broad semicircular tower reminiscent of engravings of Windsor Castle. Money could scarcely have bought more in the way of aristocratic pedigree. Transparent in intention, the trappings nonetheless had their effect. Although he had exchanged pleasantries with George MacFarlane at half a dozen soirées, Harris felt suddenly diffident. He followed a servant down an unfamiliar tapestry-lined hall with a sense that he was about to intrude on momentous deliberations.

Or perhaps the hall's length simply allowed time to reflect that MacFarlane didn't need the medievalism to inspire awe. Harris flattered himself that he knew how one became a Crane, the deals and compromises one made. Not so in the case of MacFarlane, who as early as 1840 had allegedly been worth £200,000 and who today could doubtless buy five or six Henry Cranes. To become a MacFarlane there weren't enough business days in a lifetime.

A carpenter's son, he had started trading sticks of wood. With each trade he acquired more cutting rights or property in what became Victoria County. Timber export made him a ship-owner, then a ship-builder. Some ships were simply dismantled in Britain for their timbers. Others returned with cargoes of textiles or of people he could settle on the land he had cleared. Rumour had it that he was either about to establish spinning mills in the Toronto area or about to buy a newspaper. He had contributed articles on business or culture to a variety of periodicals and, to lure immigrants, had written the novel *Flora of Fenelon Falls*, as well as a statistic-laden *Guide to Canadian Opportunities.* Mining and whaling also figured among his interests. Many more ventures he likely kept to himself, though he made no secret of financing and captaining his own company of militia.

A pair of gargoyles guarded the study door. Beyond it, Harris found an ample room lined with overflowing black oak bookcases. Behind the refectory table that served as a desk, the more than ample George MacFarlane rose from an ecclesiastical looking chair with a high, pointed back.

A senior member of William Sheridan's generation, MacFarlane was tall, broad-shouldered and corpulent. His nose resembled an inverted ship's prow. His offered hand was so large that Harris could barely grasp enough of it to shake. Blue saucer eyes gave him a deceptively ingenuous expression.

"Sit down, sit down. I was just scribbling a bit of verse on the Treaty of Paris for one of those competitions, nothing that can't wait ten minutes." His voice was both soft and gruff, like sawdust with splinters scattered through it.

He had been interested to hear that Harris believed he could find "our friend" Mrs. Crane and had asked his wife to refer any further inquiries to him. Above all, he didn't want Elsie upset. In fact, the more quietly they worked the better. There were Henry Crane's feelings to consider as well as those of society.

"I'm only doing," said Harris, "what her own brother would do if he had lived."

"Her brother?"

"A child cholera victim in '32. You knew, surely."

MacFarlane looked momentarily befogged. "The smaller the patient, the more fallible the diagnosis. I believe there was little of the disease you mention *that* year—or this far west."

Harris knew better, and knew better than to point out that the cholera MacFarlane made light of could well have reached Canada's shores aboard his own ships. He might have taken every precaution known to physic and still not have been able to stop it.

"In any case, Harris," the older man resumed, his tone benevolent and admonitory, "a brother may do what other men may not. Consider the lady's reputation. Consider your own. I need not remind you that people want only men they believe to be of the highest character to have control of their money."

In Fenelon Falls, Harris silently wondered, did men of the highest character not look out for their friends?

"Believe me, Harris. In sixty years, no one has ever faulted me for excessive caution. Now let's see what we can do within the limits of discretion."

The French teacher was identified as Marthe Laurendeau, daughter of a cabinet minister from Canada East. MacFarlane didn't know whether she had returned there or was still in Toronto. As for Theresa, he professed optimism, but his confidential view resembled the lighthouse keeper's.

"A ruffian violates her, a hanging offence. So he kills off the victim, who is also the only witness. Even if he is caught, they can't execute him more than once, and the murder decreases the chances he will be caught. Poor Crane is coming to the same conclusion."

Strange optimism, Harris reflected—and yet his own hope was beginning to feel mulish. "Do you think," he said, "you could get Henry Crane to talk to me?"

"Possibly."

"Even if she is dead, circulation of her likeness could help locate her remains."

"I'll have a word with Crane about it," MacFarlane said.

Encouraged by these accommodating responses, Harris tried again to find out if Mr. and Mrs. Crane had been happy with each other. The temperature of the monastic chamber dropped several degrees at once. MacFarlane's eyes hardened to icy sapphires. His broad right hand rose in warning.

"That's a question one does not ask," he pronounced. "This 'greatest happiness of the greatest number' nonsense would spell the death of family life. A good marriage is one in which the husband provides and the wife obeys. The Cranes have a good marriage."

Outside the heavily-leaded window, Kate MacFarlane and her girls were strolling back towards the house in solemn conversation while the boy chased the dogs in circles around them.

"In time," MacFarlane continued, "their union would

undoubtedly have been blessed with heirs."

"I gather Mr. Crane has suffered business reversals," said Harris.

"As a chap who has never laid so much as a mile of track, I don't think I should go slinging mud at public benefactors like Henry Crane. You're out of date besides. The man is as sound as a board."

Harris could overlook being addressed in this lofty way so long as he was being informed. "Your dealings with him saved him?"

"No dealings we may have had bear on Mrs. Crane's disappearance," MacFarlane scolded before slipping back into his social mask of wide-eyed geniality. "Tell me, Harris, does anything at all rhyme with Crimea? I'm afraid I'll have to get back to this poem if it's to be done today. Do come again."

"Allow me," said Harris, having tried without success to get the conversation reopened, "to repay your kind advice by suggesting that you think twice before again acting as a guarantor for Mr. Joshua Newbiggins."

MacFarlane blinked, slow perhaps to recognize the name. "Has he defaulted?"

"No, but his character—"

"Nor will he. Newbiggins is a man of push. His backers will prosper."

* * *

Sunday evening, Harris dined in the city's most luxurious hotel. The meal began with mulligatawny soup, which every serious cook seemed to prepare and no two to agree on. Here ginger and chicken agreeably predominated. If the whitefish that followed might have been fresher, the filet of veal with tomatoes and horseradish sauce truly shone. After partaking of mashed potatoes, fresh vegetables and raspberry tarts, Harris turned away both the cheese tray and the dessert of jellies, nuts and brandied fruits. Even so, he felt in a businesslike way that he had now got through his eating for the week.

That benefit was incidental to his purpose in coming. The American, at Yonge and Front Streets, was the only hotel of its class in Toronto—though two more were soon to open with locations even more convenient to the Houses of Parliament. After four years in Quebec, the seat of government had returned. Politicians and civil servants could not be expected to accommodate themselves and their dependents in lodgings designed for travelling salesmen and farmers bringing cabbages to market.

Yes, Harris was told, Postmaster General Laurendeau and his daughter were indeed guests. At least they had been until twenty hours ago when they had embarked for Canada East on the Saturday night steamer. Harris registered this near miss as philosophically as possible. He noted down the family's forwarding address.

When he had asked the hotel manager all the questions he decently could, he went in to dinner and—as the dishes came and went—chatted with the waiter. Marthe Laurendeau had been in residence since the start of the spring legislative session. She had come to perfect her English and had stayed on to continue her studies when Parliament recessed and her mother returned home. A quiet and serious young woman, *Mademoiselle* seemed refined and rather shy. She ordered veal filet whenever it was on the menu.

As she began to take shape for Harris, he regretted having wished the grisly arm to be hers.

That she was a horsewoman came as news to the waiter, who believed she kept no mount at the hotel. Harris confirmed this with a stable hand before proceeding to the University Park.

By eight o'clock, light and strollers were draining from its green expanse. Robins, whose conversational song reminded Harris of summer evenings at his parents' home, were left to skim the lawns and pick their supper from the moist earth.

No sod had yet been turned for University College. Indeed, no design had yet been approved for the £75,000 building. The chemistry laboratory meanwhile occupied a one-room frame structure, freshly painted in mustard yellow. It looked too tidy ever to have housed pigs. It smelled too foul.

Lamb came to the door in shirtsleeves and an embroidered waistcoat. Harris may have been exaggerating the smell, which turned out to be no more than the waxy adipocere churned up with strong vinegar, a general decaying mustiness, spirits of hartshorn and kerosene from a pair of hanging lamps. Beneath them, a work bench ran the length of one wall. Amid the instruments and bottles strewn there, three cleanish bones lay on a marble slab as if for presentation.

"Sit here, Mr. Harris," said Lamb, indicating a stool as might a brusque *maître d'hôtel.* "I won't show you the hand, which I have not had time to strip the flesh from yet, but these bones may interest you." He stood pointing at the largest of the three. "Note how the humerus is severed at the upper end—not pulled whole from the shoulder, mind, not chewed by an animal, but chopped with an axe."

"As we surmised," said Harris. "Before death or after?"

"There's no way of knowing. The dimensions tell us something, however." The professor stretched a measuring tape along the thinner of the two remaining bones. "Ulna—9 21/32. If normally proportioned and not a freak, our victim would have been a man of unremarkable stature or a tall woman. Between five foot three inches and five foot five in the latter case—possibly an inch more in the former."

Victim. Harris absorbed the word in silence. Theresa's height had fallen in the middle of the range mentioned.

"And here is news," Lamb continued cheerfully as he picked up the final item on display. "The radius shows evidence of a fracture."

The bone looked whole to Harris, but then the combination of the subject matter and the atmosphere was starting to make him light-headed. "Not a fracture sustained during the..."

"Certainly not. An earlier break, quite healed but imperfectly set."

"How much earlier?"

"Months or years. You see this slight change of direction here?

And the mark—not a crack, more of a scar."

Harris steadied himself against the edge of the bench. "Could we step outside a moment?" he asked.

They stepped outside. Theresa's eighth night from home had fallen calm but cloudy. There would be no stargazing at the observatory next door. From another provisional college building across Taddle Creek rose the stirring strains of a Baptist hymn.

"Some of my colleagues," Lamb remarked, "have to show that a non-denominational university need not be a godless one. If anyone challenges you, you can say we have been studying scripture."

After several gulps of leafy park air, Harris asked whether the deviation in the radius would have made an observable difference in the living arm.

"You mean," said Lamb, "would the arm have looked crooked?"

"Yes, or been so weakened that the person would have noticeably favoured it—avoided heavy work and so forth?"

"Not necessarily. I believe the chief significance of the fracture—about three and a half inches above the right wrist—is as follows. If such an injury were to figure in the medical history of Mrs. Crane, it would tend to confirm that the arm is hers."

"It doesn't," Harris blurted out in relief, before remembering that he had no idea what injuries Theresa might have sustained since her marriage. "That is, I don't know. The break *was* an accident, was it not?"

"We can't be sure of that," Lamb replied.

Harris shuddered. An assault could have been a warning if Theresa had had any friend to help her heed it.

"Mr. Crane—has he seen the—um—remains?"

"Not while they have been with me," said Lamb. "The only gentlemen I receive here are ones that have saved me from drowning. Shall we go back in?"

Automatically, Harris shook his head—no. "By all means," he said with effort.

Inside the shed once more, his eye first caught a gleam of lamplight on precious metal at the far end of the work bench. He got permission to pick the bracelet up. From the eight silver medallions linked by pairs of the finest silver chains, certainty flowed like a current into his hands. He could name the remaining four cities before he turned the ovals over. Lisbon, Marseilles, Naples, Madrid. He even seemed to know the tracery of scratches. The bracelet was Theresa's.

She had worn it on her left wrist, though.

"Professor Lamb," he said, "what did you find out from those hairs?"

"Less than I had hoped. They are neither too fine to be a man's nor too coarse to be a woman's."

"But coarser than average for a woman?"

The note of eagerness seemed to irritate Lamb. "Average?" he said, fussing with the brass wheels on his microscope. "Averages are easy for you money men. You sum ten interest rates and move a decimal point. Simple arithmetic. Anthropometry is not so simple. Have you any idea how many hairs I should have to pluck from how many arms just in order to tell you what's average for Toronto women, let alone the sex in general? They would lock me up before the job was properly begun. What I can tell you is that the shafts of the Rouge Valley hairs are thicker than those drawn from the identical square inch of my wife's anatomy. Whether Mrs. Lamb is an average woman I have no way of judging. She is to a normal degree modest, however. I know you'll be discreet."

The Lambs were expecting their sixth child, or was it their seventh? It had been mentioned at the bank during the loan discussion. Harris approached the improvident, affectionate man bent over the microscope and humbly asked if he might take a look.

While he was looking, the door rattled against its bolt.

"Open up, Dr. Lamb," boomed a voice Harris recognized as Vandervoort's. "I've brought you the rest of the puzzle."

Chapter Five

Front Street

Boisterous and dishevelled, Vandervoort entered, brandishing a soiled white cotton flour sack that rattled as he moved. His dust-stiffened red hair stuck out at all angles. His whisky breath blared like a fanfare above the symphony of laboratory odours and quite drowned them out when he turned in momentary surprise towards Harris.

"Ha! If it isn't our amateur detective, looking neat and solemn as ever. Well, stay if you like. See what has turned up."

Vandervoort told a rambling and prolix tale that was at the same time marred by irritating omissions, but the gist of it was that after landing Constable Whelan and dispatching the arm to Lamb for analysis, the inspector had made some inquiries in the Rouge Valley area and had heard about a shed that had burned down Tuesday night.

"Where was this exactly?" said Harris.

"Between Port Union and Highland Creek. On one of those abandoned farms, you understand. Nothing anyone paid any attention to at the time."

Harris understood. Many an immigrant signed a lease before discovering he wasn't cut out for agriculture. Often as not, he would drift into town leaving untended and unregretted whatever crude structures he had managed to knock together. A vagrant's cooking fire or vandal's torch might easily claim them without alarming the neighbours.

"Now that shed—I went round for a look, and that shed was not empty when it burned." Vandervoort shook his sack.

The dry clicking sound it emitted brought a pained crease to Lamb's broad forehead.

"If you've brought me bones, inspector," he said, "I would as soon you didn't reduce them to bone chips."

"Bones," said Vandervoort, emptying his haul harum-scarum onto the work bench. He wasn't clumsily drunk, just too pleased with himself to be inhibited by professorial objections. "Bones and more bones, and that's just a start."

Among other large pieces, half a human skull tumbled out. Clean and dry as a nutshell, and—from what anyone could tell in that foul chamber—odourless. It wasn't repugnant to the senses, but alarming enough in its way. The nut had been someone's brain. Harris approached warily.

"Will you be able to tell if these fragments came from the same body as the arm?" he asked Lamb. He naturally hoped they did, having already concluded from the position of the bracelet and the coarseness of the hairs that the arm was not Theresa's.

"No indeed!" snapped Lamb. "I'm no clairvoyant."

"But there can't be any doubt," said Vandervoort. "They were found less than two miles apart. And then there's the axe."

Ignoring him, Lamb continued less waspishly to Harris, "Anatomical analysis alone won't even tell us if all these *are* from the same body. What can be observed is that this pelvis," he pointed to a dish-like object, "is almost certainly a woman's. You can see from this fragment of the pubic arch. It's rounder and wider than a man's."

"Pubic arch?"

"Here, Mr. Harris." The professor pointed without embarrassment to the location of the structure on his own anatomy. "Although, in a man, it forms an angle rather than an arch. I can also say that none of these new bones appears to be from the right arm. Further conclusions must wait on measurement... Clavicle—5 1/8 inches..."

While he was measuring, Harris turned to Vandervoort.

"What axe, inspector?"

From a side pocket of his tweed jacket, Vandervoort took an object wrapped in a charred scrap of green fabric. Merrily, he prolonged the mystery. Twice he asked if Harris were sure he wanted to see inside. Finally the package was set on the bench and the cloth folded back to reveal an axe head with the charred stump of a new wooden handle protruding from it. A stain appeared to have burned onto the blade.

"Blood," said Vandervoort with a flourish.

Harris glanced at the professor.

"Sternum—just a moment..." Lamb set down his notebook and used his ruler to lift the axe blade so it caught the lamplight. "Looks like it," he said, "but whether human or animal blood there's no way of saying. Even using the microscope."

"If ever you get a really straight answer from Dr. Lamb," chuckled Vandervoort, "then you can bet your mother's teeth you're on to something. Tell me about the arm, professor. I suppose you have already made a full report to our nosey friend."

While Lamb was reporting in scientific language, and again in plain words, Harris looked at the lengthening list of measurements. Through his damp white shirt, he felt for the point where his neck joined his shoulder. The clavicle, he thought, was the collarbone—but where did it start? Over five inches sounded long. He eased the ruler out of Lamb's hand.

"Details are all well and good," Vandervoort was saying, "but what matters is the pattern. Mrs. Crane leaves home. She's attacked and killed. The killer tries to cover his tracks by burning her remains and the weapon. Tries, but doesn't do a very thorough job. Have you found anything to contradict that story?"

"I have not had *time* to. You don't seem to appreciate, inspector, how long it took simply to strip these three arm bones. Then, before I get to the hand, you bring me a whole other bag of tricks."

"These at least are clean," Vandervoort pointed out.

"Splendid. Now, if you want an expert opinion on these, leave them with me."

"Of course, but so far you can't say I'm wrong."

Lamb wearily acknowledged that, insofar as he had been able to assess, the dimensions of all bones and bone fragments in both sets were not inconsistent with their forming part of a single skeleton. Vandervoort seemed satisfied.

"If I'm not interrupting," said Harris, "I should like to ask Professor Lamb whether a woman of five three to five five with a five and one eighth inch clavicle would appear broad-shouldered."

"That, I think, would be fair to say."

"Stocky rather than slim?"

"Definitely."

"Then," Harris declared, "it's not Mrs. Crane."

Vandervoort pulled a goatish face. "Well, Dr. Lamb," he said, "you have had a long day, considering that I dragged you out of bed this morning at four o'clock. Mr. Harris and I shall go and let you get on with your work. Oh, and you might want to look at that bit of green cloth too. It's devilish like the sleeve we found the arm in."

Harris noted the *we* and foresaw that it would soon slip into *I*. When that happened, there would be no more comradely sharing of information, and every question would again in all likelihood be turned back with another question. To make the most of the momentary opening, he took the opportunity of walking south with Vandervoort.

The College Avenue, stretching from the university grounds to Osgoode Hall, was closed at night. They settled for Park Lane, which hugged the avenue's east side fence and borrowed the dignity of its parade of chestnut trees. A landau with jingling harness passed them at a trot, its occupants doubtless heading home from Sunday dinner at one of the new uptown villas. Otherwise, the city under the night clouds was as still as a fiddle in its case.

Just waiting, Harris thought, for the note-making to resume, the music of commerce.

"Pity about the smuggling charge," he said. It seemed a safe bet that this was the case Lamb had earlier referred to as having fallen through.

"There was no way of knowing." Vandervoort drank from his tin flask. "I made sure Mr. Harvey Ingram didn't have any daughters in service to the Attorney General's household or any second cousins on City Council. He friggin' near ruined one alderman tea merchant by getting lushed up and letting the light go out in a storm."

"You mean the winter before last," said Harris, "when the *China Queen* went down?"

"Beaches black with pekoe leaves till spring... Now I'm told our beloved old campaigner has 'friends' in the first rank of capital and clergy, men on whom his claims are 'not to be inquired into.' Hush!" Vandervoort drank. "Never mind—this Crane business will make me. I've got a body now. In due course, I'll get a felon."

"The body," said Harris, "isn't Mrs. Crane's."

"Fond memories—"

"Even apart from the question of size," Harris interrupted, "the arm is an obvious decoy." He was appropriately grateful to Ingram's anonymous backers, but their interference in the course of justice would be for nought if Vandervoort were to spend all his time looking for Theresa's murderer instead of for Theresa. "Yes, a decoy. Why else leave it with an utterly distinctive bracelet—which incidentally the owner didn't wear on that wrist—then lug the body two miles off to burn it? Someone wants it believed that Mrs. Henry Crane, *née* Theresa Ruth Sheridan, is dead."

Vandervoort drank. "With respect, sir, you are not one of the parties I have to convince."

"Don't you have to convince yourself?"

"I believe in results." The whisky was starting to make the inspector weave as he walked.

"What about Professor Lamb?" said Harris. "Aren't you going to have him out to the shed?"

"Waste of time. You saw what he was like at the Rouge with all his picture taking. Brilliant mind, of course, but how far does it get you? Everything is maybe this, maybe that."

Harris gave Vandervoort a cigar to distract him from his flask. "How far do you expect this case to get you, Inspector? Deputy chief? Doesn't that go by political connections rather than by results?"

At this, Vandervoort stopped walking altogether and talked about the police. Although audibly less sober than when he had narrated his discovery of the burned-out shed, he made more sense. Familiarity had given these thoughts a shape. Harris, who had the impression of eavesdropping, would not in any case have risked interrupting.

Results were what would count in future, Vandervoort prophesied, while not denying that today's force still ran on connections.

Personally, he had always depended on some of each. The son of Niagara farm folk, he had started early talking to anyone that could offer him a less laborious life. As a young night watchman on the second Welland Canal, he had discovered who was pilfering construction supplies, thus recommending himself for the railway police when work started on the Great Western. Unspecified services were performed for G.W.R. directors, who also happened to figure on Toronto's City Council. So Vandervoort's name came up when it was decided to hire a city detective—an anomalous post on what in the mid-fifties was a betwixt and between sort of force.

A wave of arson had temporarily loosened the purse strings, though the same council had economized since. As the city's population had grown, they actually reduced the number of constables. Everything went by the aldermen's whim. No policeman could be engaged, dismissed or even suspended without their say-so. Accountability, they called it.

Not that Chief Sherwood was much for suspensions or reprimands in any case. A quiet, good-natured man, the chief. He didn't even like to insist on the dress regulations, with the result that the uniformed police were scarecrows more or less.

There had been *some* sprucing up, for change was in the air. Police failure to cope with a pair of recent Orange riots had set the ball in motion. One alderman had even proposed that Orange Lodge members be excluded from the force. That had been voted down, of course, and Parliament in May had backed away from its plan to take provincial control of the police, but a British-style board of police commissioners was still a strong bet to replace City Council in the running of things. The next chief could be an army man.

Harris's eye followed the iron grill-work that for half a dozen blocks ruled commercial and residential Toronto off from the leisured walkways, grass boulevards and carriage parade. And all the while he listened and thought that—whatever improvements the future held—in the time he had to find Theresa this maddening, temporarily loquacious man was the best he had to work with in the way of official support.

"I should not want to be chief," snorted Vandervoort, coming round at last to the question asked, "much less his deputy. Keeping constables on their beats? How anybody can do that—with the human material we have to work with... You're always fighting human weakness. For the detective now, like me, human weakness is an ally. You frequent the criminal classes. You work on their weaknesses. Bend their elbow, bend their ear, grease their palm, twist their arm, tweak their nose. Above all, loosen their tongue. Before they know it—" his fist sprang shut, "—they're yours."

About the coming changes, Vandervoort had mixed feelings. He saw the necessity for a modern, professional police, and yet he feared that would mean a shorter leash for himself. Hence, his desire for advancement. His sights were set on Inspector of Licences, which carried an official remuneration of three hundred pounds a year—double what the city already paid its detective inspector and a hundred more than it paid the deputy chief—although salary was only one consideration. Harris was left to imagine what the others were, but he doubted they would have any very improving effect on Vandervoort's character or his liver. In recent years, the regulation of liquor had become an exclusively municipal affair.

Overhead, a current of air teased the chestnut leaves. Vandervoort took hold of the metal fence with both hands and stared into the confined Avenue. Perhaps he was just drunk and tired, but his stance suggested that for him this near side of the barrier was the cage.

"I can see myself in a couple of years," he said, "taking the air out there in the back of my own open carriage."

Harris didn't bother to point out that in a couple of years the fence would almost certainly have been dismantled to facilitate crosstown traffic, George Brown's *Globe* newspaper having mounted a vigorous editorial campaign to that effect.

"What if out there on the Avenue," he remarked instead, "you were to meet Mrs. Crane? *After* having convinced her husband, the aldermen, and a jury that she was dead."

Vandervoort turned sharply. "What are you saying?"

"Merely that your position will be more secure if we find the correct solution to this mystery than if we settle for a momentarily plausible one."

Vandervoort muttered grudging assent or suppressed a curse. They continued walking south.

"I wondered," said Harris, "if you would ask Mr. Crane and Dr. Hillyard about the fracture. Neither of them want to talk to me."

"How secure is your own position, Harris?" It was the first time Vandervoort had dropped the *mister.* "Do your employers know how many hours you spend on the trail of another man's wife?"

"I trust I could explain myself to their satisfaction." All the same, Harris reflected, to do so would cost time. Perhaps he was pressing the policeman too hard.

"I don't say we can't work together," offered the latter, "but remember this is detective work, not banking. That means I call the tune."

From these words and the inspector's quickened pace, Harris gathered that there was further work for them that very evening. They loped south to Front Street.

Among the brick villas ranged along the north side, Sheridan's alone showed no flicker of lamp or candle. Its emptiness seemed amplified by the extraordinary amount of glass in its symmetrical façade. Each of the nine sash windows carried eighteen large panes, all dark.

Vandervoort turned in at the low gate, crossed the unweeded front garden and climbed the three steps that led from it to the semicircular porch. Harris followed, bewildered.

"Are we going to break in?" he asked.

A street lamp caught the triumphant gleam in the Inspector's eye as from an inside pocket he produced a large, discoloured key.

"From the burned shed?" said Harris. "But there's no keyhole."

Vandervoort looked. The key in his hand moved forlornly over the blank white surface of the door.

"It's an old house," Harris murmured. "In the twenties—"

"Yes, yes—always a servant," Vandervoort rejoined quickly, showing he was quite familiar with aristocratic ways. "We'll try the back."

At the back, a sunken flight of stone steps led to the basement. Although it was much darker here away from the street, Vandervoort hurtled down them and got the key into what Harris remembered as the kitchen door. The lock would not move.

"Speaking of servants," said Harris, wondering that the house had been left untended, "ought we not to have a word with them?"

"You find 'em first." Vandervoort was losing patience with the key, which he continued to twist and jiggle in the lock. "The fire must have bent the metal out of—there!"

The door swung inward.

"The key to her father's house! Now you'll have to believe she's dead."

In the back of Harris's mind, it registered that Vandervoort did feel the need to convince him. Later he would be flattered. Right now he was too busy castigating himself for not having sooner sought out the testimony of Sheridan's housekeeper.

No one ever mentioned her. He knew of her existence only from that latest talk with Small. There had been no such person at the period when Harris had been a visitor here, Theresa having filled the office. There had of course been other servants—whose supervision, he recalled, had occasioned some friction between father and daughter.

"Papa, the man's a thief!" Theresa had burst out one evening when a new gardener's praises were being sung before Harris, and sung again. Eyes twinkling with reasonableness, her father asked what harm it did if the odd turnip went astray. Theresa, exasperated to the point of laughter, said it wasn't that. She had found two silver watches freshly buried between the strawberry plants. Sheridan's brow darkened only briefly. "I wonder," he said, "if he thought he could grow grandfather clocks." The gardener's tenure was as brief as his predecessor's, and his successor's, but Sheridan liked to point out that the rate of job change was high everywhere in this restless decade. He had felt he was made a monkey of no oftener than anyone else.

Now there appeared to be neither gardener nor housekeeper, neither a maid to air the rooms nor even a watchman to protect all those panes of glass until the estate could be settled. No one. Vandervoort led the way inside as if he didn't expect the house to be anything but deserted.

Harris followed by the light of a lung-searing Promethean match. A second, no less pungent, lit the gaselier that hung above the long centre table. Only then did the pent-up domestic perfumes of laundry, plaster, dried herbs and wood embers begin to impose themselves. Comforting enough aromas normally, but not tonight. Was Harris's nose not yet recovered from the laboratory, or was he possibly letting the recent death two floors above colour his sense of smell? Neither explanation quite satisfied him.

The kitchen occupied the entire western half of the basement, except for a narrow servant's bedroom at the front. Harris went to have a look at it while Vandervoort rummaged inexplicably through the cupboards.

There was no gas in the servant's room. Harris lit an oil lamp that stood on an otherwise bare pine chest. Its drawers were empty. So were a row of pegs on the back of the door. So were the wide sills of the two windows that gave into wells directly below the drawing room windows. He flicked the curtains back in place.

Rooms like this were often furnished with a cot no wider than a ladder. Sheridan had provided a full-width bed, its head tucked for winter warmth into the corner nearest the bake oven. Wide as it was, the bed did seem unusually low. Perhaps to correct a wobble, pieces had been sawn from each leg in turn, to the point where the yellow and brown coverlet all but swept the uneven brick floor. Harris looked under the coverlet at the bare straw tick and then under the bed. He found not even a stray thimble.

When he turned back into the kitchen, Vandervoort wasn't there, but could be heard stirring in one of the storage rooms in the other half of the basement. Looking for liquor more than likely. Harris bristled briefly, then took a deep breath. Being pilfered—"involuntary charity"—seemed almost to amuse the Sheridan he had known.

He took another breath. After the tidy bedroom, the kitchen truly did smell wrong. Behind the domestic odour lurked a sourness. Approaching the massive black cooking stove that had been set into the original fireplace, he lifted the lid of each of the pots and kettles. He worked his way around the room, inspecting crocks and churns and all the dishes in the floor-to-ceiling dresser. Everything was clean. When he looked up to see what food or laundry might be hanging from the ceiling, he stepped backwards into a slat-backed chair. He felt tired and clumsy and out of ideas.

Turning to straighten the chair, he saw he had knocked off its back a discoloured square of material that had been draped there. He picked it up. It was sticky. A sniff confirmed it was the source of the sour odour.

The housekeeper had cleared out so thoroughly and left the

kitchen so generally shipshape. Why, Harris wondered, had she not washed this pudding cloth before she went?

He sniffed again, more searchingly. His nose could detect nothing beyond the week's development of mould already noted. Suet pudding, he thought. He folded the grey and viscous rag inside a clean dishtowel for ease of carriage back to Lamb's laboratory. He might just have a look upstairs first.

Vandervoort—his flask topped up with imported whisky—intercepted Harris on the bottom step. "No warrant, you understand."

* * *

When the accountant Septimus Murdock reported next morning to help open the vault, he seemed not just his normally gloomy self but a man in pain. His chin with its smudge of Napoleonic whiskers was trembling more than usual. Out of his pasty, pear-shaped face, his moist brown eyes cast Harris what could only be interpreted as reproachful glances.

With coaxing, Murdock admitted a newspaper story had upset him. There for the moment Harris left it.

He had been alarmed himself to read—once he got past the advertisements that monopolized the front page of The *Globe*—that over the weekend one of the bank's directors had been robbed and beaten on the road between Kingston and Brockville. Crippling head injuries made the man unfit for further business. Since it was nearly ten months until the next shareholders' meeting, the remaining directors would be choosing a replacement.

The bank had been attacked. Its officers naturally felt threatened. Then again, the accountant rarely dealt with the directors. Perhaps it was the story of the Rouge Valley arm that had Murdock rattled.

Sunday night Harris had returned home from Front Street to find stuck under his door some journalist's request for an *immediate* interview on the subject, whatever the hour. This request he ignored. He was a little out of sorts at Lamb's reluctance to receive—or even smell—his latest discovery, but most of all he was exhausted.

Harris's refusal to be interviewed did not of course keep his name out of the papers. It just resulted in the publication of less accurate information. "Mr. Isaac Harris, head cashier of the Provincial Bank of Canada" that would sit well in Kingston. The cashier of the Toronto branch had better write them an explanatory note.

Probing the matter further at the noon dinner hour, he discovered it was neither the exaggeration of his credentials nor the grisly nature of his discovery that Murdock held against him. Rather it was his cooperation with those "Orange rogues" on the police force.

"Better have a seat, Septimus. Not there. The armchair is more comfortable."

"You think I'm an old woman, but you don't know what it's like to have your children taunted in the street. I'm afraid almost for them to leave the house."

Aware that no child escapes taunting on some score, Harris nonetheless felt his heart tugged. He took another of the green leather chairs in front of the desk and tried to be rationally reassuring.

"There is Orange violence in Toronto," he said. "Remarkably little of it is directed against the city's Catholics. Now wait before you answer. Let us look at the facts. Last summer two volunteer fire companies fought each other on Church Street and attacked the police. That was Orangeman against Orangeman. Twelve days later, as a result of some bawdy-house *mêlée,* a fire brigade demolished an American circus. A week ago, merchant-publican Luther Casey had his wharf and warehouse burned—"

"By Orangemen."

"His *fellow* Orangemen—to whom in their intoxicated state, it now appears, he had denied more drink. In all of this how are Catholics more victims than any of the rest of us who value a civilized community?"

Murdock shook his heavy head. "We're intimidated, Isaac. Remember, we're in the minority. There are three of you to every one of us."

"Oh, I hardly count as a Protestant," Harris protested weakly. Geology and zoology had by painless increments displaced his ancestral faith, such as it had been—but he knew that made him no less alien to Murdock, who continued as if Harris had not spoken.

"The thugs need not attack us directly. We have eyes to see that anyone opposing their power can become a victim. Even a Member of Parliament."

"You mean William Sheridan?"

"Perhaps a rising man of business is right to court their favour and—and help them hide their crimes, but it saddens me all the same to see you do it. I must get home to dinner."

"Just a minute," said Harris. "A week ago, the very first time I saw you after the event, you hinted there was sinister significance to William Sheridan's dying on July 12."

"I knew it then, and I've got the details since. You'll never read them in the press."

"Would you mind eating here?" Last night's visit to Front Street had sharpened Harris's hunger for such details. He had previously made three or four such requests, when reports from their branch had been commanded at short notice. Each time Murdock had nodded dutifully. Today—in the absence of bank business—the accountant hesitated, sighed and nodded. Orange roguery? A futile topic, his dumb show implied—but, to his shame, irresistible. As usual, Dick Ogilvie was sent to advise Mrs. Murdock and bring back from a neighbouring café sliced ham, meat pie and a jug of ginger beer.

"Septimus," said Harris, on returning to his office, "you admit the daily papers are unreliable."

Murdock shrugged as if the thing were obvious.

"Then please don't judge me by what you read there. They say I found Mrs. Crane's arm. That's false. I found *an* arm, which remains to be identified."

"They say nothing at all about William Sheridan. What a great heart that was! I would have attended his funeral myself if it had been at the Cathedral."

"Yes, well, Mr. Sheridan found St. James with its reserved pews too plutocratic for his liking. What should they be saying?"

"Holy Trinity is in the most Protestant ward in the city, and the way things are, a Roman like myself would not have felt particularly welcome."

Harris did not stop to list the French Canadian mourners, Murdock's co-religionists to a man. "Septimus, what should the papers be saying?"

The repetition of the question gratified the accountant and unnerved him. "Ask Sibyl Martin," he stammered.

"Who is she?"

"For the last three months of his life, William Sheridan's housekeeper."

Harris had been pacing. Now he went dead still, though his pulse was off at a gallop. He felt as if he had been tracking through deep woods a quarry he might have seen by no more than a quarter turn of the head.

"Where," he asked carefully, "will I find her?"

"That's a question, isn't it?"

"Septimus."

"I don't know, Isaac. No one seems to know, and no one seems to have been looking."

The housekeeper's arm? A fearful joy tickled Harris's throat. To cover his unsettling eagerness for a human sacrifice, he said, "You think after killing him she fled."

"Or is being hidden," said Murdock. "If you ask me, she killed them both."

"Sheridan and..."

"Exactly. Father and daughter."

The theory was breath-catching, but quickly fell apart when the accountant could give no account of what Sibyl might have done with Theresa's body. Burn it? Where? Not in Scarboro, surely. How was she to have got it there? Sheridan kept no carriage.

Murdock postulated accomplices—as many as necessary. He had never actually clapped eyes on the housekeeper and could give no indication as to her height or build. "Sluttish and sullen" was how rumour described her.

By the time their meal arrived, Harris had heard several more jeremiads, but no new facts.

"Look here," he said once young Ogilvie had set two places at a gate-leg table and withdrawn, "what besides her disappearance makes you accuse this woman of murder?"

"She has a twin brother in the Provincial Penitentiary. Crusher Martin they call him."

This detail made a stronger impression on Harris than he was willing to acknowledge. "I must say, Septimus, I don't see much of my own brothers and sister. Should they hang for my crimes?"

"If you had killed a man, as Martin has, a less open-hearted individual than William Sheridan might well shy away from taking your twin into domestic service. Then again, Isaac, the woman herself worked until this past March in the house of the Orange Grand Master. Whose crime is that?"

"No one's, as far as I know."

Harris felt all the more need to defend Sibyl because of wishing her dead. He had to admit, however, that the man she would have been used to hearing reviled at the Grand Master's as an apostate had indeed been a singularly unprejudiced employer. How *had* she come in contact with Sheridan? Murdock suspected intrigue, but perhaps the imprisoned brother had simply chanced to be a client. *There* was one person Harris would know where to find.

"Open your eyes, my young friend," Murdock advised between mouthfuls. "This woman with criminal relations and an Orange past prepared William Sheridan's last meal."

"Poison? But Dr. Hillyard says he died of his old complaint, inflammation of the bowels."

"And is Dr. Hillyard above suspicion?"

"Over the years he has had more opportunities to poison Sheridan than anyone. He would not have needed a servant's help."

"Then Sibyl Martin administered an irritant of some sort that brought on the fatal attack. Police were sent for the night he died."

Harris dropped his fork. Drunk or sober, Vandervoort had never so much as hinted at this.

"To apprehend Sibyl Martin?" he said.

"Why else?"

"But how do you know?"

The clock ticked. A carter's whip cracked outside the window as his team plodded by. Harris held his breath.

"A St. Michael's altar boy carried the note."

"Why didn't you say so sooner?"

"For the boy's sake," said Murdock. "Did you know that William Sheridan bought a hundred iron bedsteads for the new House of Providence? Now don't ask me for his name."

"Mrs. Crane gave him this note?" Harris didn't mention that the altar boy might have to testify at a coroner's inquest.

"'To the police with this as fast as you can,' she said."

"Who *is* this boy?" Harris demanded.

"Please, Isaac, I can't—at least, not without leave from his father."

"By all that's just, get it!"

"I can't at this moment," Murdock spluttered. "He's—"

"Tonight then," Harris cut in. "For now tell me this—did the boy say how she seemed?"

"Not crazy or wild. Firm and angry, as she had every right to be. They had to kill her too."

"I'm not convinced of that—but, Septimus, when you learn more, you must tell me. And in return—" As Harris spoke, he could see the fatalistic twist Murdock's mouth was settling into. "In return, Septimus," he said, "if I find Orange wrongdoing, I won't keep it mum, come fire or flood."

Murdock's pastry-flecked goatee trembled, then his large head shook. "You don't know what you're undertaking, Isaac. Truly you don't."

* * *

Little bank business got Harris's attention in the early part of the afternoon. His ears were still ringing from what Murdock had said.

If William Sheridan had been murdered, it was a tragedy not just for his friends and admirers but for all Canadians—the country's first political assassination. Moreover, with agents of such butchery at large, was Theresa not in all the greater danger?

Eight days she had been missing. Harris had been looking for six, and she seemed farther away than ever. He would continue. He still had to write to Marthe Laurendeau. At the same time, bound to this office, how much could he do in the few hours a day it left him?

He needed help. The rest of the world had to continue to regard Theresa as missing, not settle back in the belief that her remains had been found. This was what Sibyl meant to him. He doubted that she had killed William Sheridan—a hard man to hate personally and, in opposition, little threat as a Member of Parliament. Harris wasn't cool enough to put aside all speculation on the subject. The servant's first interest, though, was as a missing person, not as a murderess. The presence of the unwashed cloth suggested that she had left the house abruptly. Left or been removed from it. If the bones Lamb held were accepted as most probably Sibyl's, the search for Theresa would go on.

What was needed was a description, and Jasper Small seemed the readiest source. Harris was just writing his friend a note when Dick Ogilvie knocked and entered with a sealed envelope.

"On that pile," said Harris, re-dipping his steel-nibbed pen.

Dick set it down quickly, trying to make his intrusion as brief as possible. The towering pile of unopened correspondence toppled across the polished surface of the desk, shooting its topmost member very nearly into Harris's lap. His hand closed on the envelope just below the sender's name, H. M. Crane. Small could wait.

July 21, 1856

Dear Isaac,

Have just identified bracelet as Mrs. Crane's and fabric as that of the green habit she left home in. Professor Lamb may have further revelations. Still, am compelled to fear the worst.

Kindly overlook any incivility. I realize that only through your persistent and unselfish exertions has truth come to light. Thank you for that. Finding what you found Saturday ~~must have been~~ can't have been easy. Yet better to know.

The loss of both father—for so I regarded William Sheridan—and wife has made this the hardest week of my life. Shall spare no effort to find her murderer. At the same time, business will not stand still. Leave for Chicago tonight.

Faithfully yours,
Henry Crane

The hasty scrawl with scratchings out breathed the same sincerity as Crane's halting reading at the funeral. Whatever conclusions Harris had reached wavered. Theresa might have had a reason for wearing the cities-of-Europe bracelet on her right wrist. Finding her murderer could be all that was left.

Harris was reluctant to lay the letter down. The paper itself, he discovered, was agreeable to hold, thick and creamy between his fingers. The watermark was English, like the builder of Crane's brougham. The stationery of a successful man.

Crane's success carried all the more weight on an afternoon when Harris had allowed his own and his employers' business to stagnate. He pictured Crane's private railway carriage. Tonight it would be coupled to a train bound for the Collingwood dock, where Crane's steamer would be waiting. Crane would rise above grief to get on with making money. The Board of Trade approved such dutifulness. Harris fell short.

Moodily, he flicked the creamy paper. Losing to Crane in love forced him to acknowledge the other man's persuasiveness, but a lingering resentment, of which Harris was not in general proud, made him at the same time partially immune. "Spare no effort"—where then, just to start with, were the handbills?

From an inside pocket, Harris eased his flimsy portrait tracing and unfolded it carefully. With a pencil stub, he tried to darken a smudged line, the eager curve of Theresa's upper lip. The paper tore. Crane's stationery was instantly crumpled into as small a ball as the rich vellum would allow and dropped into a drawer. All the letter meant was an opening from the man Harris had most questions for.

The Ontario, Simcoe and Huron had no train till ten. Before turning to his bank correspondence, Harris sent Crane word that he would call on him at his office at four unless Harris heard otherwise.

At three fifty, he was passing through the heavily-columned entrance to the block Crane had built for himself on a part of King Street East recently levelled by fire.

"Mr. Crane is expecting me."

"Mr. Crane has gone out of town, sir," replied the porter. "Not five minutes since, his carriage was by to take him to the station."

Scared him off, thought Harris without satisfaction.

"When will he be back?"

"See me in a fortnight, I believe he said. His secretary will know, sir. Second floor, first door on your right."

Harris fled without wasting time on the secretary. King Street was the best in the city for hailing a cab, but by the same token the worst for making speed. To cover the half mile to the Union Station, Harris had the driver drop down to the Esplanade, where he could whip his horse up to a brisk trot.

They raced up beside a Great Western passenger train that stood straining for departure, steam up and nose to the sun. No private car was attached, but Crane himself stood on the front platform of one of the canary yellow carriages, in conversation with a conductor on the ground below. If Chicago still beckoned, it seemed the trip was to be overland via Detroit.

Harris had paid the driver and was climbing the carriage steps before Crane saw him.

"Why, Isaac..." Polite surprise, a tight smile.

"I wanted to catch you if I could," said Harris, unhurried now that he was aboard. "One or two matters in connection with your note."

"I'm afraid there isn't time." Over Harris's head, Crane's eyes flicked towards the conductor, who with a raised hand signalled the driver. "Next month, let us say."

"I'll ride as far as Hamilton with you," said Harris. "That will give us an hour and a quarter."

The engine's whistle sounded two short strokes.

Crane still didn't make room on the platform. The step gave him a height advantage of eight or ten inches.

"August," he said, "would be better. I'll be back in time for the inquest."

The train was starting to move.

"When did your wife break her arm?"

"As a girl—didn't you know?"

"You can't ride there, sir." The conductor, walking at a pace with the train, touched Harris's elbow.

"He's right, Henry. May I join you?"

Crane looked as if he regretted having broken his silence by writing. Perhaps he had done so only under pressure from MacFarlane and had feared more questions would follow.

"Excuse me, no," he said. "I have an address to prepare, besides which, the subject of my letter is too painful for me to discuss just now."

They had cleared the station, but were still travelling slowly enough for Harris to have jumped down safely. He did not jump down.

"What did you do, Henry, that Sunday afternoon when Theresa went out for her ride?"

Crane hesitated, then turned sideways to let Harris pass. "Perhaps you had better come in," he said.

It seemed an awkward, over-courteous manoeuvre when the natural thing would have been for Crane to lead the way into the carriage. Squeezing by, Harris was aware of an untrimmed tuft of sandy hairs in Crane's pink ear. Temptation seized him.

"Where," he dropped into the ear, "is Sibyl Martin?"

He used the door frame to brace himself against being pushed back. That was presumably why Crane chose the opposite or lake side of the train to throw him off. Had Crane been able to get his full fourteen stone behind the shove, the distance across the platform been a half-foot less, or Harris's wits a fraction of a second slower, the cashier's chin would have been the first part of him to hit the gravel shoulder—which was now jogging by at more than ten miles per hour.

As it was, his right hand caught and briefly held the stair rail, or rather the iron newel. This swung him out facing the direction of travel. He got his feet under him, but was in too much of a crouch to run properly when he fell. He tumbled forward. Tucking in his head, he managed a somersault which made his spine feel as if it were being driven out through the back of his neck. When his feet came lowermost once again, he tried to get up. His left ankle twisted in the loose gravel. He pitched sideways and rolled over twice more. Coming to rest with a head-to-toe suit of bruises and with blood seeping through his shredded trouser knees, he looked for the train. Some hundred yards ahead it swung right past the water works and began to put on speed.

Harris wondered if he might have hung on, pulled himself back up the steps. Doubtful. Of doubtful value too. Did he think he could have bullied further revelations from Crane? Harris might be the more athletic of the two, but he was no wrestler, and Crane—having built much of the railway—was far likelier to have friends aboard.

Harris stood and dusted off his clothes as well as he could with the backs of his lacerated hands. A sewage-scented breeze off the harbour cooled his face. Where the gravel ended, a ribbon of oily sand caught whatever the wavelets deposited—a fish carcass, barrel staves, cabbage leaves, a broken doll. Nothing that a brush with death could not beautify. Thanking his stars, Harris limped off towards the cashier's suite as briskly as his sprained ankle would let him.

Chapter Six
St. David's Ward

Forty minutes later, Harris entered Crane's gates, but avoided the house. He wasn't trying to be furtive—a ludicrous proposition with this ankle. Although he had bound it up when he had washed and changed, his ornamental walking stick was too slender to take much of his weight as he made for the stables. Flitting from tree to tree was out of the question, and yet he was hoping to escape the frosty butler's notice. The coachman seemed his likeliest informant.

Interviewing Crane's staff was something he would gladly have left to the police, who could have gone about it in an above-board way. Too late for that. If Harris's finest sensibilities still recoiled from what felt like espionage, the rest of him literally ached with the conviction that Crane need no longer be treated as a gentleman.

The long, low villa took some circumnavigating. Girdled with white trellised verandahs in the regency style, it sprawled over one of the park lots on the north side of Queen Street East. Around a final corner, the brougham—with horse still harnessed—stood in a shaded stable yard. As Harris approached, a man in shirtsleeves and a yellow waistcoat came out of the summer kitchen with a square of gingerbread in his thin, pale hand. He looked at the sweet with a shudder and tossed it onto the manure heap before realizing he was observed.

Harris introduced himself. "You're Oscar, aren't you?" he asked.

"That's right." The voice was lifeless and incurious. The skin of Oscar's long, angular face was uncommonly dry for that of a man who otherwise appeared not more than twenty-five.

Harris mentioned riding with him to the Sheridan interment and added something about helping Mr. Crane investigate Mrs. Crane's disappearance.

"Master's out of town. I just took him to the station." Oscar began with trembling hands to unhitch the horse. The mention of Theresa seemed to agitate him.

Harris stood with the black carriage between himself and the house. "I've missed him then," he said lamely. "I thought he was leaving tonight."

He produced Crane's crumpled letter, which he had smoothed out and brought along, then didn't know what to do with. Oscar would think him both liar and fool.

"Mr. Harris," said the coachman, turning the name over. "*You're* the gentleman who found—" He stopped what he was doing and searched Harris's face. "That *horrible* thing in the valley. We were just reading the papers and talking it over at tea, but Cook and I can't make sense of it. Can you?"

Here was a lucky opening. The man's sudden intensity surprised Harris, but then again, to any healthy nature, the news must come as shocking.

"It's the Mistress, they say. I can't eat for thinking of it, and sleep won't come any easier..."

"The remains may be of another woman," said Harris. "Do you know what became of Mr. Sheridan's housekeeper, for example?"

"Miss Martin? Left town on the Sunday." Oscar's voice went dead again.

"Where did she go?" Harris asked.

"Another posting, I heard. I don't see how she could have got hold of the Mistress's bracelet and riding dress."

"What posting? Where?"

"Master would know."

"To be sure," said Harris, with as little disrespect as possible. The manner in which Crane had reacted to mention of the housekeeper's name suggested he knew something well worth knowing about Sibyl Martin, including perhaps how her arm might have been mistaken for Theresa's. "And has no one seen her, Oscar, since Sunday, July 13?"

"None of us has." Oscar shrugged and resumed his work. "Some thought she should have stayed for her master's funeral, but then she might have lost this other position, and besides..."

"Yes, Oscar?" Harris hoped it didn't show too much that he wanted to turn the man upside down and shake everything out of him at once.

"I don't know if I should mention it, seeing it was kept out of the papers, but she must have been put out by that night in the lock-up."

"Saturday night?"

Oscar nodded. "Police were taking her away when Master and I arrived. He told her they would not put her on trial—and of course they didn't."

"For murdering William Sheridan, you mean?" Harris was impressed by how closely this story matched Murdock's.

The idea of murder, however, Oscar put deprecatingly aside. Within half an hour the doctor had come and made his finding, but the police would not let Sibyl Martin go until morning. Being suspected like that must have been hard on her. Oscar didn't blame her for wanting to slip away afterwards.

She had been agreeable enough to Oscar in terms of offering him cool drinks on a hot day. She hinted men had ill-used her, but never complained of William Sheridan. Then again, she was no longer nineteen. A morose sort of woman, Oscar thought her—not that he had any need to go prying into other people's troubles.

He had not, he admitted, worked long for the Cranes. He had come with the brougham, his first position of this sort and his first of any sort since recovering from an illness he did not care to specify. Before his arrival, the household's only carriage had been a two-wheeled chaise, which Crane had driven himself—and still kept for occasions when Oscar was not available or not wanted. A groom, since dismissed, had sufficed. Now Oscar did it all.

Harris followed him into the stable when he led the carriage-horse to its stall.

"What can you tell me about Miss Martin's appearance, her size especially?"

"Can't say I noticed. Like any woman in service, I suppose. Not slight like the Mistress. I can't believe she won't come tripping through that door, Mr. Harris, and ask when I last changed the bedding straw." Oscar again began leaning on his words. "She was very *particular*—not scolding, you understand. The past she left alone, but she wanted everything done right *in future.* Some writer—I read a lot, Mr. Harris, more than you would think—this man speaks of the soul looking steadily forward, creating a world always *before* her. That reminded me of the Mistress..."

It seemed a strange, rambling speech. Harris lost the continuation, for his attention had been caught by the animal in the next stall, a black mare with a white left hind foot.

"When was Spat found?" he asked.

"Found?" Oscar returned to earth.

"I understood Mrs. Crane's mount had disappeared too."

"She was riding Nelson." The coachman gestured towards a third stall, which was empty.

Harris stared stupidly at it. He should perhaps have been less surprised to have again caught Crane out. In fact, when Harris rehearsed that drive to the cemetery, he realized Crane had not lied to him, merely neglected to correct Harris's assumption that Theresa had been riding her own horse.

"Spat was indisposed then?" he said. "Unfit for exercise?"

"Look her over for yourself if you like." Oscar sighed as if accusations that he had neglected his charges were no more than he could expect. "I warn you, though, she doesn't take to strangers."

"Forgive my questions, Oscar, but this could help us find your mistress. Was it usual for her to ride Nelson?"

"Not usual, no. Her friend, the French lady, took him out more often."

Harris edged in between Spat and the rough boards. He had

no illusions that the horse would remember him, but found that his hand remembered the touch on the withers she found most reassuring. She nickered a greeting.

"Oscar," he called over the partition as he stroked the black muzzle, "did she give you any reason for choosing Nelson?"

"I had the day off. I wasn't even here when she left." The coachman came around into Spat's stall. "I blame myself for that... You got on the right side of that animal dashed quick. How is it you know the Mistress anyway?"

Clouds of jealousy—dark and sullen with no lightning spark of anger—overcast the stable. Oscar's mention of reading, in combination with his yellow vest, put Harris in mind of Goethe's *Young Werther* and the melancholy of loving an unattainable woman.

"Oh," he stammered, "I—I used to help her with her study of plants—years ago, before she was married."

Oscar helped Harris to inspect the frogs of Spat's hoofs for thrush, and then to go over her inch by inch to find the reason Theresa had left her behind. No defect turned up anywhere.

Harris turned his attention to the missing Nelson and found Oscar better at describing horses than people. Nelson was said to be more quarter horse than anything, but tall, sixteen and a half hands, dark brown with a drop of red, black points, fourteen years old, and not a nervous bone in his body. How long Crane had owned him neither man knew.

Presently Oscar recalled that he had promised Cook to bring in some firewood, and Harris walked him to the pile.

"Do you always have Sunday off?"

"Only when I'm not needed. Master told me Saturday night, and I set out at dawn Sunday for my brother's home in Weston. If I had been here, I might have saved her. I can't help thinking I let her down."

"We must hope she's alive," Harris said in parting.

"Hope, yes! You sound like an Archer, Mr. Harris. Are you familiar with astrology?"

Harris smiled, shook his head, and hobbled away. He

wondered if Oscar might be a tradesman's son, reduced to service by misfortune or by his own peculiarities. Modern superstitions abounded. No one need look to anything as medieval as horoscopes. At the same time, the man appealed to Harris, who had not expected to find such candour anywhere at Crane's establishment. Oscar's devotion to his mistress was also touching.

And the upshot of it all was that Harris had seen Spat, although what exactly that meant he had not yet the leisure or serenity to work out. Every step on his left foot sheared painfully through his web of thought. His foremost wish was that beyond the villa's screening lilac bushes the cab that had brought him would still be waiting as instructed.

It was. He promptly engaged it for the rest of the evening.

* * *

Gas street lamps were less closely spaced along this stretch of King Street east of the market, and Jasper Small considered himself unlucky to have one right outside his door. The glare left him no privacy, he said. On the other hand, access to the upper floors of the yellow brick building where he rented bachelor quarters lay between a wine merchant and a haberdashery, which could hardly have suited him better.

Tonight it would have suited Harris to have Small installed in a sensible bungalow like Crane's. The two steep flights of stairs felt like ten.

Although only a few blocks separated Crane and Small's residences in the city's northeast ward, Harris had not followed the shortest path between them. He had wasted some minutes calling on people that were out. Leaving Small word that he would come to the lawyer's rooms at nine, he spent the remaining daylight being driven over the dusty roads between Highland Creek and Port Union. He had found Vandervoort's shed, and in the embers something more—a second charred scrap of cloth.

Hobbling up the last few steps, he rapped briskly at Small's door. Eventually, a languid male voice said something like "Come in."

Papered in red, the gaslit salon under the roof looked as hot as it felt. Most of the subjects of the framed engravings had shed their clothes, and Small—sitting barefoot at a secretary desk—seemed to be following their example. A braid-trimmed dressing gown slipped off his shoulders as he turned towards Harris.

"She wants—this client of mine—to leave her property to her daughter in such a way that a future son-in-law won't be able to touch it. Can't be done, Isaac. Oh, the husband won't be able to sell it, but he could run it into the ground and gobble up all the revenue."

"You're working late," said Harris. "Have you thought of taking a new partner to share the load?"

Small said nothing, his ghost-grey eyes focusing somewhere beyond the walls. Likely it was too soon after Sheridan's death for Harris to be suggesting such a thing, but Small's distracted state looked nothing like anything Harris recognized as grief. Well, to business. Perhaps that would bring him round.

"Jasper, what was the housekeeper Sibyl Martin wearing when you saw her a week ago Friday?"

"The housekeeper? Homespun—why?"

"Tell you in a moment. What colour?"

"No colour in particular. Conceivably an onion-skin brown. Yes, something like that." Small was looking with the mildest possible interest at the grimy scrap in Harris's hands. "Has something happened to her?"

Scrutinizing the cloth under a hot lamp in the vain hope of further revelations, Harris voiced his suspicions. Small knew nothing to allay them. He had no idea what had become of Sibyl after Sheridan's death, had never even thought of the matter till now. Strange, wasn't it, how one could take servants for granted? Urged to assemble his scattered recollections, he found none relating to a fracture in the lower right arm of either Sibyl or Theresa, but he did think them "very much of a height."

These words affected Harris like the unstringing of a bow

long kept under tension. He sank onto a thickly-upholstered sofa.

"The thing is," he said, "if I'm to keep the search alive, I must account for the remains that have been found."

"Account away then. How did Sibyl come to be in that shed?"

"Crane knows something about her. When I mentioned her name to him, he threw me off a train."

"The devil!" A look of horror tinged with amusement rippled over the hitherto serene disk of Small's face. "A train in motion?"

Harris nodded. "A guilty response, would you not say?"

"The bandage on your foot then—is there much pain?"

Harris glanced at Small's half-open bedroom door, which he almost thought he had seen move. He could not recall if his friend kept a cat, but all was still, and he was too hot and weary to be bothered.

"Not when I rest it," he said. "Do you think there could have been something between Henry and Sibyl—of a man-woman sort, I mean?"

With a musical laugh, a woman in a pink peignoir appeared at the bedroom door. "Of a prick and cunt sort, Mr. Harris? Is that what you have in mind?"

Harris took his feet off the sofa and jumped up in confusion, forgetting his ankle for the moment. He had never heard such words in mixed company, let alone from female lips. These lips were moist and pouting.

"If that is what you mean," the woman continued, "I should say that nothing is more likely."

"She was past all that surely," Small objected in a tone of mild reproof. He avoided meeting Harris's eyes. "Sibyl had nothing left in the way of freshness or girlish shape."

"No matter. From what *I* hear, Mr. Crane's palate runs very much to seamstresses and serving women. He doesn't mind them young and sparkling, but he'll also take the older potatoes with a little dirt for seasoning. Don't go, Mr. Harris. We were expecting you."

"I didn't realize..." Harris's voice trailed off.

He wondered if his friend—bereft, overworked—had lost his mind. First, to let Harris come and talk freely without warning him they were not alone. And then, for the other guest to be a woman so intimately attired, so provocative in her speech—plainly Harris could only be in their way. He hesitated, though. Here at last was someone wading into the subject he had never got respectable tongues to broach—namely, what kind of marriage Theresa had had. Perhaps a detective could not afford to be too particular.

"Jasper," he said, "what's this about?"

"Esther Vale." Distractedly, Small hunched his dressing gown back on. "The client I was referring to."

Harris knew the name. He had the troubling impression that it figured somewhere in the records of his branch.

"You might say we are each other's clients." Esther Vale glided to a chair and sat, back straight, plump hands folded.

She looked familiar too. Physically, she could almost have been an older relation of Small's, with her round white cheeks and pale grey eyes. Unlike Small's, hers were watchful eyes. They seemed to appraise what balance she should at every moment strike between the vulgar and the demure. Beneath her henna-red hair hung bulbous earrings. Presently, she took them off.

That was when Harris recognized her as the complainant in the police station, and a second later as a depositor as well.

"I lend Mr. Harris my ill-got gains, some of them," Mrs. Vale told Small.

"So everyone knows everyone," he replied, smiling as if his own position had thereby been made less awkward. Small was drifting on the tide of events and, but for the other man's scrutiny, would apparently have been quite content to do so. "Here," he said, exerting himself as host, "let's have some cognac. Isaac?"

Harris took a glass. Over £650, he reflected, on long-term deposit at four per cent. He had wondered how a barber's widow had amassed this much and was not sure he was happier knowing.

"Is Henry Crane a client of yours too?" he forced himself to ask, his face prickling with embarrassment.

"Not for me, sugar lump," she instructed Small. "Spirits poison the complexion. Mr. Crane? Oh, no, he doesn't like to pay for female companionship."

"He doesn't have to?" Theresa's husband, Harris thought.

"No gentleman has to if a scuffle with a rough-chapped slavey is all he wants."

Harris winced, as he had been intended to.

"Last October, my dear banker, when I opened my account, I may have neglected to mention that for a dozen years I have run a sporting house in Kingston, Montreal, Quebec and Toronto—wherever the provincial capital happens to be."

"She sticks," said Small, "to the seat of government."

Mrs. Vale threw her chair cushion, which toppled Small's brandy over the draft of her will. Harris attended closely. Plainly in this world anything could happen.

"Let us say I keep track of the honourable members. If they spend under my roof, it's not for want of other opportunities, but because lawgivers appreciate smart, clean girls with soft skins and saucy notions. Ditto your Napoleons of commerce."

"Except for Crane."

"I tried to land him, I will admit. A railway man that size, with a pretty, young wife to betray—he would have been a trophy to hang over my hearth. He seemed ripe for it too. To see them together, you could tell they slept apart."

"Could you, Jasper?" said Harris.

"I was referring," Mrs. Vale corrected, "to the professional eye. As I say, though, Henry turned out to have other interests."

"Sibyl Martin?"

"He's a man the waves part for. Good-natured too. Women enough would have taken her place."

Good-natured? Selectively perhaps. Harris recalled the relentless optimism with which William Sheridan had been lobbied in '53—first for the Northern Railway, then for Theresa's hand.

"Women enough," Small echoed. "Why bother then with his father-in-law's faded drudge?"

Harris silently wondered if it might not have been, at least in part, Sibyl's position that had won for her Crane's favour. Suppose Crane wanted some new benefit from Sheridan, conceivably some information. A spy might well earn her keep in flattering attentions.

Mrs. Vale, however, would allow for no motives but perverse desire.

"Taste, my cherub," she cooed. "Disgustibus nonny-nonny."

Small struck a magisterial pose. "*De gustibus non est—*"

"Exactly." She adjusted her peignoir to reveal six pale inches of leg. "Mr. Harris, I understand that you are looking for the wronged wife."

Harris didn't know where to look or what to say. To think of Theresa as injured in this way pained him, and—while no avenue could be neglected—to discuss her with Mrs. Vale must be to expose the wound to fresh insult.

"Have you any idea," he asked, "where she might be?"

"If you pay me a call on Parliament Street, I'm sure I can connect you with a girl who will help you."

Perhaps another of Crane's paramours, Harris naïvely thought.

"Help him forget the lady, you mean," said Small, "not help him find her."

"Now, sugar lump, isn't it past your bedtime?"

"Mrs. Vale," said Harris, "with which women has Henry Crane to your knowledge committed adultery?"

"You're stern, Mr. Harris. I've no head for names, you know, just numbers. Tell me, what rate do you charge when you lend my money out again?"

His glass in pieces, Small drank from the bottle "Are you suggesting that Isaac lives off the E. Vales of harlotry?"

In a flutter of pink silk over uncorseted flesh, the individual so named swept up behind Small's chair and—leaning over the back—blew in his ear.

"Bedtime," she murmured. "Bedtime, bedtime, bedtime."

"I did oblige you by being here at nine," Small told Harris with a helpless shrug. "You could hardly expect me to change the whole evening's schedule."

Harris picked up his top hat and nodded. No comradely farewell came to his lips. He was thinking about the schedule, speculating as to how it might be written up. *Nine o'clock: Isaac, on matters of life and death. Nine thirty: p. and c.*

"Good night, banker dear." Over Small's shoulder, Mrs. Vale watched Harris's retreat. "It's Parliament just north of Duchess." Her snowy cheek brushed Small's. "If you're an early riser," she added archly, "you can even come before breakfast."

* * *

Theresa had not gone for a ride. Of all the day's revelations, that was the one that kept bobbing to the surface of his mind. To that life preserver Harris's fatigued brain clung as his fingers automatically loosened shoelaces, waistcoat buttons, the bow of his tie. Everything else he had learned swirled for the moment out of reach.

The horse she had taken was not the one she rode for exercise. She must have wanted one she could ride hard, sell perhaps along the way. After carefully training the new coachman, she could not have endured the thought of her temperamental Spat among strangers. She had anticipated a long journey, so no wonder she had not been found near town—the town Harris was chained to. She had planned to leave. Whether because of Crane's infidelities or on account of some even graver crime Harris could not yet make out, but he now knew she had fled intentionally.

And gone where?

In nightshirt now, Harris turned back the bedclothes. He expected he would think more clearly once he was lying down. A breath of air off the lake was nudging the muslin curtains into the room. The night seemed cooler, but possibly the cashier's suite just had a better location and better ventilation than

Small's apartment. Small could have done better for himself. But the question was...

Sleep took Harris quickly and for some time held him fast, but eventually his ankle must have caught as he rolled over. The twinge woke him. While unable to remember his dream, he found himself in a state of sexual excitation.

By design, this happened rarely. Quack remedies he avoided, but he had developed habits that so tired his body and occupied his mind as to leave Eros no room or sustenance. He was of too empirical a bent wholly to believe moralizing doctors on the horrors of spermatorrhoea—blindness, madness, consumption, dyspepsia, epilepsy, curvature of the spine—though there was so little untainted data on the subject that it was hard to know what to believe. Harris's aversion to physical arousal was more particular to himself and lay in its invariably focusing his thoughts on one bitter-sweet experience, which he now found himself living again.

He rose and bathed to no avail. The erection did not subside.

It was late October '52, a freakishly mild Sunday afternoon in the Don Valley. Spat and Banshee had drunk from the river and were tethered to a pair of oaks, hoofs crunching the parchment-dry leaves as they shifted their weight. Theresa was standing close. There was something about the lanceolate leaves of an aster Harris was to see. She squinted against the slanting sun, which spilled its warm tones over her face. He kissed her.

They had kissed before, briefly, at parting, never in the midst of something else.

Only after he had bent his lips to hers did he think this might startle her, but she didn't recoil. She let herself be kissed, then returned the pressure. Her hands went around his waist under his fustian jacket.

The perfection of the moment pierced him through. To a critical mind like his, every object had its limits. Every transaction with nature, art or humankind left something to be desired. Everything but this. She was so exquisitely fresh and pure and trim. Heaven on his lips and in his arms. No more beyond.

She untucked the wool shirt from the back of his trousers. Her cool fingers electrified his spine. She shivered with pleasure when he stroked the nape of her neck.

The kiss ended. She breathed his name, took his hand from her waist and held it against the pleated bodice of her dress. Above the stays her small round breast shaped itself to the pressure of his touch.

His loins' machine-like answer to this new perfection stunned him. He was out of his depth. He turned so as not to brush against her.

When she released his hand, he took it away. Her eyes sought and searched his face, where they could only have read confusion. Perhaps, he stammered, it was time to return to town. She looked startled, then lowered her gaze and nodded. She said just to give her a moment by herself first, as she was in no condition to ride. He watched her stroll off through the ankle-deep lake of rustling leaves while a crow brayed and flapped its way across the sunlit valley. Harris picked up the purple flower which had slipped from Theresa's hand. Lanceolate leaves.

They went on one more ride together, but she didn't try to show him anything. Autumn turned cold and wet after that. By spring she was Crane's.

It was still dark night outside Harris's window. He rubbed himself to a joyless climax, dozed briefly, then lay and watched for dawn.

Would Theresa have lain with him on that bed of leaves? Seductive as the scene was in fantasy, he still believed he had been right not to let it come to that.

What he regretted was his cowardice before her green eyes' ardent query. Right then he should have told her not that it was time to take her home, but that he wanted to be with her always. That regret grew fresh teeth every day.

Crane an adulterer.

Many wives put up with hypocrisy and betrayal their whole marriage through, but nothing strained credulity in Theresa's frank heart choosing not to. She could have been planning her escape for months. To spare her father pain, she had waited till after his death, but only just. Jealousy of Sibyl might have underlain the dispute Small reported the two women having had the Friday afternoon and explain Theresa's having the housekeeper questioned by police the following night.

No, Theresa would not have been that vindictive. More likely it was Crane who had tried to cast suspicion on Sibyl—had tried to dispose of someone he no longer had any use for.

Unwilling to speculate further, Harris shaved and dressed. In fiery haste, he framed a letter to Marthe Laurendeau as Theresa's closest current companion. Had she seen the missing woman since noon on the thirteenth? Was Theresa at this moment with her? Or likely to join her? Had Mlle Laurendeau any idea where else Theresa might have gone? Harris loaded the page with assurances that Theresa's safety and happiness were his only concerns. He was inquiring in the interest of neither the police nor Henry Crane.

Once this appeal was sealed and addressed, he spent the remaining hours before opening in the less absorbing dray-work of clearing bank business from his desk. Up and down Bay Street, harbour traffic quickened with its clops, jangles, groans and shouts. Nothing, however, caused his pen or eye to pause, except from time to time, always just out of sight, the buzzing of a small winged insect.

At last, Dick Ogilvie brought in the morning papers. The board of the Provincial Bank of Canada had met in Kingston to find a replacement for the director lately incapacitated by highwaymen. All deplored the necessity for such an election. They nonetheless took pleasure in announcing that their choice had fallen on Mr. Joshua Newbiggins of Toronto, in recognition of that gentleman's particular talents and of his city's remarkable rise to commercial pre-eminence in Canada West.

Harris rubbed his eyes.

Joshua Newbiggins, Pennsylvania coal importer, promoter of Conquest Iron Works, dispenser of fifty-dollar bills, admirer of somnambulistic sopranos. He said he had come north the week Miss Jenny Lind sang at the St. Lawrence Hall.

Newspaper records placed her Toronto appearance in October 1851. After consulting also the government records at King Street West and John, Harris wrote a letter to the president of the bank. Its charter, he pointed out, as enacted in 1844 and renewed in 1854, required that directors be natural born subjects of Her Majesty, or naturalized, or have resided seven years in the province. None of these conditions fit the present case. Harris went on to report Newbiggins's unsuccessful attempt to inspect the branch's books.

"It would appear," he wrote, "that Mr. Newbiggins has sought a directorship to obtain the information denied him as a shareholder. I cannot think that the bank would be served by any director's using his position against the interest of the bank's own clients, of whom Conquest's rival, York Foundry, is one of the most prominent.

"I am confident that the board selected Mr. Newbiggins in all innocence both of his statutory ineligibility and of his motives. In fact, if even one board member had been party to his scheme, it would have been an easy matter for that member to obtain for Mr. Newbiggins the intelligence he seeks.

"My purpose in writing is twofold: (1) to lay the above facts before you and (2) to advise you that if Mr. Newbiggins again presents himself to the Toronto branch with a request to see our books I shall—"

Harris had been about to write *refuse* but softened it.

"—delay compliance until I have your reply in hand."

Serving the bank was his only thought as he sealed the envelope. Not until it was bobbing its way down Lake Ontario on the noon steamer did he reflect on the contents' potential to simplify his life.

PART TWO:
Farther Afield

Chapter Seven
Great Western

Dark clouds were congregating above the millpond. Before the village church bells had quite stopped ringing, thunder rumbled in from the west and a squall of wind hastened the pond waters towards the race. Beside it towered the fieldstone mill, a waiting grey sentinel.

Isaac Harris had not communicated with his family for nearly three weeks and didn't want to stray far from Toronto without doing so. He was not looking forward to explaining himself.

Crossing the race, he climbed the plank steps towards the open door. From inside floated his father's tender baritone. The sound made his own throat tighten around his unwelcome news. Under his hand, the wooden stair rail, sweat-oiled, smooth with use, felt as familiar as everything else about the mill, and like everything else, no longer his.

"The Minstrel Boy to the war is gone,
In the ranks of death you'll find him..."

Young Alexander Harris *had* gone to war. He had followed Major General Sir Isaac Brock up Queenston Heights and—through no fault of his own—survived. Among Harrises, the charge's futility was a taboo subject. Queenston was still Canadian, after all, and Isaac bore the slain quixote's name.

"His father's sword he has girded on,
And his wild harp slung behind him..."

After battle, Isaac thought, business must have held no terrors. Years of thrift and toil had earned Alexander a half-interest in a grist mill, then a whole mill, then a much bigger mill—the present one—built to his own specifications. Wildness might still be recalled in song, but in his own boys, industry had always been preferred.

Isaac stepped across the threshold. Misgivings receded as he smelled this community hub that had been his home. Wood, water, cotton sacks, beeswax and tallow lubricants, leather belts to drive the machinery, and grain—grain in every state from kernel to dust. The empty room still echoed with farmers' weekday talk of prices and Reform politics.

In theory retired now, Isaac's father had moved out too. He had turned his flour fortress over to one of Isaac's brothers, but he still came back with his set of picks to dress the French quartz millstones. From the Marne Valley, he was fond of pointing out, champagne country.

He was kneeling by one of them as he sang, his old frock coat folded into a pad beneath his knees, white shirt sleeves turned precisely back above the elbows. He worked by touch, fingering furrow edges too fine now for him to see. He dropped the minstrel boy mid-stanza when he realized he wasn't alone. His son felt grit in his welcoming handshake.

"Taking the country air, Isaac?" he said. "Pull yourself up a stool."

"How are you, sir?"

Well, replied the elder Harris, except for the cough that kept him from joining the family at church. Flour dust in the lungs most likely. He gave a demonstration so unconvincing they both laughed.

Alexander did look well, his flesh firm, his shoulders square. They spread wider than Isaac's, and it was a shorter lift to get a sack of flour onto them. Among the features father and son shared were a long nose, eyes sloping gently away from it, a lumpy chin and a terrier-like attachment to the task at hand.

"Fellow across the river was in Toronto on July 12," said Alexander, bending again over his bed-stone. "Told me you cut a fine figure at the Peninsula Hotel dance."

"I was there briefly."

"Too briefly for the ladies, doubtless. I hear you run a good bank too."

The only stool was so low that when Isaac sat on it, his knees all but brushed his ears. Mention of the bank made him feel more awkward still.

Joshua Newbiggins had come to see him Wednesday with questions about York Foundry—how much their loan was for, whether they had been late with any payments, where they got their coal, what they were paying for it. Canada had no hard coal. If Newbiggins could get control of York's American supplier, he would have his rival under his pudgy little thumb.

"Your brothers are doing all right here, Isaac, but the railway has killed Holland Landing dead. No freight goes by water between Toronto and Lake Huron. The city is the place to be, and you're the only one of us to make a name down there."

Isaac lifted a hand against the words. He had put Newbiggins off, but on Thursday a ciphered telegram had confirmed his election. Resignation had become inevitable.

"Modesty aside," Alexander was saying, "the only one. But what I still can't fathom is you're also the only one that has not started a family."

They had played this scene before. Isaac changed the script.

"Father," he said, "I've left the bank."

There, it was out. He felt again the keys leave his hand as they had Friday morning after he had moved his effects to the American Hotel. The jangling ring had nearly slipped through Murdock's agitated fingers.

"Found a way of doing better on your own?" Alexander was beaming. "I thought you would once you had had a chance to look around. Man should be in business for himself. So what's it to be, Isaac? Shipping? Manufacturing? You'll want to marry in any case."

Alexander understood Isaac's putting the law and his clients' interests before a whim of the directors. He understood without pressing for details, which Isaac could not in conscience give. Matter of principle—of course. What the retired miller found incomprehensible was that his son had no *other* business in view, except for the rescue of Theresa Crane. Isaac tried several times to explain it.

"I'm baffled," said Alexander, getting to his feet at last. "What do you propose to live on?"

"I've savings enough for now and a property or two I can sell."

"You're too young to be drawing on your capital." A sacred axiom, delivered with the categorical gruffness that just yesterday—it seemed—had ended all family disagreements.

"It will only be temporary," said Isaac.

Alexander walked away in disgust. He went as far as the low-silled window overlooking the eighteen-foot wheel. The worst birching he had ever given Isaac was for putting his young life and bright future at risk by riding that wheel on a dare. A loving chastisement, doubtless. And yet, in the rigidity of the back now turned to him, Isaac recognized a fear for which he had no sympathy. His tolerance even was ebbing fast. Career and fortune be damned!

"It will just be till this disappearance is resolved," he said in a nonetheless cool, bankerly voice as he came to his father's side.

"I know you were fond of the Sheridan girl," Alexander murmured, "and she would have made a good match. Your taking time to help her husband look for her does you credit, but mark this—as an outsider, you can't neglect your own affairs indefinitely."

"He's not a fit husband."

"So, if you do find her, what then?"

This rather fundamental question Isaac glanced at, then brushed aside. If Theresa had run away, as he now believed, resolving her disappearance meant more than simply finding her. It meant protecting her from whatever had driven her from her home. A task of unknown size.

"She still won't be yours," said Alexander, unconsciously echoing Small's reminder.

"I accept that she will not." It was Isaac Harris's bargain with fate, *not* to have Theresa on condition that he could save her, but it would be some time—at least—before his acceptance would be tested, and there were more urgent matters to discuss.

"William Sheridan was your M.P. Can you think of anywhere she might have gone? Any family friend or refuge?"

Alexander seemed taken off guard. "In York County?"

"Possibly. She was last seen in Thornhill. With a bay gelding." Isaac had confirmed this on his way north from the city. "That was the evening of the thirteenth. Later than that, no one I have met has seen her."

"You must know other well-connected young ladies," said Alexander, back on his hobby horse. "Doesn't George MacFarlane have daughters?"

"MacFarlane? His oldest unattached girl is twelve."

"That fellow across the river sells him timber. Talk is MacFarlane is to be knighted for contributions to the Crimean campaign. Troop carriers, hospital ships and the like."

Patriotic verse, Isaac added under his breath. "Please, Father, think. Did you ever see Theresa in the company of anyone besides her father and Crane? Did either of them mention anyone she might have visited?"

"Let it go, Isaac. '...When we're far from the lips we love, we've but to make love to the lips we are near.'"

Isaac had always disliked hearing cited this couplet of Thomas Moore's, which he believed did scant justice to his parents' feelings for each other.

"I can't," he said.

Outside the window where they still stood, a bolt of lightning split the noon sky. Rain was peppering the Holland River before the thunder reached their ears. A chill wind blew between them.

"It will blight your career," Alexander prophesied grimly.

"Father," said Isaac, reaching out to him, "I should like to oblige you, but in this one matter I can't."

"Leave then. Don't wait to see your mother."

"I beg your pardon."

"You would only cause her pain. Go quickly, Isaac, and never breathe a syllable of this to her." The words poured out so fine and smooth as to leave no doubt they represented a finished thought.

"I don't see how you can ask me to—"

"Oblige me," said Alexander, compact and immovable. "Go now."

No more was said. Isaac's boots beat a brisk tattoo out the door, despite his misgivings. For his mother to learn of his joblessness, he thought, would pain his father more than her. Then again, not all battles could be fought at once. His visit had at least shown him where he stood, as well as relieving his father of any temptation to brag about him. His ultimate success must be his justification.

He walked out into the rain, around the millpond to the paddock where he had left Banshee. He barely limped now from his sprained ankle and found he could ride if he mounted from the right side instead of the left. The horse had been surprised but accommodating.

The doors of the stuccoed Presbyterian church opened as he rode by. He didn't look back, at least not until he was too far away to be identified by any of the worshippers. He had never felt more utterly alone. For now, no remedy.

From thoughts of his family he distracted himself by scouring half a dozen townships that filthy afternoon. Evening brought more rain. Not until every innkeeper and stable hand had gone to bed did he return, saddle-sore and empty-handed, to the city. The bay gelding Nelson and his lady rider had dissolved.

Downtown, the American Hotel boasted a night clerk, a preened young heron with a dazzling white neckcloth and a precise eye. Whatever the night clerk might or might not think of the mud on the guest's trousers, he knew the guest had a letter, hand delivered at 9:26 p.m. To avoid soiling the lobby chairs, Harris opened it where he stood.

Sun. 27 July

Dear Isaac,

Had to write tho' quite done in. Much work occasioned by yr. resig. Let that pass.

Lad we spoke of lodged out of town for his safety. After

mass today, praised yr. honesty & discretion till family consented to yr. seeing him. Come to me for letter of intro., but not tonight. Must rest.

Faithfully, Septimus M.

* * *

Murdock was sleeping above the bank. Until a watchman could be hired, he felt someone had to—though, as acting cashier only, he did not propose to move his large family there. Harris roused him from the mahogany canopy bed at seven on an already sultry Monday morning.

"Right, Septimus, what's the name of this altar boy?"

"Who?" Murdock pulled a paisley dressing gown about him and yawned.

"The boy," Harris stammered. "The boy Theresa sent to summon the police on the night of the twelfth. The one you wrote to me about last night."

"Oh, you mean Nicky Gunn. He's staying with his uncle, a baggage master for the Great Western Railway."

"Which station, Septimus?"

"Pardon."

"Your note said he was lodged out of town. Where?"

"Hamilton. Didn't I say? Here, Isaac, off so soon? Let me give you the father's letter to his brother first. Just so the Hamilton Gunns know who you are. Won't you have some tea?"

Harris grabbed the letter, refused the tea.

The first Great Western train of the day was just starting to roll as at 8:10 he climbed aboard. The feel of the iron handrail and a glimpse of the accelerating gravel shoulder beneath the steps made week-old bruises tender, but he didn't linger on the carriage platform.

For the short run, he had taken a second-class ticket. German-speaking emigrants occupied most of the sixty wooden seats. On the side away from the lake, however, he found one empty and slid his portmanteau beneath it. After declining a slice of the thick sausage on which his neighbour was breakfasting, he was left to such reflections as the incessant clanging of rails, wheels and couplings permitted.

Lurching towards Hamilton, he ground his teeth at the lack of speed. He doubted whether, after more than two weeks, a meeting with Theresa's messenger would repay the time it cost.

The car sizzled. It bounced on its tracks like fat on a glowing griddle. Harris found no relief in the shade of the slate-grey clouds, none in the air pouring through the open windows at twenty miles per hour. When the train stopped at Oakville, ice cream vendors swarmed to the windows. Harris bought a dish and found it already softened to the consistency of bacon grease.

It was all nonsense. In the light of day, even Murdock was inclined to see Nicky's sojourn less as a precaution against Orange reprisals than as an opportunity for the boy to visit his young cousins. Perhaps—Murdock's parting suggestion—Harris would like to wait until Nicky returned.

Harris hadn't waited even to reply.

The locomotive slowed for the last time, dragging its tail on wheels through a timber bridge trestle at little more than a brisk walk. Sixty feet below, a canal and marsh gleamed dully. In the eight months that the Toronto spur of the G.W.R. had been open, Harris had come to Hamilton once on bank business and once to shoot ducks. From today's irritable perspective, both seemed to him like pleasure jaunts.

Just after nine thirty, with a clapping of the wooden buffers at either end, the carriage came to rest in the midst of three dozen other canary yellow cars. At half Toronto's population, Hamilton seemed to be suffering from twice the railway fever.

In his corner of the throng and bustle, the lanky baggage master, Nicky's presumed uncle, wore his heavy spectacles and railway cap as if they constituted part of his head. Distraught passengers in line ahead of Harris each received forms to fill out. With no one was this complete official peevish or surly, for no one did he much exert himself. The loss of other people's trunks and suitcases was evidently a misfortune Mr. Gunn had learned to endure.

Harris reached the counter at last. Gunn had not the pleasure of knowing Murdock, but responded agreeably enough to his own brother's written request that Harris be granted an interview with young Nick. This could not, however, be arranged before the noon dinner hour, no, not by any means.

On the chance that Theresa had come west, Harris filled the interval with his standard inquiries of ticket offices, stables and hotels. By noon he had fruitlessly tramped through much of the town. Two of the main streets had been dug up for the installation of sewers, muddy planks across muddier moats providing the only access to some of Hamilton's proudest shops and homes. Fine structures, Harris guessed. After Toronto's surfeit of brick, the local sandstone would have been soothing to a less impatient eye.

The Gunn house was situated two blocks north of the railway tracks on MacNab Street. In this the port area, dwellings were frame. Inquiry of the children playing tag in the dirt street resulted in Harris's being directed to a house loyally painted in the G.W.R.'s canary yellow.

The baggage master arrived from the station as Harris approached the door. They found Nicky Gunn making candles for his aunt, who had no girl old enough to be entrusted with the task. The boy was between ten and twelve, neatly dressed, quiet and steady-looking. Straight blond hair fell over his heat-flushed forehead. Before pouring the hot tallow, he wanted his aunt's opinion as to whether he had the wicks quite straight in the moulds. He protested at having his task interrupted. At second asking, he nonetheless accompanied his uncle and Harris to the cramped and airless guest parlour.

What qualities were looked for in an altar boy Harris did not know, but he could see why Theresa might have picked Nicky above other passersby for an errand of moment. Questioning at first elicited no more than was known from Murdock. A lady had called out to Nicky from the gate of one of the villas facing the Esplanade, a red-brick villa with nine big windows in front and a round roof over the front stoop. This could only be Sheridan's. And the lady? The conscientious boy described her in such a way as to convince Harris of her identity. Slender, younger than Nicky's mother or even his aunt, brownish hair, green eyes, mouth in the shape of—here the boy drew a low-pitched gable in the air.

As for her mental state on that night of her father's death, she had been in full control of herself as far as the boy could see, strong and confident of purpose. There was nothing broken or disconnected in her speech, although he believed she had been crying.

Harris, who had never seen Theresa in like condition, suffered a fresh, hot pang of pity for her loss.

"Now, Nick," he said, leaning forward, "I want you to think most particularly, and tell me every word Mrs. Crane spoke to you, first to last, as much as you can remember."

Taken somewhat aback, the boy looked to his uncle, who nodded.

"She said, 'Here, take a message.' I didn't want to at first. I heard there were to be fireworks down the beach at nine o'clock, and I didn't want to miss them."

"July 12," his uncle scolded. "You should not have been out at all, with all that rabble about—making your mother grieve."

"Go on," said Harris. "You were reluctant to take a message. What next?"

"She said, 'You must take this to the police at City Hall as fast as you can.' I knew the house belonged to people of consequence. They all do along Front Street. The word *police* caught my notice."

"And the penny," the uncle irritatingly added. In his own parlour, he was still wearing his railway cap. "I'll bet there was money in it."

"What then?" said Harris. "What else was said?"

"That's all, sir," the boy replied after a pause. "That was when I saw the tear on her cheek. I took the sealed up envelope—and the money... It wasn't a penny either, but sixpence," he added, as if to demonstrate his honesty.

"Now think, Nick," Harris insisted. "I'll tell you why I'm asking."

"Mr. Sheridan was a prominent man, as you say," the uncle put in, "a friend of Catholic and Protestant alike. That's why all the questions."

"What's more," Harris pursued, "Mrs. Crane disappeared the day after you saw her, Nick, and neither her husband nor any of her friends has seen her since. She may be in danger. We don't know if she has come to any harm. I am working with the police to find her, which is why I need to know as much as I can of what she did and said just before she vanished."

The boy pushed off his face his shock of fair hair, which fell immediately back.

"I've told everything," he said. "May I go now?"

"Nick," said Harris before the uncle could again intervene, "was there something she asked you not to tell? Perhaps some indication as to what she needed police for? The present exceptional circumstances release you from any obligation you may feel to keep silent. You may speak before your uncle and myself. Well, Nick?"

"She...she said, 'Don't breathe a word of this to anyone, but I have the woman that murdered my father. You must help me.'" The boy squirmed a little under the gravity of this communication, but his eyes held steady.

"That's all right, Nicky," his uncle soothed. "We already knew there had been villainy. Mrs. Crane just didn't want you gossiping along the way. With all that Orange mob loose in the streets, she didn't want you telling them their game was up."

"Anything else?" said Harris, considerably more excited than he could in kindness show. "Did Mrs. Crane give that woman a name?"

She had not. The boy had nothing more to communicate, and this time was immovable. Harris thanked him.

So—prior to Dr. Hillyard's examination at least—Theresa had shared the view of Murdock and his co-religionists that her father had been murdered. Give the uncle credit. His explanation of Theresa's request for silence was as plausible as any. The unnamed suspect must be Sibyl Martin. How did so physically slight a woman as Theresa manage to hold her? Harris wondered whether the ancient physician's subsequent finding of death by natural causes had seemed as compelling to Theresa as to the authorities. If, as Murdock claimed, Sibyl had been locked up Saturday night only to be released Sunday morning, might Theresa not have fled because she feared for her own life with this murderess—as she believed—at large?

"Of course," added Nicky's uncle, "Mrs. Crane did not disappear on July 13."

"Her husband says she did," Harris retorted.

"I saw her with her husband a week ago today." The baggage master removed his spectacles to wipe them on a large red handkerchief. His naked, concave face looked as guileless as a saucer. "They were passengers on the 5:45 p.m. westbound express."

As if to see whether he had been tricked into betraying a confidence, the boy watched Harris closely.

"I find this difficult to believe," Harris stammered, tasting perspiration on his upper lip. The parlour was close and warm as a greenhouse. "May I ask if you were wearing your spectacles?"

"Uncle always wears them," Nicky asserted.

"That's so." Gunn curled the wires around his ears, and the glasses fell back into his face.

"You saw both Mr. and Mrs. Crane quite clearly, Mr. Gunn?"

"Through the window of a first-class carriage, no farther than across this room. Oh, yes. Everyone on the Great Western knows Mr. Crane, and that was his wife all right, just as my nephew describes her."

* * *

At the Great Western station again, Harris approached the ticket counter, then turned away. He couldn't determine in which direction to travel.

Wanting a cigar, he went back outside, where his eye wandered over the maelstrom of brakesmen, firemen, switchmen, inspectors, tradesmen, apprentices, porters and clerks. Whenever he noticed one less occupied than his fellows, Harris pounced. Some responded willingly, some sparingly, some not at all to his inquiries as to what reputation the baggage master enjoyed. Overall, report attributed to Gunn above fifteen years of blameless railway service in England and Canada, a good head for the names of railway employees, and eyesight—as corrected—as acute as anyone's. Nothing Harris heard resolved his vacillation.

He doubted Gunn's sighting of Theresa. Was this baggage master at all likely to be a painstaking observer of female physiognomy? Crane's, perhaps. Yes, Harris would grant him Crane. The railway builder's pink visage and portly form might well be familiar to functionaries of Gunn's rank. Harris knew from painful experience that Crane had indeed been riding the G.W.R. west one week ago, on the afternoon of July 21. That Crane was travelling with a woman, or expecting one imminently to join him, would help account for his violent disinclination to have Harris ride with him from Toronto to Hamilton.

Gunn might have seen a woman accompanying Crane. Suppose further—what was less probable—that she matched Nicky's description point for point. That description had seemed conclusive to Harris only because Nicky himself had framed it and because the woman described had been seen at the gate of Sheridan's villa. Crane was an adulterer, after all. If his travelling companion resembled Theresa, the reason might be that such was the general stamp of woman that caught his fancy. Or perhaps he wanted someone who would pass casual inspection as his wife. Whoever had sat with Crane in that first-class carriage could now be in Chicago with him, and it would be madness for Harris to pursue the couple nearly five hundred miles on so slender a chance.

Less than slender. There was no chance really that it was Theresa. If it were, her disappearance would have been mere theatre, a trick in which she and Crane had colluded for some dark purpose. Crane's approach to Harris at the funeral would lack rhyme or reason. No, Harris knew Theresa's character to be too frank and direct for such plotting, and she must in any case loathe Crane too deeply to so collude with him.

Or was that merely Harris's dislike, which he wanted her to share? He knew nothing of her feelings. His wish that she no longer be able to abide Crane's company might, he reluctantly admitted, be distorting his assessment of possibilities. What, after all, was his warrant that Crane was unfaithful? The sportive chatter of a bawd. Harris winced. If Theresa's father had fallen victim to a violent conspiracy, Theresa might surely be excused for in turn conspiring—for her own protection—to drop from view. Perhaps she had genuinely disappeared from Crane's house on July 13. Perhaps she had returned to enlist Crane's aid only after her father's funeral and after Crane's ride to the cemetery with Harris. Harris couldn't explain the grisly arm or other remains, but from Theresa's presence at Crane's side, it didn't follow that she knew of them.

So which ticket to buy? A train tooted twice and left for Toronto without Harris. He took another turn around the rail yards.

Two Saturdays ago, an ostler had seen Theresa in Thornhill, and Harris had failed to credit this authentic sighting because of his mistaken preconception as to which horse she had been riding. He didn't want to repeat that mistake. It seemed he could not yet afford to turn towards the home of Marthe Laurendeau in Canada East. He must at least find someone who had seen this companion of Crane's from closer quarters than had Gunn, someone who could render Gunn's identification either more probable or less.

Wearily Harris booked his passage on the 5:45 westbound express. He still thought Gunn's clue chimerical and did not mention it in the letter he wrote while awaiting his train's departure.

Afternoon, July 28, 1856
G.W.R. Station
Stuart St.
Hamilton, C.W.

My dear Mother,

Toronto, as you can see, is doing without me and will have to for some days more. When I do return, it will be to the American Hotel at Yonge and Front Sts.

I have left the bank. Between the two of us, I think the directors were galled that a mere cashier should have been reading the charter. I am disappointed in them, but not much put out, and have no fear for my future. In this prosperous time and province, opportunities abound.

I do not, however, propose to take up any just yet. All my energies are absorbed in the search for your late M.P.'s daughter, Theresa Crane, missing now for fifteen days and nights. Some garbled account of the matter you may have seen in the Toronto papers. Contrary to them, I believe there's a good chance she is alive and that she left home of her own volition.

My present intention is to ride the Great Western Rwy. between the Niagara and Detroit Rivers, stopping to inquire at stations, hotels, stage offices and livery stables. I am somewhat hampered by having no photographic likeness to show.

If you can think of any place she might have gone, please let me know. Her husband is of no help. With me he acts as if he would be just as happy if she were never found.

It may surprise you to hear I was at the mill yesterday morning. My circumstances appeared to upset Father, and it was at his request that I left without greeting you. Owing to the difficulty he has reading, the fact that I have written you would be easy enough to conceal from him, but I do not desire it. Preferring rather to keep everything above board, I nonetheless leave the matter of disclosure to your judgement. You best know his moods.

Love to you all from the Head of the Lake. Hamilton's motto is, "I advance." Amen to that.

Yours always, Isaac

* * *

For the next three days, Harris kinked his neck muscles sleeping on railway carriage seats and ulcerated his stomach with railway station food. It took this long to convince him that Theresa had not gone west. It took this long to bring him face to face at last with Mrs. Fitzroy, whose husband had left her for the California gold fields in '49, and whose wistful favours Crane had purchased with a twenty-dollar washing machine and a considerably costlier cashmere shawl. Apart from her colouring and a very approximate resemblance around the mouth, she was to Harris's eye nothing like Theresa. She it nonetheless was whom Gunn must have glimpsed through the glass. The preceding week she had kept Crane company as far as Detroit, then returned alone to her home in Port Dalhousie.

Her single room was hung with other people's drying bed linen and children's diapers. Believing her a loose woman, those who brought her their soiled bundles addressed her churlishly, and she replied with as much spirit as she could. Harris trod softly over what was for him unfamiliar ground. Mrs. Fitzroy had had little enough joy in her life for the past seven years and had very little more now, living as she did for Crane's occasional summons. Her brother was a railway conductor who acted as pander. Of Mrs. Crane she knew nothing and preferred not to think, while of Crane himself she would say only that he was a good man with much on his mind. All Harris got from her was a heavier heart and evidence independent of Esther Vale that Crane had broken his marriage vows.

When he left her, it was with no clear sense of direction. For a time he continued his inquiries through the Niagara peninsula. Crossing the new half-million-dollar Suspension Bridge, he fared as poorly in the States as at home.

On Friday morning, a new month began, badly. At Table Rock overlooking Niagara Falls, he had his pocket picked of fourteen pounds and a not particularly valuable watch he had used since he was nine. A constable assured him that by the standards of the resort, he had nothing to complain of. Many visitors were beaten as well as robbed, and had Harris any idea of the number that came to the Falls only to do away with themselves? In the summer months especially—sucked into the gorge as if by mesmerism.

Scarcely more cheerful was the abrupt realization that the first of August was Theresa's birthday. It caught him while he was scouring the Front for a tolerably honest and not dangerously intoxicated hack driver to take him to the station. Into the gorge beside him hurtled walls of water, their spray cool on his cheek. At the same time, he was ringed by a scum of thimbleriggers, photographers, vendors of Indian bead work and touts for everything from scenic towers and menageries to excursions on the new *Maid of the Mist* steam ferry—all of whose voices combined to outroar the cataracts. Theresa was twenty-four today. Harris decided to walk.

From the Falls themselves he felt no fatal tug. A quarter mile downstream, however, past the verandahs of the last hotel, the river racing far below appeared deceptively calm and inviting. Theresa, though, he insistently told himself, whatever her circumstances, had too much character to contemplate...

Besides, did an act as momentous as suicide not require a more tasteful *mise en scène?* Harris quickened his pace to avoid one more Irishman with goose feathers in his blackened hair, war paint on his face, and machine-basted moccasins to sell.

Just ahead, the Suspension Bridge smiled a grotesque eight-hundred-foot-wide smile in cables hung from stone towers in two nations. Scowling back, Harris made his way to the bridge's upper deck along which the Great Western as well as pedestrians crossed the Niagara River. He intended to ask how soon he could expect a Hamilton-bound train. It was time to return to Toronto and start over, from zero.

The young toll collector posted at the Canadian end of the bridge was staring at a coin in his hand, too lost in wonder to pay Harris's question any heed.

"It's a real gold eagle," he said. "See where I bit it? Ten U.S. dollars. Said he wouldn't be needing any change."

A party of sightseers had come up behind Harris and were clamouring for admittance to what a sign advertised as a "Panoramic View of the Falls from the Greatest and Safest Bridge in the Engineering History of the Planet!"

"*Who* said?" Harris asked the boy above the din.

"Fellow that just walked out there. Doesn't dress rich either. Craziest thing I ever saw to pay a twenty-five cent toll with a ten-dollar gold eagle."

"Eagle, hey?" cried stout Daddy Sightseer, his hand describing a broad arc over the wood lattice railing towards the depths of the gorge. "When he's done flying, he won't miss it..."

Harris didn't hear any more. Reflexively he ran out onto the bridge to rescue whatever unseen figure the boy was pointing towards. The plank walkway was no more than a yard wide and encroached on at every step by braces for the railing and by the suspension wires connecting the span to the swooping cables overhead. Harris had also to dodge the men and women—some in full skirts—who were negotiating this obstacle course in the opposite direction.

At last he could pick the individual out. The closer he got, the more familiar appeared the yellow waistcoat and the long head—turning now in sharp-featured profile as the man stopped above the middle of the river. He peered down at the green water marbled with foam, then consulted a pasteboard rectangle in his right hand. So as not to alarm him, Harris slackened his pace as he came up.

"Hallo, Oscar," he said.

The coachman took an instinctive step away as he looked up, tottering against the railing, which came only to his mid-thigh. Harris got a steadying grip on his right arm. Oscar's eyes were red and showed no sign of recognition. Vapours too sweet for whisky swirled around him. Cherry brandy perhaps.

"It's Isaac Harris, Oscar. We were speaking ten or twelve days ago at Mr. Crane's." To find Oscar entertaining desperate thoughts surprised Harris more than perhaps it should, given the symptoms of neurasthenia he had noted on that earlier occasion. No great blow would have been required to confound so ill-ballasted a bark.

"I remember," said Oscar. "The butler saw us in conversation at the woodpile that afternoon and gave me notice. No room for gossips. Who tends her horse now I don't like to think."

"That's disgraceful!" Harris rejoined with feeling. "Let me help you find another position." He owed the coachman that much, though Oscar's present demeanour would scarcely recommend him to anyone looking for a smooth drive.

"Don't blame yourself, sir. The things that are meant for us gravitate to us."

"How is that?" The diction suggested a third party speaking through the coachman.

"We cannot escape our good. You gave me hope of finding the Mistress—and I have."

"You have found Mrs. Crane?" Harris fought to keep a modicum of calm in his voice. "Where?"

"'A light shines through us upon things and makes us aware that we are nothing, but the light is all.' Ralph Waldo Emerson. That's the writer I was trying to remember. I re-read his essay. I'm a simple man, but I do read. Some nights I don't sleep for reading."

"You look as if you would benefit from some rest." Harris tried to guide him away from the railing, but the man would not move. "Tell me about Mrs. Crane," Harris added.

"The Over-soul."

"The which? Step this way, please."

Oscar stayed put. "The Mistress, I tell you. We see the world piece by piece, but the whole is the soul. I marked what you said about her feeling for plants and growing things, and then I read there's a kind of botanical park up here, apart from the tawdry glitter. A Garden of Eden!" He flung his free arm out towards the land between the Canadian and American Falls. His fingers moved to gather up the rocks and trees and unseen wildflowers as he would a set of reins. "That's why I borrowed from my brother and came up here, Mr. Harris. I thought I should find her in that sylvan paradise."

"Let us go there then," said Harris. "Let's go now." He had of course already searched Goat Island and interviewed both naturalists and custodians.

"No, sir. I was wrong. Man is a stream whose source is

hidden. As soon as I saw those mighty cataracts, I knew I had misread the Revelation."

"Oscar—is that a photograph?"

His eye darting to a party of passing strollers, Oscar clasped the sepia-toned pasteboard tighter and dropped his voice to a frenzied whisper. "The landscapes, the figures are fugitive as *mist.* That's how Mr. Emerson puts it. As *mist.* The soul advances not in a straight line but by meta—like a butterfly. I heard her voice in the waters, Mr. Harris. She is done with earthly gardens."

"She is alive, Oscar. We just have to look harder."

"No, listen."

"We have to keep on looking."

"Listen to the waters. She's calling me over to the other side."

"Wait."

"One blood flows through us."

"Wait a day at least. See how you're shaking. You're not yourself."

"I'm blasted with light. Read Mr. Emerson—the soul is giving herself to me. Did you not know the Mistress was born *this very day* under the sign of the Lion? A sign of fire! And I—I am a Crab."

"A which?"

"Yes, yes, a Crab, native of the water sign Cancer. She had to pass through fire, but I must pass by water."

"She wants you to live, Oscar." Harris heard a desperate passion in his own voice now. As he went on fumbling for any key to slacken the strain on the coachman's wits, he felt the taut wires of his own purpose vibrate in sympathy. "I know her character," he pleaded. "Live for her."

"Mr. Harris knows better than poor Oscar Eberhart?" Oscar shook his long head pityingly. "The soul gives herself to the simple man as to the scholar. We are *all* dreamers of spirits."

"Wait, man, and see which of us is right."

"No need. The power to see is not separated from the will to do. Look, I took this from the Master's bedroom." For the first time he showed Harris the *carte-de-visite* his right hand had been clutching to his chest. "See how the Deity shines through her."

Harris tried to hold Theresa's trembling portrait steady so he could look.

"Master may be in Chicago, Nelson in Port Hope, Mr. Emerson in Massachusetts, but *she* brought *me* here."

"Port Hope?" cried Harris. "When and where did you hear that?"

"See her lips move," commanded Oscar, entranced.

"Tell me about Nelson."

"'O, Oscar,' she's saying, 'come Over.'"

"No—"

Suddenly Harris's left hand, which all this time had been on the coachman's right sleeve, was clutching air. Harris lunged. He threw Oscar back from the railing down onto the deck of the bridge. As he moved to pin him there, thick arms encircled his own chest from behind and a voice of nightmare was growling in his ear.

"Steady there, my fine thug."

"Let go. He's going to jump."

In no longer than it took to say the words, Oscar had found his feet and stepped over the railing. He fell at attention, feet together, hands at his sides. Harris and his captor saw the spray blossom as the coachman's body entered the river 250 feet below.

"We have to get a boat out," said Harris. "He may be alive."

"He was alive enough before you got to him. I saw everything."

Fully expecting to be freed, Harris instead found other strollers laying hands upon him. Around him sputtered male and female voices.

"This one pushed the other."

"Hold him."

"An accident, you could see."

"But if they had not been fighting—"

The whistle of an eastbound train ran over the conclusion. So crowded had the narrow walkway become that there was now a real danger of someone's going over the edge by accident, or else onto the tracks.

"It was a suicide," said Harris.

Daddy Sightseer agreed, but—as he had only just come up from the toll collection point—he was given little credit.

"The poor beggar that fell," put in someone else, "he had

been knocked on the head."

"Just so. He was reeling and—"

"Not a bit of it. I saw everything."

"He was tripped."

"In any case," said the growling man who had first caught Harris, "I'm making a citizen's arrest." It sounded as if part of his tongue were missing.

"Take him into custody."

"Not that way. It happened on the Canadian side."

"Not a bit of it. This is the United States of America."

"Stand back there while they take him off."

"No, this way."

Harris was being pulled in both directions now. Space opened around him. Between the red silk or white muslin bonnets of the women and the men's felt or straw wide-awakes, he noted that the black face of the oncoming locomotive was no more than twenty yards away. If it were observing the bridge limit of five miles per hour, he calculated, he had a chance.

He drove a boot into the stomach of the growling citizen. His bare head butted that of another tormentor. By diving under the bowed legs of a third and between the suspension wires, he managed to clamber across the tracks inches ahead of the advancing iron beak of the cowcatcher. The G.W.R. drew a curtain between him and his pursuers.

He ran west. Seeing the curtain was only four cars long, he allowed himself no more than a glance into the gorge as he made for the Canadian end of the bridge. No sign of Oscar. Some bodies never were recovered, allegedly revolving forever in the Whirlpool three miles below the Falls.

At the toll booth, the young collector was rummaging through the portmanteau Harris had dropped. Twenty-five cents was owing. Squaring the debt with some small coins the pickpockets had left him, Harris instantly reclaimed his possessions. He still had a customs inspector to face.

In vain, Harris insisted he had not been out of the country. Regulations required an interrogation regarding contraband, and what—incidentally—was the blood on Harris's forehead? Just above the hairline, Harris's fingers discovered a warm wetness. He wondered if there would be blood and hair on the belt buckle of the man he had butted. If he submitted to questioning until the mob from the bridge caught up, he could find himself facing assault charges as well as having to explain Oscar's fall. The loss of hours, if nothing worse, would be unendurable.

West of the toll and customs posts, the tracks forked out into extensive freight yards with two hundred feet of open ground before the first cars or sheds that could provide any cover.

The inspector was wearing slippers. He did not appear to be armed.

Harris fled. He abandoned the luggage he had just redeemed, an eight-inch hunting knife with it. He had had to leave his hat where it had fallen during his tussle with Oscar.

The breeze rushed through Harris's hair. It seemed to him he was running full tilt.

Theresa's vivid and characteristic portrait, which Harris had actually had within his grasp, the coachman had managed to take with him into the gorge. All that he had left Harris was a name, possibly no less a hallucination than the photograph's moving lips. Port Hope.

Harris's legs were pumping faster and faster. With just fifty feet to go, he put on even more speed.

A gun went off. Metal clanged against the iron track just ahead of where his right boot was coming down. He didn't ask himself whether the ball had shattered or whether he felt the flying fragments of it enter his flesh. He had reached the corner of a woodpile. The last thing he saw as he rounded it was the growling man with a smoking derringer in his hand.

Chapter Eight
Cytherean

Harris wasn't hit. So ascertaining, he didn't tarry behind the cordwood. He had not seen if the derringer had more than one barrel, and farther shooting weapons might be out against him. He made next for a string of boxcars. In their lee, he kept running west.

Yardsmen gaped. Still, he was better off in sight than in range. His feet would in any case betray his location to a kneeling observer, but hopefully make poor targets.

The nick in his scalp was throbbing now. He was unhurt otherwise, but his left ankle was beginning to tire. He could not run much longer. There was, moreover, no departing train for him to slip aboard and no hiding in the yards with so many railwaymen about.

Open fields adjoined the freight yards to the north. As soon as he felt no eyes upon him, Harris veered that way. The first field he crossed on his belly, moving only when a gust of wind stirred the long grasses enough to disguise his movement.

In the intervals, he strained his ears for pursuing footsteps. No shots had followed the first. His principal antagonist, though armed, struck him as neither fleet nor stealthy. The pounding in Harris's chest began to subside. He heard nothing but the cicadas around him and from the direction of the river the aggrieved squawks of seagulls.

He thought of Oscar. There would not in any case have been time to scramble down the side of the gorge, find a boat, negotiate the rapids, and fish him out before the Whirlpool claimed him. Still, Harris regretted not being able to look for the body. The lightning suddenness of the man's exit—for all the warning signs—had left a sense of incompletion. He had been there, speaking, then not.

Harris felt a kinship to Oscar because of the dramatic effect Theresa had had upon the coachman. Lightning could have struck Harris as well. Perhaps it had. With neither position nor family backing, nor even a change of clothes, he was busily grinding earth into the knees of a pair of pale striped trousers and into the elbows of a bespoke morning coat. The bank cashier of three weeks ago would scarcely have differentiated this madness from that of the mystic Crab.

A row of trees marked the field's northern limit. Harris crawled to one of the thicker trunks and stood behind it. Looking back towards the yards and station, he detected no sign of interest in his existence.

He decided, all the same, on one more precaution. Rather than wait around for a train, he would try to catch a lake steamer from the mouth of the river. He had heard there was a daily departure around noon. With no watch, he could not tell what chance he had of covering the dozen or so miles before then. It might already be as late as eleven. Time to start running again.

Ahead the river elbowed left into the Whirlpool. The timbers of a boat or wharf vomited to its white surface, revolved, and re-submerged. Harris barely glanced down as he pounded past through fields and orchards.

From the next farm, a road led north. In the yard stood a team of Clydesdales hitched to a waggon-load of fruit. While the sight of a spirited saddle horse would have pleased him better, Harris nonetheless decided to ask for a ride. He paused first to brush himself down and to draw a banknote from his moneybelt. Licking his handkerchief, he sponged from his face as much blood as he could locate. He was prepared to blame robbers for the rest.

The incurious farmer spared him the embarrassment of telling this fairy tale. He was quite willing besides to transport Harris as far as the port of Niagara, but on no consideration would he be hurried. His peaches were not to be bruised or bounced from their pine crates.

By the time they had crept down the steep escarpment at Queenston, Harris doubted his father could have had much more trouble getting up it in 1812. Might greater headway not be made by water? From this point the river ran strong and straight without rapids. The breeze was southerly and stiffening. There was, moreover, not a horse to be hired in the village. Nor a dinghy either—but Harris dipped again into his reserve of paper money and bought one at a piratical price. Hoisting her triangular sail without delay, he steered her into the swiftest part of the current.

He glanced left at traffic on the riverbank road. As broad almost as long, the little boat was likelier to have brought her owner pike and sturgeon than racing trophies. She was nevertheless overtaking one farm waggon after another. Her red sail canvas, though ripped, was not rotten, and she didn't leak much. By holding both sheet and tiller in one hand, and with the other plying a wooden flour scoop provided as a bail, Harris was pretty well able to keep up. The dinghy had been beached, after all. He expected as her planks swelled with moisture the seals between them would tighten.

They more or less did. In what seemed short order, he found himself opposite the abandoned Fort George.

With the fort's crumbling earthworks still between him and the docks, he heard something like a piano's low A played on a steam whistle. The sound sucked the wind from his sail, or that was how his impatience made it feel. The departure signal boomed again.

When he finally cleared the headland, the ship was churning the river white to either side. She was gleaming white altogether, except for the black H of her side-by-side stacks and half a dozen large and brilliant flags. A ribbon of water already stretched between her and the quay.

There was no speed to her yet. Harris was able to pull abreast—but not approach. With practically no keel, his dinghy slipped sideways when he tried to come up wind. He struck sail and manned the oars.

The collision of Lake Ontario with the Niagara River chopped up the water here. To make any headway, Harris had to pull facing astern. He tried to steer by a church spire on the American shore, but whenever he glanced over his shoulder the white ship had accelerated beyond his calculations. The Greek-looking name painted on her paddle housing in black-outlined gold capitals flashed across his bows. Passengers under her rear saloon-deck awning waved him a cheery adieu.

A final, muscle-searing burst of rowing cracked the right oar and brought the dinghy's nose in contact with the steamer. It would have been no more than a brief tap that left Harris and his boat bobbing far astern—would have been, that is, but for the overhang. The ship's superstructure was built out from the hull and flush with the outer surface of the paddle housing. In the trough of a wave, Harris's prow slid beneath this projection and caught. Dragged lakewards, the dinghy pivoted on her mast. There was an instant before she shook free, an instant when the thwart on which Harris sat came within jumping distance of the steamer. He managed when he landed to catch hold of one of the long wooden fenders.

Belatedly, the paddles slowed. The one-man boarding party, it seemed, had at last been remarked.

Relieved of the urgent necessity for action, Harris found himself recalling the custom inspector's green felt slippers. Might that slighted official, he wondered, have telegraphed the steamship company?

Without haste or enthusiasm, he climbed over the main-deck rail, to which a curious throng had by this time gathered. Among them he first distinguished two individuals. One was a pained-looking purser in a jacket trimmed with gold braid. The other, wearing his usual tweeds, was John Vandervoort.

"One cabin passage to Toronto," Harris told the purser, "and could you ask the captain to pick up my dinghy. I'm afraid I let her get away from me."

* * *

There was never any question of the gleaming *Cytherean*'s turning back. Harris himself was lucky to have, in the purser's words, "been taken" aboard. His little tub with the broken oar and the red sail trailing overboard shrunk away astern to a speck and then to nothing. From Table Rock on, his morning had cost him more than any two average months.

He would consequently have settled for deck passage rather than pay the 150 per cent cabin premium had it not been for the advisability of reassuring the purser that he wasn't quite the floating vagabond he appeared. If he had dared to hope also that Vandervoort would not be admitted to the cabin, he would have been disappointed. Not even a stateroom would have ensured privacy. Vandervoort was admitted everywhere. Gratis.

That last week in Toronto, he had eluded Harris. He had regretted perhaps speaking so freely on the evening of their visit to Sheridan's kitchen. Harris regretted his not speaking of Sibyl Martin. The opportunity to corner Vandervoort aboard ship would in those trackless days have been jumped at. At the present moment, however, Vandervoort threatened to be very much in the way—and this was of course when he had chosen to make himself available.

The detective inspector would keep Harris company throughout the four-hour crossing. No trouble in the world. The drama of the banker's arrival had, friendly considerations apart, sufficed to pique his interest. On the bright side, Vandervoort seemed to have no formal complaint to bring nor any knowledge of Harris's earlier difficulties with an officer of the Crown.

Harris washed and combed himself in one of the steamer's lavishly mirrored bathrooms. Vandervoort watched. Harris entrusted his morning coat to a steward for cleaning and pressing. Vandervoort recommended he purchase cigars. Harris, who may have had water in his ears, strolled to the bow rail and watched for the smoke of Toronto's factories to climb above the horizon. The day had been grey and was growing cool, more like the end of August than the beginning. In his shirt sleeves, he felt it.

Vandervoort stuck close. "Yes, Mr. H., you showed determination in boarding this lady."

"I've business across the lake," Harris curtly replied.

"Took her by force, as it were. Not your way normally, is it?"

"Have you found Mrs. Crane, inspector?"

"There have been developments."

Harris looked at him sharply. "In Niagara?"

"No, this was a family matter. I believe I told you I'm from the region." Vandervoort drew from inside his crumpled waistcoat a silver medal. "Look," he said, "I took the pledge."

Irony edged his voice, but his hooded eyes rested with something approaching paternal affection on the shiny disk all the time it was in Harris's hand.

"Sons of Abstinence," Harris read. "Lincoln County Lodge. Be sober and watch." The full text of the pledge, including a promise to discountenance intemperance in others was stamped inside a cross on the reverse.

"A moving ceremony," said Vandervoort, "held at my mother's bedside."

Harris began to wonder if the insistence of Vandervoort's attentions had not sprung from his need to impart the momentous news of his conversion. No one could fault him with reticence on that subject.

"A new police is on the way, Mr. Harris. You'll see spit and polish and a board of commissioners, so dead wood will no longer have the aldermen's skirts to hide behind. Your temperate, businesslike officer will reap the rewards."

"As one such," Harris jumped in, "you may care to know that Mrs. Crane did sit for her photograph, at No. 4, City Buildings, King Street East."

"It must have slipped Mr. Crane's mind. Now *there* is a gentleman of whom it is said that he has never used tobacco, intoxicants, or an immodest word—and look where he is today."

"In Chicago, is he not?"

"Being honoured for his contributions to North American transportation."

"It would not surprise me," said Harris, "if he never showed his face in this province again. To what developments regarding Mrs. Crane were you referring?"

"I marvel, sir, that *your* eyes aren't green. Just think what pangs of jealousy you would have been spared if you had been as bold three years ago with her as you were today with the *Kith 'n' Kin*."

"The which?"

"This floating palace. Glorious, isn't she? And spanking new."

Harris followed Vandervoort's pointing arm back and up to the gracefully carved nude that surmounted the eight-sided pilot house. Even without sun, her tresses glittered. Their sweep followed Botticelli, Harris believed, though the clam shell she balanced on had been scaled down.

"To see that waist of hers, Mr. Harris, you would never guess she gobbles up over a cord of wood per hour. Did you notice the crystal chandeliers? She has got them. Damask curtains. Potted plants. Wood panelling. Brass thingummies—enough of them to keep a dozen cabin boys polishing their hearts out. She's perfect in every way, except for her damned name, which not one of her crew, let alone her two hundred passengers, can wrap his tongue around."

"Have you found her horse?" said Harris.

Vandervoort was still smacking his lips over the lofty image of Aphrodite, as if she were sculpted in butter.

"Excuse me, Inspector, but do you even have a description of her horse? It's bay, not black."

That seemed to get Vandervoort's attention. "Shall we take lunch in her dining saloon?" he asked. "Oil paintings on the walls. You'll pay more than at the bar, but the—uh—the tone—"

"We were going to work together, John, if you'll recall," Harris broke in impatiently. "You were going to call the tune. Well, what's it to be? Polka, jig or reel? You said you were damned if you knew what had become of William Sheridan's housekeeper, and now I hear she spent a night in your lock-up."

"What of it? No one questioned her."

"Oh?"

"It was the Glorious Twelfth, remember," Vandervoort added. "You can bet your granny's wooden leg no one with any authority was frequenting the poultry market. I believe they even let the sergeant out for the evening... Hell, you know where *I* was—stalking smugglers on the peninsula."

Vandervoort was grinning but moving away as he talked. The other change Harris noted, with a satisfaction he did his best to conceal, was that his questions were now being parried rather than ducked. He followed the red-haired policeman astern.

"And in the morning?" he asked.

"In the morning, we heard from the doctor how the death certificate would read."

"I'm so glad it didn't come to that, sir!" said a girl in a short blue cape as she stepped from a cabin doorway directly into Harris's path. "It's too romantic the way you were plucked from the waves. It was you, wasn't it? Sissy, this is the shipwrecked sailor they plucked from the waves."

Excusing himself, Harris caught up with Vandervoort under the scalloped awning that covered the rear third of the deck.

"You say, 'would read.' Had Dr. Hillyard made out no death certificate by Sunday morning?"

"Can't be done for twenty-four hours—a precaution against premature burial. He sent word, though. No murder, no murderess, and no earthly reason to see where the drudge ended up once we let her go."

Harris considered mentioning the brown dress he had found in the burned shed, but persuading Vandervoort to keep looking for Theresa no longer seemed worth the effort. As soon teach a puma to eat oats. Besides, no longer bound to Toronto by work, Harris needed the police less. All he wanted from Vandervoort was a free hand plus whatever scraps of information he could shake loose.

"What have you heard from Professor Lamb?"

"Lamb? That mad wag would take a thermometer reading before he would venture to say his pants were on fire." Vandervoort was again drifting away, this time towards the bar concession.

"You must," said Harris, "have had a report since the evening we were at his laboratory."

"What are you buying me?" Vandervoort shouted to be heard above voices made loud by whisky.

"There's no point making a secret of it," said Harris.

"I suppose it had better be buttermilk." Vandervoort's fingers were in his waistcoat pocket, clinging no doubt to his temperance medal.

"I could always ask him myself."

At this point a weedy man in the tallest stovepipe hat Harris had ever seen grabbed his hand and wrung it.

"You're the gent whose vessel was run down in the river mouth," cried the stranger. "It's shocking, sir, the high-handedness of these steamship captains. Sue the company, that's my advice. I'll gladly represent you in court. My card—"

"So *this* is the party everyone has been talking about," broke in the barman. "Your health, sir—no charge. What will you have?"

Bewildered as he was by the attention, Harris was also being reminded by his stomach that he had put nothing in it for the past six hours.

"Buttermilk," he stammered.

"Two," said Vandervoort, with a flourish becoming to the proprietor of the freak on display. "I'll say this for Lamb," he added aside. "He has changed my mind."

"How's that?" Harris forgot about being a menagerie exhibit.

"Buttermilk, sir? I'll send to the kitchen for some. Can you just tell us what happened?"

"Had his vessel sliced in two," said the emaciated lawyer. "I've never seen a clearer case of negligence."

As other drinkers bellowed competing theories, Harris pulled Vandervoort to the port rail and insisted he explain himself.

"Palm of the hand," said the police detective as if the thing were obvious. "Three and a quarter inches. Too wide for Mrs. Crane, as her glove-maker can confirm. More likely the drudge."

"Sibyl?"

"Quite likely—though we can't hope to find a record of *her* glove size."

Here was a revolution in thought. For practically two weeks Harris had heard no whisper that anyone but himself believed Theresa still drew breath. That isolation now ended—just when his freedom of movement made it matter less. Chagrin embittered sweet relief.

The *Cytherean*'s after deck was rising and falling on a long, sickening swell. Harris had not noticed before. He steadied himself against the end of one of the long, arching trusses that kept the 200-foot wooden hull from snapping in half. He fixed his eyes on the horizon. The lake's south shore was no more now than a blue line above which rose Niagara Falls' cloudy exhalation. Harris looked back in dismay over the days lost to an all-out search.

"When I collected my bag of bones," Vandervoort continued, "I did see a scrap of dun fabric that might have belonged to her. Thinking nothing of it, you understand. By the time I went back for it, someone had been tampering with the site." The inspector's boot nudged Harris's. "Foot size very like your own."

The buttermilk arrived in two crystal goblets the inner surfaces of which it had, with the motion of the ship, coated to the very rims. The only taker, Vandervoort noisily drained both glasses.

"Of course," he said between gulps, "if we had the constables to do it, we should have posted a guard over that charred rubble until a coroner's jury could have a look."

Later, when Harris's queasiness had abated, the two men sat indoors. Between their deep leather chairs stood a low chess table with dark and light squares of wood set into its surface. A circular depression in the centre of each square kept the pieces in place as the ship rolled over the waves.

Harris asked why there had as yet been no inquest. Had Crane's travel schedule occasioned the delay? Not altogether, Vandervoort protested. The arm had been discovered in Ontario County and the other bones in the County of York. There were jurisdictional questions to settle.

As to where Theresa had got to, Vandervoort was sure Harris knew better than he. That bay horse, for instance. And what had Harris been doing in Niagara? On all fours, apparently. And why was he in such a hurry to get back to Toronto? Having shared his information, Vandervoort was seeking reciprocity.

"I'll be taking closer interest in your movements in future, Isaac Harris. A fortunate accident that we met!"

"Do you play, Inspector?" Harris gestured to the chessmen drawn up in starting array between them. He had just noticed that those with the paler finish—those that moved first—stood on his side of the table. He was going to have to stay one good step ahead of Vandervoort. If he did happen to pick up a trail in Port Hope, he wasn't convinced it would serve Theresa's interests to lead the police along it to her.

Vandervoort made a throat-clearing noise and underlined his disgust by resting the sole of his boot on the edge of the table, which would have tumbled over had it not been bolted against rough weather to the floor of the salon.

"That's no pastime for men with blood in their veins," he said.

"How so?"

"You labour mightily attacking the cockalorum there." After an instant's hesitation above the white queen, Vandervoort's thick index finger and thumb singled out the white king for a rough tweak. "You strip away his guards. You check him. And then, if you win, you don't even get the joy of taking him off the board."

"You corner him," said Harris.

"You never lay hands upon him," the policeman countered.

"No need," Harris persisted. "You trap him so he can't escape—unless he traps you first."

"Too deep for me, Harris, and too standoffish for the times we live in. Bloodless damned foolery!"

Presently a steward reported sighting the twin spires of Holy Trinity Church and attempted to answer passengers' questions as to the duration of the Toronto stopover. He found it hard to be precise. There were a hundred crates of peaches to unload, after all, and soft fruit could not be rushed.

Mention of Holy Trinity roused Harris, evoking a snatch of hymn, the pink shine from Crane's inclined head, the clank of an iron coffin against the hearse's wheel. The best use of Vandervoort might be to get him questioning Dr. Hillyard's findings. A metal coffin would preserve better than wood. It was perhaps not too late for an autopsy on William Sheridan.

"Sibyl was an embarrassment, wasn't she, Inspector? William Sheridan tried to curtail Orange influence, and she had ties to the Grand Master himself. If Sibyl were a murderess, the whole Order would be implicated. Christopher Hillyard is a sash wearer too, of course, to say nothing of City Council and your own force."

"I'm not," said Vandervoort with a hint of proud independence, before remembering his ambitions. "Not yet."

"You must have your doubts then. What I'm wondering is whether a murder investigation might not uncover an unrelated motive and thereby lift suspicion from the Orangemen more effectively than the current smothering operation."

"You're thinking Mrs. Crane killed her father," Vandervoort brutally replied.

Harris glared. Having just that morning learned how it felt to be shot at, he would gladly have subjected his interlocutor to the same experience. How had he sat with this man?

"I hope you meant that as a joke," he managed to stammer. "No father and daughter were ever more attached."

"Three years ago, perhaps. But he may not have liked the idea of her leaving her husband, and she would have needed money to do it in any style. Did I mention that valuables were missing from the strongbox under Sheridan's bed?"

"You did not. Was the lock forced?"

"There would have been no need with Sheridan dead, now would there? She could have taken the key from around his neck—"

"Preposterous!"

"Oh, yes, banknotes, share certificates... Your friend Mr.

Small can tell you what all if he has a mind to."

The state of Jasper's mind was not at present a reassuring object of contemplation. At their lunch on July 17, five days after his partner's death, he had given no intimation that Sheridan had been robbed. Possibly by then he still had not inspected the box. As for Theresa, she would never have killed her Papa, but once he was dead, might she not have borrowed against her inheritance? The more funds she had, the farther afield Harris might be obliged to seek her.

"What do you say," asked Vandervoort. "You have a great many thoughts you're not sharing, and I may as well stick with you until you do."

"You may as well fly to the moon."

To preserve the fiction that he was landing in Toronto, Harris went to collect his morning coat from the steward's pantry above the engine room. The throb through the floor was slowing.

"Where do we go first?" said Vandervoort, practically underfoot. "The bank?"

"They no longer employ me."

"Their loss. Where do you live then?"

"The American Hotel, where I intend to have a bath. If you're thinking of following me into the tub, I would just as soon you obtained an arrest warrant and threw me in a cell."

"No question of that," said Vandervoort. "I'll wait."

The old Fort York Garrison's palisades and the Queen's Wharf swung into sight out the port windows, followed by the beach where the city's Baptists held their immersions. The *Cytherean* was entering Toronto Harbour.

People always swarmed to the gang-boards long before the ship was docked and gave themselves a quarter hour of being jostled off their feet for the sake of a two-minute head start in disembarking. Harris was no less critical of this habit today when he had reason himself to be among the first ashore. He wanted time in which to elude Vandervoort.

In the shuffling crowd, it was inevitable that Harris would again be recognized as the shipwrecked sailor.

"Mister," one of two chubby boys screwed up his courage to ask, "are you a runaway slave?"

"Don't be simple," jeered his companion. "Slaves are coloured, like the stewards."

"Yeah, well Billy was on a steamer picked up a runaway slave. From Mississippi."

All the time that the *Cytherean* was nudging into her berth at the Yonge Street Wharf, Vandervoort talked about crime and how most of it in this city was traceable to alcohol. Drunk and disorderlies were the rule. Tavern and street brawls, noisy whores, the occasional arson. Gunshots were rare enough to attract notice, and drinkers so careless about covering their tracks that even capital cases called for little in the way of detective work. True mysteries—like Mrs. Crane's disappearance —might not develop above three times in an entire working life. You had only to solve one to make a name.

The boards dropped, releasing passengers into the city—and harbour smells back into the cabin. Harris stepped briskly across the Esplanade towards the three-storey block of yellow brick at Yonge and Front. He picked out his window and picked up his pace. Let Vandervoort keep up as he might.

At the hotel desk, Harris waited while departing guests were informed that the Kingston steamer was late today and that they might still make it if they hurried. He then settled his account for the week he had been away, collected his mail and declined Vandervoort's offer to accompany him to his room. It all seemed to take an hour. While Harris was climbing the front stairs, he overheard Vandervoort ask about the location of the back ones.

One flight up, Harris's room faced the harbour. With no time even to change his trousers, he went straight to the window. Beside it, he had noted, a drain spout ran down the outside wall. As he threw up the sash, he caught sight of Vandervoort standing just below on the street corner with views of both south and west faces of the building. That the inspector would wait peacefully in the lobby had been too much to hope.

Three hundred yards to the south, the bustle around the

Cytherean was subsiding. Peach crates lined the wharf. Down-lake goods and passengers were practically all aboard.

Harris dragged his bed across the door. Unlocking a trunk, he removed his eight-gauge side-by-side and a flask of black powder. He poured in as much as he judged the weapon would stand.

No time to stuff cotton in his ears. Even though he was using no shot, he checked quickly that the street below was clear before discharging both barrels simultaneously out the open window. The noise was all he desired and more.

He dared not show his face to see if Vandervoort had taken the bait. When he listened at the door, his ears were still ringing so badly that he was afraid he would miss the footfalls on the stairs. He caught them—four boots—by pressing the side of his head to the polished floor. Back to the window.

As he lifted his right leg over the sill, he seemed to remember from some boyhood escapade that this wasn't the way. He pulled the leg back. Sticking out his head and trunk instead, he turned and sat on the sill, then used the hooked-back, louvered shutters to pull himself to a standing position. Sturdy hardware, he thought. Something to be said for a first-class hotel.

There would be excited voices in the hall by now. The door would be pounded, rattled, and opened soon enough with the clerk's key. The bed would not hold long after that.

Harris reached his right hand across to the spout and glanced down it. It didn't seem like much to slow his descent. Still, he could not risk a free drop to the plank sidewalk. He would need both ankles for running.

A rough seam between lengths of pipe bloodied his hands as he slid, but the sting only goaded him to greater speed as he dodged and leaped piles of rubbish across the Esplanade. If anyone were shouting after him to stop, he didn't hear.

The first airborne sound to reach his clearing ears was the *Cytherean*'s deep whistle of departure.

* * *

All eyes were on the desperate character pelting headlong down the wharf. Fleeing, it seemed, the scene of some crime.

A stevedore's foot went out to trip him. Harris vaulted over it and stepped handily across the bare two feet of frothing sewage that separated Aphrodite's side-wheeler from shore. He later learned he owed his luck to the blast of his own shotgun, which had made the inquisitive deck hands slow to cast off.

The purser's reception this time would have frozen flame.

"Before I can sell you a ticket, *sir*, you will have to explain to the captain the circumstances of your coming aboard." The very braid on the purser's jacket bristled.

The captain was less prim, but when it came out that the importunate companion Harris had been trying to leave behind was John Vandervoort, the very John Vandervoort with whom the captain had stolen fruit as a boy—why, then it was irrevocably decided to turn Harris over to the constabulary at the first port of call. By 1:15 a.m. they ought to make Port Hope. Authorities there could telegraph Toronto to learn if there were grounds to hold him.

Harris was welcome in the meantime to book a stateroom, which he would have to guarantee not to leave. Alternatively, accommodation could be arranged in one of the rope lockers. A bond of fifty dollars was settled on.

"Purser, a receipt for our friend if you please," said the captain, counting out the banknotes. "Pleasant sailing, Mr. Harris."

The stateroom opened off the dining salon and had a window onto the promenade. The furnishings included a wash stand, a large looking glass and a soft bed onto which Harris threw himself in exhaustion and despair.

He felt idiotic. He might, from the way Vandervoort had had the run of the ship, have guessed at the inspector's influence with the captain. Had storming aboard the *Cytherean* at Niagara saved any time? It would all be spent in a small-town lock-up. Harris knew enough of the personnel of Station No. 1 not to expect Toronto police to be in a position to answer a telegram before breakfast or more likely, as it would be a Saturday, before noon.

Harris rolled over to face the varnished partition wall. From this side, merry voices in the next room sounded taunting and pitiless.

Could he truly be this sorry for himself? Well, his pride was hurt, he had to admit. Look at him—dodging bullets, crawling through fields, climbing out windows, running about like a demented squirrel. How had this creature grown out of the sober, trusted, filial individual who eight days earlier had been respectably employed receiving deposits, granting loans, denying loans—sometimes to steamboat captains—at the corner of Bay and Wellington? His reputation was falling off him like the peel from a Christmas orange.

It added to his chagrin that it was inadmissible even to think of such matters while Theresa's safety remained in doubt. This search he had undertaken—he wasn't up to it.

"Can't see nothing."

A pair of children on the promenade had their faces pressed to Harris's window.

"Someone's sleeping, looks like."

Harris forced himself to his feet and the two scampered off. He washed the grit from his hands. They weren't badly cut. Then he remembered the letters that he had picked up at the hotel and found that he wasn't quite done pitying himself yet. No friend or relative had written. After ten days, there was still no reply from Theresa's riding companion Marthe. There were only bills and advertising circulars to remind him that he was earning nothing above a few modest rents and was spending like a sailor on a spree.

He should perhaps have haggled more over the bond. Then again, suppose the captain's offer of close confinement were no bluff. By the time legal remedy could be sought, the *Cytherean* might well have sunk back into the waves with Harris still nestled among the ropes. Three hundred lives a year were lost on the lake. His release would be at the top of no one's mind if storm or fire threatened.

It would not take much of a storm to roll this vessel, either, with her narrow wooden hull and her heavy walking beam up there in the sky. It would take even less to ignite her. She was all tinder, with fresh coatings of flammable varnish to make her blaze the brighter.

Harris's stateroom would blaze as bright as the rest, but was at least above the waterline and no more than fifty yards from the nearest life preserver. A happy thought.

Happier yet was the arrival of a steward asking what Harris would take for dinner. Through the open door, passengers could be glimpsed clinking crystal across white table linen and slurping down what appeared to be a thick fish soup.

Harris felt a space the size of a watermelon open in his stomach. Besides the soup, he had the steward bring him mutton with caper sauce, mashed potatoes, mixed vegetables, uncooked celery, boiled custard, raspberry tart and half a pint of cider. He requested also a small table, stationery, pen and ink.

No gourmand, Harris nonetheless took cheer as well as strength from good food, and when he had dined became considerably more resolute. Oscar had mentioned a brother in Weston, a small enough place that a note addressed to Mr. Eberhart there should reach him. Harris set down what had become of Oscar, and he didn't mince words—although the oleaginous phrase "unfortunate accident" did keep threatening to slip through the iron nib onto the page. To learn what remains if any had been recovered, he recommended applying to the Welland and Lincoln County authorities.

To the American Hotel, Harris wrote an apology for the strange manner of his departure and a request that they keep his room for him. Of three difficult letters, however, the one to Jasper Small occasioned the greatest embarrassment of all.

It was humiliating to remember his friend with Mrs. Vale's ring in his nose. Small had always liked his pleasures, certainly. Never before had he seemed their thrall. The added responsibilities Sheridan's death had thrown on the surviving partner must have overwhelmed him, and Harris had to wonder if Small were still capable of attending to even the simplest task.

Three sheets of *Cytherean* letterhead were wasted on false starts.

"My dear J.," Harris scribbled at last. "Hope you'll excuse brevity—this written in great haste. Hot on Th.'s trail but shall soon want funds. Can you undertake to liquidate real estate holdings named below? If too busy, pls. advise. Am. Hotel will forward mail. Yours always, I."

Once the three sealed envelopes were in his coat pocket, he removed the coat and closed the shutters against the last hour of daylight. He intended only a short nap, for he wished to be awake when they docked and able to take advantage of any opportunity to escape detention ashore. His body betrayed him, however. He slept until someone rapping on his door announced their arrival in Port Hope.

Having no light, Harris groped his way towards the sound. The door opened before he reached it. In the reduced glow of the dining salon lamps, stood not one of the Negro stewards but the captain himself, accompanied by a crusty old blue jacket with handcuffs at the ready.

* * *

Unmanacled promptly on reaching his cell, Harris completed his night's rest on a straw pallet from which the mice obligingly decamped. When he awoke, he reflected that—while not at liberty—he was at least in the right town. "Nelson in Port Hope," Oscar had said.

With Constable Pitt, Harris maintained the pretence of wanting to leave it. No deep cunning was required. If, in the black of night, this official had appeared seasoned, the light of day showed him to be positively elderly. The conditions of detention were not onerous, apart from the tedium of endless cribbage games. The longer the two men played, the more trouble Pitt seemed to have reading his cards.

"My eyes were getting weak," he confided, "before I took to bathing them in rock salt melted in brandy. French brandy mind. Would you care for the *exact* receipt?"

"No need at present." Harris stifled a smile and a yawn. "I was wondering how often steamers leave for Kingston?"

"For the eyes, by the way, some swear by wild violet tea."

"There's the early morning one I came on," Harris suggested.

"Every day but Sunday—and another at four thirty in the afternoon. Except on Sunday of course."

Harris was about to ask the present time when the clock in the cupola three storeys above them struck four.

It was Saturday afternoon, and Port Hope was humming. No less construction mad than Hamilton or Toronto, the small town danced to the song of saw and hammer. Behind the new Town Hall, meanwhile, the market raised its dust and voice. Bushels of grain, hogsheads of whisky, miles of lumber were offered, declined, accepted at scarcely lower prices, and carted to the docks. Waggon wheels and manure-stained boots rushed past the basement window of the police lock-up.

Only inside did life assume a pastoral gait. "Miss the four thirty today," said Pitt, "and you'll be cooling your heels till Monday."

Feigned horror at this prospect gave Harris the excuse to ask who in Port Hope might have a horse to sell. Pitt, who had been about to play a card on Harris's five, put it back in his hand while he rhymed off livery stables plus a couple of local breeders, though on reflection they raised mostly plough horses.

His catalogue was interrupted by the approach of light, brisk steps. They stopped at the police station door. An envelope was pushed under it. Then they faded back down the corridor and up the basement stairs.

This door Pitt had locked before letting Harris out of his cell to play cards. Why, though, had the messenger not knocked? Telegrams were to be personally delivered. Harris vainly watched the window for feet to fit those steps. There was in any case no necessity for anyone leaving the Town Hall to pass this way.

"A very crabbed hand," said Pitt. He was standing by the

window too, turning the envelope's contents to the light. "Of course, Sager's Hotel has a horse left by one of their guests, but I believe they are holding it for a Toronto gentleman. Ah, is your name—"

"Yes, yes," Harris blurted. After so many empty hours, everything seemed to be happening at once.

Pitt gave him the paper to read. It wasn't a telegram but a note signed by John Vandervoort, Detective Inspector of Police: "You may loose Mr. Isaac Harris to continue his travels where he will. Any breach of the public peace he may have caused on leaving Toronto can be dealt with at a later date."

"I don't suppose you would care just to finish the hand," said Pitt. "You're too late now to make that boat."

"I must try." Harris suspected that on leaving the Town Hall he would be followed by Vandervoort's messenger. "Could you mail these letters for me, constable? Here's nine pence for the postage."

The quarter hour chimed as Pitt was unlocking the door.

"Now I don't need to tell you," he said, "that those of us that have to keep a sharpish look-out need something stronger than violet tea. Salted brandy is what I recommend. There you are. Free to go. Don't worry about those letters. I'll see to them."

Swallowing his apprehension, Harris thanked him on the way out.

"Wait."

"I cannot."

Pitt shoved into Harris's hand an envelope identical to the three he was leaving. "Your bond, Mr. Harris. The captain of the *Kith 'n' Kin* asked me to return it to you."

Harris nodded and ran. Early this morning he had counted three blocks north, one west, two north. Reversing the sequence, he turned down Queen Street with the river on his left and the west side of the frame and red brick town climbing the hill to his right. He dashed between the towering, still growing, brick piers of a future railway viaduct. Then he was over Smith's Creek onto Mill Street, of which the steamer dock formed an uncommonly commodious extension. Harris found three vessels moored there.

Confusion was momentary. Harris was advised to follow a lad in a shako cap and baggy jacket, who was running for the farthest ship and glancing back over his shoulder as if expecting a companion even later than himself. Hurrying after, Harris looked back too. He still thought it possible he was being followed but could not make out by whom.

Ahead a black wall loomed. He recognized the Crane-built *Triumph*—a vessel he had in fact sailed on before. She had a sleek, iron-plated hull driven by underwater screws. For efficiency, she had *Cytherean* beat. Nor, Harris noted approvingly as he crossed the gang-board into the hold, would this steamer's sheer sides tempt dinghy sailors to folly.

"You're cutting it fine, sir," remarked a steward. The whistle had not yet blown.

Call this fine? Harris thought—but he lacked breath to answer with more than a smile.

Just as the departure signal sounded, a cab came clattering down the dock with two passengers who were cutting it finer. One was heavy-jowled and laden with luggage including a birdcage. The other man appeared tall, weaselly, and just like the sort of informant Vandervoort might recruit in the Dog and Duck. Perhaps too like.

Harris bought his ticket. Kingston was *Triumph*'s next port of call, and as he didn't anticipate going that far, he economized by taking deck passage. His morning coat he again left with the stewards for pressing.

In the pungent privacy of a w.c., he loosened his boot laces. He then transferred to his oilskin moneybelt the portrait tracing plus all his coins and banknotes, including the fifty dollars from the *Cytherean* envelope. This useful sum he had not written off. At the same time, he had not truly expected to see it again until he had leisure to present his receipt at the steamship office in Toronto. All credit to the captain and the constable!

Triumph had cast off. The water in the bowl was jiggling with the distinctive high-frequency vibration of a propeller under steam. Not wanting to get too far from shore, Harris hastened to the promenade. He chose a free stretch of rail about two thirds aft on the starboard side, away from the receding docks.

Yesterday's clouds still had not cleared. The cold grey water streaming by looked a long way down. On the other hand, there was little wind. Harris's half-mile run had doubtless taken something out of him, but for the moment he felt limber rather than tired.

He took a last look left and right. Since leaving the purser's wicket, he had seen none of the late arrivals. A thin, light-haired woman in a low-necked dress was his nearest neighbour, and she seemed absorbed in following the swoop of the seagulls through a pair of gold opera glasses.

Stepping over the rail, Harris sprang head first into the lake. As soon as he felt the water—icy even in August—sting his eyelids, he doubled up to slow his plunge. Deeper meant colder. More importantly, he didn't want to risk getting sucked into the steamer's whirling screws.

Triumph slid past him as he surfaced. Bobbing in her wake, he heard a surprised shout and thought he saw a pair of gold opera glasses trained on him from the promenade. As he had hoped, no one followed him over the rail.

To business then. Harris yanked off his hand-crafted boots and let them sink. He would find factory-made replacements ashore. From the water, the beach looked twice as far as it had from the deck. Hand over hand, he pulled it towards him.

Chapter Nine
Horse Power

At about seven in the evening of July 15, 1856, an Englishman with pink cheeks and greying hair presented himself at Sager's Hotel on the Port Hope waterfront. He signed the registry, "Enoch Henry and Dog." He also had a bay horse he wanted fed and stabled. As for his own dinner, he said with simple pride that he had already got "that little chore" out of the way.

At breakfast next morning, he told a fellow guest that a sentimental novel by one George MacFarlane had induced him to see Canada for himself. He had sailed directly from Bristol to Toronto, where he had stayed a week with distant cousins. He planned to push on to Fenelon Falls. He thought he would just inspect the railway construction first.

Work was proceeding on the Port Hope, Lindsay and Beaverton line, but the stir of the moment was the Grand Trunk, which in a matter of weeks would complete the first rail link ever between Toronto and Montreal. The last obstacle was the valley in which Port Hope nestled.

After breakfast, Enoch Henry and Dog, a pampered but mannerly black retriever, went strolling among the fifty-six piers of the Grand Trunk's Prince Albert Viaduct. High on a scaffold, an inattentive workman let a brick slip from his hand. Enoch Henry fell dead. He was buried in his straw hat, for not even the doctor could stomach picking it out of his stove-in skull.

Nothing in his effects identified his relations, on either side of the Atlantic. Only some days later was the underside of his saddle found to be stamped, "HENRY M. CRANE." Might this be Enoch Henry's Toronto cousin? The hotel manager wrote to Crane, whom he knew to be a man worth pleasing, and on July 28 received from his butler a terse reply.

Crane was said to be out of town. He was expected home on August 3, if animal and harness could be held till then. The late Enoch Henry wasn't mentioned.

This omission made the hotel manager wonder if the horse were stolen. There might still be a reward. He suspected not his deceased guest, but rather someone who had imposed on him to buy it.

"Mr. Henry was," he said, "that green."

He was speaking to Isaac Harris, freshly outfitted after his swim by a Port Hope haberdasher.

Harris looked down at the crisp black straw wide-awake in his hands. He had recently run close under two of those scaffolded piers himself. On the sunny morning of the sixteenth, as the brick was falling, he seemed to remember he had been counting new banknotes.

At some time before that, but later than anyone else Harris knew of, Enoch Henry had likely seen Theresa. The detective's thoughts hardened. Where, he wanted to know, and when?

On the pretext of helping locate Mr. Henry's people, he got permission to inspect the luggage. Two men had removed to an attic lumber room a steamer trunk full of clean shirts and romantic fiction. When Harris got back downstairs, he asked to see the beast supposed to have borne all this plus a rider the seventy miles from Toronto. He believed it would have taken nothing less than one of P.T. Barnum's elephants.

Despite dusk's approach, a lantern was supplied only grudgingly. What that horse had already cost the establishment over the past two and a half weeks! And did Harris think Crane's butler had sent money for feed? Nothing of the kind.

Harris's boots creaked as he followed the manager's young daughter across the stable yard. "Nelson," he muttered *sotto voce*, "I believe we did meet once or twice in '53, not that I should expect you to remember, and I have heard something of your recent exploits..."

The stiffness of his new tweeds added to the sense of

occasion. They were a uniform tan, not the large checks favoured by the shop proprietor, but not banker's clothes either. With them he felt he had assumed more fully his new identity. The small girl held the lantern up at the level of his new factory-minted watch chain.

Inside the stall, Harris took the light from her and quickly found what he had not been meant to see, fresh spur gouges in the animal's dark reddish-brown flanks. The girl admitted it was earning its keep and more through rental to hotel guests.

It had the short, wide head of a quarter horse and many characteristics that would make for a comfortable ride—a long neck, long sloping shoulder, knees and hocks set low, and well-rounded hind quarters. It stood roughly sixteen hands and was, Harris judged from the triangular tables of the teeth, over twelve years old. All this was consistent with what he knew of Nelson. So too was the good nature with which it submitted to his inspection.

And now his guide had to help serve the guests' dinner if the gentleman had seen what he had come for.

He had. This might well be the horse Henry Crane had ridden the first time he had called on William Sheridan and met his daughter. Plainly, though, Enoch Henry's trunk had reached Port Hope by other means.

What they were no one at Sager's had remarked. Could it have come later? Oh, yes. Earlier? Perhaps.

* * *

The steamer office was able to confirm for Harris that trunk, dog and man had all arrived on the four p.m. boat. Sans horse. That left Mr. Henry three hours in which to acquire one and to feed himself. After tramping around to all the downtown stables, restaurants and hotels, Harris rented Nelson to ride to those farther out.

Eventually he came to a prepossessing inn at the eastern limit of Hope Township. Glimpsing the sparkle of its table settings from the Kingston Road, he congratulated himself on not having dined sooner. When he had seen both, however, he would rather have touched his tongue to the floor of the stable than to the food from the kitchen. Never had he encountered so violent a contrast between cleanliness of premises and foulness of cuisine. The great consolation for Harris was to find he had a companion in misery: the English traveller had eaten here too.

"There you are, sir, a lovely bit of pork. Now soon as I have a minute I'll tell you about that gentleman from back home."

The pork set before Harris was swimming in its own grease, where it had the company of potatoes fried black on one side. A side dish contained peas boiled till they burst, then half drained. Over them floated a buttery scum. Small wonder Enoch Henry had referred to dinner as a chore.

Harris nibbled at his cider, trying to make of it a meal.

"Now why aren't you eating, sir? Drink on an empty stomach might not harm you so much if that were our own cider, but I won't lie to you. It's from a bottle..."

Harris instantly resolved to order more whenever the proprietress gave him the opportunity. She never did. She was a stout, scrubbed woman in an apron vast and white as a snowbank. Before it she held for presentation a slimy, yellow object about ten inches long.

"...It's the season, sir. No applesauce for your meat either, I'm afraid, but I have brought you a nice pickled cucumber. You're from the paper, I expect. Well, just eat up then while I take the weight off my feet and tell you..."

She told him first about the black dog. She didn't let dogs in the room as a rule, but this one was so well schooled, it never bothered the guests for a taste of their dinners. Imagine. Its master—she never knew his name—had brought it some dry biscuit of its own he claimed was good for its teeth. He was an original and no mistake.

He had tired himself walking. The Northumberland Inn looked respectable, he said, reminded him of home—though he was from Somerset himself. Then he unbent enough to tell a story on himself that was laughed at still. In town, he had asked the first railway worker he saw what time the next train left for Lindsay—which a map he supposed reliable indicated was only twelve miles from the goal of his pilgrimage, the storied Fenelon Falls. He was told he was early by a full year.

None of the other diners could help hearing. One who had just been persuaded to sit down was an anxious young woman in a travel-stained green riding habit. She apologized for her appearance. You could tell she had had a gentle upbringing. Said she had fallen while trying to ride side on a man's saddle. No injuries, she was sure. She said she was taking a deceased uncle's horse to Cobourg to sell.

She spoke to the Englishman before he left. He left on horseback.

Harris tried to imagine the transaction. The animal she was offering was not fast, but would do useful work for a humane master. She spoke of oat-to-hay ratios and of root vegetables. And Enoch Henry, who had just been making public resolve to be less gullible in future, would have been dazzled, even if the subject had been of less intrinsic interest. For he was listening to MacFarlane's heroine Flora. She spoke to him with the accent and intensity of the New World. Perhaps too he saw her chestnut hair flying as she skipped from log to log across the swift Fenelon River to bring medicine to a sick shantyman. Theresa saw a man who was good to his dog. She would have taken little of his money. Of herself she may have told him nothing at all.

"...I was just surprised she didn't stop the night here after." The proprietress sounded unexpectedly wistful as she rose from Harris's table and straightened her white cuffs. "There were not two hours of daylight. That dress besides was miles long for walking. If she had stopped with me, she could have unburdened her spirit, as I've been bereaved myself—but, no, she slipped away. Suspicious, don't you think? I wonder now if I wasn't as credulous as that gentleman we were speaking of..."

To be thorough, Harris had her step out and identify Nelson. The purchaser's death came as sad news.

"So far from his mother's hearth." She stared across her well-swept, lamplit inn yard at the plank road winding into darkness. "I've the St. George's Society expecting their monthly supper here at ten thirty, so I had best get my dining room set to rights. My, they are a splendid crew. It would have eased that poor man's heart to hear the toasts." A smile lifted her full cheeks. "You can say that in your obituary."

Harris explained that he was not a journalist but a friend of the lady in green. "Did her habit have both sleeves?" he asked.

"Sleeves? Yes, of course, but why—"

"Could any of your establishment," he hurried on, "have seen which way she went?"

"I asked, sir—no. What is it she's running away from?"

"Help me find out," he begged.

So she let him ask again, from stable hand to scullery maid. The latter tugged at her red fingers, scuffed her shoes, glanced at the floor and confessed at last. She had no notion where the lady went, but behind Mistress's back she had let the lady use kitchen shears to cut a swath from the bottom of her bright skirt. In return the girl had been given the surplus fabric for her granny to make a waistcoat.

Electricity moved Harris's legs without his choosing. By the calendar eighteen days behind Theresa, he nonetheless felt as close now as to the next tree.

He rode straight to the grandmother's and bought the waistcoat.

* * *

After a few hours sleep at Sager's Hotel, Harris set out on foot. As August 3 was the day the butler had named for Crane's return, Nelson had to be available and rested.

Harris's course lay through long-settled agricultural land, the lake on his right. Soon after five, the sun climbed from the water to fire the corn fields and set aglow farm windows. It felt like a new dawn in a long season. Last night, for the first time, Harris had spoken to people who remembered having spoken to Theresa later than July 13. If not at ease, she had at least been whole and active. Although no one so far could quote to him any of her actual words, she and he had ridden the same mount, and a piece of the fabric she had worn now girded his chest.

The hue and texture were not new to him. Allowances made for differences in weathering, they matched those of the Rouge Valley sleeve. No pleasant thought on a promising morning.

He walked faster. He must walk in Theresa's shoes now, for she had left the Northumberland Inn without a horse. Would she double back? He thought not. She would continue east, the lake on her right. Crows and blackbirds serenaded Harris as he moved from farmhouse to farmhouse. He mentioned dates and times, showed the practically illegible tracing, pointed to his ill-fitting emerald vest. One family gave him breakfast, none information.

He worked east towards Cobourg, the nearest town after Port Hope. Arriving on King Street close to nine, he considered the day half gone and was surprised to find hotel clerks still yawning and grumpy. A whisky and tobacco aftertaste of Saturday night seeped from taprooms into lobbies. Saturday's guests were unremembered, let alone those of July 15. Check the register and welcome.

At Weller's Stage Lines, however, a stable boy had not forgotten. He was busy harnessing a team of four out in the yard, and practice lent his movements a grace despite his ill-proportioned physique. Hands, ears and feet all seemed untidily large for his body.

"I found her in one of the stalls talking to Jupiter." He seemed so certain, and—mercifully for a Harris dumbfounded by this stroke of luck—he had more to say. "The light there is poor. I could not see her face, not at first. She sounded not much older than what I am, but dead tuckered out. It was morning like now. I told her if she was waiting for the eastbound, she would be more comfortable waiting in the office or at the Globe Hotel next door. Passengers aren't supposed to be in the stables. But she said she would rather be with beasts that asked no questions."

The boy grinned his approval of this sentiment. Stealthy rather than calm, Harris followed him from strap to tightening strap. How gladly would he have dispensed with questions, could he but have picked his informant up and wrung the entire encounter from him!

"What else did she say?"

"She talked about Jupiter's teeth being worn sharp and him biting his tongue and not being able to chew right. He was off his feed was all I knew. She said try filing, and it worked. No ribs showing now, eh, Jupe?" He slid a bridle over the head of a bucktoothed grey and secured the throat latch. "It was only when she came out of the stable to board the coach that I saw how beautiful she was. If I had known, I'd have felt awkward talking to her—if you know what I mean."

Harris nodded silently, remembering his silence the evening Sheridan had said, "My dear, Harris here is new to town, but from the riding," and Harris had met the gaze of large, green eyes burning in a seraph's face.

"She was just so matter-of-fact about Jupiter, not like..." The boy's voice trailed off, leaving his difficulties with Cobourg's belles to be imagined. "You're the first person I've told about her."

"Did she ask you not to tell?"

"Not in so many words. I just knew she was hiding from something. When we got outside, I could tell from the earth on her dress that she had been sleeping rough. But now..."

"Asa," an elderly man in a battered felt hat called from the office door, "you get those animals put to yet? It's nine fifty-seven."

"Now?" said Harris.

Asa finished buckling the traces and set to threading the driving reins through terrets on the horses' collars and saddles. "Well, mister, I keep wondering where she is and does she need help. Not that I can do much about it."

"You can. You are. Did she leave on the eastbound coach?"

"The ten o'clock," said the boy, "same as this one here."

"I'll be on it too then. She didn't tell you how far she was going?"

She had not told him—nor could Asa guarantee that today's driver was the one who had conveyed the beautiful lady in question. All coach drivers shouted at him much the same.

The vehicle was uninvitingly square and spartan, with a chipped coat of red paint and rolled canvas flaps in place of window glass. The felt-hatted man led three passengers from the office and held open the coach door while they climbed inside. He then hoisted himself grumbling onto the box.

Harris was about to join him when the grey horse caught his eye. "Did you," he asked the boy aside, "overhear any of what she was saying to Jupiter when you found her?"

"There was something about it being hard to sleep. And then I think—this is what I keep puzzling over because of it being spookish, and her voice so low and weary."

"Tell me quickly."

"Telling would ease my mind. It sounded like—don't ask me what it means—sounded like, 'Isaac, I must do it for her.'"

"Isaac?" Harris's scalp was tingling. "Are you sure?"

"Asa," the driver called down, "is that gentleman coming or staying?"

"Isaac's what I heard. Did she have a horse of that name?"

"Asa!"

"But do what?" Harris pleaded. "For whom?"

"'Isaac, I must do it for her.' That's all."

Harris almost went back on his decision to leave. "I'm coming," he said.

He swung himself up onto the box just as the yellow wheels started to roll. He looked back to thank Asa, but too late. The boy had already turned towards the stable. On either side of his head, his ears stood out like jug handles. Fine ears they were too.

* * *

Harris's excitement ill suited him for the trip he now faced. Asa's testimony to Theresa's exhaustion made him anxious, while the thought that she had called upon him—and he could not doubt that *he* was the Isaac she meant—reinforced in him a joyous yet desperate sense of purpose. That after so many days of flailing about, he now had a trail to follow sharpened his joy. That he was following it so sluggishly deepened his despair.

Once under way, the driver became less irritable, but denied having noticed any female passenger in green, or any other colour. His one topic was horse-drawn transport in the quarter century it had employed him.

"Winter's best of all!" he exclaimed, pulling his battered hat down against imagined blizzards. "Ice ties your steamers snug in port. Then we put runners in place of wheels and off fly our coaches over potholes, over swamps. Winter's your great road improver in this country, young sir."

He might have thought Harris freshly arrived from Jamaica and unfamiliar with the properties of snow. Long before winter, of course, the Grand Trunk Railway would be complete from Toronto to Montreal and swallowing his custom whole. Harris let him brag while himself puzzling over the words Theresa had addressed to him.

If she were running away from Toronto, it sounded as if she were also running towards some task she thought she must perform. Which task was not obvious. Easier to start speculating as to where it was to be done, and for whom.

The coach creaked and rattled its way eastward—the lake not always in view, but always to the right—and would be pursuing its laborious course as far as Kingston. Theresa's mission, though, might take her farther, down the St. Lawrence River to Marthe Laurendeau's home in Coteau-du-Lac. With more time, Harris could have mentioned these names to Asa. He mentioned them without profit to the driver.

"In French Canada, young sir? Now there they understand that winter's your time for travel and social calls. Ever hear of muffining? You take your muffin—your young lady, that is—out in a sleigh and..."

Harris wondered if "for her" could signify anything other than for Marthe. Theresa had few friends and no family, save perhaps for some cousins across the Atlantic. She had been fond of Kate and Elsie MacFarlane. Sibyl Martin she had apparently suspected of murder, which provided no motive to do the housekeeper good—unless Theresa had subsequently concluded that her suspicions were unjustified and wished to make amends. This was conceivable—even if, as Harris believed, Sibyl were dead. Nevertheless, Sibyl would still have to have a connection to some place on the road ahead.

By four o'clock Monday morning, that road had dwindled from plank to ill-graded earth. The change lengthened times between scheduled stops by fifty per cent, for at speeds above three and a half miles per hour teeth threatened to loosen from gums. Harris had by now been coaching for upwards of eighteen consecutive hours and would gladly have seen every such conveyance splintered for boiler fuel.

From Napanee on, an increasingly heavy rain softened the bumps, but deepened the ruts. Drivers too had changed for the worse. The replacement had brought an open bottle of whisky on board with him at Shannonville and seemed to be drawing consolation from it with increasing frequency at the very time road and weather conditions were making team management more critical.

In the vain hope of sleep, Harris had moved inside. There each sway and jolt seemed exaggerated by the lack of external reference points. Not only was it still dark night, but the canvas flaps had been lowered to keep the compartment relatively dry. Louvers in the door admitted air sparingly. The seats' wafer-thin upholstery had been tamped thinner by generations of passengers.

For Theresa, the journey had been worse. The most recent innkeeper had seen her on the coach more than two weeks before. Frail, was how he described her, and yet too preoccupied to take nourishment, "not so much as a cup of broth." He had failed as others before him to persuade her to stop the night. She had mentioned no destination. Harris hoped now that it was indeed Coteau-du-Lac, where she might at least give herself into the care of someone she knew, but from the inn to

Marthe's, she still had more than two hundred miles to cover.

Blackly, Harris reflected that he still had many hours in which to dust off his bookish French.

He would rather have been riding Banshee. He would have worn her out long before now. Incessantly he had to remind himself that in this limping coach he was making the best time possible. The railway wasn't finished. No steamers sailed on Sunday. Besides, only by stopping at each stage could he be sure Theresa was still travelling east along the Ontario shore, the lake always to her right. He was eighteen days behind but no longer losing ground.

The only other steadying thought in that hour before daybreak was that, in her anguish, the woman Harris had built his life around had used his name, and his alone. He felt she had asked for his protection.

Since swimming ashore from *Triumph*, Harris had had no inkling about whether he was being followed. He had been wary at each stage point, though. By now any spy of Vandervoort's who had sailed on to Kingston could have rejoined Harris by coaching west.

Three passengers had boarded at Napanee. Opposite Harris dozed a musty-smelling Methuselah in preacher's black. Beside him, his young wife clutched a suitcase that but for the rain she would gladly have got out of everybody's way by having carried on the roof. To her chagrin, her feet occasionally collided with those of an extensive traveller to Harris's right. He acted very much at home and, whenever he thought anyone awake, spoke of the virtues of various kinds of insurance.

None of them resembled any of the steamer passengers. Still, it was dark. The preacher, for example, might not be as old and decrepit as Harris assumed.

He almost put the man's resilience to the test by hurtling onto his lap as the coach bounced down a slope. At the last moment, a lateral jolt threw him instead on top of the insurance salesman. After that, the coach didn't move.

Through the downpour, the driver could be heard climbing

down from the box. He flung open the downside door and between curses told the inmates they would have to get out if the horses were to have any chance of pulling the coach from the mud. The preacher's lady had difficulty waking her husband, who had allegedly exhausted himself at some camp meeting the day before. What a shame, the salesman whispered to Harris, if the reverend died uninsured!

Once the three youngest passengers were drenched, the woman begged the driver to leave her husband in the lightened coach. Exposed to the rain, he would surely catch a chill. When the horses pulled, however, the right wheels only sank deeper, aggravating the tilt, and she became reconciled to his getting wet. He would sustain graver injury if the coach overturned.

Harris lifted him clear and set him, with his wife for support, on the rail of a short bridge just ahead. The driver meanwhile prepared to urge his team forward again. Harris knew this would not work. He had felt the ground in front of the wheels and found it even softer. A couple of yards farther on, the deck of the bridge would carry the wheels to where the road started climbing out of the gully, but there was no driving through that intervening mud hole.

"Hallo there, driver. Let's get some logs down first."

"No need for that, damn it." The rain fairly sizzled off the man's drink-inflamed face. "This here is a strong team."

He laid his long whip on the animals' flanks, and the coach came another ten degrees nearer capsizing.

Harris, his hand quickened by anger, took possession of the whip. "Now we'll have to pull the coach back before we lay the logs. Unhitch the team."

"Here, I know my business..."

"Do it," said Harris.

While the team was being unhitched, he set the insurance salesman to identifying likely looking timber along the gully. In the lee of the coach, he got a tin lantern lit and gave it to the preacher and his wife so they could alert any oncoming traffic to the obstruction. The one favourable circumstance was twilight's incipient dilution of the inky sky. The rain fell hard as ever.

The ground behind the coach was appreciably less firm now than when they had first got stuck. Harris and the driver hastened to attach the traces to the rear axle and the horses dragged the vehicle back, if not out of the mud, at least onto a more even keel.

Just then a woman's shouts rang out. Harris looked up to see the preacher's wife waving her lantern at a waggon coming west over the brow of the rise. A square, flat load stood out against the paler clouds.

The insurance salesman meanwhile sauntered up complaining that he could find no logs large and sound enough to bear the coach's weight. Whether he had looked at all was not evident from the cleanliness of his checked suit.

"Never mind," said Harris, mud from cuffs to collar. "Here's something better. Look on the waggon." To the carter he called, almost cheerfully, "Good morning there! Can you lend us ten feet of road?"

The waggon was carrying pine planks, eight inches wide. The carter, his assistant, Harris, and the coach driver laid them crosswise, three deep in front of each pair of wheels and as far as the bridge. After that it was easy. With the water-logged team back in front, the stage coach rolled to firmer ground. The lumber waggon drove over the planks in the opposite direction before they were pried out of the mud and returned to the load.

"You won't find any more bad patches before Kingston," the carter called as he drove off.

Harris waved and climbed up on the box.

"Before we start," he said, "let me have the whisky bottle."

The other three soaking passengers had already resumed their seats.

"Empty," grunted the driver. "You better ride inside."

"Show me."

Harris was shown. A tantalizing last half ounce swirled around the dimple at the bottom of the bottle. Harris emptied it into the mud.

"How is the road from here?" he said.

"All plank again in another quarter mile. Horses drive themselves. Ride in the coach, mister, dry yourself off."

Carrying enough rain water in his clothes to fill a magnum, Harris suppressed a laugh. The man was hours from sobriety in either direction, but not belligerent, and there was no reason not to let him save a little dignity.

"What's the holdup?" called the insurance agent.

"No holdup," replied Harris, jumping down and taking his place inside.

The coach moved on up the rise into a soggy dawn.

Under the circumstances, the canvas flaps seemed pointless. Harris furled the nearest one. He wanted light to see his travelling companions. Any delay was irksome, but the recent activity had lifted his spirits and—tired as he was—sharpened his interest.

The salesman struck him as handsome in a gipsyish way, a minor dandy, and avid of whatever comforts would make bearable a life of perpetual motion. He was again amusing himself by nudging the woman's slipper.

This time she ignored him, as she was devoting her full energies to drying her husband's face. Plainly its maze of furrows was not stage makeup. His years had not stooped his proud shoulders, however, nor did palsy shake him, and the wet hair that Mrs. Postlethwaite's comb lifted off his brow was thick and dark. Paying her no heed, the old man sat staring straight at Harris.

"Have you got it?" he asked abruptly.

"Got what?"

"Got religion," the wife explained.

"No," said Harris.

"It's never too late," the wife said kindly. She looked to be a country girl, full-figured and used to heavy work. Once done with her husband, she adjusted the suitcase and wiped the moisture from her own downy blond moustache.

"Have *you* got it?" the preacher asked the salesman, who nonchalantly slid back his foot.

"I've got it."

"Hang on to it," said the wife.

The preacher again fixed his eye on Harris. "The Lord works in mysterious ways," he said. "We were sunk in the Slough of Despond and He chose an Unbeliever to lift us thence and send us on our way rejoicing."

"Oh, you would have got where you're going without me." Harris hoped to stifle theological controversy, on the one hand, and envy, on the other.

The salesman nonetheless felt slighted. Smiling tightly, he disavowed any knowledge of God's ways, but savagely deprecated the state of the provincial highway—on which subject he begged leave to claim some hard-earned experience. Mr. Weller ought to get after the politicians or do the work himself if necessary to keep his coaches running. And the coaches themselves wanted replacing. This derelict must be thirty years old!

That no banker in this age of steam would advance a farthing for such a project Harris took care not to point out.

"You know not whereof you speak," said the preacher.

The salesman fell silent, but Harris was the one addressed.

"They are hanging a boy this morning," the old man continued, "an inmate of the Provincial Penitentiary. I must not be late, for without me *he* won't get where he's going."

"Amen," said the wife.

Harris opened his eyes wide, then narrowed them in thought. He was surprised to find himself so near the Penitentiary and tried to remember what inmate there he had heard referred to in the past fortnight.

"What has he done?" asked the salesman.

Looking younger than ever, the wife leaned forward and dropped her voice. "They say he beat a keeper senseless."

"He must not leave this life," boomed her husband, "without a chance to repent of his hot temper, which has been his besetting sin almost since his infancy."

"My husband made the unfortunate's acquaintance when he last visited the Penitentiary in February. That was before our marriage."

"Allow me to congratulate you—both," said the salesman. "I've seen for myself, reverend, what an invaluable support your bride is."

"It's God's work Mr. Postlethwaite does," she said proudly.

"Amen to that. For its sake, Mr. Postlethwaite, may I ask if you've yet had the opportunity to insure Mrs. Postlethwaite's life?"

The preacher blinked.

Slowly, it seemed to Harris, who had a question of his own. Murdock had mentioned a prisoner. It had not seemed important at the time.

"*My* life?" Mrs. Postlethwaite stifled a laugh.

"I don't wish to alarm you, ma'am, but the way is uncertain, the premiums modest, and with the Colonial's system of bonuses your coverage increases automatically."

"The boy that's to hang," said Harris, "what's his name?"

"His name?" The mix of subjects may have confused the preacher.

"Charles Martin, isn't it, my dear? My husband really must rest now to prepare himself for the task of redemption that lies before him."

"Not Crusher Martin?" asked Harris. Here possibly was a link to Sibyl, a very perishable link.

"He told me he has been so vilified," said Postlethwaite, revived by indignation.

"I'll go with you then. I have to speak to him."

"I don't think—"

The preacher cut his wife short. "On what subject?"

"The recent disappearance from Toronto of his twin sister, Sibyl Jane Martin. Her life is feared for."

"I see." Postlethwaite pursed his lips judiciously. "I cannot well refuse you as without your exertions I should not be in time to see him at all. May this encounter show you the necessity of Divine guidance and open to you the path of Salvation."

"Amen," said the wife.

"Amen," said the salesman before circumspectly resuming his own campaign for proselytes.

Chapter Ten
Gravity

In another five hours, Postlethwaite and Harris were set down under a drizzly sky in the ship-building village of Portsmouth. From banking days, Harris knew Kingston, but had never visited this western suburb. Before him rose the largest structure he had ever seen.

The uniform pale grey limestone of which it was constructed made the Penitentiary look even vaster. Four fifths of the façade was wall—buttressed, blind, twenty-five feet high. Into the middle of this fortress had most ingeniously been spliced something resembling a county courthouse, complete with cupola. Two magisterial columns bore up a gently sloping pediment. Through this the most elegant entrance a cage ever had, Harris trotted after the eager old soul-saver.

He almost hoped to be refused admission. He had a trail to follow. This was a distraction. He was suddenly afraid too of trespassing with his questions on Charles Martin's last hour. No, truly, it was Crusher Martin he feared. The prison stones and mortar made vivid the violent tempers they were fashioned to contain, gave weight to the girl-wife's breathless words, "beat a keeper senseless."

It was too late, however, to withdraw. Mrs. Postlethwaite had parted from her husband only reluctantly and on the understanding that Harris would look after him while she went on to arrange lodgings. There was in any case no difficulty about getting *in*, the unsmiling porter assured them. Had he come as a tourist rather than the bearer of a dry suit for the preacher, Harris would simply have had to pay 1s. 3d.

"Women and children half price," said the porter. "Makes a

nice family outing."

Harris smeared the mud more uniformly into his trouser cuffs while Postlethwaite was changing in the porter's lodge. Then they crossed the limestone-walled entrance court and climbed a grand limestone staircase to the door of the limestone cell block—where a clerk not quite up to the dignity of his surroundings pulled a face at Postlethwaite's letter of authorization. The Penitentiary had its own chaplain, he grumbled. He didn't see the need for some "circuit rider" to go sticking his nose in. Postlethwaite began fulminating about freedom of conscience in the Canadas.

"Step smartly then," the clerk interrupted. "You're late."

A young French-Canadian keeper, lent extra years by a thick brown moustache, escorted the two visitors through the iron grill into the central rotunda. From it, cell ranges radiated like the arms of a cross. An outbreak of the shivering ague had confined a few unfortunates to their cots, but most of the cells he led them past were empty. During daylight hours, he explained, the seven hundred convicts were kept busy either directly maintaining the institution or earning revenue for it in the neighbouring limestone quarry and in the penitentiary workshops.

Martin was a melancholy case, he said, and it sounded to Harris as if he meant it. The convict's quiet industry had earned him special employment. One day he had apparently been weeding the warden's garden when it came time to return to his cell. Out he hit with his rake handle. Whang!—to the front of a keeper's head. Whang!—to the side. What had enraged him was not being allowed to complete his task. His death sentence had seemed certain to be commuted, but then just three days ago the keeper attacked had—despite the most attentive nursing—died of his injuries.

This news lengthened Postlethwaite's stride. In his wife's absence, his decrepitude seemed to have dropped away. Every couple of paces now, Harris noted, carried them past one of the cells, which were scarcely large enough to lie down in.

They came abruptly to a cell that wasn't empty. A heavy man

sat slumped on the end of the sleeping shelf. His face was lined and putty-coloured. Although the Penitentiary air held no heat, he wore only the convict uniform trousers, brown in the right leg, yellow in the left. The hair on his bare, sagging chest was as grey as the stubble on his head. Everything about his appearance spoke to Harris of defeat, but nothing more so than his not looking up when the iron lattice door was opened.

"Now, I don't need to warn you he's a hothead, reverend," said the keeper, not dropping the "h" as French speakers often do. "I'll be handy if you need me."

Postlethwaite insisted on speaking to Martin first while Harris paced the areas in front of and behind the cells, shivered in his water-logged tweeds, and listened to the echoes from a multitude of hard, flat surfaces. Every door that closed or opened sounded like a dozen, and yet there seemed to be more locks than keys. Harris had no words to fit the condemned man's ears. Their worlds touched at no point—except that Harris had wished Martin's twin sister dead so that the life of another missing woman might be hoped for.

And yet Harris had come too close now not to see what Martin knew. Being spared no longer tempted him. With the execution less than half an hour away, each ebbing minute left him less composed.

The preacher finally summoned Harris at twenty to eleven. Martin raised no objection to an interview, but the keeper would be preparing him at the same time. Postlethwaite was going to see the warden about his clerk's high-church bias.

"Mr. Martin," said Harris, standing before the open cell door, "I was a friend of your sister Sibyl's late employer."

The convict stared at him with red, bulging eyes. He was in the process of being dressed in his own clothes, a farm labourer's coarse cottons.

"Forgive my intruding at a time like—at this time. Do you know where Sibyl is?"

Martin stared. "It broke her heart," he said at last. "She heard I was to swing. It must have broke her heart."

"When did you last see or hear from her?"

Martin didn't answer.

"You had a letter from your sister, Crusher," said the keeper, who was fitting irons around Martin's ankles. "It's in your Bible."

"An old letter," muttered the convict, but then he spoke directly to Harris. "Will you read it out?"

The Bible lay beside him from his session with the preacher. From between its pages, Harris shook out a scrap of brown wrapping paper, folded in four.

The letter was dated 8 July. There was no salutation, just one paragraph, pencilled in a primary-school hand. Harris read aloud:

> I never thought to have a brother hanged, but for our family there is nothing but pain. It comes of our parents' sin. I will ask the master if he can get the sentence changed. I do not expect it. You should have looked to him sooner, for now he is ill and may not last the week. When he dies I shall come to you. I shall come also if he lives, for I know he will give me leave and perhaps travel money too. Fate has given him a good life. It is easy for him to be kind. Do not count on your preacher, but you and I are of the same flesh and blood. Alas. Sibyl.

Martin's wrists were manacled now. Chilled by the letter's desolation, Harris started with awkward fingers to put it back where he had got it.

"Keep it," said Martin. "Take it back to her. She never came."

"Her master died on July 12. She vanished the day after. Do you have any idea where she might have gone, or what might have happened to her?"

The convict raised his voice and his two chained hands. "She had nowhere to go. She had no one but me."

"Steady there, Crusher." The keeper's avuncular tone sounded forced. "Come along now. Let's go for a walk."

Harris was making difficulties for everyone. He pressed on. "You don't think she had another position to go to?"

Martin's fists covered his eyes.

"Another situation," Harris persisted, "when William Sheridan died?"

"I never heard... Mister? This day will I be with my Saviour in Paradise?"

"Yes, indeed," said the young keeper, his hand at Martin's elbow, urging him up.

"You, mister." Martin stood in front of Harris. "Will I?"

Harris felt his head starting to nod assent. "I don't know," he said. "Have you had any other letters since this one?"

"They are only allowed one every three months," said the keeper, tenser than before, but—considering the circumstances—still wondrously polite.

"None then?"

Martin stared at the floor. "There was a letter Saturday, from 'a sincere friend.' No name. Said Sib was dead, that she would have come if she could. I'd like to think she would."

"Do you have it?" said Harris. Saturday was two days ago, as recent as finding Nelson in Port Hope.

"He destroyed it." Martin nodded his cropped head at the keeper. "Said he promised to."

"I *have* to take him now, sir. The scaffold is outside the Penitentiary, you see, this being a place of reform only..."

"I don't ask to make trouble for you," said Harris, "but where did you get this anonymous letter?"

"There was no letter like that. Up, Crusher."

Martin rose without protest. The moustached keeper, all business now, and one of his burlier fellows walked on either side of the condemned man. Harris brought up the rear.

"Mr. Martin," he said, remembering late a rather crucial point, "had your sister Sibyl any broken bones?"

Martin shuffled forward as if deaf. Through the stubble on the back of his head shone a curved scar. A broken bottle, Harris guessed. A tavern brawl. The scar was easier to look at than the neck below it—a thick, strong neck, about to be broken.

Who besides her killer would know Sibyl was dead? A "sincere friend" of Martin's. Mention of a letter had Harris's brain buzzing with questions—and yet he knew he could put them to the keepers later, at a time more conducive to confidences. With Martin there was no possibility of delay.

He tried again. "Charles?"

"*You* think I'll burn in hell."

"No, I don't. I don't believe so."

They passed out of the cell range and through the rotunda.

"And I'm convinced your sister didn't let you down. Someone prevented her from coming."

Outside the office, Postlethwaite and a frock-coated gentleman Harris took to be the warden fell into step at the head of the procession. The leg irons forced Martin to turn sideways on the steps down to the entrance court. His eye caught Harris's.

"Who prevented her?"

"I'll try to find out. Had she ever had any bones broken?"

"Her arm snapped when we were little," said Martin. "I snapped it."

Under the sloping pediment of the north gate, the keeper turned Martin over to a blue-jacketed village constable and an un-uniformed deputy. Both waved truncheons and smelled of drink.

"You'll have to leave him to me now," the preacher told Harris, "so we can say a last prayer together."

"Which arm?" Harris insisted. "Where?"

Puzzlement rippled Martin's forehead. There was no time for explanations. He would have to take Harris's question on trust or leave it alone.

"Here." With his left forefinger he tapped his right forearm, and away they led him through the middle of a puddle.

The warden had already gone back inside, to his garden perhaps. Before they disappeared too, Harris took the names of the keepers as witnesses to what Martin had said about the fracture. Broke his sister's arm? It didn't surprise them. That fellow didn't know his own strength. In the more than twenty years the Penitentiary had been operating, poor Taggart was the first employee killed in the line of duty. It could have been any of them, though.

What *was* surprising, they agreed, was this hanging. It should have been in Kingston at the Frontenac County Gaol, but the old gaol had been pulled down to make way for the new Customs House, and the new gaol wasn't built yet. As Taggart had been a lifelong Portsmouth man, the village had asked that the scaffold be erected here, just around the corner. And yet no one from the Penitentiary was supposed to attend. How was that for strange?

Harris set off around the corner indicated. He had never witnessed an execution nor wanted to, but was still accompanying Postlethwaite. He didn't feel quite finished with Martin either. Having in his last moments pried him open, made him promises, confided and extracted confidences, Harris found that he could not avert his eyes from the convict's end and call it delicacy.

The scaffold stood on the village green, which spectators' boots were churning into mud. The rain had only just stopped. Men, women and children continued to congregate even as the thick, drab figure in the middle of the platform was being asked if he had any last words.

Martin moistened his lips. He had plainly never made a speech, and his voice was low and mumbling. From where he stood, Harris caught the drift only. There was something about deserving death, being afraid, the comfort of the Gospel. If his sister were alive, he said, he forgave her for not coming, was sorry he had shamed her. God have mercy.

After this muffled imprecation, Postlethwaite's ringing "Amen" came as such a contrast that the crowd tittered. The preacher glared down at them while the hooded hangman stepped forward to pull over Martin's head first a white sack and then the noose itself.

It was already well past the appointed hour of eleven. Without more ceremony, the hangman pulled the lever that drew the bolt from the trap—which he stamped on at the same time. A petulant gesture, it appeared. He may have been afraid that the rain had swollen the planks and made them bind. The trap swung smartly down on its hinges. Martin fell through. The rope tautened.

The rope broke. Harris heard a mild pop, then saw a frayed tassel swinging where a hanged man should have been. The executioner evidently knew his lumber better than his hemp.

Martin fell before the front rank of gasping spectators straight into the pine crate waiting to receive his remains. Kneeling in it, he found his voice.

"Hallelujah, Lord! I'm saved!" he bawled out, his words lifting and spreading through the moist air. "I'm saved! I'm saved!"

Whether he truly thought himself dead and in heaven or believed the accident entailed an earthly pardon was unclear. Pressing forward with the throng, Harris could see little of what was occurring at ground level. Postlethwaite descended the stairs with the help of the railing. His steps faltered, for the first time since leaving the coach, as he escorted Martin back up to the platform. They were raggedly reciting, "The Lord is my shepherd..."

The trap was soon set again. Repairing the rope took longer. There was nothing for Harris to do but wait. He could not hope to get close enough to Martin to speak to him again. Martin, besides, after the bungled execution, was in such a state of religious exaltation as to be quite incoherent. The white cloth had been pulled from his enraptured face. Exclamations burst from him like thunderclaps. Some segments of the restless crowd jeered and baited him, only to be hushed by others.

Amid these exchanges, one figure's stillness caught Harris's eye. The young keeper had taken off his uniform tunic and cap, which had left a red stripe across his forehead. His oak-brown moustache looked humid and heavier than ever. Harris worked around behind him.

"Hallo, Vaillancourt. Don't be alarmed."

The keeper started, relaxing when he saw Harris was alone.

"For Paul Taggart," he confided. "Someone had to come, with leave or no."

"Employers are fallible," said Harris. "A man has to think for himself."

"I thought I should only be off my watch ten minutes. Who could have expected this?"

"Who gave you the anonymous letter?"

"I wasn't supposed to tell Martin."

"You can tell me," said Harris in a tone that left no room for doubt. "Was it a man or a woman?"

It was, said Vaillancourt, the angel Providence had brought to Paul Taggart's bedside when he had no one to tend him but his shipwright father, a gouty grandmother and the charitable women of the village. The stranger was soon doing more than the rest put together.

Vaillancourt knew. He often called by before his watch, be it morning or night. He found her, Ruth Nagle, unflagging in her attentions to a patient never at rest or more than semi-conscious. Her quiet resolve radiated beyond the sickroom to steady a community chafed raw by the length and horror of Taggart's struggle—to steady most particularly the keepers, men like Vaillancourt who had to go back among violent convicts day by day.

Last Saturday he had arrived at breakfast time. His friend's struggle had ended the night before, as Vaillancourt had known sometime it must. And yet the nurse, after fifteen days of exemplary composure, was beside herself with grief and groundless self-reproach. Apprised of his access to Martin, she begged Vaillancourt to read the condemned man a letter she pressed into his hand. That night she vanished from the house and Portsmouth.

The thought that Saturday night was less than two days ago so consumed Harris that he barely saw the second noose slip at last over Martin's re-bagged head. Theresa's middle name was

Ruth. Her mother had been a Nagle. Ruth Nagle had by the keeper's account arrived July 17, the very day Theresa's coach would have passed through Portsmouth. Why had she nursed Taggart? Harris couldn't say, but he knew for a certainty that fewer than forty hours now lay between him and her.

Theresa had written on Sibyl's behalf—done it for her.

"I know this woman," Harris whispered urgently. "Where's the letter? I must see the handwriting."

The hangman's hand went to the release lever. He raised his foot.

"Burned it," said Vaillancourt. "I had to."

"I've got it!" Martin bellowed across the green. "Brothers, I've got—"

The trap dropped. Three or four powerful spasms shook Martin's frame. After that he was merely a fourteen-stone weight swinging at the end of a mended rope.

Harris stared. He had seen a human being die for the first time. There was the body. There had not been one to see after Oscar jumped, so *that* death didn't feel quite genuine. This didn't feel genuine either. Harris felt he had missed it. Other concerns had so absorbed him that he almost had. Shame tinged his sense of wonder.

Some of the villagers were cheering, while others turned queasily away. Vaillancourt crossed himself. Nearby, a shop woman said it was a pity Martin's death could not have been drawn out six weeks like Taggart's.

"No," said the keeper, not to her, perhaps not even to Harris. "He died in chains, in public. Twice! He paid all we can ask."

Some moments later, a gentleman in black climbed up on a stool, ripped open Martin's mud-stained shirt, put his ear to Martin's grey chest, and pronounced the heart still.

"It doesn't bring Paul back," said Vaillancourt, "but it is just."

Harris swallowed hard. He could imagine being anything sooner than a cold-blooded executioner. If only the guilty would destroy themselves.

"If you see Miss Nagle, thank her." With these words the

keeper slipped back to the Penitentiary in his shirt sleeves and suspenders to face the consequences of his truancy.

The girlish Mrs. Postlethwaite meanwhile arrived with friends to take charge of her husband. The preacher was wheezing now and peevish at having had to assist at one more hanging than he had bargained for. Harris helped him promptly to the waiting carriage, then had himself directed to Taggart's house.

Whether his haste was callous or an impulse in the presence of mortality to "seize the day," Harris could not have said. The clatter of a pine crate being nailed shut lashed the air behind him.

* * *

Taggart's grandmother said nothing of gout, complaining only of sore feet. Paul had done the heavier housekeeping. She had a tired, sallow face, yellowed white hair, and enough bulk to hold down a chair in any wind. Harris had eventually found her ensconced at the apothecary's. Fever had laid up her son, Paul's father, so the family had not been represented at the execution. Mrs. Taggart was catching her breath and awaiting news.

Harris made a somewhat tongue-tied report. The farce of the broken rope was difficult to reconcile in one narrative with the gravity of a broken neck. He found, notwithstanding, that the effort to do so helped him to put some order into his own nightmarish impressions and to steady his mind for the contemplation of Ruth Nagle. Mrs. Taggart deprecated the incompetence of county hangmen and gave thanks that the world was now safe from Crusher Martin. Harris understood her sentiments and said so. Then he asked about the nurse.

Mrs. Taggart had needed help caring for Paul, but had been wary. This Miss Nagle who presented herself was so young and slight, her costume so garish and soiled. She had no luggage. She claimed, however, to come of a Montreal medical family and to have nursing experience. She gave references. Rather than waste time checking them, Mrs. Taggart simply sniffed her breath for liquor and examined her on the properties of various pills, poultices and fumigations. In a plain linen gown lent by the apothecary's wife, Ruth Nagle was admitted to the sickroom.

Harris glanced at the woman behind the counter. Yes, he thought the dress sizes comparable. Mention of the Montreal medical family didn't discourage him, for Theresa would quickly have recognized that whatever story she told would require too much effort to verify. It made no sense for her to stop here, and yet...

"When she left you, Mrs. Taggart," he entreated, "was there *any* indication at all where she might have gone?"

"The warden sent us a fancy doctor—all paid for, mind—a Kingston man." Mrs. Taggart's lips pursed sourly. "Did my grandson no good that I could see. No more than my poultices. Anyway, *he* wanted her to go work at the City Hospital there, but whether she did or not I couldn't say. She left in the middle of the night, you know. No note or notice. I never found out where to send her wages."

Ruth Nagle had been quiet, hard-working and respectful enough, if Harris were wanting her in any professional capacity. What she lacked, to Mrs. Taggart's mind, was resignation.

Martin's attack had cut Mrs. Taggart up badly. Nevertheless, when she saw how her sweet boy was afterwards—confused at best, barely ever awake at all, day after weary day—she had started preparing for the Good Lord to take him. His nurse had refused to look at this possibility. Ruth Nagle always thought there was something more she could do in the way of cleaning the room, changing the ventilation, varying the diet, rearranging the pillows. Busy, always busy, and then—she couldn't accept God's will.

"How do you mean?" asked Harris.

"Why, the way she grieved!" The fat old woman twisted irritably in her chair. "She, who never saw Paul when he was properly himself. Strong he was, sir—but gentle, trusting to a fault. Oh, I had cause to moan and howl more than any stranger. Then the way she bolted! Took only the gaudy clothes she came in and—" Mrs. Taggart seemed to see Harris's green waistcoat for the first time. "I must say, the shade improves on acquaintance. If you're of the girl's family, sir, I meant no offence. What with the strain of recent events..."

Harris hastened to assure her he appreciated her frankness.

"No one could have saved my grandson," said Mrs. Taggart, "excepting the wretch that's hanged. Without your kinswoman, Paul's end would have been harder and meaner, no question about it."

Customers were arriving from the place of execution in search of stomach medicine. Other spectators came to gloat and gossip. While grateful for Mrs. Taggart's tribute, Harris was able to get nothing more of value from her or anyone in the village.

At this point, having missed breakfast, he should have stopped for lunch. His own appetite had somehow survived the hanging. He had noted, however, that cabs were scarce in Portsmouth, so when he saw one jogging past he promptly engaged it for the drive into Kingston. If no moments were lost, the kitchen at Irons Hotel would still be open.

His head rocking against the horsehair seat back, he reckoned again the hours he had to make up—so many fewer than he had dared hope. Finding Theresa had become feasible. He wondered what stroke of fortune could have caused the interval between her and him to narrow so dramatically.

For her attendance on Paul Taggart, he simply could not account. She had not surely left Toronto for this. At the same time, if her object had been to disappear, stopping two weeks in Portsmouth, under a relatively transparent alias, represented a substantial risk. A risk, moreover, for someone there was no evidence that she knew at all.

And what of her letter to Crusher Martin? Her leaving that communication till after Taggart succumbed seemed no accident. Her attempt to save the keeper might all along have been an attempt to save the convict. If Taggart lived, his assailant's sentence might be commuted. If Taggart died, his slayer would swing. Harris wondered, though, how Theresa could possibly have incurred so heavy an obligation to the Martins.

How she must have had to mortify herself to live under Mrs. Taggart's roof! Terms like *quiet* and *respectful* fit the fugitive Harris was pursuing as ill as they did the captivatingly lively woman he had once known.

The detective picked drying mud from the seam of his boot. He felt steeped in death. Martin's abrupt fall from man to corpse re-enacted itself unbidden in his fancy. As for Sibyl, he shied away from speculating on the circumstances of her end, because he didn't want to think that Theresa might have had a hand in it. He knew she couldn't have, unless perhaps accidentally.

Enough. The point was to find her, as he soon would if she were in Kingston. On a full stomach, he would turn over every last block of grey limestone to do it.

Out the cab window to the right, the lakeside prospect included up ahead a squat, round Martello tower that marked the entrance to the harbour. Harris was entering familiar territory. At the same time, in a park to the left stood a three-storey public building he wasn't sure he recognized. An ochre-haired young woman coming from it was waiting to cross the street.

Her glance met Harris's. She raised thick eyebrows, half smiled, and was lost to view. Harris reacted slowly. He didn't stop the cab, thinking she must have mistaken him for someone else. He would have remembered her eyes. Only blocks later did he suspect she might be the passenger with gold opera glasses from *Triumph*. Tawny, those eyes looked, and sly.

Eyes that knew him, yet that he didn't know. The eyes, like as not, of a police spy.

On alighting, he asked the driver what the building opposite the Martello tower housed. It was, he learned, the City Hospital.

Chapter Eleven
Running Water

Stopping only to buy a loaf of bread, which he gnawed in the cab, Harris returned to the hospital. Theresa wasn't there and never had been, as either nurse or patient. He made sure. His tongue had become a machine for asking questions, stamping them out like tin trays. He interviewed Taggart's fancy doctor. He tried the Roman Catholic hospital as well. He looked without success for Vandervoort's tawny-eyed agent. Then he started in on his regular inquiries, which kept him several days in Kingston and its vicinity.

The gravestone-grey, monolithic city was handsome enough, built up as a provincial capital in the forties, but deserted now by Parliament, bypassed by the Grand Trunk, emptying of business, and most particularly devoid of people who had seen Theresa. As of Wednesday night, Harris had fallen sixty more hours behind her and into a state approaching automatism. His feet found their own way back to his hotel room. He didn't want to think. Having felt his forehead fanned by the wind from her heels, he would only be thinking how he had lost her again.

He didn't want to feel. He had telegraphed Toronto to forward his mail, then delayed opening the envelopes that came until he judged himself too exhausted to be much distressed by their contents. Midnight was now approaching. Without loosening his cravat, he sank onto a chaise longue and lit a cheap cigar.

The letter signed, "Yours ever, Jasper" was—those words apart—distressing first to last. Apropos of their most recent meeting, Small said "that piece" had solemnly sworn to stay in the bedroom until Harris had left, but perhaps it was just as well for Harris to know he had been overheard. Besides, to make a whore behave would take an engineer cleverer than any the age had yet produced. In this and all departments, Small confessed himself quite helpless.

"Since the Old Man's defection," he wrote, "I have so much to do I can begin nothing, except another bottle."

Clients were going elsewhere, which simply demoralized Small further. Important documents had been misplaced. As for selling Harris's properties, he didn't know what he could do, but would mention them to Esther, who was always looking for investments.

Harris hated use of the word *piece* to refer to a woman. He turned the page down in his lap and squinted through cheroot smoke at the ceiling.

The rasping tobacco scent plucked him back to a billiard haunt of Small's. "One more game, Isaac?" Jasper would ask lazily. And one more after that. Harris's eyes were smarting. Not a brilliant player, Jasper, but elegant as a prince—a challenge to beat and a pleasure to watch. Formerly at least.

Damn.

Harris wondered, though, if Jasper had really changed, or if his friends had simply failed to understand his character. Take Sheridan, for example.

As he had other of his employees, Sheridan had overestimated Small. The young lawyer worked well under direction. His greater command of his temper had saved Sheridan embarrassment, and worse, time and again. Sheridan's mistake lay in taking Small as his only partner, in leaving him no one to rely on but Sheridan himself.

This mistake magnified the impact of Sheridan's death. If his clients lost thereby, someone else's clients must correspondingly be winners. Wondering not for the first time who these winners might be, Harris glanced down and found writing on the letter's back.

P.S. As yet have lost only some business while you appear to have thrown yours up entirely. Sincerely hope you're not going quite to pieces. Rumour here is Theresa killed the servant out of jealousy and fled. All twaddle of course.

P.P.S. No need to worry about Crane's testifying against her. Under present British (hence Canadian) law, husband and wife considered one flesh, therefore not competent witnesses when spouse put on trial. There's comfort anyway. Coroner's inquest into arm etc. now set to proceed. You'll be subpoenaed if found.

Harris changed hotels instantly. Gladly as he would have given evidence two weeks ago when the inquest should have been held, he had no intention now of being found by some paper-server and dragged away back to Toronto. The move took little time. He had just bought a change of linen, but had no other luggage. He found himself sweating all the same.

To read the letter from his mother, he had to light an oil lamp. It was too hot really, but his inexpensive new room above a Princess Street coffee house had no gas or other luxuries—just a few sparse furnishings and a view of the hind-side of a brewery. All there was black and quiet now. Harris left open the sooty curtain so as not to discourage the least current from stirring the soupy air.

Then he slit open the envelope from Holland Landing. Paper money tumbled out.

Some notes were crisp as starched cuffs, most cobweb soft and veined. They bore promises of payment by banks, governments, railways and assorted other commercial ventures, including the Niagara Suspension Bridge. A vignette depicted the tangle of wires and cables.

Harris scarcely recognized them. He was too amazed. The family sometimes commissioned him to buy in the city a tool, a book, or a pair of shoes, but this looked like enough to outfit an arctic expedition.

Denominations ranged from five shillings to fifty dollars. A few bills were better tinder now than tender, their issuers bankrupt. Others to Harris's knowledge would be subject to ruinous discounts if presented anywhere but at a head office in Sarnia or Halifax. The ragtag collection nonetheless represented something close to thirty pounds.

1 Aug.

My dear Isaac,

I deliberated all of fifteen seconds as to whether to tell Father of your letter. The enclosed treasure is from him. He either has been calling in old debts or had this tucked away in odd corners. Of the mill, not the house. My establishment's dusting and scrubbing would not have missed it. I am instructed to tell you he is most anxious you not sell any of your assets so long as prices continue to climb. (Whether he thinks it better to wait till they have fallen I dare not ask.)

If this loan reaches you without mishap, I urge you to avail yourself of it rather than tempt the carriers' honesty by mailing it back.

Neither of us understands what you are about. It is so outside normal experience—although I am reminded of a businessman named Capreol who some dozen years ago chased a friend's murderers across Lake Ontario in the middle of the night when police refused to act. He was called impetuous, but I thought it rather fine. No married woman was involved.

Although Mrs. Crane's disappearance distresses us, we can think of no one particularly likely to shelter her. It is years since she has been here. She was to have come up with the Hon. William at the time of the last election, but went instead to represent him at a Mohawk funeral in Brantford.

Now her own dear father has died. She must feel it dreadfully, having in a way lost both parents at one blow.

If your quest brings you this way, you shall not be forgiven for again slighting our dinner table.

Yours, Mamma

Harris grinned wryly. The family rift, it seemed, was healed.

Gratitude to his parents then passed into sharpened anxiety for Theresa. Mention of Brantford would have meant more to him a week or ten days ago, when all directions seemed equally open. He would have been there like lightning. Having come this far east, however, Theresa surely would not double back to the other side of Hamilton.

As for the money, of course he would keep it. Borrowing from his father was infinitely to be preferred to delivering houses he believed respectable into the clutches of a bawd. Not that he would have done that, but he had not yet devised an alternative.

He slipped the re-packed envelope into the pocket of his jacket, which he folded over the foot of the bed. In lodgings of this class, sleeping with the window open was risky. Closing it, though, meant suffocation. Before it, he placed the room's one chair—an armless, straight-backed affair. On the seat he balanced the tin pitcher and basin in such a way that they would be sure to fall and wake him if anyone tried to climb down a rope and in over the sill. Having doused the light and undressed, he began to fear he might sleep too soundly for this noise trap to work. He lay down gingerly.

For the first time since his resignation, he dreamed of the bank. He and Murdock were closing the vault. The sigh of the key turning and the clunk of oiled bolts springing together into their sockets sounded vesper-sweet as always. Everything was secure.

But no, something had been forgotten this time, and the locks had to be opened. A ledger had not been deposited. Was that it? No, Dick Ogilvie—the bank messenger—was stuck in the vault and had to be saved. Only now the keys could not be found. Harris patted his pockets again and again while a chill crept down his neck. His hearing meanwhile became morbidly acute. He seemed to perceive the noiseless shuffling of poor Ogilvie beyond the iron door.

The door, Harris realized, was open. His hotel room door. Through it he felt a breath from the corridor. Fully awake now, he saw—not twenty inches from his pillow—a form gliding out. He rolled off the bed into a low crouch and dived. He caught a left shoe.

The shoe came off in his hands. A boy in a shako and baggy jacket skipped off towards an open window at the end of the dark passage. His stride, however, was broken and his stocking slipped on the oilcloth floor covering. Harris's bare feet gave him better traction.

He caught the boy by the waist and carried him back into the room. Strange as it felt, he didn't hesitate. All he knew was that after his losses at Niagara, he wasn't disposed to let anyone rob him a second time and make away with the spoils.

Closing and locking the door, he stood his captive against it. The boy was slight. He slipped around like quicksilver, though, and almost managed to duck under Harris's arm. Harris threw the room key under the bed. He tried to sound calm.

"What did you take, puppy?"

"Nothing." It was a hoarse, husky voice, feigning indignation well. "You're dreaming."

It was too dark to see his face. Harris pinned him by the throat while feeling his loose linen jacket. Something was weighing down the right-hand outer pocket.

"What's this?" It felt, when Harris pulled it out, like a pair of pointed pliers. "Don't pretend you're choked."

"Tool of my trade," said the boy. "Here, let go."

"Which trade? Thief?"

"Tinker. I fix things."

"Like locks that won't open because the keys have been put in from the other side of the door? What did you take from this room?"

"Never been in it."

Harris thrust his hand inside the boy's jacket. Brushing the shirt front, he felt beneath it and about the chest something like a bandage. Perhaps it was a hiding place. Its wearer was too agile to be badly hurt and in need of a dressing. Then Harris's fingers closed on a wad of papers in the inside breast jacket pocket.

"What are these?" he asked none too gently.

"Go ahead and have a fine old grope, why don't you? Do you a power of good."

Harris's world tilted. The throat beneath his fingers felt smoother. The words from it sounded husky as before, but in a higher register. He dropped what he believed to be his letters, dragged his prisoner to the window, and pulled off the boy's high cap. Hair the colour of ochre fell about her face.

"What on earth—"

"Were you wanting to undress me altogether?" she said and, before Harris could answer, kissed him on the mouth.

Harris prised her face away from his, but kept hold of her wrists. He didn't know what to do with her. He wanted light, and at the same time recognized that he was wearing nothing but his new undervest and drawers.

"Would you rather I scream for help?" she asked.

He would of course not, but didn't leap at the bait. It was already easy enough for her to keep him off balance. Before he had recovered from the shock of her sex, he realized she was the very woman he had seen Monday outside the City Hospital. She had been wearing lace mittens.

"A naked man confining a girl in his room," she taunted. "What will the decent folk say?"

Harris found his voice. "Dressed as a boy, you brought my release to Port Hope. On *Triumph,* you changed into a dress. You saw me jump in the lake, but you had to sail on to Kingston."

"They'll lock you up for raving alone."

"You couldn't get a ship back on Sunday," Harris persisted. "Then two days ago you saw me in a cab on King Street, and in one disguise or another you've kept track of me ever since."

"All for love, I suppose."

"No, I was to lead you to Mrs. Crane. You stole my letters because you hoped they would say where she is."

"Pooh!—to put it ladylike. I just wanted your cash, since you were simple enough to count it with the curtain open."

"A common thief then."

"I don't admit to nothing." She tried to rub her trouser leg against Harris's thigh. "We could do business, though—a little trade and commerce."

"Stop it!" Angrily he shook her, once. "I may be easy to embarrass, but embarrassment does not make me sweeter to deal with."

She seemed to think about that. "So," she said, "are we going to hold hands like this all night?"

"If I turn you over to a constable, I suppose he'll just let you go. You're in the pay of John Vandervoort."

"There's little enough of that to be *in*, exactly." A chuckle rumbled like gravel in her throat. "Look, Mr. Harris, if you want to chat, let me have one of those cigars I smell."

Wanting to see rather than chat, Harris nonetheless welcomed her change of ground. "No more tricks then," he said.

"Maybe."

"Just light the lamp, will you, without setting fire to us both."

With no drain spout this time and no rope, she would have difficulty leaving by the window. She might throw the letters out, though. As soon as he let her go, he scooped them up instead of reaching for his clothes. Modesty yielded to prudence, but not bloodlessly.

"You're pink as rare meat," said the police spy when the light came up. She might have been nineteen or twenty. "Is Nan Hogan the first of her sex then to see you in your underclothing?"

Harris glanced at the papers. They were his and appeared intact. Fumbling a little, he passed Nan Hogan a cigar to distract her while he was dressing.

When she lit it, holding her hair back from the lamp, her smoking struck him as oddly natural. She seemed a woman framed with few curves. Her narrow, rectangular face ended in a thin, tight mouth and small, square jaw. Her remarkable yellowish eyes were oblong slits.

At Toronto's Royal Lyceum, Harris had seen women in breeches swagger coquettishly in male rôles, but never one as free and natural with male ways as this. Nan Hogan's arsenal certainly included coquetry. When she played a boy, however, it was not to pique interest, but rather—it seemed to Harris—to enjoy a boy's liberty of action. She was welcome to it, out of his room.

As soon as he had on his tweeds and had patted every pocket to ascertain that nothing was missing, he pulled the bed from the wall, retrieved the key and opened the door. Nan ignored it.

"I'm letting you off, Miss Hogan. Go on."

"You mentioned Mrs. Crane. Is she in Kingston?"

"You've had time to look." He was pointing Nan's way, but let his arm fall to an attack of curiosity. "What did they tell you at the hospital?"

Nan cleared the chair and sat on it reversed, her folded arms resting on the back. "Time, yes, but I've only a wretched description—slender build, brown hair, etc. Who doesn't have brown hair? I'm better off sticking to you..."

Harris threw her bodily out.

When he was again in bed, with key and money under his pillow, Nan came back and called softly through the door for her "outsiders," as she termed the pointed pliers. He didn't answer. She was too deadly stealthy, even on these creaking floors, and the next poor devil might have his throat slit as well as his purse lightened. She would find other ways to supplement her spy's wages.

After she had stopped calling, Harris lay listening to the sparse night traffic of a port city in decline. Perhaps the lake had simply drained away down the St. Lawrence River. His mouth felt dry as sand. Then in the penumbra of consciousness his lips tingled with the memory of Nan's kiss—a mocking, brackish droplet of moisture.

He thought deliberately of Theresa, but her face was blank. It worried him not to see her face.

He tried to count. Always he had known exactly how long she had been missing. At 3:14 a.m. on August 7, he fell asleep before working out that this was the twenty-fifth night.

* * *

His first waking thought was of Nan Hogan. By now she would have communicated with the authorities, and he would be served with a subpoena before he was on his feet.

He dressed—and it didn't come.

He shaved undisturbed.

After downing a breakfast chop and a large cup of coffee, he was beginning to feel invulnerable. Vandervoort would evidently rather have him continue looking for Theresa than give evidence at an inquest likely in her absence to prove inconclusive. This plan suited Harris, except that he didn't intend to find Theresa for Vandervoort to interrogate. He had therefore to keep Nan from following him.

He assumed she would try. To draw her out he strolled down Princess Street to the harbour and back up Brock. It was her build and eye colour he had to watch for. The saucy freak could be wearing anything. He rather hoped to see her in a crinoline, for then he would simply have to hire a horse.

It wasn't to be that simple. In Market Square he became suspicious of a slight figure in top hat and a man's short paletot cloak with slit sleeves. A few blocks later, suspicion became certainty.

They spoke. They might as well walk together, she said in her deepened husky voice. She laughed at his offer of a bribe. He entertained dark thoughts of tying her up or knocking her unconscious. Then they came upon the new Roman Catholic cathedral, still towerless but some two hundred feet long and bristling with limestone buttresses. On an impulse, Harris ducked into a side entrance off Clergy Street.

He found himself near the altar rail, practically in front of two dozen kneeling papists. A priest was saying prayers in Latin. Harris felt the blood of his Presbyterian ancestors rise to his face. His straw hat in his hand, he edged down a side aisle, his discomfort lightened only by the realization that his stratagem was working.

Nan had not followed him into the sanctuary. There was no question of her doing so with her head covered. Had she bared it, however, and let her tresses reveal her sex, she would have been expelled for wearing trousers. She had no choice but to wait outside—and outside there was no point from which all entrances of this great hall of worship could be simultaneously surveyed.

Harris crossed the nave along an empty rank of pews. He waited until the pious began filing to the rail to receive the sacrament before advancing towards the door opposite the one by which he had come in. Now the guessing game began. He was certain to win eventually, and the most he risked losing was time.

The coast when he looked out was clear. His opponent must be at the far corner. He committed minor trespass by dashing between two houses on Brock Street, leaping a fence, and slipping in through the back door of a Princess Street wine merchant. ("Purveyors to Regiopolis Seminary" read a discreet sign.) In propitiation, Harris bought a corkscrew he had no use for, meanwhile congratulating himself on his own deviousness. He had won first time.

His victory would have meant no more than the fleeting pleasure it gave him if he had not already concluded that Theresa had never been in Kingston. He could find nothing of her here and had almost come to believe he could sense her absence. Oscar's disease in reverse. A cab carried him west past the commercial buildings on King Street, back out of town the way he had come.

Confidence in his decision grew when out the cab window he saw a sign. From the eastern end of a warehouse, an enormous padlock appeared to leap, and the black letters encircling this *trompe l'oeil* painting spelled, "CRANE'S PAINTS & HARDWARE."

Of course. This must have been in the back of Harris's mind. He had forgotten that Henry had been born in Kingston, and that his younger brother still ran their deceased father's business. Theresa might have feared her brother-in-law would recognize her. By inquiry, Harris learned that Mr. Arthur Crane had in fact been out of town all this past week, but Theresa could not have been expected to know that. If she meant to continue east, to Marthe's perhaps, she could well have thought to bypass the grey city by land or water.

Harris sprang back into the waiting cab. With something more now than wishful thinking to support his course of action, he felt as cocky as a heartsick man can feel on four hours' sleep.

From the first farm house past Portsmouth he proceeded west on foot. In Theresa's place, he would have been looking at first light on Sunday for a boat and boatman to take him around Kingston. No road hugged the curving shore, but he followed the one closest to the water, on his left for once, and asked whomever he could collar if they had seen her four mornings ago. Memories should still be fresh.

A farmer who had been up before dawn repairing a thresher had noticed a solitary woman hurrying west along the Front Road. He could not at that hour make out the colour of her costume. It was certainly no one he knew. His own affairs cut short any speculation as to the nature and wisdom of her errand, but he did recall checking the mercury and being surprised to find it stood above seventy Fahrenheit degrees. She had been hugging herself as if for warmth.

Feeling fortune's wind strengthen in his sails, Harris prepared to hear of further, confirmatory sightings. He was disappointed—all the way to Collins Bay. From this dead end he retraced his path, looking for the point at which Theresa's had diverged from it. Even if no one had seen her, there might be some physical evidence.

And so it was that on the afternoon of Thursday, August 7, a lean and hungry-looking man in tweeds, straw hat and startlingly green vest was observed prowling the verge of the Front Road four miles west of Kingston. He was too well turned-out for a tramp. He was too indifferent to dirt and burrs to pass as a professional gentleman. Some children thought he might be searching the ditches for weeds from which to make quack medicines and looked in vain for his circus waggon inscribed with promises of miraculous cures. A dairymaid averted her gaze from the suspicious character and quickened her pace. A harmless lunatic perhaps, but one never knew.

A shoe and harness maker simply assumed he had lost something and stopped to offer assistance. The searcher's physiognomy impressed him favourably. What he would remember was the long, straight, narrow nose and a particularly sympathetic downward curve to the upper eyelids. Age? That was hard to judge. The cobbler thought he walked like a young man, raised in the country but wearing city boots. At the same time, the grey in his dark side-whiskers, even if no more than the effect of roadside dust, did not appear out of place. Then again, his bloodshot eyes burned bright. And his complexion showed not age lines but recent strain.

The tweedy man had not just lost a gold sovereign. He was seeking a lady, and it truly was amazing in what detail he could describe her. The cobbler asked question after question. Able to offer no help at all, he at least went his way with a story to tell.

Increasingly, when such stories were told at taverns along the northern shore of Lake Ontario, one or more of the hearers would recognize the subject.

"Nose like a greyhound? The very party that came pestering me in Cobourg!"

"And didn't he stand the entire *Kith 'n' Kin* on her ear last week?—though I'm not sure he meant to."

"This week he has been all over Kingston and no mistake. You can't move without that emerald breast of his hitting you in the eye."

He made for a spot of colour in the landscape. No one was seriously annoyed with him.

No one but Harris himself.

He was by two o'clock repeating himself, going back over ground already covered, revisiting bushes he had looked under half an hour before, endlessly checking his own earlier work as if it were that of a subordinate he no longer trusted. He could not believe he had lost the trail completely. There had to be a dropped button, a swath of flattened grass, a footprint not quite washed away, a thread, a hair, a breath. Something had to have been missed. Yet even as he audited, Harris's mistrust spread to the auditor. His eyes were useless. He almost stopped bothering to look as he dragged his body up and down beneath a dull, damp sky.

Recollections of his morning smugness made him like himself no better. His glee on eluding Nan Hogan especially galled him now as he stopped by the side of the road to wipe the sweat from his foolish face. She would find him out again before he had learned a thing. He had scarcely been making himself inconspicuous.

As if he expected to see her coming, he looked back east across a shingle beach. The lap of wavelets steadied him. Even under clouds, the lake shimmered. He let his eyes slide over it away from the road out to the two promontories that closed the bay. On the nearer, shorter one stood an orchard and a farm Harris had already visited. The further, longer one he had supposed uninhabited, belonging as it did to a family settled north of the road. Now, though, against the grey sky he thought he discerned the faintest pencil line of smoke rising from a clump of trees down by the water's edge.

It was gone. No, there it was, a thickening brown smudge.

Harris's senses quickened. An entire layer of dead skin seemed to fall away. A ten-minute run brought him around and away from the bay to where the road bridged a stony creek. He had noted this feature previously, but not the extent to which the stones were shaped and spaced to form steps leading downstream—out towards the further point. By discreetly extending a natural peculiarity, human hands had provided a path that left vegetation undisturbed. Harris sat on the edge of the low, railingless bridge. His feet easily reached the first stone. He stood on it.

It wasn't quite the first. Upstream from it lay a larger, flatter rock the bridge timbers had hidden. Part of this stone's surface was not grey but rust. Iron ore, thought Harris, and was about to hasten on when he noticed the colour was flaking off. He crouched and lifted some of the caked red substance with his thumb nail. It looked like blood.

Anxiously, he followed the stepping stones towards the plume of smoke. Around a bend in the stream, the stones became sporadic, while the path climbed the right bank and cut into the trees. Harris crept forward along it. He resented the extra seconds he had to take, but didn't want a snapping twig to alarm the fire tender.

Might not that person be Theresa? If the blood on the rock weren't hers, it might—or if her injuries were light. Four days was a long time to hurt, but a short one to heal. Harris prayed for her to a heaven he believed empty. Let her be safe. Let her be whole.

Theresa's feet in any case had not created this well-worn path. One or more squatters' likely had.

On a smaller farm, this land—though damp—might have been cleared of its stands of cedar, elm and silver maple. As yet, however, the owners' appetites appeared not to have grown into their holdings. Nature here for now was permitted to take its course.

Just at first, tree trunks hid the lake, which presently twinkled between them as through a grill. Leaving the path, Harris stole along parallel to the shore. Then he saw it. Out on a patch of sand quivered the flame's pale light. Over it, a cauldron hung from a log tripod.

To the right, nestling against the rocks that marked the drop from the forest floor to the beach, a low shack had been laced together from odd logs, loam and driftwood. Harris's survey of this beaver lodge was cut short by the emergence from it of a woman in an emerald green dress.

Harris caught his breath. He tried also to rein in his imagination, to hold it back from hasty inferences.

The dress's wearer was of medium height and thin. She kept her back to Harris as she bent to add wood to the fire. A walnut-brown rag covered her head. When she stood up, she winced and kneaded the small of her back with her right hand. Whether from sun or dirt, the skin of that hand was very dark.

Harris's heart ticked off the suspenseful seconds. His vision blurred. When she bent over again, he approached—almost not daring to look. This was no Mrs. Fitzroy. Two such dresses could not conceivably turn up within the space of a week in the same square mile of country.

He could picture Theresa's face now, precisely, the line of her nose, the parting of her lips.

He didn't want to alarm her by creeping too close. He waited till he was just close enough that she could not run away without recognizing him.

"Theresa?" he called out, softly first then louder. "Theresa."

The woman turned towards him a startled, ancient face. They stared at each other a long, still moment till the greedy screeching of a seagull seemed to break the spell.

"Who's Tree-sa?"

"Beg your pardon—a woman I'm looking for." Harris tried to clear his throat. Speech came slowly. "I—took that for her dress."

"It's my dress," said the squatter woman, wiping her crooked nose on its cuff.

He saw he had exaggerated her age. The lack of teeth gave her mouth a collapsed look, and ingrained grime accentuated the lines etched by rough living. Her figure remained firm and shapely inside the fitted bodice.

"May I," he said, "ask where you got it?"

"Bought it," she sniffed. "Are you a constable?"

He shook his head. "From whom did you buy it?"

"Because if you're a constable, I can show you the bill of sale." Her voice, hitherto flat and dull, rang with triumph. "I knew I'd be suspected. As if such as *me* never came by anything honest."

"I should like to see the bill of sale."

"You're not a constable, though." She stuck a discoloured finger in the cauldron.

Drawing closer, Harris saw that the water whose temperature she was testing contained several pounds of wildflowers. Queen Anne's lace, he guessed.

"Are you," he asked, "a dyer by trade? That's honest work to be sure."

"I may be. Was there something you wanted done in that line?"

"I should like a piece of cloth the colour of the dress you exchanged for the one you're wearing."

The dye woman looked at him narrowly. The raw onions on her breath, of which they contributed the least putrescent element, flayed his nostrils. She asked his name and who he worked for.

He told her.

"I'm Etta Lansing. Mrs. Lansing to you. You would do better to tell me you're Henry."

"I'm not," Harris blurted, his heart racing, but convinced as it raced that it was avoiding a trap. Theresa could never have expressed a preference that Crane find her—Crane the faithless bully, so slow to look for his missing wife, so quick to believe her dead.

"You do sometimes go by that name," coaxed the woman in green.

"Never. I'm not Henry. I don't serve Henry. I won't tell Henry the lady in question was here or where she went. Now—was she injured?"

"She came to no harm with me... Something for your thirst?"

While pursuing his interrogation, Harris diplomatically accepted from Mrs. Lansing a tin cup of some bitterly resinous infusion.

"That's sweet fern," she said. "You find it by the edge of the road. It's good for the ague."

Harris let his cup be refilled.

"It will be five cents by the way. I can't afford to give nothing away. Much obliged. Sassafras makes a nice tea too, and a nice orange dye, but it doesn't grow in these parts. Stoke up that fire a bit, will you?"

"The water is turning yellow," said Harris. "Was this the colour?"

"That wild-carrot yellow was my favourite hue, until I saw the green." She smoothed the skirt of Theresa's dress, already stained with splashes from various dye pots—if with nothing worse. "You're supposed to get a bright green from dying your yarn first in goldenrod, then in indigo. Indigo's dear—and has to be fermented with urine. In the end, you do get a good strong green, but not like this."

"Does Theresa Crane have your yellow dress?"

"Who? The lady didn't mention *that* name."

"Mrs. Lansing—"

"Ooh, not so hot. I did keep a scarf the same, if you've time enough to wait while I get it."

Harris followed her to the square door of the shack. "The bill of sale too, please."

She supposed there was no harm. It was produced from somewhere under her garments and held for his inspection. The name signed in pencil was not Theresa's. The hand, despite a tremor, was. Harris didn't know how much acute distress to read into this distortion, as whatever her physical and emotional state, she might also have been trying to cover her tracks.

"How did she seem?" he asked.

"You wait outside." Having tucked the precious paper away, Etta Lansing darted into her hovel.

Harris stuck his head through the doorway but could see nothing in the windowless interior. The air besides made him gag. From some vomitous corner accessible only by touch, the squatter emerged with the yellow scarf.

The colour was clear and bright enough in what was coming to seem a rural way, but dull beside a brand new synthetic dye like that of the riding habit. In the yellow dress, a traveller would attract less notice. Theresa's change of clothes, her shaky writing, her mention of Henry by name all suggested to Harris—independent of the blood stain—that between Portsmouth and this beach something had happened to increase her sense of alarm.

"Look here, Mrs. Lansing, you've still told me nothing of her physical health or state of mind."

"Mind? She was half out of it, I should say. What you would expect of a woman who had just been robbed."

"She had been robbed?" The word did not slip gently into the place Harris's premonitions had tried to prepare for it.

"It's a lonely stretch of road like you get when so much land belongs to one house. I don't complain, mind. The deed-holders leave us alone, and we leave them likewise. It's lonely road, though. I wouldn't go myself except to collect plants for my colours, and then I have a good sharp knife—"

"But was she hurt?" asked Harris in a misery of suspense.

"She had no broken bones that I could see. She might have caught some bruises, but they wouldn't have flowered till after she left me. Stoke up the fire again, will you?"

"Never mind the fire," said Harris, tormented by thoughts of hurts he could not ask about. "She was robbed, so when she left here she had nothing but the four shillings and six pence that bill of sale says you gave her."

"And my yellow dress." Mrs. Lansing's puckered face clouded over with indignation. "That wasn't just a shift, I'll have you know. It had a waist and full sleeves like the modern style is. There was a deal of yarn in that dress."

"But in terms of actual coin and paper, she left here with under five shillings."

"She was welcome to take her goods elsewhere," sniffed Mrs. Lansing, "if she thought she could have got a better price. And as for her hair..."

"What about it?"

"She just threw it in the fire. Nice brown tresses, foot and a half of them. She asked me first if I could change the colour. I said, 'Certainly, missus, if you want to stick your head in that there cauldron for an hour.' So—snip, snip—off they come and into the flames. I got them out right smart."

Harris turned away. He couldn't bear not knowing Theresa's suffering and couldn't bear knowing the fraction of it which the described act of self-mutilation expressed. Then, with a self-command that astonished him, he turned back to look the hag in the eye.

"What did you do with the hair?"

"Do? Why, it's worth money, I'm telling you. If she don't need it, I do. Mr. Lansing is making an ornamental wreath of it to sell to a professor at the Queen's University."

"*How much?*"

"I can't say I'm partial to the tone you're taking. I've been more than obliging, and Mr. Lansing won't like to hear how I'm took advantage of in his absence. There now. I've said all I'm going to say until my fire gets tended."

Harris could not remember having made a more distasteful bargain. He paid four dollars for the wreath and scarf and threw his emerald waistcoat in to appease the possibly apocryphal Mr. Lansing.

And how much else of what the dyer said was true? Harris's fingers held a three-year-old memory of Theresa's hair, to which "nice brown tresses" were as tarred rope. He doubted that the lifeless filaments handed him came from his darling's head. He nonetheless wrapped them in a clean handkerchief before sliding them into his breast pocket.

Their transaction made Mrs. Lansing more trusting. All at once, she could see by his firm chin and high, smooth forehead that Harris was a man of good faith. Her pot was permitted to cool.

The lady, she said, had come by land but insisted on leaving by water and would on no consideration go into Kingston, which she called "Henry's city". By water how? In Mr. Lansing's boat to be sure, same as he was fishing from at this moment.

Harris looked south and east. Just here the lake became river. The water began not just to move but flow, down to the Atlantic Ocean, no turning back. The shores closed in. Yonder sat Wolfe Island like a pipe in the mouth of the St. Lawrence, its ten-mile stem affording a portage around Kingston.

Suppose, though, Theresa had suspended her flight. Nearer to hand lay other islands, two large enough to have been ruled into farms. Harris dared to imagine one of these had taken her in and lent her haven, far from the highway, surrounded by the waves. There she would regather her strength and spirits. He would find her in a room with fresh air, clean sheets and pillows to arrange.

"And did your husband take her over to Amherst Island?"

"Oh, no." Etta Lansing shook her head so hard she had to retie the brown rag under her chin. Vindicated pride again rang in her voice. "He put her—by her own wish, mind—in an Indian canoe headed down the river."

"I don't believe that," Harris retorted. "These days Indians travel by steamer like anyone else, not in birchbark canoes."

He had seen them at the rail, both sexes smoking their clay pipes.

"There was never anything as fancy as birchbark." The squatter woman took more pleasure in the occasion to gloat than offence at Harris's doubts. "Those two young bucks?" she crowed. "Dirt-poor, without the price of deck passage between them. Paddling a hollowed-out log like they make up there." She pointed west, towards Shannonville. "Your Treesa spoke their lingo too. How's that for strange? She arrived a lady and left a savage!"

Try as he might, Harris couldn't shake her from this story. Eventually, he drew apart to consider. His resistance started to waver.

He had passed through a Mohawk reserve Monday morning on the coach, had heard of other settlements downstream at Cornwall and Montreal. His mother had mentioned Theresa's attending a Mohawk funeral. Although her colouring was not such as to let her pass for an Indian, perhaps she thought she could lose herself among them.

A chill blew off the lake. The opaque sky heaved and spread to reveal new depths of cloud.

Two images flashed through Harris's consciousness. A woman of gentle breeding, far from home, alone and without luggage, running down a country road at night—this was desperate enough. That same woman, Theresa, still fleeing, but now destitute, ill-clad, shorn of every badge of social respectability, and riding in a red man's dugout—Harris had no words to express his fear for her. He didn't positively expect her conductors to mistreat her, but could not feel confident that they would not.

His father had had Six Nations Mohawks as allies in 1812. Alexander had always spoken highly of them. In the counter-attack after Brock's death, they had proved so intimidating that Americans had thrown themselves off Queenston Heights sooner than face Mohawk flint.

But the wars were over and the fur trade too, and now the races lived apart. Literature of the noble savage was no longer being written. Today, it seemed, it was the whisky merchants that best knew Indian ways.

And Theresa, did she know and trust them? No answer brought her closer. If Harris found her with them—by her own choice sharing their longhouse or their farmhouse or whatever it was they shared—would he know *her*, know how to keep her safe? This was his father's "what then?" question, which Isaac had always contrived to push back. Find her first, he had thought.

Very well. He would find her. He tried again to focus his every power on the search. Its field had never appeared so vast.

Harris felt the size of the land and, though it was his by birth, his ignorance of it. He knew one corner of a clearing in the endless forest. You scurried back and forth across your corner. You began to feel at home. But every grain of soil you had passed over could vaporize, and the continent would not be a thousandth part of one per cent the smaller. Harris came of island peoples. For warmth in the new world they had encircled their hearths with coastlines in the dirt, in the air. To accept the Indian story was to step out into the deep.

Before accepting it, Harris must question Lansing. There was always the chance that he'd contradict his wife. And, if not, he'd still have more immediate intelligence than she as to where the dugout was headed and what its occupants intended. When, he asked, would Mr. Lansing be back?

Mrs. Lansing, who had begun to busy herself sorting and folding rags from a heap by her doorstep, gave a grunt expressive of the impossibility of knowing. Harris said he would wait, but this didn't suit the squatter woman. Rather than have her hospitality so imposed upon, she confessed that her husband was not fishing but would most likely be found at a tavern in Portsmouth.

"Your quickest way is along the beach here as far as the big rock, look," she said, her stained fingers plucking Harris by the sleeve. "Then straight up the path to the creek."

"Good day then," he answered impatiently.

In the way of beaches, sand had managed to get inside Harris's boot, but he entertained no thought of stopping to remove it. Too many steps remained before him not to make a start.

PART THREE:
Indian Country

Chapter Twelve
Refuge

So eager was Harris to get away that it wasn't until he had gone a dozen paces that he wondered if Mrs. Lansing wasn't just a little too eager that he go. He glanced back. She nodded and waved him on from where she stood watching.

His boots crunched more slowly through the sand. He realized something had changed. But if an occurrence in the last three minutes had made him less welcome, it was nothing he could see. No vessel was approaching. Sloops and dinghies bobbed out on the bay just as before. His eye fastened on the windowless shack. Unfit, he thought, for pigs.

Suppose, in acknowledging one lie, Mrs. Lansing had told another. Suppose her husband were not jauntily if fecklessly raising a glass at the Portsmouth Arms, but rather sleeping off the effects of drink in his own unclean bed. She had her pride. She would not want it known. Perhaps she feared also that he would be abusive if wakened. Hearing him stir, she had hastened to dispense with Harris.

He walked back.

"Go on," she said. "You'll see it, by the rock." She had begun feeding twigs to the fire and, before she grasped his intentions, had permitted Harris to get between her and her dwelling. "Here!" she called. "Where do you think you're going?"

Ignoring her, Harris knocked on the low plank door. He got no answer. His hand went to the door handle. There was no lock.

"You're sure Mr. Lansing is not at home?" he said.

"With shillings I earned in his pocket?" Mrs. Lansing came scuttling over the sand, her voice shrill and scornful. "No chance of that."

She sounded convincing, but her demeanour overall was too equivocal to warrant withdrawal just yet.

"All the same," said Harris, "would you fetch a light and show me inside?"

"You mean to plunder me." Mrs. Lansing threw her weight against the door. "Get away or you'll smart for it!"

She leaned against the hinged side where she had not much leverage. Harris pulled the door fully open, careful not to stand in the aperture in case Lansing were armed. It promised to be an awkward interview.

"By what right—"

"Mrs. Lansing, I've no time to lose if I'm to find Mrs. Crane. Hallo in there! Mr. Lansing, can you hear me?"

Inside no one answered. No furniture creaked under an occupant's shifting weight. While Harris listened, Etta Lansing darted around him and into the shack. Her weapon must have been waiting just inside. Now she stood blocking the doorway, forbidding entrance with swipes of her plant-cutting knife's discoloured crescent blade. It grew from her discoloured fist like a claw.

"What the—" Harris gaped, astonishment overmastering prudent fear. It surely couldn't be her husband she thought needed such desperate protection. "What are you hiding?" he asked.

The sentry said nothing, but—

"Isaac—is it? Isaac?" A thin, compelling voice inside.

At the sound, Mrs. Lansing slackened her guard. Harris wrested the knife from her—before he knew if she still intended to use it—and in the same motion flung it up onto the hovel's patched-together roof. Without reflection of any kind, into the dark room he plunged.

This was the moment of moments.

"Keep talking," he called to the voice in the darkness. "I can't see you."

"Over here, back and—left. In the corner."

"Theresa?" Her voice was thin as ether.

But it *was* her voice. Three steps, not a continent, away.

"Thank God it's you," Theresa said.

Harris tripped over what felt like a chair, a sea chest and a nest of pots, then bit the head off a match. It flared to show a left back corner full of rags. Across three bales of rags trailed a sodden-looking coverlet with wrenchingly little in human shape beneath it. Where the blanket stopped lay Theresa's starveling face. She raised it towards Harris. Her eyes threw back the flame.

Love consumed him. The love he had tightly packed for long storage and rough transport expanded through him like bursting fireworks. His heart beat a drum roll. Trumpet fanfares blared.

"'Thank God it's you' indeed," huffed Mrs. Lansing, righting the furniture. "Told me she would see *nobody*, not at any cost. Would have saved me trouble if—"

"A lantern quick!" Harris could make nothing of her words. "A candle—anything—"

The match went out, but Harris was kneeling by the makeshift bed. His fingers found Theresa's hair. Perspiration had plastered the short strands to her scalp. He pressed his lips to them.

"What do you need first?"

"The fever..." She seemed to choke on the cabin's stench, then spoke in a rush. "The fever has broken, just don't take me back."

"If you have no injuries that prevent it," he said, "I'm taking you out for air."

"Did you," she whispered, "come alone?"

"Yes, quite alone."

Her arm went round his neck. He lifted her effortlessly. Just behind them stood Etta Lansing, bewildered still by the revolution in her lady guest's attitude towards being found.

"If missy *wants* to see you," she muttered, "well..."

Theresa in his arms, Harris brushed past her protectress towards the square of light and out into the day. He laid her on the beach by the languishing fire.

"Wait," she said, "I'll sit up." Blinking against the light, she accepted his help without reserve. "No need for the blanket. I've—got all the good I can from it till it has been dried."

Harris crouched before her, suddenly diffident. Seeing in

daylight just how little of her there was threw him. So did a malignant-looking black sore on her sweet mouth. She wasn't shivering and sounded amazingly collected, but his misting eyes gave him no faith yet in her recovery.

There was the further shock, just now catching up to him, of Theresa's presence in any form for the first time in over forty-one months. The search was over. "What then?" had become "what now?" She had so inhabited his recent thoughts that he had assumed he would be prepared. He had forgotten just how different in texture such thoughts must be from the breathing woman herself. Here she sat, weak from illness, but looking at him with thoughts of her own, an autonomous being he could no longer claim to know.

"Am I too frightening to talk to?" she asked.

Too beautiful, thought Harris, remembering Weller's stable boy in Cobourg—and too miraculous.

"She said you had gone away in an Indian canoe," he said.

"I meant to. I..."

"What *happened* to you?" He fought to keep the panic from his voice. "There was blood under the bridge."

She seemed about to answer, then looked away towards lake and sky. "Aren't the birds late flying south this year?"

"Not too late. It's only August 7."

Plainly she lacked the strength to tell him anything about her harrowing journey and was iller than she wanted him to know. He expressed sympathy on her father's death. She seemed not to hear. Besides the blanket, the full sleeves of her yellow dress were drenched with sweat. Harris hung his jacket around her shoulders.

"It's the ague, isn't it?" he said. "It was in the Penitentiary, and I believe Taggart's father had it too. Have you any medicine?"

"Sweet fern tea." She attempted a characteristic grimace he had quite forgotten. "Milk would be better."

"Should you not be lying down?"

"Not yet."

Harris moved closer. "Rest against me then."

"The keeper of this inn believes in starvation—as a cure."

Theresa rested against him. "It was all I could do to keep her from bleeding me."

This prospect stood Harris's hair on end. Theresa was in no fit state to survive amateur surgery.

"You would have been out of my way before now if you *had* let me drain the poison out of you," said Mrs. Lansing, who appeared clutching a now superfluous wand of lumpy tallow. "Do you more good than milk, which I don't have."

"You've been very patient," said Theresa without irony.

Harris found her a knot of driftwood to lean on while he built up the fire and tried to dodge the horns of a dilemma. He had immediately to obtain food and quinine. On the other hand, looking back towards the shack, he could see Mrs. Lansing's hideous knife lying up among the unmatched roof shingles. It was not permanently out of reach. Even if he took it with him, she would have others, and he feared exposing Theresa to any further risk of bloodletting, however therapeutically meant.

Taking Theresa with him offered no solution. The evening promised rain. The noisome den he had just delivered her from afforded the surest, most discreet, and most convenient refuge. She plainly could not walk any distance. If he were to carry her, she risked catching a chill and attracting attention with no guarantee of his finding a farm willing to take her in.

Commissioning Etta Lansing to fetch supplies also lacked appeal. She might take too long, talk too much, and in the end not bring what was wanted.

"Is there a Mr. Lansing?" Harris asked Theresa in an undertone.

"I have not seen him. Perhaps my fever keeps him away."

"Will you be able to manage on your own with her for three or four more hours?"

Anxiety rippled across her wan features. "We'll manage splendidly," she said.

"I don't see another way. Do you?"

"Expect you at seven." It had been her telegraphic style of inviting him to dine with her and her father at William Sheridan's Front Street villa.

Harris smiled.

"You'll want your jacket," she said, clasping it tighter around her.

He left it with her, plus a few dollars for contingencies. From the big rock, he looked back down the beach to where she was sitting. All these weeks, he had never dreamed that when he found her he would have to leave her again so soon and trust she would still be there when he got back. He didn't think he could.

Then he saw her rise and, taking Mrs. Lansing's arm, walk slowly back into the shack. He ran down the path into the woods.

* * *

"Your friend found but health poor. Will not return home. Can you give safe haven? Please reply soonest and tell no one outside your family."

Such was Harris's message to Marthe Laurendeau, Coteau-du-Lac, C.E. He imagined the stone manor house had a long verandah overlooking the St. Lawrence—the very place for Theresa to seclude herself and convalesce.

But it was a gamble in every way. Never having answered his letter, the shy and serious *demoiselle* had given him no reason to count on her—and his unciphered telegram set her a poor example of discretion. Even coming into Kingston to send it risked attracting the attentions of Vandervoort's agent.

Harris took care to avoid his hotel, which he thought Nan Hogan might be watching, but for the rest a lack of alternatives made him bold. Farm families were devoting every effort to the harvest and balked at taking in an ague-sufferer. They recommended the Kingston Hospital. So did the physician who had attended Paul Taggart and praised Theresa's nursing skills. So did the sympathetic keeper Vaillancourt, now feverish himself. The hospital, however, was not to Harris's mind sufficiently out of the way. Coteau-du-Lac was, provided Theresa were well enough to travel and Postmaster General Laurendeau willing to take her under his protection.

She had been found at least. As he went from house to house, Harris kept reminding himself. If finding her were possible, he reckoned anything might be—though in itself the discovery amounted to no more than crossing the moat of her troubles. The walls were still to scale, and allies far from certain.

Waiting for an answer to his telegram unluckily meant an additional night at the shack, which it would have taken more money than Harris was carrying to make habitable. He resisted the temptation to buy bedding. Instead he added to his other purchases a change of clothes for Theresa and oilskins.

Rain was blowing wildly enough to warrant them by the time he left the Front Road at the creek. For speed he kept to the bank this time, ignoring the stones. It was well past seven.

He almost expected not to find her. So often he had not, and part of him had not learned to stop searching. The elusive Mr. Lansing worried him. So did having spent as yet no more than twenty minutes in Theresa's company. As he pushed towards the storm-whipped beach, he couldn't help reviewing her manner to see if any of it admitted the least possibility of her having left again on her own.

Considering her debilitation, she had behaved quite naturally. Her attempts to minimize her distress ran true to character, as did her practical references to milk and blanket drying. The nurse as patient accepted a physical proximity that—considering the painful tenor of their last previous meetings—might otherwise have made them both awkward. Least like her was her incuriosity. How Harris had reached that hovel door she seemed to take for granted.

Her gratitude for his arrival he couldn't doubt. Would she, though, accept his ongoing assistance? Trusting him, him or anyone—that might be difficult, thought Harris, for a woman who had chosen a husband she could no longer bear to see. Henry had disappointed her; therefore...

Or possibly it was his own disappointment that was making Harris suspicious. Could *he* trust Mrs. Crane? The name still rasped his tongue and spirit. He believed Theresa capable of again, for some undisclosed reason, renouncing whatever comfort Harris's company gave her. She had spurned him once; therefore...

Harris's boots slipped on the muddy path down to the beach. Wind off the lake stung his face. However he twisted it, the conclusion came out the same. Suppose his suspicions of her groundless. Her perception of them could still drive her from him. His very presence could appear to reproach her for a marriage she had already cause enough to regret. Harris might not seem a possible confidant, however desperately she needed to confide. And had she not grounds to reproach him too? Unable to win her as a suitor, Harris had for three years abandoned her as a friend. With justice might she hesitate to trust him now. Therefore...

Therefore, he would find her gone—never mind that she could barely walk.

On the sand, he was able to quicken his step. Rain clouds brought early twilight. If Theresa were without shelter and her fever returned, Harris doubted if she would see another dawn. The shack at last emerged from the dusk. He had bought a kerosene lamp, which he lit immediately upon entering.

Inside he tasted mould and filth. Mrs. Lansing stood before him with a bowl of black potatoes.

"You came back, did you?" she said, as if she had bet the contrary.

"Where is she?"

The woman stepped aside. Swathed in rags, Theresa sat huddled as compactly as possible on her bale, hugging herself and rocking. Her forehead burned Harris's hand, from which she shrank as if from ice.

"Cost you two dollars, mister, if you plan to stay the night. I had food enough for her, see?"

"That's all right, Mrs. Lansing."

The legitimate landholders, Harris reflected, were providing no better. He drew a bottle of quinine wine from his bag of provisions and looked around him.

"Corkscrew," Theresa stammered between chattering teeth. "Jacket pocket."

As he tried to get some of the liquid down her throat, she coughed blood into the tin cup. Harris unwillingly remembered seeing his grandmother do this during her last bout of ague. Marsh fever some grown people had called it. He would have been seven. Or perhaps he had only heard from an older sibling about the thick black stain on the vacated bedclothes, but the nightmares had been his. With sinking heart, he scrubbed out the cup and tried again.

In two hours, Theresa had stopped shivering. Her temperature continued to climb, and she started throwing off her wraps. Harris fed her barley water before trying the milk. Having something to do helped him master his fear. As her head twisted restlessly, he watched her face and caught heart-piercing glances of recognition from her restless eyes. In a low, clear voice he kept telling her how important it was for her to rest and take nourishment, how much too he needed her, with her superior medical knowledge, to direct her own recovery and instruct him in what she needed.

Occasionally, she would assent and lie still. She spoke little, but more easily now the tremors had passed, and on one point only did she seem confused. She spoke as if Paul Taggart were alive.

"Has he wet his bed again?" she asked abruptly.

Harris felt his face redden in the lamplight. "Why—no."

"It's common enough in injuries to the front of the brain—but what about his pupils? Are they dilated? Do they respond to light?"

"He has everything he needs." Harris wondered again what Taggart had meant to her. "We'll talk about it in the morning."

The morning was still thousands of miles away. It seemed even farther when after midnight she began sobbing quietly. Harris touched her shoulder. Her face fell towards him, cambric white and crumpled. She felt and looked as if the last drops of vitality were being wrung out of her.

"I'm afraid, Isaac," she whispered.

"What's she say?" asked Mrs. Lansing, looking up from her work. To divide the interior of the shack, she was tacking together a curtain from various scraps of dyed fabric.

Harris gestured a request for her forbearance. To Theresa he said, "I'll keep you safe."

"From Henry?"

"Of course." He didn't hesitate.

"There's Judgment too."

It took him an instant to realize she was talking theologically. "Not yet, my love."

"Yes, Isaac. I'm dying and—I'm—not ready."

"Then we'll have to get you well."

Neither believed it was up to them, but he urged them to fight as if it were. She cried harder. Between sobs, she spoke of her dead parents and infant brother, alleging they would be ashamed of her, deaf to Harris's assurances to the contrary.

At length, the squatter hag came to have a look. The rustle of the silk riding habit behind where Harris knelt set his teeth on edge.

He acknowledged that, her own meager circumstances notwithstanding, she had sheltered and protected Theresa when it mattered most. Without Harris's reasons of the heart, with only her medicinal plants and teas to shield her, she had exposed herself to the risk of contagion. At the same time, her self-serving system of malnourishment had blasted Theresa's chances of recovery. Under her roof, Harris had hitherto swallowed his reproaches. If, however, she attempted now, at Theresa's bedside, to gloat or vindicate herself, he was prepared to let her taste his rage.

"There's a good sign," said Mrs. Lansing. "She's starting to sweat."

Harris had not noticed the lamplight reflected from Theresa's forehead.

"The fever was shorter this time," the woman continued. "She'll sleep now, and it will do her a power of good."

Theresa slept. Harris sat and listened to her breathing before he spread his oilcloth on the earth floor. Then he lay down and went on listening.

The afternoon's trumpets were still. Finding her was such a fragile victory—which he looked to the Laurendeaus to help consolidate. Perhaps Marthe could discover the source of Theresa's sense of shame.

* * *

The next day saw a removal to more sanitary quarters. Lansing had still not appeared. Etta nonetheless undertook "for a trifle" to summon a ferry-man from Bath. Following a short row over calm waters, Harris took a private room for his patient in that village's coaching inn.

Theresa subsequently endured another cycle of chills and fever, much mitigated by the quinine. After a late supper of beef tea and puréed vegetables, she snuggled down amid the snowy bed linen and turned to Harris.

"You look like—what?—an auctioneer," she said gravely. "Have bankers' fashions changed?"

"I'm—off duty." He wondered if he had without realizing been modelling his detective attire on Vandervoort's.

She seemed to accept his imprecise answer. "Where's your bed?"

"Across the corridor." For the sake of form, he had taken a dormitory bunk he did not intend to use.

"I'll manage on my own," she said. "I'm not planning to whimper like last night."

"I think," said Harris, "you've been very brave." He felt a rush of tenderness, as well as hope that, now her illness was receding, she would soon be brave enough to voice her other hurts.

She looked stricken at this tribute. Her large eyes turned suddenly inward, and the air of the cheery little room thickened between them, making speech sluggish and blind.

"Truly," said Harris, uncomprehendingly.

"Don't—*please* don't call me brave."

"All right then," he soothed.

"You don't know," she said after a pause.

"I should like to..." He had been about to add an

endearment, but checked himself. "Would it ease your mind to tell me?"

She shook her head.

"Tell me," he coaxed, "what happened to Sibyl Martin."

Now the head that shook shrank back into the bedclothes, and Theresa's face tightened so painfully as to close the subject.

"Oh, why did you come looking for me?" she asked when she could speak.

"I was afraid you were in danger."

"But why *you,* Isaac?"

He shrugged. "Jasper told me you wanted a friend."

"You can't stay with me, go on supporting me..."

Stung by her retreat into some private gloom, Harris opened his mouth to defend his presence, but closed it again so as not to alarm her. He feared she was in danger still.

"It's too late, Isaac," she said at length. "I'm married."

"I know you are."

He pocketed his right hand, which had been lying on the coverlet of her bed. Her admonitions were unnecessary. She had nothing to fear from his regard, nor need she anticipate its loss—for nothing he had to learn about her could change it.

"To think last night how scared I was of dying!" Theresa exclaimed. "I wish I had. I wish—"

"Well, you've missed your chance," Harris retorted.

That silenced her, and he wasn't sorry. The rags, filth and fever were still too present to his senses to render such perverse prayers tolerable. He moreover believed, as Oscar had, that Theresa was in essence forward-looking. In time she would make peace with herself. Meanwhile, he wasn't about to leave her alone—however little she seemed to want him.

From the taproom, roars of Friday night revelry rose through the plank floor. Someone was trying to sing "The Hazel Dell." At every mention of the deceased Nelly, listeners broke in to substitute other names. Hoofs and harness rattled an accompaniment from the inn yard. Harris went to the window, almost expecting to see Crane's brougham arrive.

"You've grown harder in the last three years," said Theresa. "I'm glad. Still—if I need any more tending, could you not find a woman to do it?"

"What about Marthe Laurendeau? You must have thought during these past weeks of seeking refuge at Coteau-du-Lac."

"Often." The memory seemed to make her like herself no better.

"I'll take you there. Why not?"

"Because," she said, "threats to propriety terrify Marthe, and her father's position makes it even more difficult for her to be associated with any scandal. I can't impose upon her."

Nonetheless, Harris continued to hope for an invitation from Canada East. Three days and two inns later he returned from the Kingston post office with a thick envelope. It enclosed another envelope addressed to Mme Henry Crane. The gist of Marthe's letter, as translated for Harris from the French, was sympathy for Theresa in her bereavement and ill health, esteem for her late father, regret that she had left her conjugal home, advice that she return, and—in the event that she refused—a recommendation. Marthe's mother was a benefactress of the *Soeurs Grises* or Sisters of Charity. The order's hospital on Foundling Street in Montreal had agreed to receive Theresa, although not a Catholic, and on her recovery employ her. This refuge would of course not shield her from a court order to return to her lawful husband. Pending such, however, she would live secluded and secure from worldly dangers. In time, it was to be hoped she would herself write to Henry Crane and tell him where she was. The Laurendeaus would not presume to do so.

Harris's first thought was what Kate MacFarlane had said, that Marthe wasn't truly Theresa's friend.

Mess in with the nuns? A wholesome prospect. Just as Theresa was starting to gain weight too. Her mind was also taking nourishment, from whatever books Harris found for her in Kingston. Free from fever, she no longer permitted him in the room when she was in bed, and the black scab had dropped off her lip—though deeper causes still made it painful for her to smile. He had to have more time to find those causes out.

"But we can't go on changing inns every day," said Theresa. "Otherwise, I do nothing but read. I'm shut up all the time anyway."

"Only to avoid discovery," Harris protested. "You don't require hospital care."

"I could be of use there with the nuns. I should so like to—and I have to do something to earn my keep."

Don't let her leave me, thought Harris. He wanted her good above all, and for her good had confined his affection in a strait waistcoat of service—but he also wanted her near him. In the present case, he believed the two objects compatible.

"Build your strength up first," he suggested.

"Forgetting myself in the care of others is the only way I'll get strong. Then my strength will have a purpose."

A plain white bonnet Theresa had had Harris buy to cover her cropped hair already gave her face a severe monastic outline. Her eyes and voice, however, glowed with an energy he had not felt tugging at him for years. It had become no easier to resist. At the same time, he wondered how well a house of disease and death would nurture that rekindling flame. Nursing Taggart had almost killed her.

He said so. She didn't waver. Her thirst for usefulness confirmed his supposition that she was trying to balance some moral or spiritual account. He proposed consulting a priest of her own faith.

"The nuns are godly women, Isaac. I don't intend to become one, but I don't fear their company."

Harris feared it for her. It was one thing, he reflected, within a Protestant environment to condemn Orange excesses, to encourage a Septimus Murdock, or even to walk through a vast Romish cathedral—but quite another to expose Theresa in her present vulnerable state to the risk of proselytization.

He asked whether—even if she were determined to place herself under the Pope's protection—her refuge might not rather be the modestly scaled Hôtel Dieu in Kingston. She said not. Kingston remained her aversion, and the Grey Nuns were not established there. A Catholic institution would moreover hedge her more effectively if situated in a Catholic city like Montreal. The sooner she set out the better.

Lest she attempt the journey on her own, Harris agreed to accompany her.

They boarded an eastbound steamer that very morning and breakfasted next day, August 12, at a coffee house opposite the combined hospital, asylum and convent. Foundling Street, so-called, was really more of a square. Across its dirt surface, Harris stared from their window table at architecture even more daunting than he had pictured. Behind plank sidewalks rose a limestone wall reminiscent of the Penitentiary's. Above the wall loomed a three-storey grey octopus of a building, spreading wings like tentacles over a ten-acre site. French-style dormer windows pimpled the high roofs, and from the centre of the beast a belfry surmounted by a spire surmounted by a cross struck deep into the soft dawn sky.

Theresa seemed to see none of it. She was reading a work of popular medicine and pencilling notes in the margins.

"Good strong coffee," she said approvingly. "What they served at the last inn was mostly chicory."

A customer cast her an admiring glance. The steamer had shot the Lachine Rapids just before docking, and the excitement still showed in her face. Her complexion, thought Harris, was recovering its bloom.

"You won't taste anything like it in there."

She knew this, of course, perhaps looked forward to the sacrifice, but a sweetness in her silence gave him hope.

"Don't go in," he said. "We'll keep travelling east, to Saint John or Halifax—find a secluded farm if you prefer."

There would still be sacrifices, but ones he would share.

Her forehead furrowed. Even if he were prepared to defy morality, she appeared to be thinking, why could he not remember that she didn't consider herself at liberty? She closed her book and mumbled something about the expenses he had already incurred on her behalf.

"You could work if you like," he said, "keep your own establishment."

"No, Isaac." She struggled to gather her thoughts. "I wish it were otherwise, but I must—stay here. Not forever. I very much want to see you again, when I'm more myself."

"I'll visit," he said. "I'll bring you coffee."

She looked puzzled. "I won't be allowed visitors."

"Of course not," said Harris, "but they will have to make an exception in my case."

"And not in my husband's?" She mentally rehearsed the next sentence before saying it. "You're the worldly danger the Laurendeaus want to save me from."

"And you, do you think I'm a danger?"

"Never. You're my dearest friend."

He swallowed hard. She had passed through so many stages in the five days since he had found her—gratitude, fear, self-loathing, zeal, and now a poignant regard that made separation monstrous.

She didn't know how long they would be apart. She couldn't say.

"Then as a friend," said Harris, leaning forward, "there's something I must ask you. I've spared your feelings as long as I can. The Toronto police are looking for us both. They believe your father's strongbox was plundered and that you know something about it. They believe you know something about the death of Sibyl Martin, and so do I. I'll stand by you no matter what, but I have to hear what happened to you in Toronto and after, what you did, what you saw. Tell me now."

She stammered and turned pale. She couldn't tell him, couldn't bear to live it again.

"The nuns," said Harris, "unless you become one of them, will want you to return to Henry."

"I won't, ever."

"But if he fights to get you back, he will have wealth, law and religion in his camp. Give me some tools with which to help you!"

Across the table, she took his hand, trustingly, and took courage from the contact. "When Papa died," she said, "I thought many dreadful thoughts, among them that warm-heartedness had gone out of the world—that I should never meet it again, affection without reserve. I now believe—I see more clearly every day—that I have it from you, Isaac."

"You do." Moved but undistracted, Harris returned her fingers' pressure as he urged her forward. "You also have enemies. What is it that haunts you? What's threatening you?"

"I saw him—I watched him..."

"Yes?"

"Oh, I'm a fool! *I can't say it.*" She pulled her hand back in a flash of irritation before clearing her throat and repeating in her most matter-of-fact voice, "I can't say it. I'll write it for you in a letter—within the week."

"You saw Henry kill Sibyl, is that it?" Harris had tried not to prejudge, but this way all she had to do was nod, and they would be *in medias res.*

"Not now," she said. "I'll find a way to get a letter out."

Harris doubted. Once, after an expedition to identify wildflowers, she had written him a note of correction, which read in full, "Not lobelia. Bugloss. Expect you Wednesday at seven. T." It was touching that she had not wanted him to go so much as a day with a false idea in his head, but he had never known her to write at much more length.

"Start your story now," he insisted. "Start at the end if that's easier. You were robbed."

How easy she would find the robbery to relate depended on what she had suffered from her assailant. Harris had been deferring this question. He wondered, though, if the memory of the assault might not be making it more difficult to speak of earlier crimes.

Railway workers in earth-stained fustian were by now streaming past and into the shop. Talk was of the Grand Trunk's Victoria Bridge. Above the din, an Irish serving girl could be heard announcing that if the bridge-builders wanted buns, they would have to wait.

"I left the Taggart house around three thirty," Theresa abruptly began.

"A week ago Sunday morning?" Harris asked.

"Sunday, yes. I forget which."

"Why were you at the Taggart house?"

"That is another story. When I left there, my head and joints ached. My limbs felt like lead. I thought it was because I was tired and in low spirits."

Harris perceived that she was deliberately using bland phrases to swath jagged pain. Having for an entire fortnight wrestled with a delirious patient and his soiled bed linen, only to lose him after all, she must have suffered unutterably worse than "low spirits." Such inaccuracies notwithstanding, she kept up the pretext of a scientific tone.

"What it was," Theresa continued after a fortifying mouthful of coffee, "was a warning of the onset of malarial fever. That's not something you expect in the long-settled areas. Etta Lansing says someone must have cut a stand of trees and let the sun in on stagnant water. I don't know if that's the cause."

She reached for her medical text, but Harris—impatient of diversions—covered it with his hand.

"You were walking west," he suggested, "when the first fit began."

"By the crossroads—Day's Road is it?—I couldn't walk for shivering, so down I crouched. The tramp must have been sleeping in the ditch. I suppose he was a tramp, or had just drunk too much on Saturday night to return home. He had on one boot and one shoe with no sock. He just appeared at first light..."

Harris had a guess as to the mismatched man's identity but refrained from interrupting.

"He took the pouch with my valuables," Theresa continued. "I had brought what coins and notes were left from the housekeeping and had a few pounds from the sale of a horse." A sudden query broke the trancelike surface of her narrative. "Do you know, Isaac, what became of Nelson?"

"Returned home, I believe. Crane's name was on the saddle."

"Mr. Henry is too honest," sighed Theresa. "I hope he will forgive my selling him what wasn't mine, since the proceeds are all gone."

"I'm sure he doesn't blame you," said Harris, now the one to blur his meaning. He saw Enoch Henry in his coffin with his hat on.

"I didn't haggle with him over Nelson. And Spat? I suppose Oscar takes good care of them both."

"Oscar?" A blossom of white spray opened behind Harris's eyes. Again he measured his words. "I don't know who is taking care of them. Had you spent much?"

"Nothing except for coach fare and a week's food. I had not been sleeping in inns, and for two weeks the Taggarts fed and lodged me. I also had my wedding ring and other trinkets to sell as necessary. The man got all that."

She sounded dismissive. Where she was going, she would need no money.

"Did he offer you any violence?" said Harris.

"Not at first." Theresa looked around to satisfy herself the workers' noisy gossip and disputes had their full attention. "I was too sick to resist or even to be much afraid, but he took my shaking for fear, and that seemed to—Isaac, I don't think I can go on... The idea of my fear excited him. He began kissing and stroking my hair. He had black nails and broken teeth. He said—he told me what he was going to do, and he began to tear open my dress. Then I resisted, when I felt the cool air." Her chin tilted defiantly. She *had* gone on with her narrative and resented it, not knowing if the pressure came from without or within. "Of course, my strength was nothing to his. Is this what you wanted me to say?"

"That will do." Harris moved his chair to her side of the table. *Wanted* no, but he had suspected. He would make someone pay for this violation, anyone but her, and would take as much as he could on himself. If only he had found her a few days sooner. "You needn't," he added huskily.

"Hear the story out," she replied, suddenly angry. "What happened is not what you think."

"I'm sorry—or rather, I'm glad." Harris lowered his eyes. "What did happen?"

"I vomited blood. It fell on his hands as he tried to fondle me. He dropped me with a yelp that I was trying to kill him and pushed me away with his one boot." Theresa's large eyes fixed on Harris's horrified face. She seemed at that instant to forgive him, and the bitterness went out of her voice. "His exit had a comic side. Off pelts the bold outlaw at a lopsided run, as if a fiend hung from his coattails. I didn't laugh at the time, you understand. I hid under a bridge... There, after I had thrown up again, Etta found me. My condition mercifully didn't scare her, and she was taken with the colour of my dress, which I was able to exchange for shelter."

"She paid you nothing then," said Harris. "The receipt was bogus."

"I didn't mind. She did keep her bargain, which considering how she lives is almost saintly."

Harris relaxed a little, enough to notice the homely fragrance of the bake oven, whose associations chafed him fresh. Theresa had no home. Her principles forbade Harris to give her one. He would have given her one this moment in his arms, which ached to be about her. A mere inch yawned between her sleeve and his.

"What happened," he asked, "to your hair?"

"Both the dress and my hair felt defiled—but there was more. Remember, I was light-headed with fever. Foolish as it sounds, I couldn't help believing the tramp was from Henry in some way—don't ask me how—and would report back to him." She shuddered before spitting out, "Maybe it was just that both were men whose touch I loathed."

In all but name, Harris realized, she had been raped after all, perhaps as early as her wedding night, perhaps as often as—he dared not calculate.

"How long have you felt that way about your husband?" he said.

"Long enough to be persuaded I needed different, drabber plumage that would attract no one's interest... Take *that* woman, for example, the first things you notice are her hair and costume."

Harris followed her gaze to an unnaturally violet taffeta walking dress on a girl just then emerging from the Grey Nuns' gate.

"Come back from the window," he snapped. He led Theresa by the hand past the startled waitress into the kitchen.

"Isaac, what is it?"

"Attention aux brioches!" cried a chef, sweeping a tray of cooling pastries from their path.

"Police spy," said Harris. "You won't still want to go in."

"Yes," Theresa insisted, "as soon as she is gone. I'll be protected."

"Elle est toute petite, ma cuisine. Monsieur, madame, s'il vous plaît..."

"He's askin' if you'd be so good as to return to your table," put in the Irish waitress as sarcastically as possible.

"Write soon then," said Harris. "I'll stay at..." He didn't know the city well and was momentarily at a loss for the name of a hotel.

"Rasco's," said Theresa, "opposite the Bonsecours Market. I'll write—depend upon it."

Harris dropped a couple of coins on the only clean corner of a table and ushered Theresa by way of back alleys around the nunnery's perimeter to one of the less conspicuous entrances. Their knock brought someone eventually. Admitting the sanctuary-seeker involved a reference to authority and more delay. Harris kept expecting to see Nan Hogan come tripping around one corner of the rough grey wall or another. In the end, there was no time for more than a quick squeeze of the hand before the Church of Rome swallowed Theresa whole.

"My book, Isaac" were her last words. It had been left behind in the coffee house.

"I'll get it for you," said Harris to a door already shut.

Chapter Thirteen
Recall

Twenty minutes had passed. To avoid a broken flag in the sidewalk, Harris stepped warily out into the traffic on St. Paul Street. Waggons delivering Molson's beer and Redpath's sugar rattled by, all but grazing his elbow. Hawkers, buyers, priests and soldiers jostled and swarmed on.

Harris was coming from the Grey Nuns and was in no hurry. Indeed, it seemed to him the ideal course would have been to watch the convent-hospital around the clock, lest Theresa be removed to one of the Sisters' other establishments. They had one in Ottawa, according to the portress. Another, of which she spoke with especial pride, was at St. Boniface, north and west some fifteen hundred miles.

The news had been communicated through a slide in the main door. There he also learned that, while there was no possibility of his placing the book he had retrieved for Theresa in her own hands, he might pass it in on the understanding that the mother superior would dispose of it entirely as she saw fit. *"Que le Seigneur vous bénisse!"*

Until our next quasi-meeting, Harris translated loosely, and may it not be soon. He was now wondering how likely it was that a letter should ever escape this sanctuary and how best to occupy himself while waiting.

Ahead, the potholes lay in the road. He regained the sidewalk—uneven brick—in front of a shop bursting with *Modes Parisiennes,* which French and even more English speakers were stopping to admire.

Montreal's thoroughfares might be less well maintained than Toronto's, but business was evidently flourishing. In the two years since he had last come down for the Provincial Bank, Harris had seen lithographs of the metropolis's most notable new factories and churches and factories and public buildings and factories. Lithographs, however, never show the crowds. One and a half times Toronto's population, nearly seventy thousand persons, had squeezed into residential terraces on a strip of land between the still wooded mountain and the St. Lawrence River. There looked to be more money than places to put it. Harris decided that anyone who had missed his chance to invest in real estate here might be in the market for a detached house or three in the go-ahead Queen City of Canada West. He would advertise.

His father's hoard was dwindling, and he wanted money. Of course, all his savings would not have bought sufficient watchers to encircle the convent day and night, all sharp enough to pick from among any number of identically dressed women a particular one they had never seen. At the same time, he had to be able to retain the best lawyer available in case Crane should sue for his "conjugal rights". The phrase made Harris shudder. It blandly covered a dreadful sentence and made it sound as if the verdict were decided in advance. Even so, Theresa must be represented.

He hoped the hotel she had picked out for him was not too grand. Then he was upon it, all five storeys of it, extending ten bays down the north side of the street. Rasco's could have tucked the American in its back pocket with room to spare.

Harris entered. He got no further than a plaque commemorating the 1842 visit of Mr. Charles Dickens, beloved author of...when he felt his sleeve tweaked.

"Here's your man, constable," said a husky female voice.

Harris wheeled about to be confronted by an unsmiling individual with a black mole on his upper lip. The constable appeared altogether serious in white trousers, a high-collared blue jacket and a black top hat—to the front of which the tin numeral eight was affixed. Nan Hogan's tigerish eyes beamed the satisfaction of the hunter, while her jaw looked squarer than ever and her dress more improbably purple. Only in a riot of fashion could Harris have failed to see it coming.

"Mr. Isaac Harris?" said Constable 8.

"Yes, of course."

Harris was subpoenaed to appear and give evidence "on behalf of our Sovereign Lady the Queen" touching the death of a person or persons whose remains had been found near the village of Highland Creek and at the mouth of the Rouge River. The inquest would be held at the dwelling house of Edward Wilson in the first concession of Scarboro Township at one o'clock in the afternoon of Thursday, the 14th day of August instant. Christopher Hillyard, M.D., Coroner, County of York, had signed the summons.

"To avoid a charge of contempt," said the constable when Harris had finished reading, "I am to advise you that you will have to take passage on a westbound steamer sailing no later than noon today."

"To be paid no doubt from public funds," said Harris grimly, though the expense was not at the top of his mind. Did the police, he wondered, now know where Theresa was? Was that why the axe had been allowed to fall?

"Public funds, sir? Not that I've heard." Constable 8 touched his stick to his hat brim and turned on his heel.

"Smart, ain't he?" Nan Hogan followed the man—or perhaps his uniform—with covetous glances. "Says he used to be a fireman. Oh yes, it's all one department here. And—for your information, Mr. Isaac Harris—it's quartered in the market right across the street!"

Harris heard just enough to realize he had been careless, dreadfully so. He would have to go. Cat and mouse with Vandervoort was all very well, but to refuse a summons issued under the authority of the Crown would, he feared, quite destroy his credit and impair his usefulness to Theresa in the legal battles to come.

Nan Hogan was still at his elbow. "I could take that annoying paper back," she said, "convince him we got the wrong gent after all."

"And why," asked Harris, "would you do that?"

"Save you travelling all that way to tell the world where and when you last saw Mrs. Crane. You might tell me instead."

"And if I said it has been three years?"

"An innkeeper outside Kingston says otherwise."

Nan Hogan's gravelly chuckle irritated Harris, but her efficiency exasperated him.

"Why should Mrs. Crane's name even come up at the inquest?" he demanded. "The remains are Sibyl Martin's."

"That's for the jury to say, ain't it? Now don't be coy. If you're in Montreal, the lady's stowed here somewhere. Beneath a veil perhaps. I've remarked your interest in the Church of Rome."

"Travel is no hardship to me," said Harris bravely. She might, after all, be referring only to his passage through the cathedral in Kingston. "You're welcome to look where you please."

She tried again. The girl in violet and man in tweeds formed one of several conversational groups standing about the oak-panelled lobby of the large hotel. The province's police departments, she said slyly, were swapping little favours all the time. Toronto's wanted the credit for finding Mrs. Crane. The alternatives offered Harris were, one, to reveal Theresa's hidy-hole on the spot and be permitted to stay in Montreal or, two, to keep mum now and be forced to tell all in Toronto.

Without terminating the interview, Harris continued to affect indifference. Inwardly, he was torn. If he left, he risked missing any letter from Theresa. Suppose that tomorrow, while his steamer carried him every moment farther from her, she had conveyed to Rasco's Hotel an urgent appeal for him to remove her from the convent. Harris's stomach knotted at the thought. On the other hand, if he accepted Nan Hogan's offer, police surveillance would complicate any such removal. Moreover, the sooner Vandervoort knew where Theresa was, the sooner Crane would know, and the sooner he might interfere with her.

But the decisive defence against temptation was remembering the character of the temptress. While this thieving, coquettish, tomboy spy showed initiative far surpassing what Harris had regretfully come to expect of the constabulary, he had no confidence that Nan Hogan would honour her bargain if she could.

In her presence, he took care not to register at Rasco's. He would have a telegram sent back from Lachine. He would have to count on Theresa to weather the few—he hoped—days of his absence.

The lobby tall clock struck the half.

"I've almost a mind to come home with you," said Nan, wistful, then brightening, "but there's sport and duty here."

If the duty was looking for Mrs. Crane, Harris tacitly wished Vandervoort's agent ample occasions for the other, even at some cost to property and morals.

To be quite certain he left, she walked him to the docks. She waved him off from the top of the harbour's vast limestone revetment wall, and was quickly lost in the port traffic. Vessels from as far away as New South Wales choked the river. As the quays fell astern, Harris could barely see the city's forest of church and convent steeples for a screen of schooner masts.

He thought of Theresa with a blank page before her. "My dear Isaac," he mentally dictated.

The Grey Nuns he picked out at last from its location alone. He could not say he recognized the lantern, high tin cone and cross, having seen them first through such different eyes. Earlier, the spire had seemed poised to puncture his hopes. Now it was beckoning him back.

* * *

The frame house on Parliament Street north of Duchess appeared to have started life in the Georgian style, compact and symmetrical, but to have sprawled and rambled over its lot since. Every part, however, had been kept up. An active-looking man was applying a fresh coat of serviceable blue-grey paint even as Harris approached to confirm the name on the gatepost. A brass plate was discreetly engraved, "E. Vale."

Since disembarking, Harris had looked in vain for Jasper Small at the lawyer's office and then his rooms. It was now ten thirty on an overcast Thursday morning, the day of the inquest.

The painter looked down from the ladder.

"There's an electric bell," he bragged, "right side of the door."

If the door had no slide in it, there were plainly other ways to inspect callers. Harris pushed the bell control and knocked for good measure. Batteries could run down.

The serving woman who opened was in conversation with Mrs. Vale herself, on this occasion fully dressed. She wore a burgundy skirt and jacket, trimmed with braid and businesslike. On her head she was placing a wide-brimmed straw hat grotesquely loaded with feathers, ribbons and artificial flowers. She was speaking of cosmetics.

"Lard, rosewater and coconut milk—that's all it is. I never wash my hands without applying it. Mr. Harris! I was just on my way to the bank, but you are not there."

"No, I'm here," said Harris awkwardly enough, but with no time today for embarrassment. "In which room will I find Mr. Small?"

"It's too early to disturb him," she protested, "but some of the girls are up. There's a Mexican *señorita* I'm sure you would—"

"Your own apartments?" Harris had noted costly lace curtains at the upper windows of one of the additions. He started past Mrs. Vale towards the stairs.

The servant had not shut the outside door. "Shall I call Sampson, ma'am?"

"No need." Her mistress's larded and rosewatered hands deftly disarranged Harris's cravat. "*This* way to sugar lump, if you please."

At the risk of being led astray or into an ambush, Harris followed Mrs. Vale's over-ornamented bonnet down a back passage, past a pantry full of empty wine bottles and oyster shells, down two steps, through the kitchen and the middle of a dispute in two languages on the proper preparation of cocoa, up two steps, and around a corner. He was beginning to fear, as if sleeping in a bordello were not humiliation enough for his friend, that Small had been lodged in the servants' quarters, or in the woodpile. Then Mrs. Vale led the way into another wing. She crossed a card room with four tables, its own wine cooler, and its own door to the yard. At the far side she opened without knocking the door to an office.

Small, in evening dress, lay asleep on the ottoman. His left arm shielded his eyes from the daylight, while his right trailed to the floor. He looked, with one knee slightly bent, surprisingly graceful in his abandonment.

Without preamble, Esther Vale slapped him hard between the legs. A whimper escaped him, more like a maimed rabbit's than anything human. Harris couldn't speak. He lifted Small in his arms and carried him as from a fire out of the office and out of doors.

"Hallo, Isaac," Small said thickly. "What is it then?"

Behind them, Small's assailant had thrown up the sash of the office window.

"Until tonight, little sprout," she laughed. "No later than ten."

"What is that she's saying?"

Harris didn't answer, nor did he set Small on his feet until they were on Parliament Street in sight of a cab.

"Jasper, I've found her."

"You've changed your tie knot." Small's pale eyes blinked away most of his stupor. "Found whom?"

"Theresa. I need you to come to the inquest this afternoon."

"I'm sorry," said Small. "I wish I could feel it as I ought."

"No, no," Harris corrected, "she's alive, or was two days ago."

Small looked dubious, saw that this time there was no misunderstanding, and clasped Harris's hand.

"By God, that's wonderful," he declared wholeheartedly, "the first good news all summer—but then—"

"The inquest doesn't concern her. Jasper, that's why I want your professional advice—today, right now—to keep Theresa out of it. Your old friend Hillyard is presiding."

"Professional?" The word seemed to stir a distant memory, to recall—if only one could concentrate... "Dash it, Isaac, I'm sore. Have I been horseback riding?"

"Forget what you've been doing, and hear what's to be done."

Harris's problem was how not to tell the coroner's court where Theresa was. He asked this simple question in the cab, which he directed first to Jasper's building, and asked it again as they climbed the two steep flights of stairs to Jasper's door. From Sheridan's partner he kept nothing back. By the time Small had shaved and changed into morning coat and striped trousers, he seemed to grasp that the secret of Theresa's refuge must be kept. What strategy he contemplated, however, Harris failed to discover. Small insisted on dozing away the drive out Kingston Road, while his companion counted off the fifteen miles with foreboding.

No sooner had their cab turned in between Wilson's unpainted gateposts than Harris recognized the austerely prosperous farm as one he had stopped at on July 21 when looking for the burned shack. He had not on that occasion been invited into the kitchen, which he now found to be large, clean and plain. A room, he thought, to preclude prevarication. To accommodate the inquest, high benches had been improvised from rough planks supported by barrels. Each of the fourteen jurors was on arrival warned against splinters, and not a man of them was able when seated to touch the soles of his boots to the floor. Spectators were obliged to stand, the few chairs being reserved for the witnesses and the coroner.

Dr. Hillyard looked frail and forlorn seated by himself behind the enormous kitchen table, on which rested two wooden boxes he was doing his best to ignore. On entering, Small went to speak to him. Harris couldn't hear what passed between them, but noticed the old man start and scratch his head.

Next to arrive were Professor Bernard Lamb in his antiquated green frock coat and John Vandervoort, who spied Harris immediately and insisted on wringing his hand.

"Well done, Mr. H., I knew we should find her. Where is it

Mrs. Crane is stowed? You'll soon be telling the jury anyway, and under oath."

"Have 'we' discovered," asked Harris, "how Sibyl Martin died? I thought that was the subject of today's proceedings."

Before Vandervoort could reply, Small came and took him off Harris's hands. Jasper Small, barrister and solicitor, a pleasure to see the inspector again, and would he favour the coroner with a word?

Harris meanwhile greeted Lamb, whose good news somewhat cheered the reluctant witness. Supported by the Hon. Robert Baldwin, the chemistry professor's request had been approved, his salary to increase before Mrs. Lamb's confinement. Here was one situation saved.

Farmer Wilson was by now getting impatient. He had crops to harvest, he ringingly let it be known, and so did his neighbours on the jury. No one contradicted him. He was a hard, proud-looking man with a black fringe of beard and a permanent scowl as if he were being photographed. Arms folded, he sat in the middle of the room waiting to give his evidence. Family members approached deferentially if at all.

Shortly after one, a rattle of hoofs and wheels announced the arrival of the last participant. Tall and florid, serious but not severe, Henry Crane became the centre of attention from the moment he entered Wilson's kitchen. The rural patriarch was superseded, his dampening spell broken. The harvest was set aside in a buzz of talk about the railway and steamship baron. Was it not true, a spectator leaned over to ask Harris, that Mr. Crane was involved in the laying of a transatlantic telegraph cable?

Harris didn't know, was too preoccupied even to guess. He was mentally contrasting Crane's current composure with his agitation on the occasion of their last meeting. Crane would affect not to remember the scuffle on the Great Western. And what would he remember of his wife? With rumours now in circulation of her being seen alive, should he not be showing more anxiety regarding her condition? So much the better for Theresa if he truly cared nothing for her return. Ha! *There* was wishful thinking.

Crane was today accompanied by a grey-haired lawyer Harris had met socially and had heard highly praised. Together with his client, L.L. Matheson took possession of an unused end of the kitchen table and spread out his notes. Dr. Hillyard raised no objection.

A local constable then proclaimed the court open, and the coroner began by calling over the names of the jurors. Small returned to Harris's side.

"I tried," he whispered, "to get the old fossil to cancel proceedings, in view of the uninformative condition of the remains, but it seems he needs the money."

"Was it fear of lost income that made him jump like that?"

"Like what?" said Small absently. "His fee won't reach fifteen dollars—even if he spins things out over two days."

The prospect of having things spun out made Harris squirm. He burned to be back in Montreal. Small said he would next attempt to prevent other witnesses and members of the public from hearing Harris's testimony.

The roll taken, the constable opened the two boxes. The jury were then called forward to view the two collections of bones, a complete skeletal arm in one case, calcined fragments in the other. Random gasps and exclamations brought Small to his feet. He moved that in the interests of decency the inquest be held in private. Spectators hissed this suggestion. The coroner, after calling querulously for order, rejected it.

The jurors were sworn in the presence of the bones, whose examination was the next order of business. No new facts emerged. No cause of death could be assigned. The court rituals were new to Harris, but, under present circumstances, of little interest—with one exception. Jurors were formally advised to observe the bearing and conduct of the parties in attendance, in case one of them betray a guilty knowledge.

Most eyes went scurrying around the room. Harris's went straight to Crane, who leaned back in his chair at his ease. Noticing Harris for the first time, he nodded gravely, betraying neither qualms nor bravado. The coroner's method had nothing here upon which to work; for what could observation reveal about a man so dead to feelings of culpability? Harris bobbed his head in grim acknowledgement of his late assailant.

And the inquest ground on. While directing the jury's attention to one feature or another of the remains, Dr. Hillyard incidentally criticized the police department for having removed them from the sites of their discovery. Inspection of these sites—one on the neighbouring property, one at two miles distance—consumed the balance of the afternoon.

Lamb's photograph helped direct the assembly to the exact spot where the arm had been found. After nearly four weeks, Harris stood again on the sandbar. His throat tickled with the memory of what he had at first thought a dead fish, and his sympathy quickened for a woman he had never known—but he could no longer do full justice to the horror of that other grey afternoon. His worst fears then had not been realized.

Other fears for Theresa pricked him now—relapse into illness, a nun's vocation, persecution by Crane, betrayal by an unguarded response of his own. *Observe the parties in attendance.* Harris turned to ask Small how, under direct questioning, to keep her whereabouts concealed.

Small was no longer anywhere in sight. Harris worked around the periphery of the inquest, his feet sinking in the soft sand at the water's edge. Had anyone seen the grey-eyed city man with wavy hair? Yes, a farm labourer claimed to have been asked where in the neighbourhood you could get a glass of French wine, or at least a pennyworth of white whisky.

Harris lifted his face to the heavens, which spat on it their first drops. Rain would further impede the already interrupted harvest, but the farmers took acts of God with restrained dignity. "Sent to try us" was the common view. The ex-banker wondered whether he himself would have found religious belief an asset or a liability.

Small, meanwhile, had gone for a drink.

* * *

All participants save the coroner wanted to conclude the inquest in one day, and so after a recess for refreshment, the witnesses were heard.

Towards seven thirty, evening drew in around the farm kitchen. As lamps were lit and hung, Harris noted a change in the spectators. Idlers had drifted away to taverns and not returned—to be replaced by men who, before dusk and rain abbreviated their labours, had more productive employment than cramming their heads with stories of old bones. Small did return—dulled, thought Harris, but not disgracefully drunk. He said he had planted a seed with Hillyard and they would just have to see whether it sprouted.

Farmer Wilson was sworn first. He established the time of the fire, having seen the embers smoking when he rose before five on the morning of July 16. Once satisfied that his own property was not in danger, he got on with his work. He had not snooped around, he said.

Then Vandervoort told of his discoveries at the fire site. The axe head and green fabric seemed to link these remains to the arm, while the key to Sheridan's kitchen gave the jury its first hope of identifying the deceased. Who, one member asked, had a copy of this key? Harris pricked up his ears. With a respectful nod in Crane's direction, the red-haired police detective replied that that would be for other witnesses to say.

The coroner had questions of his own for Vandervoort. Did he know Sibyl Martin? Yes, he had last seen her at about eleven thirty on the morning of July 13, at which time he had had her released from police custody. Her dress had been brown homespun. She had been William Sheridan's housekeeper and suspected of her employer's murder before it had been determined that his death was natural. She had had no keys in her possession when she left Station No. 1. She left with Mr. Henry Crane. Again Vandervoort nodded towards him.

If the assembly had shown interest in Crane before, they were now on the tips of their toes and the edge of their plank seats to hear what he would say. No one had had a chance to chat with him. During the intermission, he had retired to his carriage with his legal adviser—supposedly to consume delicacies too rare for any present but the journalists to imagine.

"It's other men's work that fills his gut," muttered one detractor. "Now move your head so I can see."

Harris had left Crane alone. The only motive for doing otherwise would have been to provoke the industrialist to some fresh hot-tempered attack, the effect of which on such awe-struck bystanders Harris judged too uncertain. Witnesses might put the wrong man in gaol, and Theresa would be worse off than before.

Then again, Crane might not have risen to the bait. The unhesitating ease with which he proceeded to the witness chair Harris had not seen him exhibit at any time in the past month. Theresa's husband apprehended no threat from coroner or jury, but it was more than that. Some other cloud had lifted from his spirit.

He readily admitted he had been wrong to let his wife go riding on July 13, the day following her father's demise. She had left soon after the noon meal, about two p.m. He had not seen her since, and his last memories of her were still painfully vivid. The silver bracelet in evidence had been on her right wrist. He likewise identified the green sleeve as belonging to the riding habit she wore.

Her father had given her a key to his villa. Crane had not seen whether she took it with her, but neither had he subsequently found it among her personal possessions. He could account for William Sheridan's own key and for the one formerly in the housekeeper's charge. He knew of no other copies.

One of the duties associated with winding up his late father-in-law's household had been settling accounts with Sibyl Martin. William Sheridan had treated servants generously, and Crane wished to honour his memory.

"I don't blame Mrs. Crane in the least," he said, "but in the first access of her grief, she had the poor woman locked up on suspicion of poisoning our father."

From where Harris stood, he could see only the back of Crane's head, with its yellowish fringe and cherub-pink bull's eye. Crane's unmusical voice, however, plainly carried homegrown authority. For all his money and turns of phrase, he was heard to be "from around here." There had already been murmured condemnations of emerald green as a colour of mourning, and now auditors seemed disposed to make fewer allowances for Mrs. Crane than did her bereft husband.

"On learning that he had not died poisoned," Crane continued, "I did what I could to deliver the Martin woman, as I'm confident her late employer would have wished."

Heads bobbed sympathetically, including Hillyard's.

Deliverance could not be effected until the morning of July 13. To make amends, Crane had driven Sibyl from the lock-up to Sheridan's villa that she might collect her belongings, and thence to the coach office. She was no longer required in Toronto and had pressing family business near Kingston. Crane had not stayed to see her board the one-o'clock eastbound, but had left some minutes earlier to pick up Mrs. Crane at church. He had not seen the housekeeper again.

He sounded most credible. Still, Harris knew he was wrong about the sleeve. It wasn't from Theresa's habit, however uncannily similar. And could Theresa really have worn the bracelet of silver medallions when she went riding on July 13? If so, then—in order for Harris to find it six days later—she must have parted with it again well before the robbery on August 3. She had told Harris, though, that her assailant had taken all the jewellery she had with her. Crane must be lying.

The coroner was falling behind in his transcription of testimony, true and false. His pen scratched ploddingly across his page. Belatedly he ruled that Sibyl's "family business" was hearsay, and the jury were to disregard it. Small roused himself to remark behind his hand that Hillyard always lost steam by this time of day, and that they might be in for a continuance after all.

"Can't you move that coffee be served?" Harris whispered back in frustration.

Small smiled enigmatically.

The jury foreman asked Crane which of Mrs. Crane's possessions besides the key were missing after her departure. Crane's lawyer objected on grounds of relevancy, and Hillyard concurred, sparing the husband any discourteous speculation as to whether his wife had meant to desert him. Crane volunteered that their years together had been very happy. He missed her every single day.

Following so noble and well-received an admission, the evidence of the glove-maker made too little impression even to count as anticlimax. Until called forward, he had been standing behind taller spectators. Harris had not previously remarked him and, still stunned by Crane's hypocrisy, could find little to remember the new witness by—a mousy demeanour, perhaps, and a rusty black suit. Given the dimensions of the Rouge Valley hand, he testified, it could not have been Mrs. Crane's. Mrs. Crane's was two full sizes smaller. From this position there was no shaking him, and he was speedily excused.

Then it was Harris's turn. He was to testify last, it seemed, for no better reason than that he had been the last witness found. He stopped fretting about Crane's deceits and resumed fretting about his own.

The state of his nerves recalled his first anxious days as cashier of the Toronto branch of the Provincial Bank, the first opening of the vault, the first closing, most of all the first letter to head office. It concerned a default. He trembled then for his career, but never considered any course other than perfect candour—whose eventual cost would be his alone to bear.

His path today was foggier. He felt heartsick at the prospect of making the jury believe what he knew to be false, doubted indeed that he could do so, and yet doubted as fiercely that Theresa's interests didn't require him to sacrifice his scruples and mislead the court. As he made unhappily to rise, Small restrained him.

"Speak the truth," the lawyer commanded *sotto voce*, "strictly the truth whatever the question. You've too much conscience and too simple a mental engine to make any kind of convincing liar. Refuse the oath."

Harris begged his pardon, but Small was now propelling him forward in response to the constable's stern repetition of his name. The coroner had Harris state it once more himself. That much was easy.

"Abode?" said Hillyard.

Harris groped for the strict truth. In Canada East he had a room he had never seen, in Canada West one where he had not slept in over a fortnight.

"Speak up, speak up."

"Toronto," said Harris, "the American Hotel." He knew the next question would be more embarrassing.

"Occupation?"

"None."

Dr. Hillyard sat up and shook the bread crumbs from his waistcoat. "According to my information, you are a bank cashier."

"Not since July 25, sir."

"'Gentleman' then," said the coroner, pursing his lips as he penned the word. "Well now, right hand on the Book. The evidence which you shall give to this inquest on behalf of our Sovereign Lady the Queen, touching the death of this person or these persons unknown, shall be the truth, the whole truth, and nothing but the truth. So help you God."

Harris said nothing. He had hoped to make even less of an impression than the glove-maker, but his very quietness was attracting attention. Spectators stopped shuffling. Jurors gawked at the silent witness. What had Small meant by telling him to refuse the oath?

"So help you God," the coroner insisted. "Say it."

"Dr. Hillyard," Small objected, "as I have already had the honour of informing you, Mr. Harris is an infidel."

The term set the farm kitchen popping with expressions of incredulity, which Hillyard did nothing to suppress.

"I can't take your word for that," he said.

"All I ask is that you question him directly if you did not have an opportunity to do so on the *voir dire.*"

Voir dire? What this see-say might be Harris had no idea, but he gathered that Small was pointing out as diplomatically as possible that Hillyard had neglected some part of his duties.

"Oh, all right, Small," moaned the coroner, scrabbling through his manual with moistened fingers. "I am to determine whether you, Isaac Harris, are such an infidel as to be incompetent to give evidence. You shall true answer make to all such questions as the court shall demand of you. So help you God. Do you believe in a future state of rewards and punishments, in this world or the next?"

"No, sir."

Harris felt a dolt for not having seen sooner what Small was about, for not having discovered this escape hatch for himself. The oath had seemed to him a pure formality. Such an out-and-out materialist as medical witness Bernard Lamb had taken it without an instant's hesitation.

"You do believe in life everlasting, do you not?"

"No, sir."

"For shame," someone cried, to general approval.

"Order," said Hillyard. "Do you believe in God, Mr. Harris. Think before answering."

Yellow lamplight cast in relief the jurors' lean, mistrustful faces. Isaac Harris had grown up at his father's mill among farmers like these, and from them he would never have chosen to divide himself by raising the present question. But he was in no doubt now, his course of action clear. Little as he relished offending the sensibilities and inciting the wrath of Scarboro's Christian yeomanry, he must prefer such consequences to perjuring himself or—by refusing to speak—incurring a charge of contempt.

"No, Dr. Hillyard, I do not believe in God."

It took Hillyard some moments to restore order. A babe in arms woke with the commotion, which it then augmented. The atheist had made the infant cry.

"Who summoned him as a witness in the first place?" Harris heard someone behind him say. It seemed prudent not to look around.

"Constable," cried the coroner, "the next person who speaks out of turn is to be shown the door. Is that understood? Now, Mr. Harris—"

Hillyard mouthed the name with distaste. Older palates are finicky, thought Harris, and sensitive to shocks. He prayed that this senescent voice of order might say nothing inadvertently to inflame the volatile gathering.

"—I understand that other witnesses can in part supply the lack of your testimony, but that it will take some days to bring them before us. You have caused an adjournment that will incommode many people. Still, I suppose you cannot have foreseen that consequence when you formed your religious beliefs. You are excused."

On rising, Harris found himself the object of Crane's study. If the witness would bear such opprobrium for the sake of disqualifying himself, he had a secret worth knowing. Crane's wide-spaced, hazel eyes had never looked so small and shrewd.

"For the accommodation of the jury," Small rose to suggest, "might the adjournment be for two weeks? By then I understand the harvest will be complete."

So urging, the man who had exposed the infidel made himself still more popular with those present, who seemed in the theological excitement to have lost the thread of the inquest in any case. To L.L. Matheson fell the unhappy duty of pointing out that so lengthy a delay was most irregular. Mr. Small's client had, moreover, been excused. Matheson challenged Mr. Small's right to make submissions of any sort.

"That will do," announced the evidently fatigued coroner. "I am not used to having my inquests punctuated by the continual eructations of counsel. I'll entertain no more of them, *from any quarter*. Risk of the body's deterioration would normally prohibit a fortnight's interruption in proceedings, but we are dealing here with bones and bone fragments. They'll keep. The jurors' attendance will be required again here on Thursday, the 28th day of August at one o'clock in the afternoon precisely."

Harris and Small slipped out to their waiting cab before the closing formalities had been completed. The evening steamers to Montreal had long since sailed. To thank his friend, Harris offered to treat him to a late supper. He had a question for Small too.

"Who are these witnesses you nominated to take my place?"

"Any of the innkeepers who saw Theresa whole after the remains were found, Crusher Martin's keepers."

"Will his arm-breaking confession be ruled out as hearsay?"

"He's dead, different rules." Small yawned. "The Lansing woman sounds an unpromising witness, but I threw her name in for luck. With that lot the jury should at least identify the deceased as Sibyl, though they won't be indicting Crane for her murder, if that's what you were hoping. Poor creature! Dismembered, incinerated. How she died we may never know."

Theresa must know, thought Harris, might indeed already have told him. He wished himself at Rasco's, with his mail.

"I should be halfway down the lake by now if Hillyard had only examined me before the inquest began."

"As he ought to have done," Small affirmed, "but the old pustule didn't want to lose a witness and flatly refused to believe so sober-looking a gentleman would publicly proclaim himself a heathen."

"I'm just relieved not to have been tarred and feathered." Harris stuck his head out the cab window into the soft, steady rain to make sure there was no sign of pursuit. No, none.

He laughed aloud. What a trick Small had played on him, the two of them had played on Hillyard! What social and legal consequences his declared irreligion might entail Harris was as far from considering as pole from pole.

"It's a fine night, after all," he said, wiping his face. "Where shall we eat?"

"Not tonight, Isaac. I'm promised."

"Not to...?"

Small shrugged. In the damp air, the horsehair upholstery smelled of neglect.

"That's madness, Jasper. The woman struck you in your sleep."

"Aha. Why did she do that?"

"Why? To show she owns you, I suppose." High spirits had passed into high indignation, without which Harris couldn't have brought himself to allude to the *liaison.* "Break with her," he urged. "You still have a talent for the law."

"The spark went with Sheridan."

"No, I saw it today. Break with her before she kills it. I don't advise whoring—but you can do better, even among whores."

"You've acquired some experience then." Small settled more snugly into his corner of the rattling cab. "Dear wicked Esther," he mused. "You know, I've been drawing inspiration from her plump thighs all evening. She does own me—and I advise you to keep well out of sight of the police. Forget about eating in public. Crane will insist on your being questioned within an inch of your life, oaths optional."

Resignedly Harris let Small and his inspiration be. Small's warning made sense, however, and Harris thought of Theresa's precarious cloister. He thought of her slender ungloved hand laying a compress on a sick child's forehead in the Grey Nuns' foundling wing.

Unknown to him, she sat before a blank sheet of paper.

Chapter Fourteen
The Letter

Grey Nunnery, Montreal
Friday, 15th August

Letter writing harder than I thought. Am sorely out of practice. I used to write long letters to my mother, though she died before I was ten days old. Addressed them to Heaven and gave them to Papa to post.

Because she had cholera, they would not let her hold me. It's not a quiet end. I've read that when your body is drained dry, you groan with cramps for hours. It's mostly fatal still. Papa never talked about her illness, but in his own last days he railed against the ship-owners for bringing us the cholera epidemic of '32. Many at the time blamed the immigrant passengers, even tho' they suffered worst. Here in Montreal, the Grey Nuns marched bravely off to nurse them in the fever sheds at Point St. Charles, where the rwy. bridge is being built.

They did the same fifteen years later when typhus broke out. Parliament was sitting in Montreal. I was in lodgings with Papa. I wasn't allowed out, but from my window saw these women pass in their drab, Quakerish dresses and black bonnets, and marvelled that they always made a point of visiting those with infectious diseases.

Must collect the eggs now. If diligent, hope to be allowed to nurse, but perhaps the sisters consider me the infectious one on account of my Protestant religion. More soon.

17th August

Have suffered a mild relapse and been ordered to my bed. While I no longer have access to quinine, the dispensing sister has administered an herbal febrifuge. All that is prescribed now is rest, which I intend to borrow from to write to you. I promised you an explanation. Here it is.

The sisters will suppose I am making peace with my husband. You will read how likely this is.

I don't propose to enter into detail as to why I married Henry. I admired his mature energy. I don't say I loved him for his steamships or his railways, but he made you believe he was contributing to his age. His eye saw the future. His shoulder turned the wheel of progress.

My pampered upbringing made me no keen judge of character. Furthermore, though I doted on my father, I didn't believe he had that variety of judgment to teach me. I dispensed with Papa's guidance, and he indulged my choice.

At the time I accepted Henry, I believed you wanted no more from me than the fraternal companionship we had been enjoying. Too late, I knew I had mistaken you both.

Isaac, our marriage brought no joy.

Perhaps Henry didn't notice. Once a project is completed, he looks to the next. Once his bride was secured, he cared only that his wife decorously perform her duties. He had no more conversation, no more visions to unfold. He had expended all on courting. Apart from his physical attentions, which were never other than painful and perfunctory, he paid me scarcely any attention at all. Why had he wanted me? As a catch, I think, to be mounted and displayed.

The abruptness of his transformation from persuasive suitor to indifferent husband stupefied me. For months, I doubted it. I had never met such coldness. I tried to find out if I were doing something to displease him, or whether he had learned anything to my discredit, but he would admit to no change in his feelings towards me. Eventually I began to suspect there were other women and by then was grateful to them for sparing me his company. I filled my days with study and charitable work. I visited Papa.

You must not suppose, Isaac, that I loved my father too dearly to make a good wife. When I married, I took my husband a whole heart, moving into his house without regret. While Henry professed to understand and to admire the strength of my filial sentiments, so long as I had not quite despaired of his esteem, and for a good while after, I gave him no demonstration of those sentiments that could incite the least envy of his father-in-law. Years passed.

Now for Sibyl Martin. I'll introduce her as I first made her acquaintance. You ask about her end, but if I am to make you understand anything, I must take each fact and impression in order.

While law and Parliament absorbed my father's keenest energies, his servants came and went. You know how Papa was. Last March or April, without taking advice, he engaged a new housekeeper.

I had misgivings, starting with her family.

Sibyl and her twin brother Charles were born out of wedlock in the back woods of Simcoe County. My father had defended Charles Martin on a murder charge and saved him from the noose once by adducing evidence that his victim had a weak heart and that a healthier man would have survived his blows. Martin's life was spared, but even a Penitentiary sentence was too much for his parents to bear. Considering it a judgment on their unsanctified union, they drowned themselves. A violent heritage and no mistake.

My alarm grew when I learned Sibyl's former employer was Orange Grand Master. Orangemen hated my father as they did Robert Baldwin, hated them for being Protestant Irish and still having campaigned to suppress the Lodge. The bill didn't pass, but it made Papa enemies. I read his mail.

He tried to assure me that Sibyl took no interest in questions of politics or religion, but I thought her possibly just close-lipped. She was quiet certainly, to the point of stealthiness. She made too little noise. I would be discussing something with Papa, look up, and there she would be, clearing away the tea things. "Tell her not to come till she's rung for," I suggested. He didn't see the necessity.

You will recall how he used to wink at informality. She took ample advantage. Or perhaps it would be fairer to say that mistrust quickened my sense of her shortcomings.

In the keeper of my father's house, I should have been reassured to see good spirits and a spruce demeanour. Sibyl showed neither. While she kept his villa clean enough, her skin looked grey and waxy, as if personally she never scrubbed. She had a slovenly slouch. Her perpetual mud-brown dresses she wore loose, sacrificing smartness and convenience to her comfort. And still her mouth took a grudging twist. In her fourth decade, she seemed to want it known she had lived through a long succession of unrewarding years. Papa paid her well, gave her a full day off each week, seldom criticized. You would never have thought it to see her. By the time she entered his employ, I suppose her discontented mien was set.

You will think me harsh, Isaac, possibly jealous. It was true that this woman occupied the place for which I should have bartered my own chilly hearth in an instant. I tried to think better of her and succeeded pretty well until Papa's last illness.

The legislative session that ended 1st July left him exhausted. I expect you know as much as I about the political tug of war that has been going on. Your friend William Sheridan had fought his proudest battles as a reformer, but George Brown's party of radical reform was sounding increasingly anti-Catholic, while progressive conservative John A. Macdonald spoke more appealingly of making friends with the French. Both sides wooed Papa fiercely. At the same time, he was undertaking a case or a cause of some kind which seemed to shake him to his foundations, and yet which he did not feel he could ease his spirit by telling me about.

He enjoyed robust health generally, as you'll recall. In recent years, however, he had suffered recurrent bouts of debilitating abdominal pain, diagnosed as iliac passion or inflammation of the intestines. They chose this moment of nervous strain to flare up once more.

Over the next days, I spent less and less time at Henry's, more and more at Papa's, till I was in effect living there. Then Sibyl was the jealous one. "You go on home, Mrs. Crane," she would say. "I can do everything here." This although she knew nothing of nursing. Used to free rein, she apparently considered herself mistress of Front Street and resented dilution, however temporary or exceptional, of her authority.

Unluckily, her brother's devastating news arrived this same week. He had committed another assault and was in a month's time to hang for it. I offered Sibyl leave and her steamer ticket. She said she preferred to wait till her master was out of danger, as we all believed he soon would be, but I should have insisted. She became positively obstructive in the kitchen. Accidents happened.

On Friday, 11th July, I went down early to light a fire after sitting up all night with Papa. He could not sleep for stomach aches. His temperature had risen above 100, and I feared peritonitis might have set in. Dr. Hillyard had left him morphine. He would not take it. He didn't complain, but kept rolling that enormous, white-thatched head of his as if to avoid meeting the eye of some impudent lobbyist or favour-seeker. Pain had dug deeper the furrows that ran from his nose to the corners of his mouth. The skin seemed to have lost its resiliency.

Isaac, I cannot tell you what I felt. I have not the skill, the time, or a steady enough hand. That night I believed Papa and I were coming as close to a goodbye as we ever would, and I was right, even though he got better.

He asked me to read him his favourite verses by Thomas Moore. I have always read badly, too fast and without enough expression. It didn't matter. More often he recited from memory:

"Row, brothers, row, the stream runs fast,
The Rapids are near and the daylight's past."

And from the *Irish Melodies*:

"The heart that has truly loved never forgets,
But as truly loves on to the close..."

At ten to four, he stopped tossing and reciting. When I let the lamplight fall on his face, his eyes under his great white brows were purposeful, though weary. He said the pain was subsiding and, in answer to my question, that he thought, yes, he might sleep, but he would like to shave first, as he expected Jasper that morning with documents pertaining to their new case. I said I should scrape his face gladly if he were still awake by the time I had heated the water.

On bare feet, I slipped down to the kitchen. Sibyl's room adjoined it, but I didn't hear her stirring, and it was too early to wake her. My guard was down, as you can imagine. After what had seemed a death watch, I felt blessed release plus the fatigue that anxiety had kept me from admitting. I went straight to the stove. As I raised the top to see if a fire had been laid, I glimpsed a flicker of flame at my elbow, just under the sleeve of my light summer nightgown.

"That's my job, Mrs. Crane," said Sibyl, reaching forward and dropping the lighted match into the stove.

I jumped back with I don't recall what exclamation. As soon as I had ascertained that I wasn't on fire, I gave Sibyl the day off and insisted she leave the house before breakfast, which I made myself. I intended once Papa had rested to ask him to dismiss her altogether.

Towards noon, a knock at the front door awakened him. It was not Jasper, whom he had been expecting, but Henry, who was usually too busy to appear during the day or for that matter the evening either.

Henry and his father-in-law were not bosom friends. Having married freely, I never complained of my choice, but if my marriage had been conspicuously happier, I suppose Papa would have found it easier to warm to Henry. He sincerely admired Henry's initiative. Both were self-made men, albeit with a difference characteristic of their generations. Papa required a competency. Henry has always hungered for a fortune. Papa believed good government would as a matter of fact be good for business. Henry thinks the sole measure of whether a government is or is not good is whether it advances business interests.

Perhaps the two could never have been close. In argument, Henry kept making the practical mistake of invoking profits rather than ideals. You observed justly, Isaac, when years ago you said that Parliament itself was Papa's El Dorado, its civilizing rituals his streets of gold. A man's right to elect his legislators or stand himself for election, the legislators' right to topple a ministry in which they lack confidence—these were his spoils of office.

William Sheridan and his gang fought the constitutional battles of the age. Henry Crane's attitude is: now that that's settled, let's get rich.

He was cordial with Papa but never seemed to succeed in interesting him in his schemes and rarely called unless he had a scheme in which he wished to interest him. This Friday, I asked Henry to keep his visit short.

I went to get him after fifteen or twenty minutes, and the two of us spoke for a moment in the upstairs hall. He looked grave but calm, and tall and pink as ever. I caught a whiff of the sandalwood soap I had once liked so well on him. He never smells of liquor or tobacco.

"Your father seems out of the rough water," he began stiffly.

I assented, hoping he would go now.

"It has been a trying time," he rushed on. "Very hard on you. On the housekeeper as well."

"Has she told you this?" I asked. It typified relations between us that my feelings meant no more to him than Sibyl's.

Henry shrugged. "Better leave the cooking to her."

"On the contrary," I said, "Sibyl has shown she's not to be trusted with fire. I'll fill her place."

"Papa tells me he's not dissatisfied with her. As for you, you are too little at home, our home, as it is."

You can guess how I resented this appropriation of my father against me. In aversion rather than submission, I dropped my eyes. From where I stood squeezed between Henry and the topmost stair, the freshly waxed banister spiralled down in a long, graceful oval. Its normally pleasing curve dizzied me. Mastering my tongue, I suggested we pursue our talk below, farther from the sickroom. Henry said he had not time. Business would not stand still. His last words to me before shutting the front door on any chance of rebuttal were an injunction to compose my differences with Sibyl.

Jasper arrived mid-afternoon. As I came down to answer his knock, I was astonished to see Sibyl had already let him in and was busy brushing his bowler hat. He was late, he knew. He had just come from successfully defending an illiterate nine-year-old girl against the enforcement of an indenture. He thought, rightly, his senior partner would be pleased. I sent him up to wait for Papa to waken while I had words with the unsheddable housekeeper. What did she mean by returning so soon?

She professed anxiety for her master. As soon as ever he was on his feet, she would gladly leave for Kingston. Meanwhile, idle hours were torment to her. What with "the Honourable" indisposed and her brother under sentence, she had passed a weary night of it and risen in a fog. She professed herself contrite for her carelessness at the stove. Henceforth, she would submit to my orders. I made her no promises, but neither did I throw her out the door, and presently she served Jasper and me tea in the parlour.

He found me in more distress than Papa's condition seemed to warrant. I hesitated to explain.

I have known Jasper since girlhood, of course. Our fathers

did business before he thought of a legal career. He was my first dance partner. He used to tell people whom he didn't think it would shock that our courtship never went farther because his limbs would not fit over a horse and mine would not fit under a card table. The truth is he's so easy and pleasant with everyone that I could never imagine him forming any restrictive attachment.

This afternoon he had papers for Papa he wished he could tell me about. Toronto's social order might be shaken, but the implications reached beyond that, much. I thought such excitement best deferred till Papa was stronger. Jasper fidgeted and remarked on my agitation. He had sworn secrecy. I didn't press him. Nonetheless, he insisted on advising me, as an old playmate, to see less in future of the MacFarlanes. He could not say more.

To change the subject, I complained of the hot sun beating in and made some adjustment to the curtains.

He had said enough to make me quite lonely. I had fallen away from all the girls I had gone to school with. They had married well or supposed I had. My friends would be few indeed without Kate MacFarlane and her daughter Elsie. In whom could I confide regarding the mad-seeming housekeeper? Jasper? Confidences plainly weren't safe with him.

I thought then to ask him about you, Isaac, hoping his indiscretion this time might work in my favour. It did, in the end. I could not approach you directly when you had made such a point of keeping away. You certainly owed me nothing. What I was hoping was that, if you had stopped thinking about what might have been, I should be able to stop too, and together we could solve the riddle of Sibyl's behaviour.

A moment later I glimpsed around the door jamb a twitch of brown worsted in the hall. The mirror didn't need polishing, the pictures straightening, the clock winding. I rushed straight out to see what reason other than eavesdropping Sibyl could have for being there. Jasper doubtless thought me mad.

Sibyl had "meant no disrespect" by loitering in the hall. On the contrary, she said. She had not wanted to anger me, either by interrupting my conversation with Jasper, or by failing to consult me regarding Papa's supper menu. Did I not think a suet pudding would lift his spirits?

I rejected the suggestion firmly. Intestines which barely twelve hours earlier had been so excruciatingly inflamed would rebel afresh, perhaps fatally, at such a greasy mass. A glass of buttermilk was the most that should be thought of. Buttermilk, yes, missus. How fortunate, said Sibyl, she had come upstairs to ask my wishes before proceeding!

Again that night I sat up with Papa. He slept well and, not having been to bed for several days, I dozed from time to time myself. On the morning of the "Glorious Twelfth", I brought him from his own garden a bouquet not of orange lilies but of white English daisies and made as unalarming a case as possible for helping the housekeeper to another situation. He had often employed charitable cases before, but never, I pointed out, in such a position of trust.

"I'm sure you have your reasons, my dear terrier," he said, "but her brother's last trial seems to have been such a rushed business, and the sentence too harsh for a simple assault. I should hate to lose sight of Sibyl until I've done what I can in the way of appeal. Brother love runs strong in their family, too strong, I'm afraid."

I asked what he meant.

"Did you not hear why their parents couldn't marry?" he said. "Not to put too fine a point on it, their uncle was their father, their mother their aunt."

This news made Sibyl more pitiable in my eyes: guiltless, she must bear not only the shame of illegitimacy but the more intimate taint of inbreeding. Justice herself must weep. Pity, however, was beside the point I was urging. Let the poor woman be treated with exemplary kindness, let her be lodged with every comfort in the American Hotel, so long as she was removed from the possibility of doing harm in this house. Not as a punishment, but as a precaution.

Papa nonetheless hesitated at this anxious time to add to her burdens by any show of want of confidence. The matter remained unresolved when Dr. Hillyard arrived.

Some think Christopher Hillyard should have retired from the practice of medicine years ago. In fact, he did and went to live abroad, but he pined for his city and his profession and last April returned to both. (That he also lost his savings in a railway stock swindle is a rumour he won't confirm.) Dr. H. attended my birth and my mother's death. As a family friend, he is supposed to be above censure, but I should frankly have wished a different physician for Papa this summer.

I do not share Jasper's objections to the porriginous eruptions on the doctor's scalp. These are not communicable. What I do regret is the doctor's refusal to speak to me in anything but platitudes. The practitioner's traditional reticence towards the laity has in his case been reinforced by prejudice against any female who interests herself in indelicate subjects, especially one he recalls and still thinks of as an infant.

On 12th July I asked if, now that Papa's pains had subsided, the danger of an abscess could be ruled out. Dr. H. would not say. I asked if I might attend his examination of Papa. Dr. H. refused.

The two were alone together so long that after forty minutes, I tapped on the bedroom door and entered. I overheard Papa say, "Never fear, Chris. I have the document here safe in my box." When he saw me, Papa begged I would excuse them a little longer and assured me the consultation was no longer medical but legal. His words were cheerful. And yet the weight of grief in his eyes convinced me they were discussing that society-shaking lawsuit on which I partially blamed his attack. I gave them the time it would take me to fetch the doctor a dram of Irish whisky. After that, business talk must wait till Monday.

On his departure, Dr. H. authorized his patient to get out of bed for an hour or two. Wrapped in a pearl grey dressing gown, Papa went straight to a window overlooking the harbour. As you know, Isaac, no house in town has windows the size of his, as his bills for heating fuel each winter can attest. This day, however, no window would have been large enough. He must throw up the nine-pane sash, stick his great white head out into the street and have a proper look around.

The panorama he commanded was of Toronto on semi-official holiday. Orangemen in a position to do so seemed to have given themselves a Saturday off work, while the rest made work as little burdensome as possible. Stevedores passed whisky bottles between lifting bales. More pleasure craft than usual sat with limp sails on the glassy bay, and the steam ferries to the peninsula wove less certainly than usual between them. At the foot of Bay Street bathers waded into the foul harbour waters for some relief from summer's heat. Behind them on the Esplanade, an impromptu horse race almost bowled over wearers of the newest and brightest hoop skirts, while a locomotive lazily shunting cars into the semblance of a train counterpointed with its puffs and clangs a brass band marshalling for the parade.

When at last I coaxed Papa inside and combed the smuts from his mane, his thick eyebrows were bristling gloomily. He fretted that the open view his house enjoyed would not be open much longer. When the aldermen had allowed railway track to be laid along the water's edge, he said, the Esplanade's fate had been sealed. It was axiomatic. Where railways ran, warehouses and factories would cluster. City Council, dominated though it was by railway men, would have to move their City Hall uptown just to escape the stench. Villas such as Bishop Strachan's and Papa's would become uninhabitable, valuable only for the land beneath them.

I reminded Papa he was not in Parliament and need not repeat himself.

"Well, terrier," he replied, "I've constituents with more pressing problems. I had best look to my long-neglected correspondence."

"I'll be your amanuensis," I said, fetching his lap desk. "Answer a pleasant letter first."

He replied that pleasant letters rarely required the quickest answers, but that here at least was a diverting tragedy, a constituent's complaint against his neighbour's goat. We were both laughing when Sibyl came up with an urgent message for me. She took the opportunity of asking, now her master was sounding so much improved, whether he had yet asked the Governor to pardon her brother.

"Not yet, my dear," he said, wiping a tear of mirth. It plainly embarrassed him that he couldn't quite stop smiling. "Come back in half an hour, Sibyl. We'll speak of it then."

She glided out in sullen silence, her eyes on the floor.

My envelope contained Henry's summons home. I doubted it was urgent but could not disobey. I prepared Papa a light lunch, obtained his promise to rest after eating it, and left him for Queen Street East.

I never heard his voice again.

Hours later

Ague chills compelled pause. I'm now in fever stage. Thoughts tumbling, but hand steadier.

Don't expect me to remember all the pretexts Henry had for detaining me that Saturday afternoon. Believe I was to organize a 12-course dinner for 20 princes of capital, or perhaps the other way round. He was jealous. I suspected no further motive.

While he was home, I kept up the charade. I clipped roses for his table from trellises running the length of the south verandah. And I dragooned Oscar into cleaning French windows. The dining room is lined with them. Ten minutes after Henry left (for his office, he said) so did I, although our butler tried to detain me with every vexatious excuse.

At Front Street, I found Papa napping: his pulse strong and steady. Sibyl served me tea in the parlour. Bitter taste, but did not complain. Very tired after nights of watching and struggles with Sibyl, doctor, Henry. Reclined on sofa for five or ten minutes as I intended. The hall clock had just struck five.

Awoke mildly nauseous. Perspiring heavily, although sun no longer beat in through south windows. Knew it must be late. Bestirred myself. Through twilight saw room door closed, unlike before. Not locked. Went out into hall and found clock hands stood after eight. Three hours gone.

No whisper from anywhere in the house, just a cooking smell that seemed out of place.

Run upstairs felt like snail's crawl. Papa lay peacefully on his back, not a characteristic sleeping posture for him. Skin clammy, no pulse. I lit a lamp and one by one lifted his cooling eyelids. Neither pupil reacted to light. No breath clouded a mirror held under his nostrils.

My Papa lay dead, and I still suffered from a drugged intoxication that kept my tears from flowing. It was a special hell. All I could think was how magnificent he looked, his features neither delicate nor rugged, but boldly, clearly sculpted. Chiselled by a Master.

I felt no swelling in his abdominal region, nor did I anywhere find a wound. What had caused this wreck? Presently I saw on the far night table the supper tray, the all but empty soup bowl, the dessert dish half covered with suet pudding. The other half clean but for a shiny smear and a stray, solitary, darkly gleaming raisin.

I opened the night table drawer: Dr. Hillyard's morphine salts were missing. Thought, breath came slowly. The opiate. Had it been divided between us? One large, deadly dose. One smaller and merely stupefying. The amount that I had been fed dulled feeling, but did not quite obliterate memory. Sibyl was answerable for something. I took the poker from the hearth, and I began to look for her.

I met her on the stairs from the ground floor down to the kitchen. She was climbing as I descended. My lamp showed her coarse features pulled to one side of her face in an unfamiliar expression of anxiety. She said something about going up to fetch Papa's tray.

"You can leave that, Sibyl." My head burns as I write the words, but it didn't when I said them. My voice was drowsy, soothing. If my thoughts too rolled sluggishly, they were in compensation preternaturally clear. "Have you anything for me to eat?" I asked.

She stepped back into the kitchen and took a bowl from a dresser. I held the poker behind me. She was no taller than I, but sturdier and, given my present state of torpor, quicker. She might bolt out the kitchen door and up the outside steps to the back yard or, if I moved to block that exit, up the stairs I had just descended and out the front.

"Oyster soup?" I said. "That will do very well."

My long sleep had tousled my hair. While Sibyl was dipping her ladle in the pot, I removed pins to cause further havoc.

"I'll eat at the table here. No need for ceremony. Just lend me a hairbrush before I sit."

She looked at me askance. The request was so unlike me, and she didn't know for how much eccentricity her doctored tea could account. The fearful grimace twisted her mouth higher into her left cheek. Her eyes slid towards the back way out.

"My hair wants brushing," I said blandly. "I'll just help myself, shall I?"

I counted on her to protect her nest and was not disappointed: Sibyl bustled into her room. Now I had only one hole to plug. I stood in it.

"Give me your keys, Sibyl."

She turned and made to rush me. I held the poker in both hands, aimed it up and towards her breast like a bayonet. I held it short so there was very little but the point left for her to grab. She might still have prevailed, but something held her back. I've often wondered what. Physical fear, consciousness of guilt, the habit of a servant, a sense of fatality stronger than her panic, perhaps a combination of the four.

"Missus," she pleaded, "what has happened?"

"You've killed your master, Sibyl. That's what has happened."

"No. He can't be dead."

"Poisoned by your hand."

"Never!" She advanced upon me so that the point of my poker actually touched the bodice of her gown. "If I had done such a thing," she wailed, "I should never have waited here."

"You'll explain that to the constables," I replied, standing my ground. "You'll deny poisoning me as well."

"A sleeping powder, Mrs. Crane, for your good. Anyone could see you needed rest."

"I'm rested now, Sibyl, and I'll take charge of the keys."

I locked her in her room, then sat at the kitchen table. Sickly, I pushed aside the bowl of oyster soup. I still smelled pudding: the cloth it had been steamed in hung over the back of the opposite chair. I put my head down on my arms and wept. The excitement of the late encounter must have helped flush the blunting morphine from my blood.

I wept at first for every selfish reason. Also for the loss to Papa himself of a life he kept finding, for all its sorrows, pleasure-full. But the longer I lay there, the more the public character of the tragedy overcame me, the loss to the voters of York County, to Parliament and to the country, to Catholics and Protestants, to the accused and impoverished, and to the miserable woman in the next room (I didn't care if she heard me), who with her employer's death, had lost the best friend she ever could have had.

And she the author of her loss. Here truly was insanity, worse than that which condemns many a poor woman to the harsh, stone cells of this convent's lunatic wing. How cunning did Sibyl's previous fits now seem! Her efforts to drive me from the house by words and fire were to make way for the grand insanity of destroying her good angel.

What sense could one make of such things? I shed fresh, baffled tears.

A musket *feu de joie* along the Esplanade finally roused me, together with shouted insults of the Pope. I wrote to summon doctor and police. Henry had left standing orders to advise him should Papa's condition alter for the worse. My note enjoined him send whatever black cloth we possessed. Although I didn't expect badges of mourning to chasten Orange tongues, I wanted the revellers to know, howl as they might, that William Sheridan had no more to fear from their malice.

From Papa's doorstep I engaged a neat, respectful boy to bring the constables. I used the word murder. The other two commissions went to a likely runner.

Two constables arrived soon after nine. When I opened to their knock, the one calling himself Devlin did up a button on his tunic. He was all angles but for his limp black hair. His more compact, blond companion, introduced as Morgan, was already buttoned up and looked in every way more reliable, but said very little. Constable Devlin thought it unfair that he should be on duty when the whole town was celebrating, but murder was murder, the public had to be protected, and where was the deceased? He slapped Papa's cheeks and pronounced him dead. Constable Morgan turned down the bedclothes, put his ear to Papa's chest and nodded. Neither wished to touch the supper tray, which might be evidence. Better leave that till the doctor arrived.

Of greater interest was the suspect in the basement. Morgan for once seemed to speak for both of them when he admitted he had never laid eyes on a murderess. Devlin wanted to lay hands on Sibyl as soon as possible and remove her to the cells of Station No. 1, where she could be watched at every hour of the day and night. I might think her secure enough in a locked room with barred windows. But could I swear she had no second key? No means to harm or even make away with herself before she could be properly questioned? I could not.

I didn't (and don't) have enough faith in human justice to wish Sibyl preserved for the scaffold, but for examination yes. I needed to understand. They led her from her room with hands chained together and hanging in front of her loose brown dress. She didn't raise her eyes to meet mine.

"Why did you do it, Sibyl?" I asked.

She didn't answer.

"Sibyl Martin," said Devlin knowingly. "You were discharged from Grand Master Gowan's four months since for loose behaviour."

"The goings-on were none of my doing," she muttered. "I left because I had a better place to go."

"And look what you've made of it!" I said.

Such perversity beggared belief. What I had been considering a private act of madness appeared now in the light of a political assassination. Plotters could not have furnished their Corday with a story apter to secure access to her victim. Papa was a notoriously celibate widower. Mr. Gowan is a widower *tout court.* Allegations that improper advances had been made to Sibyl or to anyone else under the Grand Master's roof would have disposed Papa to offer his client's sister employment where such indignities were impossible.

My hope of understanding dimmed. Such police as I had so far seen might not be competent to solve a murder, however much they wished to. To expose an Orange conspiracy they would have no wish at all.

"I'll see she minds her tongue, ma'am," said Devlin, pushing Sibyl towards the stairs. "Constable Morgan will wait here for the doctor."

But Morgan didn't want to miss his chance to walk beside a woman in shackles. I saw what I must do. Whatever her desserts, parading Sibyl along the Esplanade as part of the evening's spectacle ill became a society that long ago abandoned the public pillory. I pinned about her shoulders a shawl long enough to cover the handcuffs. I placed her most concealing bonnet on her head. No one thanked me. I didn't mind.

Left alone, I hunted the morphine bottle. I was prepared to look long and treat its absence or emptiness as suspicious. It came to hand among a number of patent medicines in a locked compartment of the kitchen dresser. The contents appeared little depleted. Before I could inspect them further, Henry's carriage arrived.

His step was brisk, and his knock, but I had never seen his skin so pale or eyes so red.

"Theresa, I can't tell you how sorry..." Of course he couldn't. It would have spoiled the effect.

I stepped back deeper into the hall as he stepped forward, and he halted as if he perfectly understood.

"Dr. Hillyard has still not arrived," I said as evenly as possible. His note was to have been delivered before Henry's, and how much rather I should have seen Papa's misogynistic old pal than my crocodile husband!

"I've just—" Henry shook his head and waved his long right arm to the east. "Just seen Sibyl being taken into custody. I've never misjudged anyone more. I don't expect your forgiveness. Only understand I should give anything for today not to have happened."

I believed him. A murder in the family was something he would survive, but it couldn't benefit his projects. I was grateful for his not defending Sibyl to my face.

He wanted to see Papa. Considering what their relations had been, I dreaded the encounter. I begged him to wait for the doctor and was relieved presently to hear that gentleman's cab at the door.

Dr. H. was always frailer by evening, but the change in him today was extreme. He walked with two canes. The sores on his forehead were raw from scratching. He would not speak a word until he had with laboured breath hauled himself all the way up to Papa's room. Ten o'clock struck while he was doing it.

He opened Papa's eyes. He opened Papa's mouth and sniffed inside. When I pointed the half-eaten pudding out to him, he placed a spoonful of it in his own mouth, depositing the matter after a time in a folded handkerchief. At Henry's urging, he likewise tasted the oyster broth.

"A relapse, my dear," he said to me. "No one's to blame."

I showed him the bottle he had left. These crystals, he confirmed, were morphine, not some filler added to hide misappropriation. A small, non-fatal dose might have been removed. I could not bring him a sample of the tea, which had all been cleared away while I slept.

"The housekeeper drugged me so I couldn't protect Papa," I insisted. The sight of a rosette on Dr. H.'s lapel kept me from mentioning the Orange Lodge. "She can't be innocent."

Henry promptly seconded me. "As you know, sir, Mrs. Crane is of a scientific turn of mind and not given to wild assertions. If she says the housekeeper killed our dear father, it must be true."

"Administering a sedative," the doctor said distinctly, "is not, one must hope, the same as murder."

And that was all he would say: my pleas for a post-mortem went unanswered. He gave my arm a sorrowful pat and wearily accepted Henry's offer to dismiss the doctor's cab and drive him home in our brougham.

Our coachman had meanwhile trimmed Papa's door in black as I had wanted. It was ghastly.

Chapter Fifteen
The Letter *(continued)*

Thursday, 21st August

Have for four days been too ill to write. Sister Saint-Jacques today allows me to sit in a corner of her cabinet-lined dispensary while she grinds her herbs and prepares her tinctures. She wants me to know that no church but hers allows women to be pharmacists. I suspect, however, that I owe my returning health to no product of her garden, but rather to her having turned her budget inside out to buy me quinine. She will say only that Peruvian cinchona bark is a Jesuit discovery, which Oliver Cromwell died from refusing.

One cabinet contains her medical library. I have just confirmed there what I knew the night Papa died: an abscess could not possibly have formed and fatally ruptured in the few hours of my forced nap. However unwholesome, the suet pudding had not caused death, not without some quicker-killing additive. I spent Saturday night wondering which, for I had made his spirit a vow to find out how he died.

Henry had meanwhile determined that it would overtax me to watch by my father in a servantless house and had arranged to have Papa removed to Ogilvie's establishment. The body could be professionally laid out, for viewing at our own villa on Monday, and interred the day after. I protested this extraordinary arrangement to no avail. Later Saturday night, when I asked Henry what progress he had made with Dr. H., he replied that the doctor had persuaded him (with details Henry could not for reasons of delicacy repeat) to accept Papa's death as natural after all. Conceive my sense of betrayal. I scarcely can now myself, for it presupposed a trust in my husband I should long since have put aside.

Sunday morning, I wished to see Papa. I was told the undertaker's sabbatarianism made this impossible, so I went to church instead. My father had for the decade since its construction supported Holy Trinity, but a house of worship without reserved pews wasn't smart enough for Henry, who preferred his wife to be seen at the Cathedral, not that he often went himself. I sometimes rebelled, but today indulged his preference. Having given Oscar the day off, Henry drove me in our old chaise to King and Church. When he handed me down, he as usual pleaded business at his office two blocks east and engaged to come back for me in an hour and a half.

Worshippers who had heard of my loss waylaid me in the porch, until Kate MacFarlane and her daughters swept me up. I was alone? Then I must join Kate, for with her husband truant as well, there was ample room in her pew. Her brusque kindness promptly overrode any scruple Jasper had planted in my mind regarding the MacFarlanes. I stipulated only for the aisle seat.

At the time I was aware of no plan to leave during the service. I simply felt stifled, as if I needed open space through which to receive God's Word. Kate sang the first hymn like an angel at my side. Her clear, rounded voice would grace any concert hall, but I believe she imbued it with exceptional strength and sweetness for my special consolation. I added my thinner warble and was consoled, until we reached the words:

"The flowers beneath the Mower's hand
Lie withering e'er 'tis night."

I whispered to Kate not to follow me and left.

An empty cab was passing on King Street. I got in. I should not have found one outside Holy Trinity, and it would have been twice as far to Papa's. That Henry had relieved me of Sibyl's keys presented no obstacle. In a hiding place convenient to Papa's kitchen door, I kept a key of my own. When I felt it turn in the lock, I believed that something inside must show me why William Sheridan had withered e'er night. I entered and locked the door behind me.

The doctor's word would free Sibyl, if it had not already done so, free her to melt with her secrets back into the bush. I started my search in her room. I was looking not only for a murder weapon, but also for any document indicative of a conspiracy. While locked in here, she would have had ample time to burn evidence, so I supposed I had to look for ashes as well.

None of the plaster was loose nor any of the bricks in the cleanly-swept floor. It's a bright room for a basement, with two south windows. I opened each and, reaching through the bars, set aside the dead leaves and scraps of paper that had fallen into the window wells. Nothing.

On the back of the door hung a spare shapeless gown and a winter cloak. Nothing was tucked or sewn into either. From the pine chest I yanked the three drawers, turning each over to ensure nothing was pinned to the back, sides, or bottom. The stockings and chemises that tumbled forth I turned inside out and, finding nothing, threw back without refolding.

On top of the chest beside an oil lamp lay a volume of popular theology. Also one of popular history which seemed to place a lurid emphasis on all the bloodiest episodes of regicide, insurrection, crime, war and suppression: the Roman Empire, the Spanish Inquisition, the Crusades, the Borgias, Napoleon. Nothing was concealed in the spines or between the pages. The bindings showed no signs of tampering.

My task grew harder. There was still the bed, but I couldn't pull all the straw from the tick and set the room to rights again in time to keep my appointment with Henry. While deliberating how to proceed, I glimpsed my grim, white face in a mirror I'd neglected to look behind. I unhooked it from its nail. Out of the back fell a folded piece of brown wrapping paper, which I've managed to keep through every chance that has befallen me since. The round, childish hand I recognized at once as Sibyl's. I read:

Who finds this please send to Chas. Martin, Provincial Penitentiary. Brother, we are cursed indeed. My master is dead and your best hope of pardon with him. Do not look even to see me in Kingston, for I am suspect of murder. Mrs. Crane has shut me in and means I think to break my skull, innocent though I am. She should sooner look to her Henry. You know I have a carnal nature which I abhor but cannot fight. And where could I have learned to resist a man who bends wills as he bends rails? Henry told me the old stag was failing, and I must find a new protector in him, although the master's help I never had to earn by sin...

Sin with Sibyl? Again I caught my breath at Henry's capacity to deceive me. Once his total dupe, I still had not learned to doubt him enough and perhaps never would.

Adultery I had suspected, as I've said. I've seen him help a red-cheeked laundress with her basket, or whisper in a parlour maid's ear, or follow a seamstress with his eyes, or let his hand brush that of a pretty shop girl. I've seen him come home late, and early, too flushed and languorous to have come from the business he alleged. But I never guessed he would prey on my father's servants. Besides, Sibyl was not pretty. Could she really be to Henry's taste, or had he seduced her for reasons of policy, precisely because she served in Papa's house and might do his bidding there? I shuddered to think.

Involuntarily, my eye measured the bed. I couldn't assimilate the thought of Henry, sleek and scented, lying here with grey-skinned Sibyl. There wasn't time to assimilate it, for an even graver and less credible charge still hovered in the wings. I hastened to read on.

...For Mrs. Crane's health, he persuaded me to give his wife sleeping medicine. While she slept, he visited the master. I heard voices raised, and afterwards, Henry left without seeing me. The house was still. I couldn't move. If I had left then, I should be safe

now, but if the master was alive, I couldn't leave him, and I was too afraid to go upstairs and look. I have seen dead folk, some like our drowned parents pretty bad. My legs, forgive them, would not take me up into the master's room where I might meet the sightless eyes of our one benefactor, brought to grief through me. I waited and listened. I practised believing Henry had not done it. The master if dead had died of his own weakness, like the man you hit. At length I heard Mrs. Crane stir. If she should scream or call out I should fly. She never did. She went up to her father and came down again, her step so calm I thought my fears were groundless. It was only the drug. So I am tricked by my own trick, and now if she don't kill me she'll have me put in gaol...

Sibyl's paper slipped from my fingers at the sound of a key in the outside kitchen door. Instinctively, I slid the drawers back into the dresser and hung the mirror. Nothing else was obviously misplaced. Through the room door which I had left ajar, I heard the indistinct voices of two people who had entered the kitchen, one male, one female. I didn't long debate a hiding place: there was but one. Scooping up the letter from where it had fallen, I rolled beneath the low bed.

Along the side, the coverlet fell to within inches of the floor, but the foot of the bed had no such valance. Turning on my side, I bent my knees hard lest my shoes betray me. Three layers of petticoats complicated this manoeuvre. A hoop skirt would, for good or ill, have prevented it.

Once anxiously compressed, I listened again for the voice that had warned me into so amazing a posture. It was Henry's voice, in its peremptory rather than its solicitous register.

I had never known Henry to be violent, merely ungentle, and yet I realized that of late I had been increasingly apprehensive in his presence. It was possible some intractable, undisclosed problem was altering his character. Or even some physical process in his brain. Desperate as my concealment may appear, I was still not convinced that an industrialist of such achievements as Henry Crane's could be a murderer. I just did not want to take the risk of his finding me.

I did, however, want to hear what he and Sibyl were saying. Although it would increase my danger, I actually willed them to come into the room where I was. Presently my wish was granted.

"Come along," Henry was saying, "you must gather your belongings now so I can take you to the coach office."

"The eastbound doesn't leave till one," said Sibyl in her usual sullen tone. "Well, I won't be watched while I pack. Wait in the kitchen."

So, before I had another chance to confront her, Sibyl was being bundled out of town. She plainly felt the want of ceremony. She naturally would not want Henry to watch her retrieve, and perhaps to insist on reading, the letter she believed to be still behind the mirror, but to address him so provokingly she must have done a very thorough job of convincing herself he was harmless. Or perhaps she simply did not regard her own welfare.

Through the gap between coverlet and floor I saw Henry's brilliant black boots stride across to the dresser, before which he dropped a carpet bag of Papa's. I heard him open a drawer. Sibyl's preference was nothing to him, any charm which she had once had for him exhausted. Huddled practically beneath his feet, I was scared enough for her if she wasn't for herself. Yet I stayed quiet.

"Here," Sibyl protested, "someone's been through my things. I never left 'em so tangled."

Henry was filling the bag. When he asked if she had anything stowed under the bed, I almost cried out.

She told him she wasn't going on the coach, not now, for she had to make sure nothing had been taken. Tomorrow's steamer would get her to Kingston soon enough, and in "a damned sight" more comfort. She must have known how Henry detested blasphemy.

"What possessed you to tell Dr. Hillyard yesterday morning that I wished Theresa given a sedative?" he burst out.

For fear of missing the answer, I struggled to stifle my

sense of Dr. H.'s treason.

"I had to ask him how much to put in the teapot," Sibyl retorted. "If I gave her too much, we'd have her death to answer for."

The sentence ended in an unspoken "also".

"I've patched the damage," said Henry, going down on one knee. It seemed he was about to look under the bed after all. "Just watch your unclean tongue."

"Ask me civil, and I won't tell anyone my Henry was the last person to speak to the master."

Her Henry and welcome. My distress owed nothing to their endearments. I was torn between fear of Henry's lifting the hanging edge of the coverlet, which alone concealed me, and fear of what he might have done yesterday evening while I slept. Sibyl's suggestion, contained also in her letter, he did not deny.

He withdrew the hand reaching towards me. Slowly he rose.

"Sibyl," he demanded, "did you go up to Papa's room after drugging my dear wife?" His boots stood so close to Sibyl's scuffed slippers that I thought he must be holding her shoulders. "You move so softly, Sibyl. Did you creep upstairs so quietly that no one heard you coming? It's dangerous to creep about, you know."

"I stayed downstairs," said Sibyl. "I didn't watch you kill him."

She seemed bent on discovering by direct experiment the worst of which my husband was capable. I winced in anticipation of I knew not what.

"Who speaks of killing?" His voice was starting to tremble. "Your master had a relapse, or did you fool the doctor?"

"How would I do that?" Sibyl persisted.

"By Jesus, I'll show you!"

A loud, full curse. I had never known his temper to break free like this. I lacked confidence that anything could check it now.

Henry must have thrown Sibyl down onto the bed and climbed on top. From where I cowered, I saw her slippered feet lift simultaneously from the bricks and heard a thump above my head. Then Henry's feet rose from view one by one. Under the double weight, the ropes that held the ticking stretched and sagged. A knot pressed down into my left shoulder. I was too horror-struck to move.

"Perhaps you took one of Papa's pillows like this," he cried, "and held it over his face."

I come now, Isaac, to those events I felt least able to speak of when you found me. I concluded that the story to be told at all had to be set down in full, but now wonder if my long-windedness has been any more than a form of reticence, a way to avoid mention of my lying quietly under a bed on which Papa's housekeeper was being smothered. Worse was to follow.

Sibyl knew how to hold her tongue and might, I think, have got away scot-free. Perhaps it was remorse for her part in Papa's death that made her tempt fate with one goading word after another. And yet she did not want to die.

She squirmed and fought so the ropes creaked. She may have landed at least one good blow or kick, for she managed to roll out from under Henry onto the brick floor. She fell on her side, so close I felt her breath. She saw me. Her eyes opened wider than I had ever seen them.

"Spare me!" she cried.

Then Henry was kneeling astride her again, with his left hand twisting and pulling her face up into the pillow that with his right hand he moulded over it. I tried to scream, but as in a nightmare no sound came out. One of Sibyl's arms was pinned beneath her. Henry sat on the other. Her kicks could not reach him, nor me once I had pulled back farther beneath the bed. The thrashing of her legs served only to show that she was alive and that I still had time to try to keep her so. I shrank back, and the time passed. It ended abruptly with the snap of Sibyl's neck.

I didn't see how it happened. It must have been the way

Henry held her or a combination of his pulling her shoulders up while pressing down the pillow. Afterwards, when he laid her supine, her head lolled on the bricks at a sickening angle.

He was breathing heavily. He put his right ear to Sibyl's chest, turning towards me his smooth circle of scalp fringed in short sandy hair. Had he listened with the other ear, our eyes would have met. From the back, his head looked innocent, peculiarly childlike. He left it some time on Sibyl's bosom, to which his right hand stole caressingly. He had stopped listening and was resting.

This turning for comfort to the woman he had killed revolted me, but I no longer had any wish to scream. I bit my hand so no sound should escape me.

Rousing himself, he dressed Sibyl in the shawl and bonnet I had placed on her the night before. Then he lifted her limp-necked carcass in his arms. I heard his footsteps recede through the kitchen, the outside door open and close.

The sense of release was neither immediate nor lasting. Lest he return, I huddled where I lay some minutes more. When at last I crawled out and started to rub my cramps and bruises, my one thought was to get as far from Henry as possible as soon as possible. But how? No steamers sailed on Sunday. I had no mount and no capital but my wedding band and three shillings for the poor box. Papa's strongbox lay just upstairs. I should have raided it without scruple, had the key he wore about his neck not gone with his remains to Ogilvie's and the spare not been locked in his office vault on Yonge Street. There was nothing for it but I must return to Henry's villa. I must face Henry.

Service had ended, his vehicle not yet arrived, when I returned to St. James Cathedral. The MacFarlane girls were peering behind every shrub in the close while on the steps Kate fired questions at the verger and pointed in a succession of directions with her fan. Ah, there I was! Where? How? What? She had never known "God Our Help in Ages Past" to affect anyone so adversely. I said I had merely wanted air, exercise and solitude, but she must not speak or let her children speak of my absence as the news would unwarrantably distress my husband. I pretended to agree I should have stayed home altogether.

The known strength of my attachment to Papa earned me a degree of indulgence. I needed it, for I am no actress and was desperately hoping Henry would also interpret my inconsolable anguish in this light. But where was he?

I was on the point of accepting a ride with Kate when his carriage-horse Providence came trotting up with the old, green, two-wheeled Boston chaise in which we had left the church after our wedding. The black leather hood was up against the noon sun and projected so far forward that the upper half of Henry's body remained in deepest shadow. Only his black-trousered knees showed there was a driver at all. I thought how easy it must have been in such gloom to spirit Sibyl's body from Papa's back lane through the unsuspecting summer streets. To where? An ice house, perhaps, or the firebox of a locomotive.

When Henry emerged to hand me in, I couldn't look at him. His apologies for his lateness I didn't hear. I was finding it next to impossible to climb into the dead woman's seat. Again my distress was excused. Young Elsie MacFarlane threw her arms around me and begged me to come sketch with her soon in her garden. I would see how the growing things would "buck me up."

I don't know how I rode home with Henry or how I ate dinner with him, except I believed I had to. This meal might be my last for some time. Fortunately, the full horror of what I had witnessed from under Sibyl's bed had not yet had time to permeate my soul. I would give it none until after I made my escape.

I would not cross him as Sibyl had. The closest I came to alluding to his crimes was when he announced in cool, defensive tones that the housekeeper had been released from the lock-up and had left town. I said it relieved me to know that a servant Papa had trusted had not killed him. My previous suspicions had slandered his discernment.

Henry scarcely listened and seemed as impatient to leave the table as I. His professed intention of returning to his office spared me the necessity of arguing that mourning was compatible with horseback riding. I told him I should rest. Understandably, but for him most unusually, Henry had that day cut his cheek in shaving. When on his trellised verandah we took what I pray was our definitive leave of one another, my last impressions were of the glancing touch of his deadly hands and the scent of not sandalwood, but zinc ointment.

I didn't dress wisely. Once decided on a man's saddle, which would be easier to sell, I should have taken men's clothes and changed into them when clear of Toronto. At that moment, however, no practical consideration could make me contemplate putting my legs into Henry's breeches.

Our cook looked askance at my gaudy green costume. I wanted exercise, I said. Back soon. I rode north, thinking (insofar as I thought anything) to lose myself in the endless woods.

From campaigning with Papa, I knew some of the less travelled roads of York County. My terror abated the farther down them I rode. I had money for food. I would not chance letting anyone know where I slept, but the warm, clear sky assured me I should come to no harm out of doors. My bed was the dry, fallen needles of a stand of pine that still awaited the settler's axe. I awoke before daybreak, feeling comparatively safe and utterly tormented.

Not all the thoughts that follow burst on me at once or in so pointed a form. (I've had ample time since to sharpen them for my own discomfort.) The exact sequence is forgotten and unimportant. The first, however, was this: she who does not speak gives consent.

Qui tacet consentit. William Sheridan's un-Latin tongue used to mangle this maxim as invariably as his just protests honoured it, in Parliament and out. For all I knew, his raised voice had cost him his life. Even if my speaking had resulted in two women's deaths rather than one, my silence had authorized the one.

Practically speaking, could I have stopped Henry? I was ill-equipped and worse placed to pose any physical threat, nor have I any influence over him. He doesn't respect or care for me. And yet I could have complicated his task, whereas by doing nothing I had made it easy.

"Spare me!"

I wondered to what extent Sibyl's words had been directed at me, to what extent at him. By not addressing me more explicitly, she had spared me. Perhaps I was attributing too much design to a spontaneous outburst, but my musings went still further.

Her wide eyes haunted me. I wasn't sure if they had really held surprise. Suppose she had known I lay beneath the bed, known not clairvoyantly, but having felt my shoulder through the mattress. Or suppose much earlier she had heard me close the drawers. I imagined Sibyl leading Henry to reveal himself to me, Sibyl risking everything so I might denounce him.

Instead, I had broken bread with him, Sibyl's murderer, my father's butcher. It was plain enough now, as stark as a crow's call or a dead stump in the milky dawn. The man I had admitted to our family had destroyed its chief. Such was my cowardice, however, that even in my own thoughts I had been unable to arraign Henry Crane for parricide until I was well out of his sight.

Sibyl he had used to prevent my interference. Vain of Papa's trust, she might have needed little persuasion to try sending or scaring me from Front Street, but where persuasion was required, Henry had been ready with caresses and promises of protection. Possibly Sibyl had even been convinced that morphine in my tea was for my good. Plainly, though, she had neither wanted nor foreseen her master's death. She had not conspired at murder.

If there had been an assassination plot, as now seemed far less likely, it had not included her.

When it was light enough to read, I took out her letter. Who could she have hoped to discover it? Who but me? Not Henry or some unlettered servant that would have brought it to him. It concluded thus:

...now if she don't kill me she'll have me put in gaol. That wife of Henry's is too proud to believe any of what I write. I only wish some kinder soul may deliver this to you, so you do not suppose I of my own will let you die alone. Sibyl.

I knew then I must turn east towards the Penitentiary. Only on arriving some days later beneath its walls did I realize I could not honour Sibyl's request. Officials would read her letter. Its contents, if they got out, would alarm Henry without disabling him.

For Charles Martin, it contained few words of consolation anyway. Rather than deliver it immediately, I worked for the commutation of Martin's sentence by nursing the keeper he had attacked. When Paul Taggart died, and the execution seemed certain to proceed, I had conveyed to the condemned man that his sister had not forgotten him. A feeble gesture? I felt so. Far from making the peace with Sibyl I had intended, I had let her down again. I fled Portsmouth ill and exhausted, as you know, in defeat and despair.

I can still see no light through my guilt. Good works elude me. Nor do my solitary and unguided prayers show me a path. I had thought to unburden my heart to one of this convent's clear-eyed Christian women, but have not done so. You are the first to be told its secret shame.

Isaac, it seems I have a visitor. The sister describes him in such terms (variola scarred, beetle-browed, dolichocephalic) that it cannot be you. She knows or will say nothing more. I fear it may be some agent of Henry's, in which case I nonetheless pray, like Sibyl, that my testament may reach its addressee.

Yours always,

T.

Chapter Sixteen
Reinforcements

Following the adjourned inquest, just as Theresa was beginning her letter, Isaac Harris telegraphed Rasco's Hotel to ask whether any communication for him had arrived. Their negative reply made him no less eager to reach Montreal.

A night in Toronto remained to endure. Remembering Jasper's warning that Crane would want him questioned, Harris avoided the address he had given the coroner and bedded down instead at Randall's stable in Banshee's stall. This nest proved even less restful than expected. Ribs showed through the mare's dapple-grey coat, from which the gloss had all but vanished.

Next day, although the horse made him more conspicuous, Harris secured a stall for her on the cargo deck of the steamer that bore him down lake. Starting to undo the liveryman's neglect would occupy some portion of the weary voyage.

Another portion he spent anxiously perusing Toronto newspapers from the fortnight since his August 1 flying visit. Had anything been published prejudicial to Theresa's name or safety? While he looked, three articles on other subjects caught Harris's irritable and restless eye.

One from The *Leader* of a week earlier coincidentally concerned an inquest. Harvey Ingram, of Aberdeen, Detroit, Presque Isle and latterly Toronto, aged forty-six years, had been found at the foot of the Gibraltar Light, which he kept. The jury said he had not fallen, but been killed by drink alone. Beside him lay a partially consumed case of champagne, which reminded Harris of the dropped smuggling charges. Stricter treatment might have lengthened Ingram's life. It seemed remarkable that one inured to bad whisky should die of good wine, but perhaps the pleasing taste made stopping harder and the knowledge that it was only wine made stopping seem less urgent.

Harris thought of all the champagne bottles in Mrs. Vale's sprawling establishment and of lives poured grossly or languidly away.

The next story to engage his attention was one of progress and enterprise. The *Globe* reported the mayor's ceremonial removal of the first shovelful of earth from the foundations of the future Conquest Iron Works. Company president and Provincial Bank director Mr. Joshua Newbiggins had spoken on the occasion to warm applause. "Our friends at York Foundry," he warned, "will soon feel the bracing winds of competition whistle through their forges whenever railroads tender contracts for track." Other engagements had prevented the attendance of Conquest's newest and most prestigious backer, Mr. George MacFarlane—but that Titan of timber and other ventures innumerable was said to have been instrumental in reassuring aldermen that an iron foundry would in no way compromise the residential character of Front Street. *Sir* George, as the next honours list must have it.

The addition would not change the fact that MacFarlane had questionable taste in partners.

Harris turned finally to the papers dated August 15. He had been avoiding these for fear of seeing his own disreputable name in print. He found in the end only one item, alarmingly headed, "Infidel's Testimony Rejected," but mercifully short and hidden away near the bottom of a middle column on page four. The writer slyly asked if Mr. Harris's barrister anticipated trouble collecting his fee after exposing his client to public obloquy. Traced to an address he preferred not to make public, Mr. Jasper Small replied that he liked to think even atheists had some sense of honour and that he, for his part, looked forward to representing Mr. Harris for many years to come.

Small, it seemed, was offering his services. Good.

Nothing in print gave any hint as to Theresa's location. Better yet.

Harris proceeded immediately to a writing desk in the steamer's lounge. With Ingram's fate as well as Theresa's needs in mind, he scrawled a note to be mailed back to Toronto when they next touched land.

Friday
On Lake Ontario

Jasper,

If in truth open to new commissions, borrow against whichever of my properties the mortgage brokers like best and come at once to Montreal. The ornate house by the Parliament buildings, e.g., would make a very serviceable horse-nail factory. The secret you so ingeniously saved yesterday is bound to leak out soon, and then legal manoeuvres will begin in earnest. Find at Rasco's your faithful, if godless, client—

Isaac

The next six days passed in waiting. The steamer crawled down the St. Lawrence and through its locks, delivering Harris at last to the metropolis. At last! But in thriving Montreal, nothing had happened. Nothing continued to happen. The public clocks at long intervals announced one empty hour after another.

The saving of Harris's sanity, meanwhile, was seeing to Banshee's recovery. As with gradually increased rations of oats and hay she put on weight, he stretched her legs with longer rides, up the orchard-covered mountain and down past the limestone quarries on the other side. Then he would trot her back to his hotel to find the clock hands a little advanced—and no messages.

Small neither came nor wrote. Nor did Harris see anything of Nan Hogan or the police, though he was careful whenever he ventured near the convent to make sure he was not followed. They seemed not to need him.

Tuesday morning, the promised week passed without a letter from Theresa. Inquiries availed Harris nothing.

He felt helpless. He needed to hear from her both some reassurance as to her present condition and some information he could use to protect her. Crane's crimes might be guessed at, but guesses have no public standing. Harris resembled a knight who, hearing rumblings from the forest, can execute no plan of attack or defence until he establishes the nature of the beast. For her chains to be broken, Theresa had to break her silence. He saw no other way.

Two days later, with dense cloud pressing on the island city, uncertainty had so paralyzed him that even distressing news came as a clarifying mercy. Without touching his fried eggs, he sprang from his seat at the breakfast table. Thursday's *Montreal Herald* reported that Mrs. Henry Crane, missing from her Toronto home since July 13, had found her way to the Grey Nuns' hospital, where she was receiving care until she could be reunited with her husband, the well-known etc., etc. The announcement originated with Postmaster General Armand Laurendeau, whose family had long supported the sisters' charitable work.

Article in hand, Harris rushed out of the hotel. What deprived him of breakfast was the need to take measures rather than any overwhelming sense of shock or betrayal. In her letter to Theresa, Marthe had undertaken that her family would not volunteer information to Crane, but suppose that Crane—knowing of Theresa's connection to Marthe—had eventually made an approach to Mlle Laurendeau's father. Perhaps the two men had business dealings, negotiating agreements for the transport of mail. No venal motive need be imputed to the postmaster general. Crane's quite natural wish to find his wife must have overborne the wife's unexplained wish not to be found. Could Laurendeau in conscience have refused Crane's blunt request? Most unlikely.

These thoughts, however, occurred to Harris only now that the secret was out. He had expected it kept somewhat longer.

He was hastening to the Anglican diocese, where he presently asked for any priest who might have known Theresa or William Sheridan when Parliament sat in Montreal in the late forties. He was told he wanted Philander Bray. Besides his duties at Christ Church Cathedral, Philander Bray taught dead languages every morning at McGill College.

Harris hastened up the sapling lined, dirt avenue north of St. Catherine Street towards a square, stone hall surmounted by a thick lantern. Cowed young men were filing out after Bray's lecture. The cleric had no charm of person or manner and remembered no Sheridan girl. With the father he had disputed the relative importance of faith and works, he recalled with asperity and a marked New England accent. St. James *versus* St. Paul—deeds versus piety.

Harris could imagine Theresa's benevolent father holding each one severally sufficient to save a soul. Likely neither would find favour in Bray's eyes, which were too deep-set and thickly shaded ever to feel the warmth of the sun. Nipped by their frost, Harris stumbled frequently in explaining his errand.

"Let me understand you, Mr. Harris." Philander Bray rolled his lecture notes and tied them with a black ribbon. "You are a family friend, who allowed this Protestant Episcopalian woman to enter a Roman Catholic convent, from which you naturally find yourself barred. You now fear *inter alia* that she may be forced to return to an adulterous husband."

Harris noted the particular distaste with which his interlocutor alluded to adultery. A spark of hope flickered before yielding to the next icy blast.

"As her late father's former pastor," Bray continued, "I am to insist on seeing her, to persuade her to leave the Grey Nuns if I can, and to otherwise convey from her a letter."

"An account of her husband's crimes." Harris was saying what he wished rather than what he knew Theresa's letter to contain. "Which document," he added, "must not fall into unfriendly hands."

"Legally," Bray retorted, "his crimes are little to the point. In this very city, a judge recently ordered a woman back to a husband convicted of assaulting her."

"I don't know the law, sir, but even if I make my case badly, please do not refuse me your help."

Bray sniffed noisily. "And what religion do you profess? Are you a churchman?"

"My mother is a Presbyterian."

"I have no motive for helping you and no authority. Your request would have to pass through Bishop Fulford to his homologues in the Church of Rome."

The professor-priest set off at a brisk strut down the college avenue towards the city. Beyond it dully gleamed the swift St. Lawrence, highway and sewer. Harris let him go and wished him drowned—for all of fifteen seconds—then caught him up and tried again.

Bray didn't turn his head, which Harris observed for the first time in profile. Its prominent parietal and occipital lobes would have spoken to a phrenologist of such unencouraging traits as self-esteem, firmness and conjugality. It was all charlatanism anyway, Harris reminded himself.

"There isn't time for bishops," he said.

"For Miss Sheridan's sake then, I must see what can be done. Don't thank me."

Harris was too surprised by this apparent reversal either to thank or to correct him. Here was one man Crane's name did not impress.

"Show her the article, Mr. Bray."

The gentleman addressed sniffed again, evidently suffering from hay fever.

The two men proceeded straight to Foundling Street, where Harris said he would wait. From a window table at the coffee house, he watched Philander Bray, in flapping black tail coat, approach the Grey Nuns' gate. For some minutes Bray faced the slide in the door, then turned away. He remained nearby, however, which kept Harris from despair.

After twenty minutes, Bray spoke again through the slide, and Harris wished the clergyman all the firmness his head shape was supposed to signify. The slide closed. Bray paced the plank sidewalk another quarter hour before—without a backward glance—he was admitted to the convent.

Now the real waiting began. As the lunch hour arrived and faded into afternoon, it became tempting to fear that Bray had removed Theresa, or left without her, by another door. Clouds drifted lower across the square. Harris tried to make each cup of strong black coffee last an hour, and had just drained the final chilly drops from his third cup when he realized the fog had become too thick for his watering eyes to make out the urn-shaped adornments on the convent gateposts. He settled his account and went to shiver on the sidewalk where Bray had been pacing. The temperature had dropped with the clouds.

Eventually Bray emerged alone and—but for his own lecture—empty-handed. Harris bit back the keenest disappointment. Having just taken a short turn to keep warm, he hastened towards the clergyman through the mist. Might not his tailcoat pocket contain a few pages from Theresa at least? A line even in her hand? Impossible to imagine that Bray had spent so many hours in the convent without seeing her.

"Mr. Bray—"

Bray halted all questions with a raised hand and looked back towards the Grey Nuns' door, which was still open. Presumably after some parting words with the portress, Theresa herself stepped out.

Seeing her made the dank air summer sweet. Although thinner than nine days ago, indeed painfully thin, she greeted Harris with a smile from the heart. He felt his own face kindle at her flame. She wore the same plain gown and white bonnet as when she had entered the convent, and she carried a roll of papers she declined to let Bray relieve her of.

"Isaac, did you send me Mr. Bray?" she asked cheerfully.

Bray sniffed at the suggestion of having been sent.

"I approached him, yes," Harris managed to say, his pulse racing with coffee and emotion. Her presence in any form enraptured him. "Are you well?"

"Well enough," said Theresa. "I didn't recognize Papa's old friend at first, nor he me, but I remembered Mr. Bray's preaching when I heard his voice. My father valued your support, Mr. Bray, on the disposition of the Clergy Reserves."

"*Tempus fugit,*" said Bray. "Let's be off."

He takes no pains to appear congenial, thought Harris, recalling that at the college the priest had chosen to speak of his disagreements with William Sheridan rather than of shared causes and common ground. Now he took two or three steps west on Foundling Street and beckoned Theresa irritably. She did not follow immediately, but when she spoke again sounded wearied, as if by a long and uncertain purgatory.

"Mr. Bray has offered to let me stay with him and his family. That's best, Isaac, I think. We don't know what Henry may do."

"A great improvement," said Harris, giving her his arm. Whatever his misgivings about such a berth, his first task was to remove her from the doorstep of the convent now famous for sheltering her. "Where to?"

"St. Peter Street to Craig," said Bray. "Your company is not required."

"It's freely given." Harris walked north with them on the fog-filled street indicated, keeping himself between Theresa and the carters driving blind.

"Mr. Bray prefers I not have callers yet," she said, "but we can write. That is, if you like..."

Through his shirt and jacket sleeves, Harris felt her grip tremble.

"Count on my liking," he said. "Is that for me?"

Two steps ahead, Bray turned east on Craig Street towards the Champ de Mars.

"Is that the letter?" Harris asked.

"I wrote it for you." Theresa pressed the roll of papers into his hand. "I have to give it to you, I suppose, but you won't like me better after. It can't be helped. Goodbye."

"Don't say that," said Harris. Her resignation told him she was not "well enough"—perhaps not well enough to be left with comparative strangers. "Let me take a hotel room for you instead," he urged. "I'm afraid you'll starve yourself."

She smiled then. "Under Mrs. Bray's roof, I understand, I'm as likely to be trampled by wild buffalo."

"Take your leave, sir." Bray stood sniffling before the door to a narrow house in a neat stone row. If only he would blow his nose and be done.

"I *shall* thank you now, Mr. Bray," said Harris, taking his hand. "As long as you have anything to do with this lady, you will have to do with me. I should like her seen by a physician."

"So I intend," replied the clergyman, "this very evening. The city's most knowledgeable attend Christ Church, as I trust will you."

"You are most kind."

To Theresa, Harris mumbled a ragged, unsustaining farewell. It almost choked him. As soon as she went indoors, he returned to Rasco's and wrote Bray with an offer to pay her keep as well as any medical bills she might incur. Then he read her letter.

* * *

Harris read with growing consternation. The evidence of ague in Theresa's very handwriting all but sent him back to Craig Street. He had just sense enough to realize he was too overcome by the rest of the letter to speak coherently to anyone. He did believe also that the gruff Philander Bray would without further prompting call in as good a medical man as any Harris could find in equal time. Finally, the regularity of Theresa's script in the most recently written passages kept him in his room, if not his chair.

He washed his face and started again from the beginning.

A second reading complete, he went back out into the fog and walked at random until after nightfall. Through his mind, meanwhile, ran a rope of many strands. Sometimes it ran, sometimes inched. It knotted up at others or reversed itself. It started independent of his volition, burning and binding as it would. Harris walked until he had it enough under his control to pick the strands apart and look at them.

One strand was awe—dread mixed with wonder at what Theresa had experienced. He would never know her as he felt he once had, for since then she had lived horrors closed to him. Sheridan's assassination grieved him, but what must be *her* grief?

He would never be obliged to submit to a brutal husband, to watch him murder and still to sit at his table. Harris remembered Sibyl's room. He could picture the low bed, the space between the yellow-brown coverlet and the brick floor—but, through no deficiency of Theresa's manuscript, the most vivid images it gave rise to could encompass no more than a fraction of her ordeal. Imagine being kicked by a woman in her death throes and being unable to move a muscle to help her. Imagine living with that memory. Harris couldn't imagine. The contemplation of such a moment humbled him. He could presume neither to blame Theresa nor to tell her not to blame herself.

His own conduct was another matter. She had mistaken him and married elsewhere because he had not made himself plain. She couldn't approach him when she needed a friend because he had "made such a point of keeping away." Guilt was the second strand in his rope.

The third was sympathy, harder to pick apart because of its breadth and strength. It moved Harris that Theresa had so generously and unassumingly opened herself to him, had indeed been dissecting the tenderest corners of her conscience at the very moment Bray had reached the convent. Even more moving was her courage. "Don't call me brave," she had begged him during their second night together outside Kingston. She *was* brave, though, tremendously. She had struggled alone not only against Sibyl, the treacherous Dr. Hillyard, and Crane, but also with Small and her father himself for his protection. After Sheridan's death, she had not collapsed. She had shown extraordinary initiative and run enormous risks to find out its cause. Harris thought of her, groggy from morphine, calculating the deadliest grip on a poker. He thought of her beneath the bed, willing Crane and Sibyl to come where she could hear them, discovery in the end dependent on with which ear Crane listened for Sibyl's heartbeat. Theresa's need to understand was one Harris both admired and shared.

It was more than sympathy. From the extent to which he recognized his world in her depiction—the constables, Kate

MacFarlane, Jasper Small, William Sheridan—it was manifest how far the two of them saw and thought in harmony. There was no one on earth with whom Harris could ever be as certain that he belonged. Her letter confessed that she too had dreamed of life with him.

At present, however, justice and safety for Theresa had to take precedence over softer musings on "what might have been." Through Harris's rope twisted the revelation of Crane's crimes. The forest foliage parted. Harris had the beast in view.

Crane's murder of Sibyl had been half suspected, although the manner in which Theresa had witnessed and been marked by it went beyond anything nightmare could have foretold. And there was more.

Harris forced himself to sift the facts coolly. That Crane had also killed Theresa's father, medical evidence had previously seemed to preclude. Here, though, were grounds to doubt Hillyard's findings: (1) a fatal relapse would have required more time, (2) the doctor's examination—confirmed by Lamb's inspection of the pudding cloth—had excluded poisoning but not suffocation, and (3) Hillyard had a motive for pronouncing Sheridan's death natural. Namely, he had conspired to administer the drug that had left his friend unprotected.

And Crane's motive? Might he, rather than Sibyl, have been the agent of political vendetta? Harris scarcely knew how to think about these questions yet. He was still accustoming himself to the unprecedented fact that a leading industrialist had slain a parliamentary hero. In such a world, anything could happen. Crane could kill again. One consolation was that he apparently did not know he had been seen breaking his mistress's neck—another that, when the hangman snapped Crane's own, Theresa would be free.

The contrast between Crane's victims could hardly be starker. Harris wondered if the supposed Master who had chiselled Sheridan's features had had any hand in shaping Sibyl's. Her lack of family and position had apparently not been offset by any personal attractiveness, and yet she had been mocked with what she called "a carnal nature." A masterful jest indeed! Sheridan's assassination amounted to a national tragedy, but his servant's was tragic too. While she should have acted better, someone who did not find it easy to be kind might have acted worse. She had made sure she was not giving Theresa a fatal dose of morphine. She had seen Theresa and not given her away.

Once separately examined, these lines of thought and feeling did not stay separate but continued to cross and intertwine. The heart-swelling vision of a girl writing to her mother in heaven might be followed by the desolating one of a man resting his head on his victim's lifeless breast.

Still Harris walked. Eventually the gas jets in the street lamps ahead burned more distinctly. The fog had lifted. The streets were better lit than in Toronto, and Harris began to take note of the life around him. He was by the river. To his right waggons and drays loaded with barrels laboured up ramps from the piers to the street. To his left the Old Countryman Inn was turning away passengers slow to disembark. Not a bed left. People were everywhere. The evening's steamers had arrived.

When he returned to Rasco's, he found Jasper Small sipping port in the lobby. A scuffed but elegant portmanteau turned on end sat by the lawyer's chair and served him as drink stand.

"Just the man!" cried Harris, sated with his own company. "Pour me some of that and let me tell you—" He noticed that Small was sipping rather briskly, and that the bottle was already half empty. "Did you—ah—have a tolerable journey down?"

"I don't know why I came," Small confided. "I have cases in Toronto I'm neglecting, including that of a mechanic disabled by... I forget by what exactly, but it's just the sort of suit for damages the old bear would have taken to heart. *Garçon!* Another glass."

"His daughter's case," said Harris, "would hardly have left him indifferent."

But Small was in no state to reason, and serious consultation would maddeningly have to wait.

The waiter brought another glass. Harris filled both. The fortified wine was agreeable—warm and celebratory. Yes, Harris had had grim news of Crane's deeds, but tomorrow began the campaign to bring their author to justice. Here was cause to celebrate. Theresa would not be returning to Crane. It wasn't altogether in order to prevent his friend's finishing the bottle alone that Harris enjoyed a further three ounces of port before bed.

He gave Small the couch in his room and roused him from it as soon as the first two breakfasts could be ordered up. Small's heavy-lidded eyes made him look morose and sleepy even when he was not. This morning he confessed he was both—but no, he had not drunk heavily on the steamer, where he had found ladies enough with whom to promenade, play cards, and in the evening, polka. A capital dance, the polka—lively as an Irish jig, intimate as a waltz. Only the want of society while awaiting Harris last evening had made him think of toasting his fair-skinned bawd.

Harris moved him off this topic by asking for news of the inquest. Small had none, but had heard from a passenger embarked at Kingston that a squatter named Lansing had been arrested. He had apparently raped a farm girl at the very crossroads where Theresa had been attacked. A broken-toothed fellow whose shoes didn't match.

"No mystery then," said Harris, "why Etta's husband didn't show his face at their shack while Theresa was there. We must get Crane locked up too."

"Aren't you missing a few steps?" said Small. "I don't think you had better have any more of that French coffee."

Harris read or summarized for Small the parts of Theresa's letter he believed supportive of a murder indictment. At the suggestion that a pillow had been held over his partner's face, Small shook his head.

"The letter's genuine? You're sure?"

"Absolutely," said Harris.

"A pillow—what a strange, soft, dreadful death! Poor bear." Small again shook his head while absently smoothing his dressing gown over his folded knees. All natural emotion in him seemed muffled, muted. "Then I was unjust to Hillyard, the old quack. No wonder Theresa fled." He cleared his throat. "Still, where's your case?"

"Jasper, she didn't just hear Crane kill Sibyl. She saw it." Thinking to jolt Small out of his melancholia and to prepare him for battle, Harris read on to the breaking of the housekeeper's neck.

"Henry Crane?" said Small. "'Iron-hull' Crane?" He gazed out the fourth-floor window at a dull patch of sky while groping for an adequate response. "This is news indeed—but as I believe I told you, Isaac, it doesn't help in the least. Wife and husband are one flesh, not permitted to testify against each other."

"Surely not in a case like this!" Harris exclaimed.

"In any case except when the spouse is him or herself the victim."

"She can't be one with a murderer!" Harris set his cup down noisily. "What of the other evidence, Jasper? Sibyl's letter—"

"—is the undated and uncorroborated allegation of a serving woman that Crane had the opportunity to murder William Sheridan, when the death certificate says there was no murder at all. Theresa was right not to let that pathetic scribble fall into official hands."

"A serving woman is negligible, of course," Harris retorted. "Your late partner had more confidence in her than that."

Small said nothing. His expression became very distant. Harris reflected that Sheridan's faith in Sibyl would not necessarily communicate itself to judge and jury.

"Forgive me, Jasper. I should not have used him to reproach you."

"You know that pyramid he has in St. James's Cemetery? One side should be engraved THE PEOPLE'S CHAMPION, and around the corner WHETHER THEY DESERVED ONE OR NOT." Small had been touched on a tender spot. His voice gathered pain as he continued. "Who would be so trusting? Not you, Isaac. By God, not I. And yet trust as ample and generous as William Sheridan's would be part of any paradise we could imagine. He was irreplaceable because one cannot even quite *want* to be like him. Oh, hell."

Harris left a silence. He had never heard the lawyer talk so explicitly about the weight of Sheridan's legacy. While sympathetic, Harris was too preoccupied to make use of this opening. He didn't seek to discover whether any individual aspect of that legacy, any single act committed or neglected by Small, any particular lack of faith, might have triggered the surviving partner's collapse or might be preventing his regeneration. Was there one specific failure for which Small reproached himself above all others? Harris didn't ask. The best Harris believed he could do for Small was to interest him in Theresa's worsening predicament. That would benefit all concerned.

While Small was dressing, Harris wrote to Theresa. Her sleep and appetite were asked after. Small's arrival was mentioned—with more optimism than it yet seemed to warrant. Of her long letter, Harris said only that, although distressing, it had no effect on his regard for her other than to increase it. This note he consigned to a hotel messenger for immediate delivery.

The messenger returned some forty minutes later, while Harris was suggesting—and Small rejecting—ways to incriminate Crane without Theresa's testimony. What of Crane's perjury at the inquest? Her husband said he had seen Theresa off on her July 13 ride. He had in fact left the house first. Small doubted much could be made of this, and Crane's servants were unlikely to contradict him in any case. Harris acquiesced, but perhaps inquiries at the coach office... Small asked with a yawn whether after nearly six weeks anyone could be expected to remember the presence—let alone the absence—of so drab a passenger as Sibyl Martin. Besides, Crane had not claimed to have seen her board a coach or even buy a ticket. Harris remembered how difficult it had been to get Theresa's likeness to show. He despaired of finding one of Sibyl.

At this point, the door was knocked upon and Harris was handed back his own envelope. It seemed then not to have been accepted. A further setback. Finding the seal broken, however, he removed his letter and saw that Theresa had answered on the back.

"Mr. Bray," she wrote in her former laconic style, "leaves for McGill College shortly after ten. T."

Chapter Seventeen
The Bonds of Matrimony

Harris took Small to Craig Street. The lawyer's company would make it easier for Theresa to come for a drive with Harris, who moreover hoped that *her* company would inspire Small to exert himself on her behalf. Small acquiesced—fatalistically for the most part, since he had left Toronto for just this purpose, but with a hint of trepidation. He sat fidgeting in the rented coach while Harris rapped at the Brays' door.

Theresa opened it and promptly slipped out into the street. The proposed outing suited her. She appeared ill at ease, but swore she had eaten and rested well and that the physician who had called the night before, a man she knew and trusted from her previous stay in Montreal, had given her no reason to keep indoors.

"Jasper," she said, climbing into the seat beside him, "how good to see you! Papa's comrade in arms."

Small winced, owing presumably to his recent neglect of business.

"My sympathy on your loss," he replied stiffly.

"I value it. And mine..." She faltered before his evident embarrassment.

Only after Harris had had a chance to recount Small's contribution to the inquest did the lawyer's spirits begin to revive.

"Well, infidel, where shall we go?" said Small. "Now that Theresa is out of the convent, perhaps she would care to look at some clothes. The French Empress Eugénie sets the style in this city, I'm told."

"I had thought we might drive up Côte des Neiges," put in Harris, remembering too late that the final "s" was silent. "The air will be better on the mountain."

"I'm not going to shop," said Theresa, "but I should like to see where they're building the Victoria Bridge."

"A capital plan," Small responded in a thoughtless, agreeable way. "I'll see if the driver knows where it is."

On the way out Wellington Street to Point St. Charles, Theresa showed the men a telegram that explained much of her apprehensiveness. It had been forwarded from the Grey Nuns and was from Crane. Having heard from the Laurendeaus the wonderful news that she was safe, he looked forward to being at liberty to set out for Montreal within the next day or two. Meanwhile she must stay with the good sisters and build up her strength. A letter would follow.

"He sounds in no hurry," said Harris, falsely cheerful.

"He may already have left. Jasper, what happens if I refuse to see him?"

"If he insists on your return," said Small, "his lawyer will likely write to your hosts. Court action will be threatened."

"Could I not get a divorce?" asked Theresa. "Mrs. Bray was divorced from an adulterer in Connecticut before she became an Episcopalian and married Mr. Bray."

Small looked out the window for a gentle answer. They were crossing the Lachine Canal, whose flow powered grey limestone mills and factories for as far as could be seen. Hard surfaces multiplied the din.

"Jasper," said Harris, "her testimony would not be required to prove adultery against Crane."

"My friends," Small replied, "a husband's infidelity may be grounds for dissolving a marriage in Connecticut or Massachusetts where the Puritan influence is strong, but not in the united province. In Canada West, only two divorces have ever been granted, neither on the petition of the wife. Here in Canada East, divorce is unknown."

"That's clear, at least," said Theresa with a brave tilt to her chin.

Harris pityingly recalled having to explain banking rules not of his devising, but he had always tried to suggest to the client some course of action. Small seemed to leave them with nothing.

Before more could be said, the coach stopped and promptly had to move again to make way for waggons bringing limestone blocks to the bridge-head. The three passengers stepped down to find the St. Lawrence before them. Stone piers at intervals Harris estimated above three hundred feet marched away across the river towards the south shore, almost two miles distant. Stone-laden barges approached a coffer-dam surrounding one pier not yet built above water level. Derricks lowered blocks to the river bed. And over barges, dams, derricks, piers and waggons swarmed Irish-accented workers in the hundreds.

While impressed with the scale of the undertaking, Harris wondered why Theresa—with no known interest in engineering—should have wanted to come here when so much else claimed her attention. Then he saw she had turned away from the bridge towards three apparently unremarkable rows of mostly open sheds. He joined her.

"Don't lose heart," he advised. "We're not done picking Jasper's brains yet."

"I admit I can't quite shake Henry out of my thoughts," she replied, "but this is what I wanted to see. This must be where emigrants were quarantined during the typhus nine years ago."

Harris noticed that the sheds, many of which now held building supplies, were fitted with plank bunks. He shuddered. This was evidently nothing Small wanted to see, as he promptly wandered off to inspect the works. Theresa made no attempt to detain him.

"I told Jasper some of what you wrote in your letter," Harris confided, "whatever I thought might be legally useful in keeping Crane away from you, and in bringing him to justice."

He watched Theresa's face in profile, the thoughtful curve of her forehead, the unblinking gaze under soft brows. She was perhaps seeing the bunks loaded with bodies—in place of lumber—and courageous nurses passing among them.

"I hope you approve," he added.

"I don't mind—if you think he can help."

"He wants to, I'm positive, and he's capable enough, only Jasper doesn't stand very high in his own opinion right now."

"Doesn't he?" said Theresa, suddenly attentive. "Is that what the condition looks like? Isaac, what you wrote in your letter this morning about your regard—even though I could not wholly believe it, I was grateful, and pleased, until this telegram..."

Harris was starting to stammer back some tender reassurance when—

"Stone dust dries the throat," Small called out, approaching. "We should go somewhere for a glass of wine."

"Work first!" Harris replied somewhat tartly, even though he was unsure how to proceed now that hanging and divorcing Crane had both been ruled impracticable. "We'll continue our deliberations as we roll."

But Theresa wasn't quite ready to climb back into the coach. She asked a succession of labourers the location of the emigrants' burial ground and was eventually told that the road they were standing on had been laid over top of it. The graves had not been marked in any case.

On the drive back down Wellington Street, Harris thought about the shiploads of Irish who had fled famine in the old world only to die of fever in the new. Something from early in Theresa's letter came to mind, and he rapidly put it together with other miscellaneous facts.

"In his last days," said Harris, "William Sheridan railed against ship-owners for bringing not the typhus of '47 but the cholera of '32. In that epidemic, he lost his wife and son, Theresa her mother and brother. I think, Jasper, it's time you told us about William Sheridan's last case."

Alone this time on the backwards-facing seat, Small looked questioningly from Harris to Theresa.

"That case didn't touch Crane," he said at last.

"But just before his death," Harris rejoined, "your partner was arguing with Crane about something. Sibyl says voices were raised."

"I don't see that it could have been about—"

"I know you don't, Jasper, but let's spread out all the cards first and play what hand we can with them after. That is, if Theresa doesn't mind."

Far from minding, Theresa at Harris's side leaned forward and joined the inquisition.

"You told me, Jasper, the case touched the MacFarlanes," she prompted.

Small squirmed. "A mistake."

"But not a misstatement!" Harris raced on. He might be racing down a blind alley. Still, the detective muse had so neglected him lately that no inspiration could be thrown away. "Now George MacFarlane was only one of many ship-owners in 1832, so to become the focus of legal action after twenty-four years, and to warrant his family's being seen less of by Theresa, he must have done something especially discreditable. Come to think of it, I can believe his conscience chafes him, for when I mentioned the death of Theresa's brother to him on July 20, he pretended the 1832 epidemic had never happened. Theresa's disappearance had me too distracted to dwell on his words at the time, but they seem amazing now. Six thousand deaths conjured away!"

"Done what, Isaac?" Theresa demanded. "Don't spare my feelings. Knowing what I'm married to, I can bear anything."

"You must ask Jasper. The evidence is or was a document, which you heard your father assure Dr. Hillyard was safe in William Sheridan's strongbox. Following his death, Jasper told Inspector Vandervoort that items were missing from that box. Facetiously or otherwise, Vandervoort suggested to me that you, Theresa, had removed them, but it didn't occur to you to open the box—did it?—until you were no longer in a position to do so."

"No—not until Sunday noon. Papa's body went to Ogilvie's Saturday night with the key around his neck."

"Well, Jasper?" said Harris. "*Was* the MacFarlane document taken?"

"Why, yes. I thought..." Small uncrossed his legs and studied Theresa with a look of inscrutable wonder.

Harris was still arranging the cards. "You said, Jasper, that Crane had had business worries. Was that so, Theresa?"

"He never talked about business, but he did start asking me to economize, whereas previously he had scolded me for not making enough of a show."

"Yet by July 20, MacFarlane was pronouncing him 'sound as a board.'" Harris paused and nodded. "I think," he said, "that we have stumbled upon the motive for murder, and that it has to do with the transport of emigrants rather than with religious zealotry or the Orange Lodge. What was it, Jasper? William Sheridan's fortune couldn't have saved Crane, but George MacFarlane's could. What was the piece of paper he sold MacFarlane—the paper that didn't touch him, but for which he suffocated Theresa's father, your partner, the People's Champion?"

The coach had stopped at Bray's door. No one got out. Drawing a plain white handkerchief from her sleeve, Theresa blew her nose.

"Jasper?" she said, her voice thick with emotion. "Who is the author of this document?"

"I thought," said Small, "you knew."

"I know no more than Isaac has said."

Small sat up straight. He seemed to grow half an inch. The look of surprise passed from his pale grey eyes, leaving them clear and steady, expressive of thought. Harris was too preoccupied to take much notice, and even if he had been inclined to see a positive change in his friend, he would have had his hopes restrained by the apparent irrelevance of Small's next remark.

"Christopher," said the lawyer. "I believe I heard that was the little boy's name."

"After the doctor." Theresa grimaced to show how deserving she thought Hillyard of that honour, then spoke in simple sadness of her brother. "Our lives overlapped by four days, but Papa says we were never in the same room. He used to say."

The poignancy of this quiet correction only intensified Harris's feeling that she was owed an answer. Even if this document's secret didn't help protect her from Crane, which protection must be their principal object, still she needed it to satisfy her vow—the vow that had taken her to Sibyl's room and under Sibyl's bed, the vow to find out how her father had died.

"Was it a letter, Jasper?" Harris demanded. "A signed confession? What?"

"I should have to get Scabby Hillyard's permission first," said Small.

More obstructions, Harris thought and gritted his teeth to keep from saying. Small might as well be working for the enemy.

"Open the door then," Theresa said, disappointment palpable in her face and voice.

Harris opened it and jumped out, ready to hand her down.

"Can't you dine with us?" Small asked, disappointed in turn, as if her company on this occasion truly mattered more to him than the meal itself.

"No, Jasper. Mr. Bray will be home directly, and I do not intend that he should turn me out. He has promised to bar his door against Henry."

Well said, thought Harris. He undertook to write her that evening at the latest. She surprised him by kissing his cheek. With Small she set an example of graciousness, taking his hand and warmly thanking him for coming as far as Montreal on a hopeless case.

"Oh, I'm glad to find you didn't—that is, to find you so much recovered, and I look forward to being of *some* use, somehow or other..." Her first dance partner seemed caught on the wrong foot. "You can tell the Brays I'm C. of E. at least."

* * *

So, the secret of the strongbox was Hillyard's to disclose. Very well. Harris directed that the two remaining passengers be driven straight to the telegraph office.

Then—as the coach pulled away from Theresa's lodging—he

tried to get back in humour with Small, whose features beneath the rim of his black bowler hat appeared commendably grave and alert. This Small, Harris saw, differed markedly from the depressed individual that had accompanied him to Craig Street.

"Jasper," he inquired, "why does it make such a difference that Theresa did not remove the MacFarlane paper?"

"Because of my indiscretion," Small promptly replied. "You see, as Theresa says, I mentioned the MacFarlanes to her, and I was desperately afraid that slip of the tongue had cost me any chance of completing William Sheridan's last project. I've cursed myself black and blue over that. A bad conscience has made it tremendously hard for me to pull myself together."

"You thought she might have taken the document to protect her friends—but would she really have put her friends before her father?"

"Her father was dead, remember. No, Isaac, I should not have expected her to feel the same obligation to pursue the matter as I did. For one thing, she couldn't have read the letter. It was in cipher, much like the telegrams your branch used to exchange with head office. Theresa would have seen only an unpronounceable and—without the key—meaningless handwritten sequence of characters."

Tantalized and encouraged, Harris rubbed his palms over the knees of his trousers. A ciphered letter then. If Small could be led on at this rate, they might not have to wait for uncertain permission to arrive by wire from Toronto after all.

"Tell me, Jasper, can MacFarlane be sued for what he did or neglected to do twenty-four years ago?"

"By no means. Every action shall be commenced within twelve calendar months."

"Then," Harris reasoned, "perhaps Dr. Hillyard isn't strictly speaking your client and needn't be consulted."

"The case is more complicated than you imagine," said Small, but not discouragingly. "Let's consider the matter while we eat."

Harris made sure a telegram to Hillyard was sent first.

Small planned the lunch, but in the interests of health and

economy acquiesced to Harris's veto of three of the courses. Apples from the mountain were in season and formed the theme of what remained. They came steamed with the roast goose, baked and served with custard in the tart, while John McIntosh's Reds took pride of place in the fruit bowl. Harris would happily have drunk cider as well. He compromised, however, on a Beaujolais at a fraction of the cost of the Clos de Vougeot his friend was urging.

While they ate, Small talked. He started at some distance from the secret. It was less than clear, perhaps least of all to Small himself, where he intended to stop.

He spoke first of Theresa's mother. As a bride of eighteen, she had accompanied William Sheridan to the New World in 1823. Harris had perhaps noted in her husband's office Emily Sheridan's watercolour likeness—showing a narrow, animated face like Theresa's, but with a merrier cast and her auburn hair curled six inches out either side of her head. Harris might not know that whenever he saw that portrait in Sheridan's office, there was in Sheridan's bedroom an empty nail waiting to receive it. It had gone to Yonge Street with him every day and returned to Front Street every night.

Emily loved games and entertainments of all kinds, especially cards. Small wished he had known her. The couple's new friend Chris Hillyard had considered her the most enchanting whist player since Mrs. Simcoe left town in '96. By the twenties, Hillyard was already an old bachelor, but he never made any secret of the fact that in all his long and undistinguished medical career, Emily was the patient he most regretted losing.

Late in the 1840s, Hillyard began to feel his years and moved south. Which of the Caribbean colonies he settled in Small couldn't say, but in Bridgetown or Georgetown or Port of Spain, the septuagenarian one day found himself at the bedside of a feverish sea captain. A less superstitious patient might have thrown the malady off. This sailor, however, believed he was being punished for his part in bringing Asiatic cholera to Canada. Hillyard dug the wax out of his ancient ears and attended closely.

Small supposed he was being indiscreet, so he had best say no more—unless Harris would be sworn to secrecy. Harris barely nodded before Small was off again.

Hillyard's patient had in '32 been master of the brig *Katherine,* carrying timber east across the Atlantic and emigrants west. In May she was bound for Quebec City, but contrary winds had kept her at sea more than fifty days, and many of the passengers had used up all their food. She accordingly put into New Brunswick's Miramichi Bay for supplies before sailing on up the St. Lawrence. Because of the cholera scare and the master's report of ten deaths at sea "from a bowel complaint," the *Katherine* was kept offshore and under guard. No one was allowed to disembark.

Now it happened the owner was in New Brunswick looking for more trees to cut. When he heard of the *Katherine*'s situation, he had a letter carried out to her master, along with the requested food. George MacFarlane had far fewer ships then than now, and he made it clear he wanted none of them tied up in red tape for any part of the short navigation season. The *Katherine* had already lost enough time.

"Have you a copy of this letter?" Harris broke in. He had stopped eating and was anxious to see the exact words that might have cost Christopher, Emily, and—ultimately—William Sheridan their lives.

"I have a reference copy in the vault at the office—not here." Small uncharacteristically let the waiter take the wine bottle with a last half glass still in it. "The gist of it, though, was this: as the *Katherine* approached Quebec, she was to put any ill passengers ashore under cover of darkness and to sail past the quarantine station at Grosse Île without stopping."

Harris blew a breath out slowly. He was picturing men, women and children writhing with cramps on the inky strand of an unknown continent while their ship, now purged of them, sailed serenely on.

"I knew individual captains acted to frustrate the quarantine," he said, "but I had never heard it was a policy of any of the owners. Poor Kate MacFarlane, having that vessel named for her."

"She won't feel it," Small rejoined, "and MacFarlane will be spared the loss of her esteem. Neither she nor the public will ever know."

"Go on, Jasper. Finish the story."

The dining room was closing, so Small bought two Havanas and finished the story in the smoking lounge. There three men with Carolina drawls were commenting on the autumnal coolness in the air and agreeing it was time to collect their wives and daughters and go home. The room's only other occupants slept soundly in their chairs, far removed this year from any fear of plague.

And had the captain followed his instructions? From what Hillyard heard at that tropical bedside, he had. He had had misgivings, certainly, on account of the cannon at the quarantine station, but MacFarlane had vouched for its being no more than a toy and for the impossibility in any case of British troops firing on British ships.

At night and with the blessing of a following breeze, the *Katherine* slid up the broad St. Lawrence three miles off Grosse Île. Four blue-skinned passengers were meanwhile spewing fluids from both ends. Below Quebec there remained some thirty miles of river, and for two dozen of them the master procrastinated, hoping some or all the sufferers would expire before dawn. When it became clear none would, he had them and their inseparable friends rowed to a farmer's jetty. Two hours later, the *Katherine* reached port without a health certificate but presentable enough to brazen out any attempt to make her retrace her wake all the way back to Grosse Île. The long-confined emigrants cooperated fully in concealing evidence of the cholera. Who could blame them?

As of that date, 5th June 1832, no case of the disease had been diagnosed anywhere in British North America. Within the week, it had taken two hundred Canadian lives. The *Katherine* crossed the ocean twice more that summer, and by the time she was back in Quebec in September, thousands more were dead, as far west as Hamilton and London. In York—later renamed Toronto—Emily Sheridan and twenty-six others succumbed on 9th August, five days after her eldest child.

That winter the captain sailed for an Argentinian owner, whose niece he in time married. After the briefest twinge of remorse, he forgot MacFarlane and wasn't even aware of having kept the fateful letter until his wife's death fifteen years later obliged him to clean house.

Grief and guilt now reinforced each other. When in the next port he fell ill, he wanted a confessor no less than a physician. Hillyard filled both rôles. Whether the patient-penitent was Scot or Swede, ample or compact, white-haired or red—Small couldn't say. His account derived from William Sheridan's memorandum of several conversations with Hillyard, and perhaps neither older man cared to put a human face on this cog of destiny.

Before dying, he had given the letter to Hillyard, who now saw whose hand had upset his whist table. Never mind that other vessels had evaded the quarantine. Never mind that even those that passed through it often brought cholera ashore. MacFarlane was an assassin.

For some years, even after returning to Toronto, Hillyard did nothing with this knowledge. He told no one. He saw no legal means to call MacFarlane to account and lacked any stomach for scandal-mongering. Only when it appeared that MacFarlane was to be knighted for service to the Empire did the doctor break his silence by writing to the Governor General.

Sir Edmund Head was in this case ill-served by a functionary, who improperly told MacFarlane what was being alleged and by whom. The intent was not apparently to have the damning evidence refuted but to have it suppressed. MacFarlane threatened Hillyard with an action for defamatory libel. The same day—late June this would have been—Hillyard took the entire story together with the 1832 letter to Sheridan.

"MacFarlane sued Hillyard and lost?" said Harris.

"No, Isaac. Listen..."

Harris had been listening, but restlessly, with frequent prods and queries to hasten the narrative. After barely a puff, he had let his cigar go cold. He was too disgusted to taste it. He was thoroughly disgusted.

He had once admired George MacFarlane as the supreme exemplar of energy and enterprise. And now? MacFarlane was clearly not a murderer as Crane was a murderer, but now it seemed that to save a week in port—*one week*—the shipping magnate had recklessly gambled with the health and lives of his own family, of every family in his country.

Harris's imagination leaped ahead to the state in which Dr. Hillyard would have found Theresa's father two months ago. By her account, the latter was at the time torn between the solicitations of Prime Minister John A. Macdonald and those of oppositionist George Brown, and the strain was settling as usual in his stomach.

"I have," Small resumed, "traced the cholera letter's effect on, firstly, the sea captain and, secondly, Christopher Hillyard. Now this flimsy sheet of paper passes to a third reader, William Sheridan, whom it hit—his very words—'like a kick in the gut.'"

The old bear had left Parliament early that day, too sore and sorry for acrimonious debate. He had gone home to rest. While resting, he had deliberated.

A righteous urge to denounce the timber baron tickled his throat, but the MacFarlanes were Theresa's friends, and more innocent parties would suffer than guilty. Little Elsie had sketched the harbour from Sheridan's window. Kate had played his piano. The other pan of the balance held Sheridan's own wife and child. Were they not past suffering, though, the angels?

When he found himself weeping, he realized he was not the man to advise Hillyard. All the same, some maggot of inquisitiveness made him stagger to a bookcase and take down MacFarlane's novel *Flora.* He read the inscription.

"Let me see if I recall it," said Small, looking for words up among the pendants of a crystal gaselier. "Yes, more or less—'To Theresa Crane, a refreshing young friend, who may discern in her lively self some resemblance to the heroine of this simple tale. In doing so, she would confer the greatest honour on journeyman author'—large signature here and flourish—'George MacFarlane.' Henry thought his wife was being called a backwoods bumpkin. He refused the volume houseroom."

"Sheridan compared the hand with that of the *Katherine*'s instructions," Harris suggested.

"Those instructions," said Small with a sigh. "How Willie cursed their author for not using a secretary!"

"Perhaps there was no time to collar one before the brig left New Brunswick."

But Sheridan had hoped the scripts would differ. Their congruence had made it harder to put the matter out of his mind. Besides, Hillyard was always there to put it back in as through the ensuing fortnight the stomach pains repeatedly dimmed and flared. "Iliac passion," Hillyard had muttered by way of diagnosis. Small thought the later attacks as much due to a misguided over-prescription of laxatives.

MacFarlane's lawyer was asking Hillyard for a withdrawal of the allegations made to the Crown's representative concerning his client, for an unqualified written apology to his client, and for an immediate return of any property of his client's, including any documents or correspondence pertaining to his client's vessels or former vessels. How, Hillyard persisted in asking, should he treat these demands?

After a number of unavailing recommendations that his friend seek other counsel, Sheridan suggested there was no immediate need to do anything. If MacFarlane sustained no injury, Hillyard would pay no damages. In his defence, moreover, the doctor might plead that he had written to Sir Edmund neither falsely nor maliciously, but in all honesty and for the public benefit. Finally, the *Katherine* letter was its recipient's property, not its sender's.

Hillyard calmed down sufficiently to leave his scabs

undisturbed, for a day or so. Then, on the night of July 8, he woke Sheridan up to announce that his house and surgery had been broken into. Nothing had been taken, but everything had been disarranged. Yes, he could tell. He had left his effects in an informal order very different from the shambles in which he had found them. Locked drawers had been forced.

As to motive, physicians were widely—if baselessly—reputed to be rich. Then again, the less educated relatives of patients whom no medicine could have saved sometimes fancied they had scores to settle. The object of this crime, however, Hillyard believed to be neither booty nor vengeance.

"The letter," he said. "Good thing I gave it to you."

Suspicion that he was right made Sheridan no friendlier to the prospect of "Sir" being prefixed to George MacFarlane's name. Ultimate responsibility in the matter rested in England with the Secretary of State for the Colonies. To him Sheridan began to think of applying. If he got no satisfaction before the start of the next session, he might even have the matter raised in Parliament.

While briefing Small on these subjects, Sheridan began vomiting freely, hideous bilious matter such as Small had never seen, and promptly took to his bed with his worst attack of abdominal pain ever. When Small visited on 10th July, he was instructed to prepare a letter to the Colonial Office. Sheridan would decide the next day whether to sign and send it.

"None of us," said Small, "was thinking rationally. From declining to represent Hillyard, the old bear had almost reached the point of taking on Hillyard's crusade himself, risking his life in ways at least some of which should have been clear to him. Hillyard? He was not trying to kill his friend. He just couldn't bring himself to forget MacFarlane and practise medicine. As for me, my senior partner was a second father—more hot-blooded certainly but also more affectionate than my own. I feared for his life. I feared for mine without him. I've always seen myself as loyal Second-in-Command rather than as Officer Commanding. Now I was doing Sheridan's work as well as mine, an unwanted promotion seemed imminent, and I was expected to confide in no one."

Small spoke collectedly, but Harris could sense his loneliness. Society was Small's oxygen. His need for others made him want to be loyal, but also made it hard for him to be unflinchingly reticent—and, open-hearted as he was, Small must have felt the strain of bearing unassisted and unconsoled the full weight of his ailing chief's ideals.

"On July 11," said Harris, bringing them to the eve of Sheridan's murder, "you were in court regarding an indenture."

"Gratifying that someone noticed. The employer had flouted the educational provisions, wantonly stunting a young girl's mind. My pleading would determine her future. I had by the same date to draft a letter to the highest Imperial authorities on behalf of all the victims of the '32 cholera. Thursday and Friday I neither ate nor slept."

"Then on Friday afternoon you didn't even get a chance to show Sheridan your draft," said Harris. "Did he tell you Crane had come calling that morning?"

Small shook his head. "On MacFarlane's business?"

"Presumably." Harris didn't try to hide his disappointment. Significant and shocking as Small's revelations had been, they had not so far yielded anything of immediate use to Theresa.

"All I know of Crane's involvement," Small confirmed, "is what you pieced together in the coach. The idea that he took the *Katherine* letter by arrangement with MacFarlane—that relieved my mind of even less congenial hypotheses."

"You suspected," Harris said bluntly, "that Emily Sheridan's daughter took it to protect a spreader of the plague."

Knowing the letter's contents made this suspicion monstrous—but Small hastened to deny that those contents could have been known to Theresa.

"She would have recognized MacFarlane's hand and nothing more. The first three letters she would have read are *qlb*. How could she have known they stand for *put*—as in, 'Put ashore...'? Because of my warning, she might have thought it a document harmful to her friends without realizing its gravity. Without further inquiry, she likely would not have either destroyed this paper or returned it to its author, but her own disappearance put it just as effectively beyond my reach. I confess I came to Montreal hoping to recover it from her."

"And you meant to use it as her father would have," Harris added.

MacFarlane would by now have burned this compromising manuscript. Harris regretted its loss. The smoke of the fire stung his nostrils. It was a minor loss compared with the loss of a man like Sheridan, and yet Harris understood how Sheridan—as legislator, democrat and widower—could have defended the letter with his life.

"Deuce knows what I should have made of it, Isaac," said Small. "Perhaps nothing. With William Sheridan gone, perhaps MacFarlane didn't need the letter. Hillyard had given up. I was so distracted I didn't even open Sheridan's strongbox for a week after his death. Then, when I did, I felt—well, you know the rest."

Small supposed a sense of culpability gave some people the will to do better in future, but he had in the past six weeks discerned no such improving effect on himself. He was as happy without the shame and expected to be more productive as well.

Harris acknowledged his point, ungrudgingly but briefly. Now what evidence might they produce against the actual remover of the *Katherine* letter—a double murderer and Theresa's pursuer? Was there anything they could take to the inquest when it resumed in six days?

Small considered. The old set of summer migrants had long since left the lounge, and a new set was arriving for a last smoke before facing afternoon tea. Harris was restless from too much sitting. Small continued to consider.

"I wonder," said Harris, "if Crane knew the letter's contents. From what you say, the key to the cipher was not in the box."

"It applied to all communications for the year. The sailor told Hillyard, and no one who has once heard it has ever found it necessary to write down—'Britons never will be slaves.'"

"Expressing heroic resistance to health regulation. Delightful!" Harris saw MacFarlane planted on his Queen Street battlements, untroubled victim of his own charades. "He'll have schooled himself to find Sheridan's death surprising. I don't see how we could get him to rat against Crane, do you?"

"Sir Rat, you mean? He would have to incriminate himself."

"If only your damned law would let Theresa testify... Look, Jasper, I'll just put a bullet in Crane's head, and you can defend me after."

It surprised Harris to hear bubble from his lips a daydream unacknowledged in his darkest thoughts. Some dank fold of his brain must have been secreting it, though, for with the words the act presented itself complete to his senses.

Next Thursday he could be in Wilson's farm yard. He would have a clean shot just after one p.m., when Crane stepped down from his brougham. Wait till Matheson the lawyer was clear. Crane's chest would make a better target than his head, of course, keep the bullet lower too, reduce the risk to Farmer Wilson's livestock. Harris felt his Sharps hunting rifle steady against his shoulder. No anger shook his aim. It would be as easy as cancelling a cheque. In fact, he was always at his calmest with a firearm in his hands. You had to be.

While Harris was dreaming only, and by no means planning Crane's death, still the absence of any plan to free Theresa drew the dream into its vacant place, as lungs will draw foul air when denied fresh.

What was Small saying?

"I should be better qualified for my part, Isaac, than you for yours. One does not become a man-slayer all at once. Degeneration takes time... Come to think of it, why not look back over Henry Crane's life for another felony?"

"How's that?" said Harris. "Are you saying a man can't break necks without having picked locks, or kill without having coined? I should have thought that crimes of choler such as Crane's proceeded not from a sky prepared with clouds, but rather from the blue."

"And was Crane never in high temper before 12th July?"

Harris saw Small's point, yet doubted. "We have to keep him from Theresa. Have you heard rumoured any misdeed grave enough to meet that need? Adultery, you said this morning, is not enough?"

"Quite insufficient," Small airily replied, "and in Toronto he is such a public figure that any meatier scandal would have been difficult to keep hidden. However, he was not always so well known."

"His early career," observed Harris, still far from sanguine, "lies buried far away in the Northwest."

"Along with his first partner—who died, I understand, a violent death."

"An accident."

"Perhaps." Small retreated into his Buddha smile, then straightened his cuffs, seeming to recall his new-found sense of purpose. "Perhaps an accident," he said. "Would it be heartless to hope not?"

Chapter Eighteen
Steadfast

To give himself and his horse a stretch, Harris parted from Small for a couple of hours. He wanted as well to reflect upon Small's advice.

Banshee's sides were plainly sleeker than a week ago, her eye brighter. When Harris mounted, the animal wobbled her head, expressing readiness for action. Instead of taking her up the mountain as usual, he rode south and west through the factory district. Despite the city clatter, he felt himself just as effectively alone.

Jasper was no help. Willing as he now professed himself to be of service, his best thoughts amounted to no more than wishes. Harris had no idea under what circumstances Crane's unfortunate partner had perished—not so much as whether he had been burned, crushed or drowned—and Small knew nothing more. Inquiries could be made, yes, but were they worth the time?

How much simpler, Harris told himself, how much more expeditious in view of Crane's imminent arrival in Montreal, to simply remove Theresa from the jurisdiction! She must see that too. Crane would leave her in peace in New Brunswick, or New England, or New Zealand, or...

Harris couldn't quite persuade himself to this course either. Steam power had so abridged distance that no place on earth seemed quite far or new enough.

The cotton and cordage mills behind them, Harris had his mount pick up her gait. They were following the tow path of the Lachine Canal, up which chugged paddle-wheelers Harris had last seen four hundred miles away. There went the gleaming

Cytherean. Her banners tumbled on the late summer breeze, and her Botticelli goddess rose on a clam shell from the pilot house. Time and space shrank.

They must have been shrinking for Crane as well. The part of Crane's life that he had left on Lake Superior, perhaps in the belief he was leaving it forever, his own steamships and railways had been bringing closer every year. Somewhere between Sault Ste. Marie and Fort William might lie a youthful shame he had counted on never to overtake him.

A shrinking world penalized the fugitive, but benefited the pursuer. Better at these odds to pursue.

At the instant it formed, this insight struck Harris as pivotal. He felt its heft and shapeliness. It fell into his dialogue with himself like a greased pin into a hinge. In truth, however, without having made any conscious decision to do so, he was already pursuing Small's suggestion. He was already proceeding full gallop towards the Lachine offices of the Hudson's Bay Company, the likeliest place on the island of Montreal to obtain information regarding Crane's northern years.

Eight miles west of the city's heart, the Lachine Canal drank in the St. Lawrence River through a trio of mouths, each of a different age, before blending the water and sending it east to turn the wheels of industry. By five o'clock, Harris was tying Banshee to the rail of a bridge that spanned the oldest and narrowest of the three channels. Stone banks and shade trees sheltered the waters that no vessel larger than a canoe could have ruffled. Two brown ducks, mallard hens, paddled tentatively from beneath the bridge. To either side in park-like calm stood the Canadian headquarters of the company that owned half the continent.

Harris turned first to a massive, dressed-stone villa on the north bank. Thick columns and balustrades hung about the entrance. Thick mutton chops hung about the face of the immaculate porter. The visitor was briefly conscious of his own dusty riding clothes.

He was led to an office which, in the late afternoon, exhibited as much spruceness and bustle as if the work day were just beginning. Bookkeepers' and copyists' pens scratched briskly across the pages of neatly bound ledgers. Harris had heard that Governor Simpson kept long hours, rousing his voyageurs as early as one a.m. when travelling in the Northwest. Evidently a similar regime applied at home. The governor lived upstairs, but was currently absent on just such a northwestern tour of company trading posts, a clerk briefly intimated. No one familiar with Lake Superior in the forties was just now in the office. Perhaps if Harris would step across to the warehouse...

Outside, he crossed the bridge and made for a long, low fieldstone building on the south bank of the old canal. The door was open.

"Pack 'em tight, curse you," someone inside was grumbling. "You can get six or eight more in that piece, up to a hundredweight—but snug, mind."

Harris entered the dim and mostly empty storeroom to find a lad of perhaps fourteen struggling to tie a tower of blankets into a bale compact enough to be transported by canoe or portaged.

"Bear down on it with your knee there. Press out the air... Who are you?"

The speaker, noticing Harris, stepped forward out of the shadows. He wore a ragged, salt and pepper beard and an old-fashioned brown frock coat startlingly patched in blue, green and red. His right hand rested on the butt of an old single-shot pistol tucked into his belt.

The boy was all but standing on the blankets now and seemed paralyzed for fear the jack-in-the-box would spring rafter-wards once more. Before this could happen, Harris seized the encircling rope and knotted it tight.

"I've some questions regarding the Northwest," he told the parti-coloured warehouseman. "The office referred me to you."

Considering that the region alluded to extended twenty-five hundred miles, all the way to the Pacific Ocean, Harris prepared to be laughed at.

"I know the Northwest body and soul. Anything *worth*

knowing about its commerce, its redskins, its fur-bearing animals, its rocks and rivers, its storms and freezes I can tell you without your even asking. Now I'll thank you to undo that bale you've been meddling with. The brat has to learn for himself."

"Mamma will be looking for me, Uncle," the boy quickly interposed. Taking advantage of the distraction Harris had provided, he grabbed a shotgun from beside the door and left with a promise to come again tomorrow.

The uncle grunted scornfully. He was a powerfully built, apparently once vigorous man, who now moved stiffly and carried a paunch. The face behind the beard was weathered but no longer firm. Long service on rougher ground had presumably earned him this custodial position, which if it made few demands afforded little in the way of society—no captive ear for his counsel, no permanent target for his ire.

Having by now had some practice questioning strangers, Harris bet this one would talk. Whether to the point remained to prove.

"Well, state your business now you've spoiled my lesson," he said, taking the only chair. "I've leisure enough till October, when the canoes come back down river with the furs, and there'll be plaguey few of those. The land this depot serves is all trapped out. Who wants beaver hats now anyway? I suppose silk's the thing in Europe, although where the warmth in silk is you tell me. Has fashion done away with winter there?"

"Excuse me, Mr.—"

"Cuthbert Nash. I thought the scribblers yonder told you. They know me. Marten you can sell and arctic fox, but they go out through Hudson's Bay, not Montreal..."

In time, Harris extracted the admission that, while he had never been as far as the Pacific, Nash had from 1830 to '49 managed a trading post north of Lake Superior, the only barrier to his attaining higher office being his lack of formal education. Not lack of shrewdness, mind. The mid-forties had seen a copper rush on the U.S. side of the lake and the arrival of steamships. The first were side-wheelers, but Nash had made a young boat-owner's fortune by convincing him that the lake was too rough for paddles, and that he and his partner should build a vessel powered by screws instead. A sandy-haired fellow from Kingston, son of a deceased hardware merchant.

Harris, who had been pacing about the warehouse, glancing at the piles of blankets, guns, kettles and hatchets used in trade, stopped in his tracks.

"Was it Henry Crane? What more can you tell me about him?"

Nash expressed irritation. He wanted to talk about his own solid success as post manager and what a capital chief factor he would have made, not about some here-today, gone-tomorrow speculator.

"He left suddenly?" said Harris. "What were the circumstances of his departure?"

"I know nothing about it. I thought you wanted to hear about the Company's activities in the Northwest. The key is managing the Indians. Your Ojibway is unpredictable, but my experience taught me just when to extend credit and when to come down hard."

"You did say 'here-today, gone-tomorrow,'" Harris persisted. "Why did you use those terms?"

"He was gone the last time I came through Sault Ste. Marie, wasn't he? That would have been in November '49."

"Gone where?" said Harris.

"South, damn you," Nash exploded. "Where else? The canal around the rapids there still hadn't been built and kept getting delayed, so you couldn't run your ships down into Lake Huron. He must have got tired of waiting."

This hardly sounded to Harris like a guilty departure. "What exactly happened to his partner?"

"No, you tell me now—what's your interest in Crane?" said Nash, tugging at the greasy lapels of his harlequin frock coat as if it were a barrister's gown.

Harris looked for an answer he could give with some show of conviction.

"The truth, mind," Nash scolded. "The Ojibway will bear witness I've a sure nose for any sort of lie."

"I'm making inquiries on behalf of a lady," said Harris.

"Go on. What inquiries?"

"My object is to discover whether there is anything in his past to indicate that Henry Crane would make an unfit husband." Harris wished he had had this mission years ago.

"Not married yet?" Nash snorted. "I had a country wife, three children too, but Governor Simpson would not let me bring them to Montreal. He left two families in the Northwest himself before he married Lady Frances that's dead. Now we're both alone."

"I see," said Harris, pausing briefly in acknowledgement of these domestic upheavals. "What became of Crane's propeller ship?"

"Last I saw, it was sailing under the Stars and Stripes, so he must have sold it to the Michiganders once his partner died. Now don't go asking *his* fool name or how the deuce he got so scalded up. I had my own affairs to think of."

"Scalded by the ship's boiler?" Harris doggedly inquired.

"After nineteen years," said Nash, "I was at last to receive advancement, all the way to Hudson's Bay House in Lachine."

"I understand, but as for Crane—"

"For Crane I didn't give a—look, Mr. Question Mark, there used to be a lighthouse keeper up there who knew the story. Anything you want to ask about Crane you ask Harvey Ingram."

"Harvey Ingram?"

A gunshot close outside underscored the repeated name. Window glass rattled. Banshee snorted.

"My sister's brat is shooting ducks again!" exclaimed Nash, pushing Harris towards the door. "He'll blacken my name with the Company if I don't put a stop to it once for all. Get along. Time for me to lock up here anyway."

Harris looked first to his horse. Ears pitched forward, she was staring down into the old canal. There the boy whom the blankets had so vexed was acting as his own dog. Wet to the armpits, his shotgun held over his head, he floundered through the silted-up channel towards the remains of a brown mallard. She floated on her side, the blue speculum on her wing turned up to the clouding sky.

"Just wait!" Nash cried. "I'll break that gun over your backside." He was so excited he could barely close the padlock on the warehouse door. "Shooting up Company property—blast this lock."

However he felt about his own children whom he had left in Indian country, it was hard to imagine that his sister's pleased him better.

"Mr. Nash," said Harris, seizing perhaps his last chance to wring a *living* informant's name from the former post manager, "can't you tell me of anyone else who—"

"Talk to Ingram. Climb out of there, my boy, or I open fire! Ingram that kept the light at Presque Isle."

Not another coherent word could Harris get from him before Nash's thick, unsupple legs bore him away, the pistol from his waistband waving in his fist. There was no time to explain that French champagne had made Harvey Ingram unquestionable.

* * *

Unknown to Harris at Lachine, his lawyer friend had that afternoon also been looking for witnesses to Crane's boreal endeavours. Small took a cab from Rasco's to the Jesuit College at Bleury and Dorchester streets. To the missionary, he reasoned, no corner of God's earth is remote.

On the pretext of preparing a biographical sketch of Mr. Henry Crane, he gained access to a white-haired priest of gentle disposition. Father Gouin consulted a journal he had started in 1849. From it he read aloud in clear, deliberate English translation from his native French. He read the first entry plus whatever passages touched, even glancingly, on Small's theme.

24 May 1849

I arrived last week at Sault Ste. Marie, where our Jesuit predecessors first founded a mission in 1668. It is not properly speaking a *sault* (waterfall), but rather a set of rapids. In the space of half a mile, the level of the river joining Lakes Superior and Huron drops some twenty feet. The Indian canoes ride down this current with apparent ease and even stop to fish from it.

I live on the right or American bank, there being as yet no church on the other. I shall, however, be crossing often, above the rough water or below. It is only in the past half decade that the Society of Jesus has been permitted back into Canada for the first time since the English Conquest of New France. There is much work to be done.

The American settlement, with a summer population approaching one thousand, boasts a substantial fort, a fur trading post, two hotels, various shops and a horse-drawn railway for the portage of freight around the rapids. Two years ago, the state of Michigan became the first in the union to abolish capital punishment. I fear that, as news of this excessive leniency spreads, the Sault may become a mecca for cutthroats as it has for copper miners, though at present it is no rowdier than parts of Montreal.

I eat some trout and more whitefish, which is slightly longer. Potatoes and pork, seasoned with cranberries, are also staples of my diet, for all of which I give thanks...

15 June

I have now made a number of crossings of the St. Mary's River. The Canadian bank is thick with alder bushes and evergreens, beyond which are to be found a Hudson's Bay Company post and practically no other amenities. The one stone house stands unoccupied. The settlement counts fewer than a dozen white residents and between one and two hundred Indians.

Among the latter I make slow progress. They are under the

impression that the religion of the Queen of England must be the best. The Protestants have furthermore profited from their head start by assiduously translating their *Book of Common Prayer* and other tracts into the Ojibway tongue.

Notwithstanding the left bank's general backwardness, I have made the acquaintance there of two enterprising young Englishmen. Both born like myself within sight of the St. Lawrence, they now operate a side-wheeler between points along the north shore of Lake Superior and are adding a screw-driven steamer to their armada. Both men are affable. The more gifted in a mechanical sense, Mr. Colin Ewing by name, is a Montrealer and a Catholic...

20 August

Colin Ewing has just paid me a call before setting off for Chicago. There he will supervise completion of the screw-driven *Steadfast*, so named to advertise her advantage over side-wheelers in rough water. Also, so Colin says, to characterize his partnership with Henry Crane, who seems to be the chief raiser of capital and finder of cargoes. I understand they met in Kingston, C.W. some three years ago. As far as the business goes, they have made each the other's heir.

For the next month I shall miss Colin's visits. This son of the Church is a good match for me at chess, though a trifle prodigal with his pieces. I fear he is careless generally, for almost every time I see him he has some part of his anatomy bandaged. Last week, when I expressed an idle wish to have one of the skilled Ojibway canoeists conduct me down the rapids, Colin insisted on taking me himself. A rock punctured our craft, and we should have drowned but for the buoyancy of birchbark and his adroitness as a helmsman. I valued his company (on dry land) no less after, for he is generous and lively and has a quick, engineer's mind.

I encourage him to turn his talents to bringing his partner to the one true Faith. He promises to do Mr. Henry Crane that inestimable kindness, but I see no results yet. The two share a wooden house and an Ojibway servant.

I have also urged Colin to marry now that he is in a position to support a family. He is without doubt handsome enough to turn the Chicago girls' heads with his boyish, wind-swept looks, his fine black hair, and his ready smile...

26 September

Colin Ewing has conducted *Steadfast* on her maiden voyage up through Lakes Michigan and Huron to the Sault. Here for the past three days he and his partner have been feverishly tearing her apart. Since to steam up the rapids is quite out of the question, she must be reduced to pieces of a size to be hauled over the horse railway, and must then be reassembled on the shores of Lake Superior where Henry Crane has urgent and lucrative commissions waiting for her. Chess games will have to wait. My adversary has barely found the time to tell me that he has accomplished what I bid him and is engaged to be married after navigation closes in November. His excitement is contagious. God bless his ventures...

9 October

A fearful accident has occurred. Colin Ewing was brought to the presbytery this afternoon with deep burns to his face and upper body. From his distressed breathing, I infer the interior of his nose and mouth have been scalded as well, perhaps also his throat and lungs. I have tried to give him water. The lightest touch of the cup to his inflamed lips makes him yelp in pain. His features glow the brightest red and have been swelling alarmingly. His eyes are half-closed. I don't believe he has the use of them in any case. Frequently he lapses into unconsciousness, which I can only count as a merciful dispensation of our all-loving Father.

Not by my choice, Colin's body as well as his soul are in my charge. We have but one doctor at the Sault, who, although a former blacksmith, understands nothing of burned flesh and in all emergencies prescribes calomel and jalap in various proportions, none of which meet the present case. Henry Crane, furthermore, chances to be away on business in Detroit, though expected back here any day.

Colin is too sore to move in any case. I sent to the Canadian side for his own servant to attend him, and this respectable old squaw watches by his bedside as I write.

It has been blowing hard all day. This evening such an autumn gale howls about our chimneys that I should hesitate to venture out of doors on land, let alone on the water. The mate of *Steadfast* who brought him ashore has given me some account of how Colin sustained his hurts.

Bound to demonstrate his vessel's seaworthiness, the co-owner insisted on steaming up lake this morning despite the weather. This, he said, would be her first "great blow." Not an hour from the Sault, a sound as of timber splitting was reported to the wheelhouse. Colin went below decks to investigate. It appeared the violent rolling had shifted or loosened the engine from its mounts. (I am no steamship expert and must paraphrase according to my understanding.) The failure of some of the ship's wooden elements put intolerable strain on the copper tubing. While Colin was inspecting, the next great wave caused a pipe joint to separate. Escaping steam enveloped him. The crew subsequently managed to shut down and secure the engine. Sails were set, and *Steadfast* was returned to port without further mishap.

The mate has put it about that his master cannot live more than a few days. I trust that he is mistaken, but must pray for composure in Colin's presence for his condition is most pitiable...

11 October

Angry blisters consume Colin's face. In contemplating the martyrdom of Father Brébeuf, burned by the Iroquois two centuries ago, I have never pictured heat-tormented flesh like this.

Once these blisters are lanced, I still hope my patient may mend. His chest and shoulders are in somewhat better condition, having benefited from the protection of his clothing.

To give him strength, I have forced sugar and water down his throat, though it took all my courage to do so. I believe he recognizes my voice. It is a blessing his fiancée cannot see what has become of his good looks, which even if he live are gone forever. He has not mentioned her, though this evening he did manage to speak. He asked if Henry had returned. I said no. He seemed perplexed, then asked the date and the weather, which, in the two days since the storm, has been calm. His perplexity only increased, but he did not speak again...

13 October

I yesterday completed the ghastly task of releasing the fluid from Colin's blisters. His condition does not improve. I should like to give him laudanum for his pain, but have nothing except brandy, which is too fiery for him to swallow. Prayer must suffice...

16 October

It is a week since Colin's accident, and his Calvary continues. His sweat soaks his bed linen. His pulse is weak and rapid. I must now assume his end is near, for I would not have him pass from this life without the consolations and sacraments of our Faith. I judged him unfit to make a confession, but gave him extreme unction. While I was touching the consecrated oil to his ruined eyes, and asking the Lord's forgiveness for his sins of sight, I thought he wished to speak. Afterwards, supposing he had meant to ask again about his partner, I told him, "Not yet, perhaps tomorrow."

24 October

Henry Crane arrived two days after Colin's death, which I had not the heart to describe here. As soon as the surviving partner heard the heavy news, he came to me to express both his gratitude for my care of his friend and his sincere regret that he had been kept away so much longer than anticipated. In the five days since his return, he has had *Steadfast* repaired and reinforced. He will not sail her, however, for he is winding up his affairs at Sault Ste. Marie and intends to move south, away from a place with painful associations and towards new opportunities...

10 November

When Colin Ewing died, I considered it my first duty to write to the woman he was engaged to marry. I have just received her gracious reply. By it I learn that, on disposing of the partnership's assets, Henry Crane sent her a portion of the proceeds. So brief was her acquaintance with Colin Ewing that a major share of her grief must be for the lost opportunity to know him better. This noble gift, she writes, helps her to do so, for like my letter it shows her what friendship Colin was capable of inspiring. I have also received a most welcome sum from Henry Crane for the work of the mission.

Someone has tried to put it about that Mr. Crane's delay in returning was deliberate and that he did not wish to face his disfigured and dying partner, but the rumour-monger is a heathenish lighthouse keeper, who supplements his income by selling liquor to the Indians, and no Catholic or Protestant on either bank of the river believes him...

William Sheridan had encouraged Small to learn shorthand from the moment they first worked together. All that Father Gouin read Small gratefully took down and made reading it in turn to Harris the first item of business when the two met at supper.

Harris practically gaped in amazement. He felt himself in the presence of the Small of Sheridan and Small, a Small serene yet tireless in a good cause. Yesterday's idler seemed a shadow dispelled by the reignited flame of self-respect.

Were Small's discoveries useful? For the moment, wonder precluded deliberation—wonder at Small's exertions and increasingly at the story he was unfolding. By the end of that story, Harris felt his heart simultaneously go out to Colin Ewing in his long, raw torment and shrink back from the wide, wind-flailed region that had taken Ewing from city comforts forever.

"A Montrealer," Harris mused aloud—as if this detail threw the spartan amenities at the Sault into more meaningful contrast with the prosperous city he could glimpse over the white table linen, between the silver epergnes, and through the plate glass of Rasco's dining room.

"Son of a widowed rope and rigging manufacturer of St. Sacrement Street," Small briskly replied. "I paid the father a call. He never approved of his son's mid-continental steam ventures, has never met Crane or the fiancée and has nothing to add to or subtract from Father Gouin's account."

"Admirable, Jasper—and admirably thorough." Harris began to think practically. "At least we can rule out any thought of Ewing's having been murdered."

"Easy there," Small cautioned. "Ewing's marriage would have disinherited Crane. Conscience money paid to the cheated bride still left Crane profiting from his partner's death."

"There's motive, I'll grant," said Harris. "However, the accident as your missionary describes it would have been too difficult to arrange. How could Crane guarantee that on the next rough voyage Ewing and no one else would be mortally injured, or that the loosened engine would not puncture the hull and drown all on board? Ewing might not even have been of the party."

"Bound to have been, Isaac. He was waiting to test his ship in a 'great blow.'"

"But," Harris objected, "would Crane have risked sinking the principal asset he wished to acquire? Insurance rarely matches what a ship can be sold for, and when it does fraud will not go unsuspected."

"The Roman emperor Nero," Small slyly observed, "launched his mother in a disintegrating boat."

"Not in order to inherit the boat! No—I'm sorry, but I still have to think Crane's first murder victim was *your* partner, not his."

"I don't pretend we have grounds yet for an indictment," Small conceded, "but suppose Crane did avoid Ewing after the scalding, stayed away on purpose. What but guilt would have made him do that?"

"Squeamishness," said Harris. "To be blunt, he hates squashed things. I believe that's why, when he must face what he kills, his preferred method is suffocation."

Small refolded and pocketed his notes with equanimity.

"I feel rather queasy myself," he said, "surveying the carcasses of these quail. Let's have them bring us some cherries in brandy, and you can tell me what you unearthed this afternoon."

"Very little, I'm afraid, except perhaps the name of Father Gwynne's rumour-monger."

"Gouin," Small corrected. "Rhymes with *soin*—care—and *loin*—far. Yes?"

"Harvey Ingram," said Harris. "The same Harvey Ingram who until his recent death by drink kept the Gibraltar Light in Toronto."

Small raised his eyebrows, but held his reply until the waiter had effected the change of cover.

"Two years ago, Isaac, the individual you mention wanted our firm to defend him against an accusation of blackmail, arising from some transaction on a yacht between a prominent educator and his grand-niece, which transaction Ingram happened to observe through his spyglass in the course of his lightkeeping duties. In the end he said we meant to overcharge him—a fantastic notion. He intimated he had his own way of dealing with the case, which certainly never reached the courts."

"A blackmailer," said Harris. "Why didn't you tell me before?"

Arriving at Police Station No. 1 with Vandervoort, Ingram had looked the sprucer of the two in worn but sound grey breeches of a military cut, and then had shown quite convincing confusion about the Reciprocity Treaty and its provisions. He had appeared to be too fond of his bottle to be truly cunning—and so it turned out. He had, though, been considerably more devious than Harris supposed.

"Before today, nothing tied him to Crane," Small unanswerably replied.

"All right, Jasper." Harris experienced another moment like the one at noon in the coach—the moment when out of the fog looms a shape, or when the accumulating points in a plane first indicate a geometric figure. He hastened to sketch it. "Suppose Crane does have a guilty secret, dating from 1849. Not simply a delay in returning. I can't see that that would be worth much in blackmail. Ingram found this darker secret out and used it to siphon shillings from Crane's pocket into his own. Shillings at first, later guineas. The more success Crane enjoyed over the years, the dearer would have been Ingram's silence."

"I even wonder," Small mused, "if Crane might not have had a hand in securing Ingram's appointment in Toronto. It seemed an odd choice. I mean to say, Ingram had done lightkeeping work all right, but until three years ago he had been doing it in Michigan."

"Quite possibly Crane *did* get him the job," Harris concurred. "By '53, Crane would have had the ear of some politicians. In prosperity, Crane could afford not to quibble, but then he suffered reverses. The unabated need to pay blackmail would have reduced him all the sooner to accepting MacFarlane's help on MacFarlane's terms, and led ultimately to the two murders we know of."

"Better moral economy," said Small, "to have killed Ingram."

"Crane must have thought, 'Better late than never.' Did you mark his ease at the bones inquest?"

Small grinned. "Satisfaction at Ingram's passing?"

"Nothing would surprise me less. I'm wondering if Crane might not have made his last payment to Ingram in a form he knew would prove fatal. Namely, alcoholic drink."

Small wiped brandy and cherry syrup from his mouth with a corner of napkin and remarked that their time would be better spent in ordering and drinking their own champagne than in returning to Toronto to discover the source of Ingram's. Another blackmail victim might have sent it. Even if Crane were found to be involved, they would have little power over him. A case of wine from an abstainer was anomalous, but not criminal, or even—outside the Temperance Lodges—sufficiently embarrassing to be the subject of hard bargaining. What they needed to learn was not how Ingram died, but what Ingram knew.

Harris shifted uncomfortably in his chair. He felt saddle sore from the afternoon's twenty-mile ride, and there was something else. He suggested taking their cigars outside.

Nine o'clock had sounded, and the moon was up. They strolled down to the harbour, passing along the short side of the now quiet Bonsecours Market. This recent limestone structure in the neo-classical style—prodigiously long in comparison to its width—extended with its pavilions, bays and columns nearly five hundred feet along the quays, and a northerly breeze made the two smokers content to walk up and down for a time in its lee. Crowning the market's midpoint rose a noble silver dome, doubly noble in the silver moonlight. Glancing up, Harris felt drawn to this temple of healthy commerce—and repelled by the quite different dark market of secrets he was about to enter.

Small's logic unsettled him. Small's reference to "hard bargaining" suggested that whatever so-called crime Crane had committed might not be one for which he could be hanged or locked away from Theresa in the Penitentiary. What they were hunting might simply be a source of scandal. Something, it might be, public knowledge of which would intolerably damage Crane's business or personal reputation—something comparable to the cholera letter MacFarlane had taken such extreme measures to suppress. Possessed of whatever Ingram had known about Crane, Harris would find himself in Ingram's shoes. If he managed to get his hand on the lever with which to pry Crane away from Theresa, Harris would also be a blackmailer. The idea revolted him.

At the same time, a high-minded contest seemed hopeless when Theresa's champion surveyed the armour shielding her antagonist—the company directorships, the private railway coaches, the King Street office block, the iron-hulled steamers, the mechanics and labourers to command. At the centre, invulnerable, strode a parricide libertine, Theresa's legal husband, breaker of necks as well as hearts. How shameful *was* it to shame him into effectively renouncing her?

Perhaps Harris should be prepared to incur shame for his lady's sake, even if she shun him for it. His pre-eminent goal must be her salvation, not his honour—nor yet her approbation. And still, though he lose her, he would dearly have liked to deserve her, which a blackmailer could not hope to do. Or could he?

What reprieved Harris from this maze of conscience was the difficulty of discovering what, if anything, Crane had to conceal. The double murder could not be bargained over. To admit knowledge of those crimes would be to place Theresa in mortal danger. Harris wondered how to proceed. In Montreal there was little more he could learn. He would see Theresa tomorrow and question her in the light of this afternoon's developments, but unless she showed him other paths to follow, he supposed he would have to set out for the Northwest.

Harris felt a chill disproportionate to the breath of autumn in the air. He was thinking, as he had just before finding Theresa, of the unearthly vastness of the country. He had read enough accounts by travellers of both sexes to know it was possible to live and move and receive hospitality up north, and yet he himself had travelled too little, lived over the shop too long. When he pictured the setting of Ewing's death, Harris's fancy drew in waves and trees three times the height of any he had seen, sketched rocks more massive than the Bonsecours Market itself, and painted all with frost.

Such was the country that beckoned. He could not send or take Small, whose particular talents would be better employed making sure Theresa received the best possible care from the

Brays and putting as many obstacles as possible in the way of any action Crane might take to reclaim his wife.

Small and Harris walked out to the edge of the revetment wall. As they listened to the harbour waters lap against hulls destined for the farthest reaches of the globe, Harris laid his project before his companion. He would sail from Montreal tomorrow night. In order to follow as closely as possible Crane's northward route of seven years ago, Harris would journey first south and west all the way to Detroit. There he would take passage for Sault Ste. Marie. He tacitly wished Small might devise some alternative.

"When you go," said Small, "try to find that man who served as mate on *Steadfast* and see if he thinks the ship could have been made to break."

* * *

No one spoke while the mantel clock in the Brays' front parlour struck four. Despite its title, the room was cosily informal—its light clutter of books, child's letter blocks and sleeping cats tending to steer guests into deeply cushioned armchairs of long service. All the same, no one but the hostess seemed at ease.

Harris had never to his knowledge seen a divorced woman and, while she was far from the focus of his attention, did not altogether take Mrs. Bray for granted. To divorce an adulterer, he believed, was not to slight the marriage vows but rather to enforce them with justified austerity. And yet she remained easy in small matters, not indiscriminately austere like her husband. She was broad-jawed, stout, fair, something over thirty, and German-speaking to judge by her *w* and her *v*.

"We have more tea if anyone is ready," she offered. *Ve haf...*

No one was.

Philander Bray had set an icy tone by announcing to Harris that as long as William Sheridan's daughter lodged with his family, she was to see no one except by his permission. Theresa, he said, understood and accepted this condition and regretted having gone driving with Harris and his friend the previous morning.

"Is that not so, my dear?" he now asked.

"The fault if any was mine," Harris interposed, fervently wishing Bray might be called away from his hearth on some urgent and lengthy ecclesiastical errand.

In writing to Theresa the previous evening, Harris had requested an interview. She replied that Mr. Bray would not be lecturing Saturday morning and wished to work undisturbed at home, but that he would "not refuse" a call Saturday afternoon. Harris marvelled at such cordiality and filled the morning with preparations for a northern journey. He bought maps and arranged transport. He questioned Father Gouin, confirming if not much extending the story as he knew it. Activity increased his confidence in his project. Now he needed to discuss it with Theresa.

"Your fault was great, Mr. Harris," said the clergyman, "but I wait to hear from her."

Theresa's eyes blazed forth. She wore no cap and her short, chestnut hair gleamed richly as she swung to face her catechist. Her hands lay folded in the lap of a new striped gown, folded not like linen but like wings, ready to rise on the instant to great tasks. She looked to Harris more vital than at any time during the past half-month. He let her speak for herself.

"You and your family, sir, have been most kind," she said with utter conviction, despite her annoyance. "I'm grateful for your help on any terms."

"You're very welcome," said Mrs. Bray. Plainly she felt it was time to change the subject. "But Mrs. Crane has a decision to make and naturally she wants the counsel of an old friend like you, Mr. Harris. Won't you tell him, Theresa, what you have in mind?"

"Mr. and Mrs. Bray urge me to go to the United States as the surest way to escape Henry's grasp."

"Immediately?" Full of his own—admittedly tenuous—plans for her protection, Harris was taken by surprise.

"Henry may arrive at any moment," Theresa replied, "and I don't see how I can ask this family to place themselves on the wrong side of the law for my sake."

The clergyman and his wife protested simultaneously.

"They won't want us in gaol!" exclaimed Mrs. Bray. "Have no thought of that."

"A just battle is a joy," Bray grimly intoned, "but I am advised that in this case, a delaying action of one month at the outside is the most that can be hoped for."

Harris wavered. As a temporary measure, Theresa's going abroad would certainly buy time—enough time for him to discover what, if anything, Ingram had been holding over Crane.

"Our friends in Boston would help her to the nursing work she desires," said Mrs. Bray. "There is even a Female Medical College where she could qualify as a physician. But she won't go without your blessing, sir, in view of your great services to her, so don't you think you could give it?"

"You see how persuasive Charlotte is, Isaac," said Theresa. "What do you think?"

Harris thought many things he did not say. The first was that this didn't sound like a temporary change of residence. The second was how few friends of her own sex Theresa had had and how natural it was that this sensible and kindly European woman should have the power to persuade. Mrs. Bray's very lack of marked American characteristics made her proposal the more seductive. Travel was easy, borders permeable. There was nothing in Charlotte to remind Theresa of her father's distrust of Yankee republican notions of government, or to remind Harris that his father had at Queenston stared down the barrels of Yankee muskets. Harris wondered if he had been too quick to dismiss the option of exile—and yet he wanted a chance to explore the alternative first.

"Mr. Bray spoke of delaying Crane," he said. "It has just occurred to me that—whatever he may say—Henry is bound to appear at the continuation of an inquest in Scarboro next Thursday. He cannot be expected here in Montreal for at least a week. I wonder, Theresa, if you might not postpone your decision for a further week or two after that."

"To what end?" said Bray.

"To allow time for me to travel to Sault Ste. Marie, where I expect to make discoveries that will prevent Mrs. Crane's husband from persecuting her further."

Theresa started to speak.

"What discoveries?" demanded Bray. "Explain yourself."

"I should like to do so first to Mrs. Crane," said Harris.

At this, Mrs. Bray claimed to hear one of her children crying and excused herself. A marmalade kitten followed her out. Her husband remained.

"Mr. Bray," said Theresa, "I don't know what impression you can have formed of my father's friend Isaac Harris. This man has given practically all he has for my welfare, without prospect of reward. Trust him as you would yourself. Even if I were to forget that I am a married woman—a plain impossibility—he would not forget. There can be no impropriety in my speaking to him alone."

This tribute aroused in Harris such longings as belied it, but it had at least some of the desired effect on Bray.

"You may speak apart. I shall sit by the window and read." The cleric promptly took up a pamphlet entitled *The Immaculate Conception Exploded: A Protestant Episcopalian View.* With the grey light from Craig Street pouring in at his back, his eyes were in deeper shadow than ever.

Harris somewhat self-consciously moved to a chair nearer Theresa. The rustle of her new dress—doubtless one of Mrs. Bray's taken in, but very becoming—did nothing to steady him. His cheek tingled where her lips had touched it the day before. She misconstrued his flushed face.

"I see my watchdog has angered you too," she whispered, "but we must remember he would be poor protection if he were as easy and affable as some of our British priests. Why do you wish to go to Sault Ste. Marie?"

So Harris got his chance, of which he proceeded to make very little. Theresa didn't know if Crane had ever been or might have been the victim of blackmail—and if Harris intended to blackmail Crane into leaving her alone, she thought it a dangerous plan, not to mention an ignoble one. She did not want Harris to make this trip on her behalf. She would rather he not go. No, she knew nothing of Harvey Ingram, Colin Ewing, the latter's death, Crane's movements at the time, or indeed what Harris was talking about. Henry had killed Papa and, before her eyes, Sibyl. These events so filled her heart she could not begin to contemplate wrongs more remote.

Harris understood—in her place would have felt the same. Still, it was awkward.

Then Theresa, for her part, wanted to know the contents of the document for which her father had died and about which Small had made such a secret at their last meeting.

"You must have wormed it out of Jasper by now," she whispered.

"Dr. Hillyard has yet to answer our telegram."

While this was true, it failed to satisfy her.

"But hasn't Jasper told *you?*"

"In confidence," Harris replied miserably, setting himself and Theresa even more at odds. Their differences distressed him the more for being of necessity expressed in the most intimate undertones.

Bray cleared his throat and looked pointedly at the mantel clock.

"I could try to get Jasper to tell you while I'm away," said Harris at something approaching normal volume, "but I take it you won't wait."

She had reasons not to wait. She didn't believe in Harris's errand, whereas by turning Bostonian she could have work, training and perhaps a New England divorce that would cancel Crane's legal hold over her—so long as she never came home. If she would have him, Harris would join her in the republic, but with the heaviest of hearts. It seemed intolerable that the monster who had already taken so much from Theresa should deprive her of her native land as well, the land whose governance her Papa had helped shape. And still in Massachusetts, law or no law, Crane might molest her.

"I'll wait because you ask it," she said coolly and distinctly. "Please don't try to explain."

Harris hated to avail himself of such deference—a most inauspicious substitute for mutual sympathy—and hoped that this was the last time he would ever have to do so.

"Theresa," he murmured, "I'm sorry..." It was too late, though, to continue privately now that they had spoken aloud.

"So, my dear," said their host, "has he given you reasons for procrastination?"

"I find I need more time to compose my thoughts," Theresa replied, "that is if I may stay here another fortnight or so."

"Let us say three weeks. Now perhaps Mr. Harris will accompany us to Evensong."

"With pleasure." To Theresa he whispered, "Thank you."

Christ Church Cathedral on Notre Dame Street was a neo-classical temple over whose altar imposingly stretched a painted Last Supper—after da Vinci, Harris supposed. The subject, together perhaps with the time of day, led him into far from pleasant speculations. During the Lord's Prayer, he stole a glance across at Theresa, seated between the Brays' young daughter and son.

"...deliver us from Evil."

Lips moving soundlessly, head gracefully inclined, she would have afforded the greatest artist a model of saintly devotion, except that her eyes—instead of bending heavenwards or resting serenely closed—were clenched shut. In leaving Montreal, Harris wondered, to what fate would he be abandoning her?

The children clung affectionately to her on the short walk back to Craig Street, but ran ahead as soon as their father had the door open. Theresa squeezed Harris's arm.

"When Henry comes knocking," she said, "I hate to think you'll be a thousand miles away."

"Come with me," he suddenly urged, braver at the mere thought of her beside him on those northern shores. "We'll succeed better every way."

Already, though, she was following Charlotte Bray inside. While it still lacked an hour until sunset, in the front hall a lamp was being lit. Theresa turned in its glow.

"Forget I spoke, Isaac. I know no harm will touch me under this roof."

Harris did not forget, even when five days later a gale on Lake Huron was doing its utmost to pitch all food from his stomach and every thought from his head.

Chapter Nineteen
A *Thousand* Miles

Theresa picked a child's pair of breeches from the mending basket beside her. When that was empty, there was in the Brays' basement another hamper of clothes donated by more affluent Anglicans and needing repairs before distribution to those in want.

"Should I patch this pocket or just shorten it?" she wondered aloud.

There was no one to hear. Philander was on his way to McGill to distinguish between three Greek words for "love," Charlotte and the two chicks on theirs to the market to choose between pyramids of rosy apples. And the surviving child of Charlotte's first marriage no longer shared the Montreal house. Now that he was sixteen, Theresa had been told, he had gone to learn civil engineering with his father in Hartford. Well, it was weather to be going somewhere. The sun shone for the first time in days, falling through the shutters to trace on the worn carpet a fiery grill.

The parlour otherwise felt drowsy. Theresa had opened the casements but dared not unlock the shutters, for the low windows gave directly onto the sidewalk. To keep alert, she instead moved to a straight-backed chair.

She would get more items done, clothe more people, if she just stitched across here above the hole.

"So my terrier thinks the poor don't need deep pockets," she heard her father chuckle. "Why not sew them shut altogether?"

She wanted to answer that there was other work she was better at. She shared much with the Brays, including more and more a healing sense of family, but their small household could never employ her fully.

"And that one Talent which is death to hide,
Lodg'd with me *useless...*"

Not blind like Milton, she would not pity herself overmuch, though she could not help thinking with envy of Sister Saint-Jacques in the Grey Nuns' pharmacy. Theresa craved employment as never before. Her inaction she felt had killed Sibyl. She simply couldn't believe what Mr. Bray preached, that faith alone would justify her before God. Or perhaps she hoped by good works to demonstrate the strength of her faith—to prove it to others and to herself. Besides, even if God doesn't need man's work, God's creatures do.

From an end of sailcloth, she irritably cut a patch strong enough to hold several dozen gold coins.

The pharmacy was closed to her, for the Grey Nuns thought she belonged with Henry. She must wait. To make her yoke bearable, she tried telling herself that Isaac would be back soon. He had been gone nine days already.

She did not truly wish to be a pharmacist—much less a physician, which was why she did not find herself pining for the Female Medical College in Boston. What healed the sick, she thought, was not appearing briefly at a hundred bedsides, but rather sustained personal attendance at one or two. Admit it freely: to physic she owed her life. But no less beneficial than quinine had been the tender nursing she had received from Isaac and the nuns. What good were the most ingenious medicines absent such simple restoratives as clean linen, warm blankets, appropriate nourishment, a kind word and a reassuring touch? Indeed, not a few sufferers would with less risk forego the former than the latter.

Theresa's thoughts and hands stopped dead. Listen!

Out of the more or less regular beat of hoofs along Craig Street, the sound of a horse slowing distinguished itself, as if the driver were seeking a particular house. The shadow of a carriage stopped outside the Brays' closed shutters. Through their louvers, Theresa smelled the dust from its wheels. She held her breath.

She heard the latch of the carriage door disengage, boots cross the plank sidewalk to the house door, and then six-quick-knocks-in-a-block. She had teased her suitor once for sounding so eager and insistent. Most gentlemen found a double knock sufficient. Crane's touch never changed.

From it, through walls and air, Theresa's flesh shrank with a will of its own. Insistence is just his habit, she told herself consolingly. He doesn't care. This was the first time she had heard from him since his telegram of 22nd August. The promised letter had not appeared.

The six knocks came again, louder and slower. The Brays' maid-servant worked for them afternoons only, so Theresa was quite alone. She had no reason to panic, though. Henry would not try to break in, certainly not in daylight and with no direct evidence she was here. She had only to wait quietly. She had only to avoid capsizing the sewing table or dropping her scissors, which felt perversely slippery in her grip.

Henry left without knocking a third time.

Next day she received his letter announcing his arrival in Montreal, expressing conventional concern for her welfare, and asking when he might call. With Philander's concurrence, she sent no answer. She had been going out only to attend services at Christ Church. Now she stayed in altogether.

On Thursday, 4th September, while the family was at dinner, she again recognized Crane's knock. She urged Philander to ignore it. He said that his own vocation made this impossible, but that she was to take the children and lock herself in a bedroom.

"Shall I still have my pudding?" the boy shrewdly demanded.

Assured that he would, and the livelier he stepped the sooner, he raced his sister upstairs, where Theresa had little trouble interesting the two of them in a picture book. She read to them of Moses in the bulrushes. Above her own somewhat mechanical voice, she picked out by snatches those of the two equally imperious men on the doorstep below, the baron of steam and the shepherd of souls.

"I told him you would not see him," Philander reported to her later. "I declined to give reasons. When he threatened to speak to my bishop as well as to the commissioner of police, I said he might do whatever his conscience prompted, short of trespassing further on my family's peace."

"Such a big man!" Charlotte added with emphasis. "Perhaps he would try to push past Philander and come inside, if he had not seen me behind in the hall. I stood behind with in my hands a musket."

"Calm yourself, my dear," Bray enjoined. "You forget your English when you allow occurrences to excite you."

Theresa wished he would not say "my dear" in that peculiarly flinty tone that had nothing endearing about it. Charlotte's excitement was natural, her taking up a weapon extraordinary. Theresa put her arms around the stalwart woman, who misconstrued this expression of gratitude as one of fear for Henry.

"I would not shoot your Mr. Crane," Charlotte hastened to say, enfolding her guest in turn. "I showed the gun only to keep him from foolishness. When he is reasonable, he will leave you alone, I am sure."

These words made Theresa flinch back from the embrace, for they reminded her under what a grave misapprehension she had left her hosts and to what risks she was exposing them. She had thought for her own safety to tell as few people as possible what she had witnessed from under Sibyl's bed. To the Brays she had accused Henry of unfaithfulness only. For that crime alone, they were prepared to drive him off at gunpoint, but Charlotte plainly thought Henry no worse than her own inconstant first husband.

"My first husband is a reformed man," Charlotte had recently said, with a touch of pride, as if by divorcing him she had set his reform in motion.

How easily she referred to him! With how little animosity or resentment! She even entrusted to him the education of their son. Surely she and Philander had a right to know that in Henry they faced something much more dangerous.

Theresa told them now. Philander sniffed and said this was where fornication led. Charlotte coloured, bit her tongue, and finally scolded Theresa for not speaking sooner.

"You're right!" Theresa blurted out. "I've betrayed everyone my life has touched, and now you two, you four." Bray's scowl steadied her. "I don't mean to," she said more softly. "I try to even the scales, and every time I tilt them more askew. Send me away before I bring you more misfortune. I'll go tonight."

"We will not hear of it!" Charlotte exclaimed, truly alarmed. "Sweet heaven, now we understand what griefs and shocks you have had to suffer. Would we expose you to new ones?"

Philander concurred, advising Theresa against vain self-reproach. The Brays' protection would without question continue, though some different arrangements would have to be made. From now on, either the servant or Charlotte would be in the house at all times. No stranger's knock would be answered unless by Philander. The children would be sent away.

"No, please don't divide your family," Theresa entreated. "I'll go to Boston now."

"Madam," said Philander, "you are in no state to say what you should do. Be wise enough to accept guidance."

"Wait until your Mr. Harris returns." Charlotte's eyes were still red, but her characteristic good-humour began to reassert itself. "Just another week or so. The change of scene will do my babies no harm, and the days will fly by fast enough, you'll see."

The days flew like snails. The very seconds crawled. Once the boy had been parcelled off to one vicarage and the girl to another, Theresa was left with even less occupation. She mended clothes, dried fruit, pickled and preserved. As a great favour, Philander let her catalogue his library, which contained nothing more scientific than Browne's two-century-old *Religio Medici.*

She wrote to Marthe, without ill-will. Having enlisted her parents' help in lodging Theresa with the Grey Nuns, Marthe would have been helpless to prevent their publishing this address when they judged fit. Theresa, moreover, had never revealed to the Laurendeaus the principal argument for silence. Her lonely confinement on Craig Street made her all the more conciliating.

"Dear Marthe," she urged, "dragoon one of your brothers

into escorting you down the St. Lawrence from your *belle seigneurie* and bring me all the country news, or any news."

Astonishingly, Henry did not return. Where was he? What was he doing? Perhaps he had gone back to Toronto. Days passed. He sent neither message nor representative. No legal papers were served, and no alteration in Philander gave grounds to suspect that Bishop Fulford had censured the priest's conduct. The continuous suspense hung further clogs upon the clock.

Theresa began having suffocation nightmares. Because of its associations, she slept without a pillow. Now she removed stuffing from her mattress till she was lying on little more than a double sheet over the supporting ropes. Nothing soft must come near her nose or mouth.

To avoid thinking of Henry, she thought of Isaac, with whom she would have liked to find fault. He was too fond of her, for one thing. Furthermore, he was neglecting her.

It distressed her not to know what he was doing. As the week wore on, however, it became clearer that the bare fact of his absence was what distressed her most. She began to catch herself in daydreams. Her imagination elaborated recent memories of his hand in hers, his cheek close to her own.

His long face had become sharper over the years, less boyish, though his mouth had kept a contour of youthful sweetness, neither bitter on the one hand nor complacent on the other. Since they had ridden together, she reflected, Isaac Harris had known some worldly success. Unlike worldly men, he had remained trim and lithe. If he had, at least since embroiling himself in her affairs, become less fastidious about his appearance, still his appearance had not suffered. And through his eyes, through the pores almost of his skin, shone unmistakable new purpose. This time he would approach as close as she would permit.

How close was that?

Needle and thread could not shut out temptation. To tame her fancy, Theresa threw herself into the most physically taxing chores, practically depriving the serving girl of occupation.

A visit from Jasper Small on the following Tuesday drew her

thoughts another way. His previous calls had been brief. Thanks to Henry's inaction, there had been no legal threats to discuss with him. Philander's puritan strain of episcopalianism seemed moreover to scare Jasper off. This evening, by contrast, the volume of his inconsequential talk made Theresa suspect he had something to delay saying. She interrupted one of his racetrack anecdotes to ask him straight out whether Dr. Hillyard's leave had at last been obtained to reveal what document had cost her Papa his life. Small nodded and collected himself.

"It dated from 1832," he began. He knew he need not explain the significance of the year. "It was George MacFarlane's order to a ship's captain to evade the quarantine, as captains often did on their own initiative."

Jasper's account included all essential facts, though it left the anguish the letter had occasioned Theresa's father as much as possible to her own memory and imagination.

"You've understood what I needed to hear," she said calmly when he had done, "and told it most considerately."

Later, though, when he had gone, disillusionment seeped quite through her, poisoning any friendliness she felt towards human beings.

She had known George MacFarlane as her friend's husband, an elderly plutocrat who lived in a castle, a patron of art and charity, and a payer of harmless compliments to women little older than his daughters. She had assumed that in his various commercial dealings, he must have cut a few corners—but not this. Nothing like this.

Cholera was no abstract term to Theresa. In ordering its victims abandoned, George MacFarlane had not killed her mother directly, but together with other venal or merely reckless men, he had made his contribution to the hecatomb. Suppressing the documentary evidence had cost more lives, but what of that? Castle life must be protected. If Theresa called on the MacFarlanes next week, the laird would take her in to dinner on his arm, calling her his muse and inspiration.

Having been wrong about Henry, wrong about George, she

began wondering if everyone were not worse than he seemed.

"All is vanity," she thought, "and vexation of spirit." Fear and love alike.

She reread Ecclesiastes. Thursday afternoon of the third week of Isaac's absence, the bleak phrases tumbled through her brain as she washed the pine kitchen floor. Theresa was alone in the house. Charlotte was on a charitable errand, Philander on episcopal business in Three Rivers and not expected home until midnight. With Theresa's permission, Janet the serving girl had stepped next door to borrow something. Presumably, Janet had stopped there to gossip.

"God hath made men upright; but they have sought out many inventions."

Like a fury, Theresa bore down with soapy brush on some obstinate, tarry stain and, when that failed to remove it, picked at it with her thumb nail. Stung by splinters, she lifted the filth with a knife and resumed scrubbing.

She had not been pleasant company for Janet and could, for her part, well do without people just now, all and each. Charlotte resented separation from her children, however she struggled to hide it. Marthe had not come, and in today's mood was not missed. Jasper had been neglecting to see that Banshee was tended and exercised. While rinsing her bucket and drying her hands, Theresa recalled Jasper's confessing that except for betting purposes he and horses were "outside each other's spheres." He had seemed unconcerned.

"Whatsoever thy hand findeth to do, do it with thy might; for there is no work in the grave, whither thou goest."

Theresa went to the front door and opened it a crack. The street was empty. When she closed the door, the house air felt sluggish and dense. How long had it been since she had been outside, in health and mistress of her own footsteps? Weeks past counting. She tied a scarf of Charlotte's over her head. She again opened the door. A butcher's cart was passing—driven by a meat-fed boy of complacent mien and pulled by a nag with flanks raw from whipping. When the street was again empty, Theresa went out.

A chill breeze from the factory district followed her towards Rasco's Hotel. Coal smoke notwithstanding, freedom tasted heady.

* * *

Harris stayed on deck throughout the storm, though in the dark night he saw nothing beyond the next mountainous wave and a few feet of slippery rail. To the latter clung a soggy fellow passenger who in shouts told him they were crossing the mouth of Saginaw Bay. The *Lady Elgin*, a fast side-wheeler, creaked and groaned on the heaving water. Mindful of Father Gouin's account of *Steadfast*, Harris listened through the shriek of the wind for the sound of splitting timbers. He had no time for mishaps.

None occurred. By dawn, the gale had exhausted itself, and presently they approached the fuel stop of Presque Isle, Michigan, three fifths of the way from Detroit to Sault Ste. Marie. The recently violent Lake Huron caught slivers of light in smiling wavelets, ruffling the reflection of autumn's first yellow foliage along the shore. Sun kindled the landscape without taking the clean, crisp edge from the morning air.

It seemed a promising day. The storm had after all been little fiercer than ones Harris had known on Lake Ontario. The northern landscape too was, so far, much less desolate than he had feared—and there across the bay rose the lighthouse formerly manned by Harvey Ingram. Harris was the first passenger to step from the gang-board onto the dock.

Yesterday in Detroit, he had had some luck. A steamship company had permitted him to inspect the old passenger lists, and there he found the name of Henry Crane. Crane had sailed from Detroit on October 10, 1849 with fare paid as far as Sault Ste. Marie—where he *should* have disembarked two days later. He should have disembarked on October 12, *one full week* before the date Father Gouin gave for Crane's arrival at the Sault. Presumably Crane had learned something en route to change his plans. A glance at the schedules assured Harris that

Ewing's scalding on October 9 could well have been reported at Presque Isle by the time the vessel bearing Crane had stopped here for fuel on the eleventh. From seasoned sailors among the *Lady Elgin*'s crew he learned that it had been lightkeeper Ingram's custom to meet refueling vessels with cheap whisky and the latest gossip.

Now Harris's own boots were crunching over Presque Isle's shingle beach. While the *Lady Elgin* was taking on cordwood, the detective meant to see what more he could learn at the lighthouse itself.

Atop a cone of rough stone sat a brick cylinder, both sprucely whitewashed, the whole rising less than half the height of Toronto's Gibraltar Light. The red door stood open. Down the spiral stairs trailed a string of whistled notes, which Harris followed unhesitatingly to its source. The timbre and intensity led him to expect a hale individual of roughly sixty.

That presently was whom he saw at work polishing the eight sides of the cast iron lantern. The keeper was closely shaved and mostly bald, his head gleaming with perspiration in the greenhouse warmth of his glazed crow's nest. He greeted Harris and continued plying his cloth. He did stop whistling, however, which Harris took as sufficient invitation to seat himself on the top step—the only place there was room—and ask if he had the honour of addressing the immediate successor to Harvey Ingram.

"Can't say I thought much of him," the lightkeeper declared in a New World voice without overtones of Europe. "Ingram left a shambles here. Premises in disrepair. Drunk when he handed me the keys. Said he was celebrating his new appointment to—I forget where."

"Toronto," said Harris, pleased to encounter such candour. "It seems odd he should get postings in two different countries."

"He was a U.S. citizen—but from Scotland, and with that burr, I guess he seemed British enough. Good riddance, if you ask me. And he had a backer there, in Toronto."

"Who would that be?" asked Harris. "I'm from Toronto myself."

"A railway and steamship man of some size, I believe he said." The American grinned wryly. "Some size for the place, at least."

Harris wondered with amusement whether the other half dozen residents of Presque Isle would be equally contemptuous of a city of forty-four thousand.

"Henry Crane?" he asked. "Have you ever heard that name?"

The lightkeeper folded the cloth he had been using on the ironwork and from the pocket of a blue jacket took a softer one for polishing the lens.

"Never have," he said after a period of reflection. "Ingram mentioned no name. An unwilling backer, he said—and he offered me some advice I never asked for. Powerful friends, he said, are no substitute for a well-stocked mind."

"What do you think he meant?"

"Underhand dealings—if a bamboozling fool like that means anything at all. I don't know what your interest in Ingram is, mister, but even if you are his friend, I can't tell you anything different. I served with the U.S. navy till '53. I got this post because the Lighthouse Board said I was the best man to fill it. That Ingram of yours knew nothing of shipping or navigation, not that I could see—but then there was no Lighthouse Board when he came here."

"Harvey Ingram is dead," said Harris. It seemed unnecessary to disown friendship with the deceased. "I should just like to know what claim he had on the backer you mention."

"He didn't say. I didn't press him, wanting no more of his foul breath than necessary. If he's dead, it's of drink, I suppose."

No more could Harris learn, however his questions were phrased. In '49, the lightkeeper had been sailing the Atlantic Ocean, and so had never heard of Colin Ewing.

On resuming his voyage north, Harris felt justified in making certain suppositions.

Suppose that on October 11, 1849, Lightkeeper Ingram sees Henry Crane at Presque Isle and tells him what *Steadfast*'s mate is putting about—namely, that Colin Ewing is hideously burned and will last no more than a week. For that week, Crane hides. Later, Ingram learns the date of Crane's tardy arrival in the Sault. Ingram starts the rumour that business in Detroit was not what kept Crane from Ewing's death bed. Because of its disreputable origin, this rumour is ignored, and Crane moves south before he can be much embarrassed by it in any case. In Toronto, Crane's fortune and influence grow.

Further, suppose that eventually Lightkeeper Ingram learns the more-than-embarrassing secret of Henry Crane's delay, the where and why. This time he tells no one but Crane. Now he has enough power over Crane to get himself appointed lightkeeper in Toronto. Crane would have had to call in some favours for that, considerable favours as Ingram is an American, but still Ingram wants more. Pressed for ever larger payments, Crane eventually turns for help to MacFarlane.

So much it seemed safe to assume, but to the secret itself Harris felt no closer than when he had left Montreal. What had taken Ingram from '49 to '53 to find, Harris must uncover in three weeks, most of them necessarily consumed by weary travel.

What card had Ingram held? What tool or device had worked the extortion? Still, after all these miles, the only guess was Small's. At parting, the lawyer still clung to his idea that Crane had risked wrecking *Steadfast* in order to kill Ewing. That was no way to make money.

From the deck of the *Lady Elgin*, Harris once more sent his eyes around the horizon. The shore behind was now a hazy thread, the shore ahead not that even. He wondered if Crane might have had a non-pecuniary motive for wanting Ewing dead.

Harris had previously discounted Crane's lechery as the source of blackmail. Crane must at the Sault have had at least one mistress, if not what Cuthbert Nash called a country wife—but what of that? Even a plurality of country wives had taken nothing from the prestige of Sir George Simpson, Governor of the Hudson's Bay Company. These were Indian women, after all.

Of course, a Theresa Sheridan contemplating legal marriage could be expected to hold less worldly views. During courtship, Crane might have paid to keep word of his paramours and any children by them from Theresa's ears. Coincidentally, it did seem that Ingram's blackmail had commenced in the year of that courtship, 1853. Later, though, when Crane's bride was securely bound to him and her good opinion of no further value or interest, and when the favours expected from his father-in-law were not forthcoming, Crane would have been less spendthrift in concealing what no one else would hold against him. Ingram must have been paid to hide something else. By the same token, discovering a concubine or even an unofficial family would not give Harris the bargaining power he needed over Crane.

For these reasons, as well as from aversion to the subject, Harris had thought little of Crane's northern amours. Suppose, however, Crane had killed his partner over a woman both wanted. To this woman Ewing might have been expected to surrender his claims after becoming engaged to a girl in Chicago. Suppose he had not. He still had a month or six weeks before his marriage in November. Having counted on being left in sole possession of the field, might Crane not have become jealous? Certainly.

Might he have become murderously jealous, even to the point of jeopardizing his own steamer? Unlikely.

Nevertheless...

A new avenue of inquiry opened before Harris. He would much rather discover a murder than a scandal. Considerations of honour and security alike made him prefer arraigning Crane to threatening him. Harris wanted a hard indictment with all the daylight power of the Crown behind it, not hard bargaining in the shadows with only his unseconded nerve flickering between Theresa and her tormentor.

"When Henry comes knocking," she had said, "I hate to think you'll be a thousand miles away."

A helpless desire to shield her from all unkindness, an ache that never left Harris, grew painfully acute. His fingers tightened around the steamer's wooden rail. Until he returned he had to trust to others, to herself, but trust was difficult so long as his arms remembered how pitifully light and fragile Theresa had felt when Harris carried her from the Lansing shack a bare three weeks ago. She was stronger now, he knew. Under the Brays' roof, she would come to no harm. And yet he needed as a wound needs stanching to fold his darling once more in his arms.

First he must rub his nose in her husband's debauches. He had to find and question any woman that had shared Crane's bed in the north. Somehow this had not before been quite clear to Harris's mind. It was now.

As he looked for the unknown land ahead, he felt the frontier he was crossing in himself.

* * *

No healthy nature can grieve and fear uninterruptedly. On Thursday afternoon, 11th September, Theresa's gloom began loosening about her the moment she stepped from the Brays' monotonous sanctuary into the city streets. Retracing her steps some minutes later, she left Rasco's Hotel in a veritable bubble of cheerfulness. She had banteringly impressed upon the ostlers that the grey mare Mr. Harris had left with them had friends in Montreal. She extracted a promise that in Mr. Harris's absence Banshee was to be walked for half an hour in the stable yard every day without fail. Surprise visits of inspection were hinted at.

How little exercise she could herself afford she did not mention. The ordinary jostle of traffic on a shopping thoroughfare like St. Paul Street came as a rare luxury. Gratefully she breathed everyday odours of cheese and tobacco and lard. Brighter snatches of Ecclesiastes came to mind.

"Truly the light is sweet, and a pleasant thing it is for the eyes to behold the sun."

She turned right on St. Joseph Street and crossed the Place d'Armes in front of Notre Dame Cathedral. To this point she was sure she had not been followed. On Craig Street she became more cautious. From the intersection, she noted two men standing in conversation on the sidewalk opposite the Brays' door. She took a turn around the block only to find them still there. She had to get back to the house. The servant, if not Charlotte Bray, would by now have returned and be concerned about her. She reconnoitred the back lane.

The houses pressed their faces to Craig Street in a row as flat as ironed ribbon. Out there, everyone stood in plain sight, but back here a jagged succession of sheds and broken fences afforded hidy-holes in plenty. If Henry's spies could not see Theresa coming, neither could she see them lurking.

A sun-dazed dog sniffed the back of an outhouse. Otherwise the lane appeared empty. Then, from where the Brays' yard must be, their serving girl ran out, her straw-coloured hair coming undone, the hem of her Saxon blue dress trailing in the dust. She looked both ways, too quickly to see anything.

"Mrs. Crane," she called timidly, and then with anxious force. "Oh, Mrs. Crane, do come back. What will Mistress say?"

Theresa had not the heart to conceal herself before the young woman glanced her way again.

"Mrs. Crane? Oh, thank God!"

"Not so loud, Janet, please." Theresa advanced to meet her. "Let's go in."

"But where have—?"

"Don't stop out here," Theresa interrupted, taking the girl's arm and propelling her forward.

The dog whined as they passed the outhouse. Theresa turned her head and into her face was thrust a thick cotton pad, covering nose, mouth and eyes. Both her arms were seized from behind. Janet was screaming.

Theresa could pull no air into her lungs through the cloud-soft layers of fabric. All the strength of fear flowed into her limbs. She squirmed and twisted to shake off what seemed a light grip above either elbow. Each constraining hand closed just enough to convince her it was irresistible. Her shoulders were pulled flat against her captor's chest.

This was it then, death by suffocation. Another, less assured pair of hands not only kept the pad against Theresa's face, but so increased the pressure on it that she thought her nose must break.

Father in heaven, no! *Truly light is sweet.*

Blindly she kicked out, but could feel her slippers glance harmless off sturdy legs, while the exertion made her all the more desperate for the oxygen denied her. She kept kicking anyway.

"Help, murder!" cried the servant.

"Hush now, miss," a paternal French voice instructed her. *"Chut, hurlez plus.* This lady is a danger to herself and others. *Son arrestation aux ordres de son mari est parfaitement conforme à la loi.* See how her infirmity makes her struggle."

"You're choking her, sir. Do let her breathe."

"Oui, mon enfant, à la bonne heure. Now, Mrs. Crane, will you calm yourself or must we use the chloroform?"

"Tilt back her head," said a younger, quavering voice. "Shall I pour it now?"

Theresa scarcely heard any of this for the sound of her own lungs bursting.

Chapter Twenty
The First Crime

The *Lady Elgin* docked at the Sault on the morning of Saturday, August 30. When Harris set foot on the Canadian bank of the St. Mary's River, he found himself on a low, not totally flat stretch of ground, bounded in the middle distance by round-topped, rocky hills. Nearer the water, bush fires had evidently consumed the larger trees. Their charred stumps were still visible, but as much as ten years of new growth already wreathed the village in green and autumn gold. This was again not the forbidding scene Harris had anticipated. There was no beauty here to stop him in his tracks, but still a pleasing novelty of configuration combined with a humanity of scale.

At the edge of the settlement stood a few birchbark wigwams, also round, like bowls turned bottom upwards. They reminded Harris he had strayed beyond the territory of the Mohawk, traditionally longhouse-dwellers. Shipboard talk had it that still more than nine residents in ten of Sault Ste. Marie, C.W. were Ojibway Indians or half-breeds, although plainly most had built their habitations to the white man's pattern. That is, a single storey of timber squared and covered over in clapboard. West of their houses, some fifty of them or more, rose the tall peaked roof and taller flagpole of the Hudson's Bay Company post—and to the east a distinguished, two-storey edifice of red fieldstone, put together in a hybrid French and English style. Towards the stone house Harris directed his footsteps. Built for a fur trader when furs were wealth, it had recently—since Father Gouin's time—been converted from an unused private residence into the Stone House Hotel.

And a comfortable hotel it was. The innkeeper and his wife

were instantly inviting him into a parlour crammed with sofas, armchairs and footstools. They were offering him a glass of dandelion wine while he waited for a room to be made ready and a lunch to be served. What they could not do, having arrived too recently at the Sault, was assist him with his inquiries.

These he attempted to pursue among the Indians, starting that afternoon. He approached one of the clapboard houses.

An Ojibway man, lately returned from fishing, sat on his doorstep in buckskin trousers and no shirt, although the mercury stood below sixty Fahrenheit degrees. A red kerchief tied his long, black hair behind his head. His long, oval face remained still and solemn behind his clay pipe as he pretended not to notice his visitor. Harris introduced himself.

"Would you like to buy some fish?" said the man.

"Thank you, no, Mr..."

The fisherman, who barely moved his lips when he spoke, now made a sound something like, "Kabaosa."

"Excuse me," said Harris. "Would you kindly say that again?"

"Andrew Jones."

From the Ojibway's unchanged expression, there was no telling whether he was offended or jesting. Unaccustomed to Indian ways, Harris had thought the use of a name might be courteous, but he seemed to be making a mess of it. He was distractingly aware that red men—whether called Kabaosa or Andrew Jones—would predominate at Sault Ste. Marie only until the place became prized by newcomers of Harris's own complexion. Suspicion of the white man was natural. Best for him simply to plunge ahead and let it be seen that his present business had nothing to do with driving people from their homes.

"I was wondering, Mr.—uh—Jones, whether you knew Mr. Henry Crane or the late Colin Ewing when they were living here."

"They bought my fish." Andrew Jones permitted himself what might have been a smile, but it was gone too soon to be confirmed.

It transpired that the partners had bought many local fishermen's catch, both to feed their sailors and to salt for resale in other ports.

"I understand they had a woman to cook for them," said Harris. "Where would I find her."

"Why ask about a cook?" said Jones. "Don't they cook for you at the Stone House?"

"Very well, thank you, but Henry Crane is famous now—and, when a man is famous, people want to know the story of his life." Harris had not mentioned that he was staying at the Stone House, but he supposed it was a safe guess as it was the only hostelry on this side of the river. Although he had been considering citing Hiawatha as a sample famous man, he decided not to complicate matters.

"You won't spear many fish in the forest." Jones now chuckled openly. "Why not talk to Henry Crane?"

"I need," said Harris, "to talk to many people. Now about this cook..."

"I don't know where she is."

"And before her, did they have another woman to look after them?"

Jones shrugged.

"Perhaps you could direct me to another informant," Harris suggested, "someone who knew Henry Crane better. You couldn't? Tell me this then, if you will—did Crane and Ewing get along well together?"

"I never saw them fight."

"Did Mr. Crane show interest in any woman?"

"Steamboats interested him," said Jones, "and fish."

Baffled at every turn, Harris tried a bolder question. "Mr. Jones, did Crane have a mistress or what they call a country wife?"

"This family is Christian." Andrew Jones knocked the ashes from his pipe and rose with dignity. "We know nothing about country wives."

The interview was terminated, but was to be repeated with negligible variations before other doorsteps. Some men had had no dealings with Crane closer than having cut fuel wood for him one winter when hunting was poor, while others had the by now familiar excuse of having arrived at the Sault too lately to have known him at all. Some had come from Fort William or Michipicoten on his steamers—though none had been a passenger on *Steadfast* on October 9, 1849. One man said Crane and Ewing's cook had died of old age. Another claimed she had moved away. Whether Crane had paid attention to any woman on either side of the river was a question that none would answer and that many seemed to resent as a slur upon the chastity of their female relations.

The Ojibway women Harris spoke to, often found at work in their vegetable patches, would be even less communicative. They would have too little English or pretend to. Many referred him to their husbands. One pretty mixed-blood girl burst out laughing at the mention of Crane's name. She would not at first say why. Harris pressed her.

"'Crane' is one of the clans of the Ojibway," she replied at last, "the first clan at Baw-a-ting. That's the Sault here. It's funny to hear of a white man with that name."

"Did you know him?" Harris asked—but he could learn nothing further from her and soon realized she would have been a child of only seven or eight when Crane left.

Over the following days Harris continued his inquiries with no more success. He paid a call on the customs officer. He visited the Hudson's Bay Company post, which no longer received furs in any number and was in essence an imposing retail store. He visited the Indian reserve at Garden River. He would have sought advice from the Anglican mission, but the priest was tending his flock on Manitoulin Island, a part of his parish some 150 miles distant.

Harris also tried his luck on the south bank of the St. Mary's River. He found the American settlement still recognizable from Father Gouin's description, the chief improvement being a year-old canal with two locks of 350 feet each. From May to November, a ship or two a day now passed up to or down from Lake Superior.

Unfortunately, *Steadfast* no longer plied these waters. Her new owners had her serving ports on Lake Michigan now, nothing this far north. Harris had been hoping to see with his own eyes how this steamer's engine was mounted—and where, in her first year of operation, the copper pipe had broken. He doubted now if he would have time. It disappointed him to hear that the vessel that had so elaborately been broken up, portaged in pieces, and reassembled above the rapids should so easily have slipped back below them and away.

The mate who had brought Ewing to Father Gouin had also left the Sault. Sailors familiar with *Steadfast* were to be found in the American taverns, but none believed Ewing's injuries could have been other than accidental. The Sault in '49, as now, had been no more than a trading post. There had been no machine shop or skilled shipwrights, and a screw-driven vessel would have been novel anywhere. Harris's best information was that some defect in the way Crane and Ewing's steamer had been put back together after the portage had led to the accident fatal to one of its owners. Ewing was the one who knew engines, but had a reputation for impatience and neglect of detail. What a dreadful price he had paid!

As for Crane's reputation, he was the one for raising funds and wooing customers. Not a drinking man, but affable—no wearisome temperance fanatic. Always ready to do business. In fact, Crane had left the Sault to confer with mine officials in Marquette before reassembly of *Steadfast* had been completed and a final inspection made. If he had weakened the mounts, it could only have been through an accomplice. Of such an individual Harris could uncover no trace.

The sailors had never heard Crane speak of a woman, much less seen him with one, but then he lived on the Canadian side of the river, where they rarely had occasion to go.

On Thursday, September 4, Harris went in to dinner in low spirits. It would have required more hope than he could muster to keep seven weeks of anxiety and exertion from showing in his face. The innkeeper's wife noticed his dejection when she came to tell him that, although the steamer from Collingwood had not yet arrived, she would wait for it no longer before serving the evening meal.

"You must find us dull here, Mr. Harris," she observed, "compared to the cities of the South."

"On the contrary," Harris protested in all honesty. "My preoccupations make me poor company, I'm afraid, but I begin to feel quite at home at the Sault."

He was developing an affinity for the place—perhaps because Holland Landing had during his youth there played a similar rôle on a smaller scale. In that gateway village between Lakes Ontario and Simcoe, his first notions of commerce had formed. How Harris would have exulted—with less pressing inquiries in hand—to survey as he now could all traffic passing between the continent's two largest bodies of fresh water! Here was opportunity, here excitement. Even now, he could not but spare a thought for the forest and mineral wealth of the Superior shores, most particularly for the iron ore deposits. The future would be built as no age before it on iron and steel.

His mood, notwithstanding, remained bleak. His bright and sweeping prophecies showed Harris nothing of his immediate path. Either he must gain somehow the confidence of the reticent Ojibway, or he must leave Sault Ste. Marie. In the latter case, he would begin to retrace his path towards Presque Isle and try to find out where Crane had disembarked—or, possibly, jumped overboard—while Ewing was expiring. The wrong choice would prevent Harris's timely return to Montreal or force him to return empty-handed. There might be no right choice.

Under the circumstances, he could hardly do justice to the succulent whitefish, followed by caribou, wild rice, squash and beans. Nor did he find that he cared that the bread was made from maize, a subject of some complaint.

"The Hudson's Bay factor has wheat flour shipped in for his personal use," grumbled a fellow guest, a mining man who passed through the Sault regularly. "Hang the expense! The Company coddles him out of its own vanity."

The innkeeper's wife was starting to explain that with farmers now settling in the area, there would soon be wheat flour in plenty, when to Harris's surprise a more pugnacious reply erupted from the doorway behind his back.

"Not a word against the Company there, whoever you are. Not in my hearing."

The irascible voice was one Harris had heard just days ago. It hardly seemed possible, but on turning in his chair he found the new arrival was indeed Cuthbert Nash, round-bellied, grey-bearded, motley-dressed, the warehouse clerk from Lachine. The steamer from Collingwood must have just landed him. From the luggage in his hands and on his back, it looked as if Nash had brought all his possessions, but he mentioned to his hostess that his furniture was to follow. He had found he was not suited to life in the South. Next day he intended to present himself at the local Hudson's Bay post in the hope of obtaining work nearer his Indian family.

"And proper bread," the mining man snorted.

Harris saw good fortune in Nash's arrival. Here was someone who, for all his eccentricities, both spoke Ojibway and had known Crane in the forties. Nash, however, treated the detective's first overtures with unaccountable suspicion. Yes, he remembered Harris—only too well!

By now every portion of every bed at the Stone House had been spoken for. While Nash warmed himself with a glass of toddy, Harris quietly arranged to swap his own private room for half of the ex-manager's shared one and lay disguised under the bedclothes by the time Nash retired. He took care not to sleep for fear of missing his chance. He need not have worried. Nash's cursing and stamping on entering would have wakened a stone, to say nothing of his smell on undressing. Clothed, he emitted a conventionally repulsive perfume of grease and sweat, but the removal of coat, shirt, boots and trousers released an odour of human waste stale and filthy beyond even that of Mrs. Lansing's shack. Harris braced himself.

He had taken the half of the bed nearest the door. As Nash climbed into the other side and made to extinguish his candle, Harris sat up. He felt ridiculous, but forged ahead.

"Mr. Nash, I must talk to you."

"What? You?"

Nash's voice rose almost comically with the shock of the encounter, but Harris was too busy dodging the candle flame being waved in his face to think of laughing.

"Steady there," he said.

"This is another of your blasted tricks!" Nash withdrew an inch or so, his face an angrily flushed island in its grey sea of whiskers. "Too late to find another berth," he grumbled, "but you'll keep your mouth shut if you prize the teeth in it."

"You can't box in bed," Harris advised, calm only because desperate for Nash's help. "This meeting apart, how have I tricked you?"

"Ask your friend Mr. Crane."

"Crane?"

"It happens I ran into him as I was preparing to leave the island of Montreal." His left hand still clutching the candle, which drizzled tallow freely over the blankets, Nash stabbed the accusing, black-nailed index of his right hand into Harris's chest. "He set me straight on one or two points, you can be sure."

Proof against Nash's physical threats, Harris nonetheless felt at this announcement an icicle of fear press against his spine.

"Yes? What did you say to him?"

"Told him the kind of question you were asking."

So Crane knew his secrets were being probed. This Harris had wanted above all to avoid, believing the industrialist would make life harder for Theresa in proportion as he felt himself hunted. His wife had run away from him. He might not know how much she knew, but he must doubt her loyalty. If attacked, he would try to prevent her giving comfort to his enemies, would place her under lock and key if nothing worse. Such was her abhorrence of him, Harris dreaded that worse would follow without Crane's further contriving.

"Well?" Harris demanded. "On which points did he correct you?"

"You said he had no wife, when all the while you had designs on Mrs. Crane."

"I said I meant to find if he was a fit husband, as I know he is not."

"Cock-and-bull equivocation."

A squall of wind rattled the shutter. The room was getting colder. Nonetheless, Harris slipped from under the covers and lit a candle of his own. It cheered him little. His return to Montreal was made more urgent by Nash's revelation, and in the interim Nash seemed ill-disposed to assist him. Well, with the cat partly out, he might as well open the bag.

"Crane murdered his father-in-law," he said.

"I spoke to—"

"Kindly note, Mr. Nash, that I do *not* equivocate," Harris broke in. "On July 12—not two months ago—the man you spoke to smothered William Sheridan in his bed."

Even if he believed Harris, would Nash care? By the standards of the post manager's frontier existence, Crane's bloodless crimes might appear rather tame.

Nash scratched an unwashed armpit consideringly. "The name," he said, "means nothing to me."

"A Member of Parliament, former Minister of the Crown, a friend to the poor, champion of responsible government and of reform." Harris saw that none of these attributes meant anything to Nash either. "A widower constant to his wife's memory," he continued more urgently, "a devoted daughter's tender father, a gentleman of your own age, in the prime of life, cravenly suffocated—with a pillow." Seizing one from the bed, Harris brandished it for emphasis. "And the next day this same Henry Crane broke a serving woman's neck. He was seen doing it."

"Why then is he not arrested?"

"The witness is prevented from testifying. That's why I need your particular help, Mr. Nash, in uncovering any wrongs Crane may have committed here, in the North."

"I have my own affairs to occupy me," Nash replied testily. "I must see the factor—"

"Yes," Harris agreed, "but you speak the Ojibways' language and know how to gain their confidence, I'm convinced."

"Never doubt it! Gentleman in his fifties, you say?"

"Laid in the earth at age fifty-three. Will you come with me tomorrow morning?"

"If I am at leisure, and my mind doesn't change." Nash snuffed out his candle and lay down, taking some time to arrange the pillow. "Doesn't surprise me about Crane," he said a moment later. "I've a keen nose for any character defect."

Next morning, the two stepped from the Stone House together, as Harris had wished. Misgivings nevertheless assailed him. For Nash's abilities he had only Nash's own boastful word, whereas Nash's temper he had had more than one occasion to observe. Might the former post manager not spoil all by want of tact?

From the first encounter, such fears were wondrously dispelled. Cuthbert Nash's character showed quite another facet in his dealings with the Ojibway. Red skins did not appear to inflame his anger as did white. With the Indians he was by appropriate turns grave and dignified or merry and droll, but—so far as Harris could judge by tone of voice—never critical, never exasperated.

"Your Ojibway," he remarked to Harris, "doesn't like to utter his own name. So if there is no third party to do the honours, you're best to dispense with introductions."

Harris doubted if his ignorance on this point had caused his interview with Andrew Jones to miscarry, but clearly he had put his foot wrong at the start.

Finally, he learned something to his purpose. Nash had them directed to the village's greatest gossip, from whom they heard that Crane and Ewing's last servant—mentioned in Father Gouin's diary—had perished in a cholera outbreak three years ago. She had been in her sixties. Before her, they had employed a much younger woman. Susan Iwatoke had left the partners' household and the Sault in May of 1849. Some said she had kin in Michilimackinac.

The clue was slender enough, but there at least was a possible place between Presque Isle and the Sault for Crane to have disembarked. Nash would not further delay reunion with his own unofficial family. Harris set out alone.

* * *

Theresa supposed she must have stopped struggling. She was not chloroformed. The cotton was tied so she could breathe a little, though still not see. She felt herself bundled into some conveyance and driven away from Janet's wails at a pace sufficient to prevent the servant's following and on a route with enough turns to confuse Theresa's own sense of direction.

Wedged between her abductors, she tried to note what passed between them. They had been awaiting this moment for a whole week, without thinking she would ever be fool enough to venture out. At last they had her, a nice clean catch. Not a mark on her. Theresa's panicked pulse all but drowned out their mutual congratulations, and yet suspicion crept upon her that the younger voice for all its huskiness was female.

The carriage stopped. A large, loose, confident hand on her right arm and a small, tight, nervous one on her left led Theresa indoors and up a broad staircase. Pretending to stumble, she managed with her shoulder to loosen the blindfold. On her left she glimpsed a boy's baggy jacket and shako hat, but the trousered legs did not swing from the hips as a boy's. Then also, the throat was smooth, the chin and cheek unwhiskered. Theresa believed she had seen this girl once in feminine dress, but when and where she could not think, and other matters presently took her attention. At the man on her right she never got a look.

They were no longer climbing. Theresa was pushed through a door which locked behind her. As soon as her hands were free, she tore the hated pad from her face.

From what she could see, she was alone. The room was square and high-ceilinged, with one fireplace and only one door. A Brussels carpet in a floral pattern covered the middle of the floor, while a few thinly upholstered chairs and a sofa stood with their backs to the walls. A parlour then, but with two peculiarities. On the one hand, it was quite bare of movable ornaments or other small objects such as vases, table lamps, busts, books, mirrors, sewing boxes, fire-tending implements or even hanging pictures. On the other hand, and this darkened the room considerably, an armoire had been dragged in front of the only window.

To prevent the casement's opening, thought Theresa. The ton of oak defeated her utmost exertions to budge it.

A vertical ribbon of glass remained uncovered. Theresa peered through it and blinked, for there across Foundling Street rose the stone walls, tin roof and spire of the Grey Nuns' convent. The sight of her former refuge did not wholly reassure her. Of greater promise was the traffic passing just below her. She must attract someone's attention.

With the key to the armoire, which by some oversight had been left in its door, she began tapping on the window glass. One or two pedestrians glanced up. Apparently unable to see her in the darkened room, they shrugged and hurried on. Theresa tapped harder till the window cracked, then hammered a hole in it with her shoe, sending shards of glass down onto the sidewalk. She listened a remorseful instant for the cries of the injured. Hearing none, she put her mouth to the opening and set about yelling "Help!" and *"Au secours!"* for all she was worth.

But no, her cries would alert any enemies in the house. Better to throw out a note. She took the white cotton blindfold as her paper and carefully cut open her finger on the broken glass.

"H," she traced out, "E."

It was a small cut, and the blood came slowly. She was attempting to knead it down the arteries towards the wound when the door opened and closed.

Henry Crane was in the room. He advanced slowly. From where Theresa crouched, her husband looked menacingly tall and broad-chested, although his florid face expressed for the moment bemusement rather than intimidating purpose. His eyes weren't yet used to the semi-gloom.

"Theresa?" He stepped closer. "What are you doing?"

"Stop there!"

"Oh, you're bleeding." He stopped with a shiver. "Do you want attention?" he asked, glancing over his shoulder as if to assure her that the attention would not come from him.

"No, thank you, Henry."

Never had she spoken with such icy contempt. Her blood, she realized, was her surest protection against her weak-stomached antagonist. She stood up, but stayed pressed to the wall by the window so as to keep something sharp within reach.

Determined to guard this advantage, she didn't altogether listen to what Henry said next. By his tones of sincerest tenderness, she knew some trick was intended, and she heard as through a benign mist.

"...overjoyed to see...so many weeks of not knowing...dreadful weeks...your crushing bereavement...shared bereavement...I too...I—" Something here about his still not understanding why she had run away. Pain in his voice, then promise. "...agree to forget...dispense with explanations...all I ask...consent to return quietly with me."

Through the mist, a warning bell. If her consent was sought, she had better attend.

Crane moved a chair into the middle of the room and held it invitingly.

"You won't have to plan any dinners, Theresa," he announced in an expansive voice. "You won't have to pay any visits or play hostess at any entertainments. All that is over. You'll have peace and seclusion just as you would in the country. You know how sheltered from neighbours our villa is. You'll be at liberty to read soothing books and to enjoy your orchard. The fruits are at their loveliest ripeness now. I know you won't want to miss them."

His pose of providing for her welfare, convincing once, had become clownish. Why did he bother? It didn't take Theresa's educated eye to see that what Henry intended was an Edenic prison, justified before the world by his wife's feeble-mindedness.

"You're welcome to all the apples you can eat," she coolly replied, still standing her ground. "All I ask from you is to be left alone."

"Will you not live with me, wife?"

"No, Henry, I won't. Now that's understood, I should be obliged if you would permit me to leave."

Silence hung between them.

"My friends will be anxious," Theresa added self-consciously. "Your messengers gave their servant a scare."

"Are you sure you're quite well?" asked Crane. "You don't sound like yourself."

He's determined, Theresa thought with a shudder, to have me confined as a lunatic, a prisoner in his house or somewhere worse. Disdain gave way to apprehension.

"Please let me go," she asked meekly. "Forget me. I am not the woman you married."

These simple words seemed to appal Crane. His eyes flickered uncertainly. He stepped towards her, and his voice, almost theatrical before, dropped to a hoarse whisper.

"Hush! Don't ever say that."

"Stay back," Theresa cried. "Oh, why need I say anything at all? Just call me inconstant and let me go, and I swear I'll never do anything to harm you."

"You've already hurt me a great deal," Crane pronounced with a show of sorrow, and at his former volume. He turned away from her and stood mournfully contemplating the empty mantel shelf. "You left our conjugal home eight weeks ago without a word of warning," he went on. "Can you tell me why?"

Theresa judged it safer not to answer.

"When I came all this way to Montreal, you would not see me." Henry shot her a glance. "Why is that?"

Theresa said nothing.

"You have set your friend Isaac Harris snooping into my affairs." Henry gestured towards her in some agitation while he played this trump, although his voice continued clear and even. "What reason can you give me?"

So he knew. A foolish venture from the start. Not that she was about to utter a word in blame or praise of Isaac before this creature.

"Your refusal to answer," Crane observed, "does your understanding little credit."

Her resolve wavered. Maybe she should speak, she thought. Dumbness betokens illness. Theresa felt like a mouse lying with one paw held in a trap while the cat with all deliberation unsheathes its claws above her.

"Why can you not bear me, Theresa?" His voice pushed at the walls of the room. Once again he stepped forward. "Why do you cringe at my approach? Have I ever so much as raised a hand against you?"

The genteel parlour was shrinking as evening closed in, Henry's provokingly smooth pink face growing larger and larger. No ravages of conscience there. His thin lips gleamed waxily, as if smeared with some anti-chapping salve.

"Have I?"

Theresa jumped at the emphatic repetition. Fear jolted her into speech.

"Against me, never."

"Against whom then? Speak up." Crane stepped closer.

"You killed my father in his bed," Theresa spoke up and said. "You killed his housekeeper Sibyl Martin." The cut in Theresa's finger had closed. To open a fresh and more alarming wound, she dragged her right hand roughly across the edge of the hole in the window and thrust her lacerated palm into Crane's looming face.

He recoiled at her touch as if stung by acid.

"Why do you flinch, Henry? My family's blood is already on you, and you'll never get it off!"

Crane all but tripped over his boots, then over the chair he had placed, as he backed quickly away. His eyes never left Theresa's. His chin and nose bore red smudges. His hand went up as if to remove them, but could not be brought to touch them. Theresa pursued him to the door, which he flung open to reveal a stout, bearded gentleman with a medical bag.

"Examine her, dress her wounds," Crane commanded as he pushed past into the upstairs hall.

"The man you killed was no such coward," Theresa flung after him. She was a hair's breadth from tears.

The unsqueamish doctor took her right arm in both his thick hands, elevating her hand to slow the bleeding, and conducted her back into the room into the chair. Behind them the door closed again. Theresa turned at the sound and saw that Henry was not inside. They would bully her one at a time, she perceived. Choking sobs shook her.

"Be still, Mrs. Crane," said her new gaoler, "quite still. I am here to see that you are treated as your condition warrants, so if you'll comport yourself like a rational woman..."

For some time, she heard no more. She was now beside herself with grief and fear and rage. The checks imposed on her by one muscular man after another made her too frantic to marshal her thoughts. The accusations she had flung at Henry had stimulated in her the most corrosive memories and passions. It was too much. It had gone on too long. She knew she was not mad, but awareness of her husband's villainy, George MacFarlane's part in her family's woe, her own galling remorse as regards Sibyl, Paul Taggart's protracted death, the ague, the isolation and the strain of endless waiting had so torn at her nervous organization that she could not now collect herself for this inquiry into her sanity.

That's why the doctor was here. Plainly, he had been listening at the door. Above it, she saw, the transom window was tilted open, so he must have heard nearly every word that passed between Crane and herself. Between the baron of steam and his lunatic wife. Even if the diagnosis had not been bought in advance, what other inference could be drawn? Ghastly moans issued from her throat.

Finally, she understood the doctor to say, "Mrs. Crane, how did you come by these wounds?"

The doctor had a kind Irish voice, she noticed as her hand was being turned and held to the light, the fingers gently straightened. She winced. She could feel the self-inflicted cuts but not explain them. A danger to herself. Even if she forced her tongue to utter human sounds, what could she say? That self-mutilation was her only defence against a public benefactor?

The doctor had finished looking at her hand and was wrapping it in a clean linen bandage. Although he did well, she supposed, it tormented her to be so utterly in his power, scared her that he did with her what he would.

"I must warn you," he said in his considerate, methodical way, "that obstinate silence creates an unfavourable impression of your state of mind, most unfavourable. Not too tight, is it? Now, the examination I am to perform requires me to ask you certain questions. Try to answer, do."

Theresa stared at him helplessly.

"For a start," said the doctor, "what are your feelings towards your husband?"

* * *

Bored and ill at ease in Montreal, Jasper Small one fine Tuesday night took a woman to his room. His quixotic friend Isaac Harris had been gone ten days exactly. Duty and inclination alike made Small Theresa's interim protector, and he was keeping an eye out for her decidedly dangerous husband. That task, however, left many hours unoccupied.

With no attempt at secrecy, Henry Crane had arrived from Canada West by the 8 p.m. steamer on Saturday, 30th August. This was the earliest he could have been expected following the conclusion of the Scarboro bones inquest. The jury there, Small read, had pronounced the bones those of Sibyl Martin, but had been unable to say at whose hands she had died or why her arm had been disguised as that of Theresa Crane.

On his arrival in Montreal, Henry had taken a suite of rooms on Foundling Street for the space of a fortnight. Possibly he had arrived under the impression that Theresa was still with the Grey Nuns. In the three days since, he had written to but not seen her, nor yet—to the best of Small's knowledge—called upon either church or state to restore her to him. Was he indifferent or simply playing a close game? He most definitely did have other business in town. The *Herald* had reported, and

Small independently confirmed, that Henry Crane was spending much of his time with officials of Hugh Allan's Montreal Ocean Steamship Company, to whom he was representing the advantages of steel-hulled vessels for carrying the mails between Canada and Britain.

All very innocent, Small mused as he tied and retied his neckcloth. Good. Small wasn't burning to do battle with his partner's murderer, who had too much law on his side. Better to wait and see what Isaac turned up—and if it was nothing, as Small was realist enough to expect, then to pack Theresa off to foreign parts and trust William Sheridan's patriotic ghost to understand. Small could wait. He thought of himself as a patient man.

His face in the mirror looked anything but. A grimace of irritation compressed his lips and creased his forehead. Having dallied over bathing and dressing as long as possible, he was wondering how to get through the rest of the evening. So long as Theresa was not threatened, there was little for the lawyer to do but think about the quantity of hard work and soft flesh awaiting him in Toronto.

Perhaps he would try a local sporting house, *un bordel est-canadien.* Why not? He left his room and started downstairs.

In truth, Esther's smooth contours represented but a fraction of her appeal. The smooth immodesty of her caresses and endearments expressed an imperviousness to feminine convention Small found as sublime as a sunset or a storm at sea. Precepts, slights and warnings had not tamed her. The cant phrase "fallen woman" simply did not do justice to the courtesan's strength.

The mauve-gowned imp who moments later approached Small in Rasco's lobby—before he could get out the door—necessarily partook of that strength, for if she had borne herself in the slovenly, defeated manner of a common streetwalker, the hotel porters would promptly have put her out. There was vigour certainly in her small, square jaw, and her startling golden eyes impressed him with their predatory gleam. She said she had heard of Mr. Small's courtroom skills. She had a matter of business to discuss, if they might go somewhere quite private. She called herself Nan Hogan.

Small didn't unreservedly believe a word she said, but she piqued his curiosity as nothing lately had, and he doubted that she could do him any serious harm. She might do him good, one way or another.

He could comfortably have taken on extra work, but it was in the end he who employed Nan. As soon as they were alone, she threw herself in his arms. Small enjoyed the novel feel of a woman who was all bone and sinew, with no need of stays, the novel taste of tobacco on female lips. She tried first to exchange her favours for information regarding how Sibyl Martin had died. Small regretfully declined. By midnight Nan, wearing nothing but Small's white shirt and black morning coat, lay sprawled across his bed having her vulva licked and nuzzled to her audible satisfaction, and it had been agreed that for a further consideration she was to infiltrate Crane's Montreal establishment and report back on his doings.

"You had better put on an apron to attract his notice," Small advised as she arrayed herself in her own violet finery. "Crane is keen on women in service."

"I'll be an active and useful boy," she retorted, cracking her knuckles. "Whether through his landlady or through his secretary, I'll wheedle my way into a position. Depend upon it."

"As you wish, Master Hogan, but might I have my pocketbook back with the rest of my clothes? Much obliged." Small counted the bills inside and, finding all present, tucked one into her bodice. "Here's something on account."

* * *

In subsequent days, Small refrained from setting great store by a bargain concluded under such circumstances. He naturally did not mention it to Theresa. For more than a week, he saw nothing more of Nan.

Then on Thursday, 11th September, as he was sipping his

dessert wine in Rasco's emptying dining room, a waiter intimated that a lad calling himself N.H. was waiting for Mr. Small at the desk with a supposedly urgent message. Small found Nan trousered, covered in dust, and fidgeting impatiently with an inkpot. To the desk clerk's relief, Small sent the monkey to the stables.

"Engaged him to exercise a horse," Small explained with an amused shake of the head, "and he presents himself in the middle of the night. Suppose I had better see him all the same."

The clerk commented sympathetically on the fecklessness of youth and lapsed into bored silence. Once satisfied that he was of no greater interest to anyone else in sight, Small ambled off, his show of indifference facilitated by the cushion of Sauternes on which he continued to float.

In truth, he expected no emergency. To see Nan again made his wine-thinned blood sparkle with remembered delight. To see her for the first time in boyish disguise—her hair bundled up under a worn and dented shako, the nape of her neck bare—spiced memory with novelty and made delight fresh. Might Nan's excitement not reciprocally derive from seeing him? Small liked the way she rushed towards him as soon as he entered the stable yard.

"She's in Crane's hands," Nan began in a quick, husky whisper. "He means to have her seen by a medico and locked up as a madwoman."

"Locked up where?" Small said coolly, but floating no longer. "When?"

"Grey Nuns, the lunatics' wing. A living tomb, from what I hear. Now she's in a flash boarding house across the street, but she goes to the other after dark." The words leaped from her narrow mouth. Her breathing was accelerated, her yellow eyes unusually round and steady.

"It's dark *now*." Small tilted his watch face towards the gas lamp in the deserted stable yard. "Five to eight. Has she gone already?"

"Not likely. They were cooking her supper ten minutes ago when I left."

Nan was credible enough so far, thought Small, and so agitated that she must have had a hand in the capture. When she lied, it would be to minimize her rôle. Small would want to believe her.

"How did you get away?" he said.

"My job was done, wasn't it?" An edge came into Nan's voice. "I was set to watch the priest's house."

"And kidnap Mrs. Crane from there?" Small couldn't imagine that Henry Crane, a killer careful of appearances, would have ordered an action this reckless.

"From the lane behind, and not for my own pleasure either."

"You might have told me beforehand. No—never mind." Small knew she would say something about being watched every minute, and he didn't want to lose time hearing it. Having a problem to solve made him calmly practical, but he was distressed too that a woman he had enjoyed should have helped deliver Theresa to Crane, albeit for the purpose of bringing himself to the captive's aid. None of this should have happened.

"What was Mrs. Crane doing in the lane?" he asked.

"She didn't confide," Nan retorted. "Guess she wearied of being shut up, which is what she'll be now, poor wretch. I had never set eyes on the lady, and when I did, the last thing I wanted was to lay an ungentle hand upon her."

"Was she injured in the abduction?" Small's voice became stern enough to suggest that all future friendliness between them depended on the answer to this question.

"No more than winded, and for certain not by me." Nan laid her boyish, grimy right hand against the left side of her flattened chest. "Rough-and-tumble has never been my game, I swear, and kidnap never would have been either except so that I could tell you where they took her."

She sounded as if she truly wanted Small to think well of her—think of her, that is, as a peaceable whore and cutpurse.

"Were you followed here?" he asked.

"Me? Never!" This slur on her elusive stealth offended Nan worst of all. "You waste precious minutes doubting me," she chided. "The question is what will you do?"

"Aha. Her husband sent you to ask me that."

"Sweet Jasper, no! You know why his missus left him, and I don't, but I'm sure she had her reason. The man is all for show. Henry Crane is never as pure as he pretends, with his scented soap and his 'can't smoke here.' I wouldn't spy for him for love or money."

Small thought he believed her. "You're working for the police then."

"I was curious is all."

Small didn't believe that. "The first thing you ever asked me, remember, was about a serving woman's death—no affair of mine, but one that greatly interests a certain Inspector John Vandervoort."

"I admit nothing." Nan dropped her eyes and kicked a pebble against the wooden gate into St. Claude Street. "Still, as to police, I know a good Montreal constable if you need one."

The clock on the Bonsecours Market was striking eight. Theresa's supper might now be ready. If, as seemed likely, she were too upset to eat, she would perhaps be delivered to the convent immediately. Small continued to deliberate.

"Tell me, Nan. Were there two doctors to examine Mrs. Crane or just the one?"

"One is all was mentioned. What does she know that her husband has to muzzle her?"

"Let's find your constable," said Small, stepping towards the gate.

"I'll have my money first."

"You'll have it soon," he promised. "Come on."

A single medical certificate, he was thinking, plus a close relative's statement would suffice in an emergency to get a patient confined—but if either document proved defective, Crane would have no backstop and Theresa would go free. Under those circumstances, the presence of a uniformed official would deter any extra-legal interference with her.

"Come on yourself," said Nan, tugging at his sleeve to quicken his gait. "If they get her walled up in the nuns' asylum, she won't walk out again so easy. Mr. Isaac Harris will have your hide for it, he's that wild about the lady, and all my pains in coming here will go for nothing!"

This unexpected mention of Harris stopped Small in his tracks with a new idea. Isaac was due back any day, any evening.

"Get your policeman to the Grey Nuns' front gate right away," the lawyer instructed. "I'll meet him there."

* * *

Before the doctor had finished examining Theresa, she was able to repeat her accusations against Henry but not marshal in any cogent or coherent form the particulars that would give them plausibility. If only she still had her letter to Isaac. It was all set down there. She tried to think, but was distracted by the fact of her captivity, by her need to speak convincingly, and by her simultaneous conviction that speech was feather-weak to derail her settled fate. *Should* she even be fighting a finding of lunacy? It might be the sole condition under which Henry would let her live.

As she once more lost the thread of her narrative and fell silent, the doctor leaned forward, tenderly stroking his coal-black beard.

"Would you like to be revenged on your husband?" he asked in tones no less tender. It sounded like an invitation.

"All I've ever wanted is to be free of him," said Theresa, confident for once she was making the point she intended. "Let his Maker be his judge."

The doctor took Theresa to a room where a supper table was laid and left her there. The only cutlery was a spoon. She ate in the same utilitarian spirit as she had lunched that last Sunday at Queen Street East. Each laborious mouthful fortified her against an uncertain future. She tasted only to satisfy herself she was not being drugged or poisoned.

Presently Henry and the ample medical man returned from their own meal. They seemed to be in dispute as to whether Theresa would have to be removed by force.

"No, no, sir," said the doctor, gesticulating with a silver toothpick. A shred of pork flowered from behind an upper cuspid. "We call this a reasoning madness. Her speech has been wild and incoherent to be sure, but see how quietly she sits now." The speaker's tongue located the food morsel, and—after pointing to the docile patient with his toothpick—he turned that implement to its proper use.

More than words, this unabashed display impressed Theresa with the verdict passed upon her. She was judged unworthy of courtesy, perhaps insensitive to it.

"Despite her delusions regarding her great father's death," the doctor continued, "and despite her fixed idea that God will smite you for the crimes she falsely imagines you to have committed, she has enough understanding to hear that we are taking her somewhere for her good."

"I trust," Crane murmured, "you have restraints in your bag in case of trouble."

"Yes, of course, to be sure, but we have only to speak gently and keep her from sharp objects, and I vouch for her docility. Now, Mrs. Crane, you must know that you are sick. Will you not come with us to the hospital where you may be made well?"

With the courage of the condemned, Theresa rose and accompanied them. Henry did not try to touch her. When the doctor offered his arm across the street, she took both it and the opportunity to point out to him that the word "smite" had not passed her lips.

"You should know," he said, calmly ignoring her, "how much good I heard of your late father, and not just on account of his fine words either. No, indeed. When Montreal was last provincial capital, the House of Parliament used to stand on this very square, right there."

Theresa did not follow his pointing arm. She was looking at the Grey Nuns' high wall and thinking of the lunatics' wing with its cold, stone cells and the narrow slits through which food was handed into them. What a different welcome awaited her from the one she had received from the good sisters four weeks ago! She tried to feel nothing.

Henry was a pace or two ahead.

"Yes," her companion continued, "and when in '49 the enemies of responsible government broke in with fiery brands to burn Parliament down, William Sheridan did not turn tail. He stayed to gather in his arms the records of debate. He got them to the street, where the Tory mob dashed them from his grasp to heap back on the blaze, and the building was destroyed as you can see, but it was a gallant deed he did, and the country owes him thanks. I'm truly sorry, madam, for your loss."

"A mad deed, some would say," Theresa rejoined. "A danger to himself."

This hideously malapropos tribute from one of her gaolers would further have discomposed her had her attention not that moment been taken by a short, dapper figure who was accosting Henry at the convent gate.

"If Mrs. Crane were in the least need of legal advice, Jasper," her husband loudly explained, "I should see that she got it."

"I may as well look over the papers, in your own interest as well as hers." Jasper met Theresa's eyes and inclined his head.

"Our interests," said Crane, "are one—"

"All the more reason—"

"—and adequately protected," Crane continued, "without your interference."

"Who might this gentleman be?" asked the doctor.

"My late father's law partner," Theresa promptly replied, "and my own legal representative. I should like Mr. Small to read the grounds on which I am to be deprived of liberty."

"I must overrule you, Theresa."

Crane began rapping forcefully at the slide in the wooden gate and pulled the bell rope for good measure. Bridge workers came and went from the taverns and coffee houses across the square, but here on the south side little traffic passed at this dark hour, and no one turned his head at the prolonged tattoo. Grateful as she was to Jasper (how ever had he known to come?), Theresa believed Henry would as usual have his way.

"Stay a bit," said the doctor. "Our proceedings will bear scrutiny. I've the two forms right here and no objection to letting William Sheridan's partner see them."

Before Henry could raise further objections, the portress opened the slide, and he was obliged to explain his errand. Small held the medical certificate under a street lamp, and Theresa read along. Then the slide snapped shut. The sister in charge of the lunatic wing was being sent for.

"Everything in order?" Crane swept the first document from Small's hands.

"It's full of distortions," said Theresa. Her need to appear sane resulted in a pursed, bitter calm that still did not feel like her but soon might. "I've no wish, Henry, to see you punished."

"In form, however, it's quite correct," Jasper murmured at her side. "The sisters will have to accept it—but let's see the husband's signed order for the patient's reception. Does it mention what emergency prevents her being examined separately by *two* physicians?"

"Self-inflicted wounds." The doctor tendered the document.

"Wounds or no wounds," Henry snorted, "hiding cat-and-mouse from her husband has made the matter urgent enough. Stop to collect two opinions, and we'd have her running off again who knows where."

From the direction of the steamer docks, a cab was bearing down on the foursome at breakneck speed. The hoofs' crescendo made everyone look. Theresa might have taken the opportunity to flee, except that the doctor had seized her right wrist to show Small her bandaged palm. Just before the cab arrived, a door opened in the Grey Nuns' gate. A robust sister in the order's Quakerish brown dress and black cape and bonnet gave permission to bring "the afflicted soul" in.

"After you, wife," said Crane, condescending as before, sweeping her forward with his long arm.

Isaac Harris leaped from the box of the cab through clouds of dust raised by the braking wheels. An apparition.

Theresa shuddered. Isaac's long, handsome face burned with

purpose. His suddenness disconcerted her even as she admired it.

How many other pairs of eyes were turned upon this man landed like a meteor in their midst, she could not have said. Henry kept pressing her through the convent door.

"Don't go in, Theresa," cried Harris in a firm, warning voice. "Henry Crane is not your husband."

Not her husband. Later these words would amaze her, but the shock wasn't felt at once. So little was it felt that she imagined she must have had a presentiment from the moment she heard the nearing hoof-falls of the cabman's horse, or even from long, long before.

Other hands came now between her and Henry. She didn't see whose. She was still under the stars, in the open air. It bathed her brow in blessed coolness and tasted sweet in her lungs, and yet after so much buffeting, she mistrusted it and breathed with pain.

Henry was not her husband. His neglect of her from the day of their supposed wedding had already told her heart that this was so. He had a living wife when he made his vows to her in church. All through their years together, she had felt a shame without knowing what it was, and now she had a name for it.

Around her, everyone spoke at once. The nun and the doctor vented their astonishment, while Crane—now confidently, now indignantly—denied everything.

But she knew it was true. Perhaps it was this knowledge, however liberating, of three years concubinage, however innocent, that she had just now wished to run from. How could she acknowledge having been so duped?

How could she face Isaac, strong in his love, and truly most lovable? She could not even thank him. She hoped he would not expect her to fall into his arms.

Jasper was calling for the evidence of the bigamy. Isaac was producing it in a steady voice that somehow pierced the babble.

"A certified copy," he said, "of Number 309 in the Marriage Register of Mackinac County, Michigan. It reads, 'Henry M. Crane of Sault Ste. Marie, age 28 years, and Susan Iwatoke of

Mackinac, age 20 years, married 29 September 1849 in presence of...'"

Yes, yes, Theresa knew it must be so, but could not at this moment attend to the particulars. She felt assailed rather than freed. Around her, the assembly on the sidewalk was growing. Isaac's cab had not departed, and from the interior there alighted a second man, very young, and cassocked like a seminarian. He was a stranger to Theresa at a moment when strangers were little welcome.

Then, however, the seminarian turned and handed down from the selfsame cab a lady whose delicately chiselled features Theresa recognized as Marthe's.

Marthe had come in answer to her summons. Marthe, soul-saving companion of many rides and more *causeries* during the cold Henry years. Marthe, in whom Theresa had confided so imperfectly, and who had in her partially informed state given Theresa what help she could and what counsel of wifely submission her faith taught her she must. Marthe looked about her, her lovely countenance flustered with affectionate concern. Theresa reached towards her.

The womens' arms went round each other. They had not embraced much in the time before, but this was what Theresa wanted most in the world, this companionable shoulder on which to wake from the nightmare. Through Marthe's rich pelisse, she felt that shoulder tremble.

"*Je viens te consoler, ma pauvre Thérèse, et tiens—c'est moi qui pleure.* Pardon my tears."

Theresa shook her head to show it did not matter. Words came with difficulty. "*Ton frère?*" she managed to say.

"My brother Armand," Marthe rejoined, "and what a scholar! See how he devours those papers."

"It is sworn here," Armand exclaimed with the greatest possible interest, "that Susan Crane was alive on 1st January 1856."

"This is beside the point," Crane burst out. "Sister, will you take charge of this dangerous madwoman?"

A constable in a stovepipe hat bearing the number eight had

strolled up and was also inspecting Harris's documents.

"Si monsieur n'est pas le mari, je ne le peux," said the nun, throwing up her hands.

"It would require a second medical certificate," the doctor put in.

"What the good sister says," offered Armand, "is that if you are not the husband—"

"I am most assuredly the husband!" Henry Crane's forehead bulged with indignation. "These scribbled pages are worthless forgeries, and this individual"—contemptuously indicating Harris—"a known mischief-maker whose sole motive is to usurp Mrs. Crane's affections."

Theresa tightened her grip on Marthe's right arm, for she heard in Henry's voice the authority that directed great enterprises and always carried the day. Might others present not hear it too?

"But *is* this lady Mrs. Crane?" demanded Isaac, posted at her other side. "Both convent and physician will want to satisfy themselves on that point before proceeding."

Would they? Theresa couldn't see where this was written, but something in her responded to the speaker, the disconcerting angel descended from the cloud. When she heard his voice, Isaac's voice, Henry's seemed less certain to prevail.

Henry pretended deafness. "Do your duty, Sister," he commanded. "Constable, assist her."

Constable 8, stiffly erect in his high-collared blue jacket, was perusing the medical certificate prior to intervening on either side and *sotto voce* was asking the doctor to explain that document to him.

"It may be as you say, Mr. Crane," declared Theresa's examiner out loud. "It may well be." He gave his black beard a vigorous tug. "But while the issue is in doubt I shall not be responsible for depriving William Sheridan's daughter of her freedom." Removing the certificate from the policeman's hands, he tore it across. Without pause, he aligned the halves and again tore across, pocketing all four quarters. "I withdraw my finding."

Exclamations of surprise or approval burst from several throats.

"Oh! Oh my—"

"What else could he do?"

"Jamais je n'ai vu de la sorte!"

"So much for the madwoman!"

"Very well then!" Henry flared out, glowering at all, but with especial fury directed towards what he had supposed a compliant medical man. "There's more than one lunatic here, and I leave you to your own lunatic devices."

This last phrase struck Theresa as comical, though likely it was sheer relief that made her at that instant want to laugh. She exchanged glances with Harris and saw the temptation in his face too. She dared not give in. She dared not open her mouth for fear she would find herself screaming hysterically at her release.

"Excuse me, Henry." Small did not smile. "The crime of bigamy carries a minimum sentence in Canada of two years' confinement. You had better come to the police station."

The diverse gathering murmured assent. Crane looked around the circle at the lawyer Jasper Small, the detective Isaac Harris, and the postmaster general's daughter Marthe Laurendeau—at his own bigamous spouse Theresa Sheridan—at the seminarian, the Grey Nun, the doctor and the Montreal constable—at (who was this?) the yellow-eyed boy in the battered shako whom Crane had engaged a week since to watch the house on Craig Street.

Henry was outmanoeuvred. For now. But he could never have prospered in so turbulent an age without powers of resilience. Anger would currently avail him nothing. Anger accordingly drained from his pink face, which composed itself to his latest reversal, and even assumed an expression of sober helpfulness. Theresa had seen him thus with injured workers' families.

"I'm glad you're here, Mademoiselle Laurendeau," he said, believing it. "With so kind and pious a friend to look after her, Theresa will come to no harm."

Marthe nodded confusedly.

"My thanks," he said. "Go with Marthe, my love, and believe me your friend too... Well, Jasper, the police station it is. That may be best. If I just stop by a telegraph office first to instruct my own barrister and solicitor—Mr. Lionel Leonard Matheson, as you know, never loses a case—we'll soon have this straightened out to everyone's satisfaction."

Believe him her friend? Don't concern yourself with what I believe, Theresa was thinking. Would she ever believe anything again?

Isaac was at her side, his honest voice a balm to her ears, but what he was asking escaped her. Her hand, something about her hand. She could not speak yet or take her eyes from her un-husband.

"How badly," Isaac was asking, "are you hurt?"

She did not know.

Chapter Twenty-One
Grand Trunk

No victory dance shook the earth, not then nor weeks later. Unshaped to their wearers' heads, the laurel wreaths felt unnatural and precarious—to be snatched away by the autumn winds, or discarded as a mockery.

After bidding the Brays an appreciative farewell, Theresa accompanied Marthe to the Laurendeau estate forty miles up the St. Lawrence. The single-storey fieldstone manor house had been sheltering seigneurs since the seventeenth century. A roof of red tiles fell steeply past two tiers of dormers, then flared out over a long, hospitable verandah. The refuge denied Theresa as a runaway wife welcomed her at last.

Harris was welcome as a visitor. Through September, each visit saddened him more—and, when he had returned Banshee with lathered flanks to the ostler at the Vaudreuil coaching inn, he would drink an extra glass at dinner and sit up smoking long into the night. Theresa was painfully kind and uncommunicative. She said she felt numb inside.

In the wake of so many shocks, perhaps all she needed—besides country air and moderate exercise—was the passage of uneventful time. Harris would never have begrudged it but for Crane. Theresa unmarried was a competent witness to murder, and Harris encouraged her to lay an information.

"Lay one immediately!" Small advised before returning to Toronto. Unless the capital charges could be brought to trial during the October assizes, they would have to wait unresolved till spring.

Theresa felt no inclination to testify. Arguments of justice and filial duty she quietly set aside. Man could not be just, and she would not believe her Papa in heaven was crying for blood.

"But as a precaution, if not as a punishment," Harris urged one sun-drenched Indian summer afternoon on the Laurendeaus' verandah. He was practically citing her own letter. "Think what further harm such a man might do, to others if not to yourself."

It was, of course, of herself he was mainly thinking.

"You want my words to hang him?" she asked without inflection.

"No preventive surer. A conviction for bigamy will ruin his credit but won't hold him long, or sweeten his temper."

Theresa rocked in her *berceuse*. Her large eyes slid away across the meadow to the water's edge. Early frost had withered the normally hardy asters and goldenrod, leaving only the gentian in bloom—azure patches beneath the trees' red and yellow flames. The united province actually boasted half a dozen members of the gentian family, which Theresa had once expected Harris to distinguish—but when one day he asked her which subspecies graced this river bank, she said she did not know.

September passed into October. In Toronto, Henry Crane was to be tried for having two wives, and the press took note. Pious tongues wagged. Wits were honed on the sultan of steam and his harem. The most powerful voices, though, denied that any civilized court could recognize the fleeting connection between a father of Canadian transportation and a wilderness squaw, however the business might be registered by what Brother Jonathan up in Michigan chose to call a Justice of the Peace. Different mores governed backwoods and town.

It worried Harris to be absent, but as Theresa was not required to give evidence in this case, he had elected to stay near her.

Mrs. Henry Crane would not be appearing either. It was curious. On her existence everything depended, like the letter π in an equation, but she was known only very approximately. Harris had not in fact seen her on his recent travels.

At the straits between Lakes Huron and Michigan, he had found the principal settlement and county seat situated on

Mackinac Island. Susan Iwatoke was not there. This community, however, differed from the Sault in that at Mackinac—or Mackinaw, as residents seemed to call it—she was not wholly a stranger to the white population. Seven years ago, she had cooked for officers of the garrison, without references. She claimed to have left a previous situation to escape an employer's advances. One obliging United States Army major—in '49 a captain—described her for Harris. Instead of falling straight in the usual Indian manner, her hair reportedly waved softly. Her features, by contrast, were accounted less comely than forceful. She permitted no liberties. In her first months at Mackinac, she had had visits from a Canadian suitor no soldier particularly remembered, but when these attentions stopped, she discouraged all male company. Soon after, she had moved away, returning only for a brief visit last winter, then removing farther west.

Farther west than it was in Harris's power to follow—but it did not matter, for now at last the grain had been added that tipped the balance. The drop had fallen that set the mill wheel in motion. The major's circumstantial account had been enough to give Harris the idea of inspecting the marriage registers. And there he found Crane's secret—as Ingram must have found it before him. Suddenly it seemed obvious. What had blocked Harris was his preconception that what he sought was an illegal rather than a legal act.

He would always remember sitting overwhelmed by gratitude before that Mackinac County ledger. Here was Theresa's release. Here was justification for so many miles travelled on such vague and slender hope.

What had Crane done on hearing of Ewing's accident? Rather than face his mortally injured partner, he had come to Susan Iwatoke and married her. He must have felt horrified and afraid, and in desperate need of consolation. When the moment of need passed, his new wife was abandoned, likely because he could not see her in the illustrious future he pictured for himself.

Harris had blessed Susan Crane. Praise be to her rectitude in holding out for legal union, in holding out against the seducer's charms to which so many women had yielded. Thanks be to firmness of principle, as well as to any lucky stars that had brought Harris at last into the presence of this wondrous book.

Finally, he had bestirred himself to the tasks that remained. First, note the names of the witnesses. Then, before racing back to Montreal, find one willing to be brought to testify in a Canadian court. A shopkeeper named McCann filled the additional requirement that he had seen Susan Crane in robust health as lately as the turn of the year. No, he had not talked to his neighbours about the marriage or kept track of what became of the husband—but, if Crane was a bigamist, McCann would testify all right. He had great respect for Mrs. Crane.

Mr. McCann's passage and all other arrangements Harris had in the end delegated to Jasper Small, who had demonstrated such trustworthiness on the night of Harris's return and of Theresa's near immurement.

In Crane's trial for bigamy, Small himself acted for the Crown. The city's more cautious barristers little sought the office of prosecuting so influential a defendant, all the less so when that defendant was represented by L.L. Matheson. Under oath, the shopkeeper answered both lawyers' questions soberly and to the point. He convinced a jury of shopkeepers that Susan Crane was no mere country wife, but as validly married to the accused as was Mrs. Franklin Pierce to the President of the United States. Small telegraphed to Harris a sixty-word account, including verdict and sentence—guilty, two years.

This was the minimum term allowed by law and the only one short enough to be served outside the Provincial Penitentiary.

Notwithstanding, Crane's partisans roared in protest. Next day's *Montreal Gazette* reported the launch of a petition to have him pardoned in recognition of his service to the country. Meanwhile, he was to occupy the least dismal cell in Toronto's Berkeley Street Gaol.

Theresa took the news calmly. Now, Harris begged her, now—while Crane remained in custody—was the time to proceed with the murder charges. She saw no necessity. For

Sibyl's sake, he urged. She appeared to waver, but would not make up her mind.

He spoke to Marthe. His acquaintance with her dated from the moment he had heard a steward on the Montreal steamer address a passenger as Mlle Laurendeau. Handed Jasper Small's note on disembarking, he had brought her and her brother by cab—not a moment too soon—to the Grey Nuns' gates. Since that rescue, Marthe's mistrust of Harris had dissolved. She now heard attentively what he had to say regarding Theresa's state of mind.

Unluckily, though, her own quiet and reserved temperament blinded her to her guest's distressing torpor. Theresa looked well—did she not?—*béatifique même*, walked a mile a day, ate what the city-trained cook prepared, attended mass with the family, and taught the younger children English.

"When herself," Harris suggested, "she likes to be of use. Give her more employment if you can."

Towards mid-October, he encountered a change. For the first time, Theresa was not in when at the end of the hour-long ride from Vaudreuil he knocked at the manor house door. She had gone with Marthe's mother to visit the neighbourhood sick.

The next day on his return, Theresa told him without animation but at some length about a farmer with lockjaw. While temperatures no longer permitted sitting out on the verandah, tall casement windows and pastel striped upholstery made the front parlour almost as bright. Mme Laurendeau presided—a handsome and articulate lady of fifty—but left the story to Theresa.

It was feared this poor *habitant* would starve. A Saint-Polycarpe widow who dabbled in medicine was on the point of knocking out some of his teeth, that he might be fed. The proposal horrified the man's wife. She would, however, acquiesce if no less drastic measures would save him.

After ascertaining how long the sufferer had been without food or drink, Theresa sat by him and asked if he could nod his head. He nodded stiffly from the shoulders, bowed rather. She asked if he could swallow. Again he bowed.

"He was in no imminent danger of starvation, but I thought

lack of fluids might be aggravating the cramps." Theresa fell silent, afraid perhaps of boasting.

"Racontez donc à monsieur ce que vous avez fait," Mme Laurendeau softly prompted.

"By all means," said Harris with quickening interest. "Tell me."

For too long, he was thinking, Theresa had not only been acted upon to her disadvantage, but had seen most of her own best intentions miscarry. The experience must be paralyzing. It was time for her to become the heroine of her own life.

"I simply had him recline at various angles and with a teaspoon introduced water between his lips until we got it to flow around and between his clenched teeth."

"Two hours she sat with him!" exclaimed madame.

"In the evening his wife got him to swallow some beef tea," Theresa added.

"Using your method," said Harris.

"Whose else but hers? And this morning, gently, gently, his mouth was beginning to open."

"With all his ivory still in it," Harris observed. "Not a bad day's work."

"It could not have been a serious case," said Theresa, glowing a little with the compliment in spite of herself. "Truly, Isaac. I believe four in five tetanus victims do not recover."

Ten days later, days full of similar work, she told him that she thought it was time she went home to Toronto.

* * *

As the morning of October 31 took hold, the season's first sprinkling of snow melted away, leaving the fields around Coteau station smelling fresh and fertile again. The iron rails, which stretched at last unbroken to Toronto, glistened dully. Banners hung to inaugurate the line just four days ago shook the damp from their still crisp block letters:

VIVE LE GRAND TRONC
VOIE DE LA PROSPÉRITÉ

27 OCTOBRE 1856

Eastward across the level countryside, a slanting column of wood smoke already stood out against the lighter grey of the sky. The train was coming.

Its approach brought that long track to life. Harris caught his breath like any sightseer at the scale of the enterprise, while his thoughts centred on the grim business awaiting at the journey's end. Impatient on all counts to be off, he was no more than half listening to Marthe's father, who was genteelly boosting his riding as a place to invest—now that Coteau-du-Lac was "served by rail!" Down the platform, Theresa was strolling in conversation with Marthe.

"Parliament won't remain forever in your delightful city of Toronto," the postmaster general was saying. "No—size and racial balance make Montreal by far the likeliest choice for a permanent capital, although little Ottawa is beginning to be spoken of as a compromise. Either way would make this county's fortune."

The honourable member was two yards tall with an imposing French nose and an excellent English tailor. Harris's Port Hope suit was freshly pressed, but loose and worn. His largest recent investment had been twenty dollars for two first class tickets to the delightful city where he would have to sell his last real estate holdings.

He thought little of them. In that city next day was supposed to start an inquest into the death of William Sheridan. Harris still secretly doubted it.

In the past week, he and Small had spent freely on telegrams. Theresa, Harris reported, was now willing to give evidence. Under the combined pressure of Crane's bigamy conviction and her murder allegations, Chris Hillyard at last ceased defending the death certificate he had signed. He ordered Sheridan disinterred. The autumn assizes had ended just the day before. The surest way to hold Crane now was to have a coroner's jury arraign him—a finding, said Small, equivalent to a grand jury indictment. Bail would be denied, and the petition for pardon on the bigamy conviction would be rejected, if not first withdrawn.

The smoke pillar was rising straighter. Beneath it, a crow-black locomotive had rounded the last bend and was gliding towards the waiting four, the long beak of its cowcatcher ready to dispose of all obstacles of flesh and blood. The baron of steam was about to find himself in its way. His accuser would be on its back.

Perhaps, thought Harris—but by the same token, Crane would know better than most how to wreck a train and who to get to do it. Harris would give odds that Henry had another one or two cards, at least, up his sleeve. It was too soon to be feeling quite snug and secure.

"*Monsieur* Laurendeau," he said in parting, "although my business plans remain...unsettled, I shall always think warmly of Coteau-du-Lac. Here as nowhere else, Miss Sheridan has been safe."

"If only we had known that Crane had over her no moral or legal right..." sighed the postmaster general, then added with gratifying directness, "Her father was my mentor in politics, *monsieur.* I regret deferring to his assassin."

Marthe shook Harris's hand and promised to care for his horse until he had leisure to fetch it. Six carriages and a mail car constituted the entire train. Harris did his comically inadequate best to see that the wheels were attached to the axles. Then the two passengers climbed aboard.

"It's hard to believe we'll sleep in Toronto tonight," Theresa called down through the window in the pause before starting.

Her words might have made Harris suspect she too was apprehensive—had her tone not expressed rather the agreeable wonderment everyone felt at the newly-opened line. Theresa was entitled to her share of wonder. Often enough had she accompanied her father between the Canadas by the more leisurely conveyances of steamer, coach and sleigh.

"Don't forget to set your watches back twenty-three minutes," Laurendeau called up, as if neither Harris nor Theresa had ever ventured so far before. "When you travel west, you see, the sun reaches its zenith later and..."

His further explanations were lost as the train rolled away from the station, and the journey began.

Harris closed the window before sitting down. He squirmed in his seat. Mixed with his vague forebodings was the excitement of spending the next thirteen and a half hours at Theresa's side, her sole companion. A black quilted carriage mantle hid nine tenths of her. From under a matching bonnet, chestnut brown hair—three inches longer than in August—spilled out over her forehead in a freakishly ravishing sheepdog fringe. Harris's fingers yearned to be among the wisps.

Aware of his eyes upon her, she looked up, smiled slightly, and bent again over her book. Whether or not she would in fact sleep the night before facing Crane in coroner's court, she showed no anxiety yet. The volume she held was a journal. In it she pencilled sentences as the motion of the train allowed. Harris wondered if the composition of that harrowing letter had not had the delayed consequence of showing her she was capable of assembling her thoughts on paper, rather than merely keeping lists.

"It amazes me," she said, reading his mind, "how much time I spent cataloguing wildflowers. You must have been bored."

"Not at the time. What are you writing now?"

"An essay on the sickroom. Listen: 'The name is apt. Too often it is a tight box to contain and reinforce disease rather than a light and open place where the sick may mend.'"

"We must see that it's published," said Harris.

"The observations are my own, but from the late war Miss Nightingale draws the same lessons. True originality would be putting them in everyday practice."

Even as he applauded this goal, Harris judged the admirable Miss Nightingale too monogamously wedded to nursing to make a reassuring model. How soon might he broach the subject of his place in Theresa's future? Not today, not tomorrow. He tried to look no further than the next telegraph pole, then the next, then the next.

The poles appeared to pass the window slowly. A boy on

horseback confirmed Harris's impression by easily overtaking the train. Only after six or seven minutes did the rider again come in sight and fall behind, sparing his mount spurs and whip to save its life. A lordly passenger threw him a coin.

By staging a hundred such horses between the metropolises of Canada East and West, one might arrive sooner, though exhausted. The appetite for speed grew with feeding, speed over comfort. The *Cytherean* and all "floating palace" steamships on Lake Ontario and the upper St. Lawrence were superseded, and the train still took too long. Soon passengers would resent any slackening of pace. They would even want to bolt down their meals in the jolting carriages. Harris wanted to.

Lunch was served briskly enough at the station restaurant in Brockville, dinner at the one in Cobourg. By now night had fallen, and drizzle beaded the carriage windows. Theresa, however, was becoming more aware of her surroundings, which began to remind her of her flight. East of here she had slumped inattentively in a stage coach. Cobourg was where she had spoken to a bucktoothed horse named Jupiter and a big-eared stable boy whose name she did not know.

"Asa," said Harris.

"What did happen to Enoch Henry?" she asked when the train slowed to cross the Prince Albert Viaduct at Port Hope. "I should like to repay him what he gave me for Nelson."

"You need not worry about that. He's dead."

"Of what?" Her lovely lamplit features expressed concern rather than alarm.

"A head injury," said Harris to test her nerve, and hoping too by frankness to cut the distance that remained between them. "A brick fell on him—from this very bridge."

While the town spreading out below them lacked gaslit streets, individually illuminated house windows defined the valley sides and floor.

"An accident then. People suffer such misfortune." To these commonplace words Theresa looked as if she expected some rejoinder.

Harris nodded. He found he could not after all tell her how

the Englishman's misfortune had contributed to her rescue—nor yet did it seem timely to apprise her of Oscar's drowning at Niagara. To slice away all misunderstanding was too brutal a surgery. Either they must go on forever as companionable strangers or peel truth like an onion one layer at a time. In a speed-drunk age, a task of infinite patience.

Theresa spoke again. "Death followed..."

"Instantly."

"A mercy there. Tell me something, Isaac, since you persuaded me to testify for Sibyl's sake. Why does this subpoena mention only Papa?"

Harris explained that a prior inquest had identified Sibyl's remains, but not named her killer. On Sibyl, no second inquest was permitted. Nevertheless, so long as Crane could be kept in view, he would be indicted for her murder at the same spring assizes, where Theresa's evidence would convict him.

"But I didn't see him smother my father," Theresa objected. "How can I speak to that?"

"You heard him confess," said Harris, "and witnessed a demonstration that gives his confession credence. If in performing his post-mortem examination Professor Lamb finds William Sheridan was smothered, Jasper believes Crane's fate is sealed."

"Poor Papa... I wish it were spring and we were done with Henry."

The final portion of the journey was plainly trying for Theresa. Just past Port Union, as the locomotive began struggling up the steep incline to Scarboro, a pair of new passengers let their eyes rest on her while passing down the car.

"When *will* this hair grow?" she cried. "It attracts notice—and tickles my forehead."

"Let me tuck it up for you."

"Don't." She pushed his hand away. "This near the city, someone is bound to recognize me."

He touched her arm. She shook him off.

"I suppose," she added, "because I'm neither widow, maid nor wife, I have no reputation to lose. Kind of you to remind me! Well, everyone knows what sort of women most nurses are, so it seems I've chosen the perfect occupation."

"That's enough," said Harris. "I had no such thoughts."

She turned irritably away, then back to face him.

"I'm sorry," he said less gruffly. Although the anomaly of her position reflected no discredit on her, her sensitivity was understandable. Its remedy coincided with Harris's dearest wish. "As soon as you like," he went on, "or think compatible with your bereavement—"

"It would not stay tucked anyway," she said, forestalling his proposal. "I don't know why this business of going home is becoming so difficult. My only friends were the MacFarlanes, and the cholera letter already makes it impossible to see them again. Give me your hand to hold, Isaac... That's good."

She held it hard until her fear seeped away through the contact. For Harris, the first good was her appeal to him for strength, and his being there to respond. Then presently she began to feel and explore—so slackening, shifting and tightening the pressure of her fingers on his as to keep sensation fresh. This delighted and disturbed his entire body, and at the same time, squeezing back in answer to her lead, he felt engaged in silent conversation that after so much separate experience brought them closer together than words.

She held his hand till Scarboro. She dropped it abruptly when, at that station, an imposing personage in black climbed aboard and surveyed the occupiers of seats as if they were so many usurpers.

"Who's that swell?" said Harris.

"George MacFarlane's secretary," Theresa breathed.

When MacFarlane joined him, the secretary—shrunk in height and bulk as might an elephant beside a whale—pointed out two empty places well behind Theresa and Harris. MacFarlane nodded affably and with heavy tread followed his minion. Theresa pretended to look out the window, but Harris saw they had already been recognized.

"Hallo, George," he said.

"A great thing, this railway, isn't it, Harris?" MacFarlane let one massive hand rest on the younger man's shoulder as the train resumed its lurching march. "And a great burner of my trees, but they will be gone soon enough."

"I believe," said Harris, "you'll find a seat further back."

"Yes, plenty of room—but coal is the coming fuel, as our mutual friend Mr. Newbiggins never tires of saying, and if you will follow my example, coal is where you will put your money. Flora, my muse, what a pleasure to see you safe after all this time!"

Theresa looked up into his wide blue eyes with cold dislike.

"Your poor father," said MacFarlane, "a loss to all who cherish British freedoms. And this imbroglio of Henry's—unspeakable. Accept my sympathy."

"Henry's affairs will be spoken of at tomorrow's inquest," Harris felt impelled to observe. "You may find your own freedoms touched upon."

Hillyard would not be the coroner presiding and might therefore testify regarding the document taken from Sheridan's box. Harris expected that prospect to ruffle the would-be knight's good humour. He was disappointed.

"You prophesy boldly, Harris, like a true Kelt, but when better than on All Hallows Eve? I've written a slight essay on the topic for tomorrow's *Globe*. In the old country, though, it was matches and marriages young people like yourselves chiefly tried to forecast this night."

"Mr. MacFarlane," said Theresa, "do give my regards to your wife and children."

"Gladly, dear girl, but we must chat." MacFarlane clapped Harris's shoulder. "This cavalier won't object to exchanging seats with your ancient friend for the balance of the journey."

Harris rose, welcoming the chance to escape from under the sexagenarian's weight. MacFarlane mistakenly thought this meant compliance. He made to sit.

"Out of the question." Harris's arm barred his way.

"I see you think you know something to my discredit, but I assure you no imputation will touch me. Let's be agreeable."

"By all means." Harris wanted to ask whether the cholera

sufferers had agreed to be put ashore. Nothing would be gained. He was still looking up, up into the craggy face of one of the two or three richest men in the country. "We shall agree, George, that you'll sit with your secretary."

"Theresa, perhaps you would care to join me."

"She declines," said Harris.

"Can you not let Miss Sheridan speak for herself?" MacFarlane chided. He smelled of peppermints, good Cavendish and even temper.

"I have been spoken for," said Theresa. "Please leave us."

MacFarlane withdrew, smiling Keltically at the ambiguous turn of phrase. However much Theresa meant by it, or knew she meant, Harris felt for her a surge of affection that for some moments obliterated all the world besides.

Finally, the Don River trestle rumbled under the carriage wheels, none of which had come off. They were entering the city. Ahead, through the rain and dark, loomed its first two landmarks—the chimney of the new gas works and the Berkeley Street Gaol, site of public execution.

"Why did George have to mention its being Hallowe'en?" Theresa said. "According to Papa, the old heathen, this is the night when spirits walk, everyone who has perished in the past year."

On the left now, out the far window, stretched the peninsula and the harbour it cradled. All ships but one lay dark and still. At the same time, a surprising number of men were moving purposefully about the docks. Some wore police tunics. The near, right window framed the market, asleep below City Hall's clock tower, and then the broad plain of the Esplanade sweeping up towards Front Street. Again for this late hour on a wet night, there seemed an abnormal bustle. Harris set his watch back to ten fourteen.

"You have no enemies among the spirits," he said distractedly.

"No, mine are living—but you start to count and see how many dead there have been since the twelfth of July. Look, is that Jasper?"

Harris leaned across her to open the window. The lawyer was

running hatless beside the slowing train, his wavy hair rain-plastered to his head, his overcoat unbuttoned and flapping like a neglected sail. He had not seen them yet.

"Jasper!" called Harris. "Jasper, what news?"

Small looked up. Normally remote and enigmatic as the moon, his round face was a drenched image of consternation.

"Crane," he panted. "Crane has escaped."

Chapter Twenty-Two
Triumph

An untypically scowling Inspector Vandervoort was stepping out of the railway station telegraph room onto the platform. His tweed cap sat low over his eyes. The skin by his nose flamed with drink, almost to the redness of his side-whiskers. It seemed a safe bet that the medal inscribed "Be sober and watch" was not in his waistcoat pocket.

"What happened, John?" said Harris, flanked by Theresa and Small.

Vandervoort showed no surprise at their presence. "He's out. He's wounded."

Harris bit back a reproach. He was familiar enough with the shortcomings of the present police department, and with Vandervoort's own. Theresa addressed the lapsed Son of Abstinence.

"Where did he go?" she said.

"Without offence, Mrs.—Miss Sheridan, surely *you* are the *expert* disappearer. Your guess is worth two of mine. I'm doing what I can to find him, but I've too few men. Most of the ones I have are idiots. Some are in Crane's pay. What I'll say for certain is that no train or vessel has left Toronto in the half hour he has been loose."

"Then he'll try to reach the States by land," said Harris, "or to reach another port. Can he sit a horse?"

Vandervoort shook his head. "He took a rifle bullet in—" The police detective glanced sideways at Theresa and decided against naming the spot. "Between here and here," he concluded, successively slapping abdomen and upper thigh.

"By road then," said Harris, not much encouraged.

"If he's shot," Theresa observed, "he'll be very scared. That is, if he's conscious at all."

She spoke without sympathy or cruelty. Her practical tone reassured Harris on her account—and yet he continued for some reason to discount this wound, as if Crane could somehow buy his way out of it.

"I've just asked the next constables east and west to stop every vehicle on the highways," said Vandervoort, "but that leaves a dozen or more back roads."

"I'll see if the Attorney General will request help from the Garrison," Small volunteered.

"Attorney *General*? If you have pull in that quarter, Mr. Small, pull away." Vandervoort's old grin flashed briefly, more sardonic than ever. "I'd have to go crawling from chief to aldermen through all the approved channels."

Small left at a run.

"We'll find him," said Harris, alert to the need, though at heart weary of searching. "Where in town are you looking?"

"Crane's house and office, of course, and those of his closest associates."

"His own brougham and chaise?" Theresa aptly inquired.

"Both accounted for, Ma'am," said the policeman. "That is, Miss. We believe he meant to sail on his propeller ship *Triumph* yonder, so we're turning her inside out. Now, Harris, I've learned better than to tell you not to stick *your* nose into this, and frankly I'd be glad of your help—but before you do anything, take Miss Sheridan somewhere safe. We don't want her standing in the path of a bullet."

"Crane's not armed?" said Harris.

"He's never even owned a gun!" Theresa exclaimed.

A constable was now at Vandervoort's elbow, importuning Vandervoort to settle some dispute with the sergeant.

"Navy Colt revolver," the inspector threw back over his shoulder as he permitted himself to be led dock-wards. "Shot Morgan dead with it."

A policeman's murder—that must be driving the search, even

if the inspector made it sound an afterthought. Harris remembered the deceased struggling at his ledger, registering a Colt Navy revolver.

"Morgan was one of the constables that came for Sibyl," said Theresa, "the quiet, more conscientious one. Shall we find out from the livery stables what carriage has most recently been hired?"

"I don't want you out on the streets getting shot at," Harris quickly replied. To lose her now...

"Nor I you, not without me."

Searchers called unproductively to each other along the docks and through the rail yards. Wind whistled in the telegraph wires. Under the overhang of the station roof, gaslight fell full on the bright face tilted up towards Harris's. Theresa's great-hearted words stirred Harris without undermining his resolve.

"Come," he said, "I'll see you to the hotel."

"Don't take the time, Isaac. If you won't let me go with you, I can wait for you up there, in Papa's house."

Harris looked up in surprise. There it stood on the north side of Front Street, grand and neglected pending probate of William Sheridan's will, facing the harbour with semicircular portico, centre gable, and nine enormous windows, now dark and vacant.

"You have no key."

"I know where one is hid," she said.

"You have no key, but Henry does. Listen, Theresa, tell me about the hidden key and then wait for me—wait, mind—here at the station."

"Take a constable, Isaac."

"You heard the inspector," he said. "There are none to spare, and the constables can't be relied upon in any case."

"Take me then. Rely upon me."

Her face shining out of the black bonnet overwhelmed him almost. "There has been shooting," he said. "It's too dangerous."

"Take a gun then, dearest Isaac, please, at least."

"There's no time. Where's the key?"

"I'll show you," she said, setting briskly off across the open ground between the tracks and Front Street.

Harris overtook her. "Theresa—"

"It's *my* home." She walked on.

"Then walk so I'm between you and the windows," he said.

According to Vandervoort, Crane had a thirty-six calibre pistol. Unused to firearms, he would not shoot accurately with it at this range. All the same, Harris led Theresa in a wide arc around to the back lane. The windows in the west and north faces of Sheridan's villa were as dark as those looking south. At the rear of the property, there were no lamps by which their approach could be observed, and the rain kept the dead leaves from crunching beneath their feet. They reached the house. Backs to its red brick wall, they stopped to catch their breath.

Was Crane inside? He would need a cab or carriage to leave the city, and a place to wait while one was found. None would have been arranged in advance if he had meant to leave by water. Perhaps this residence of Sheridan's was too much in the public eye for a hiding place, but also desirable because above suspicion. And the back lane was discreet enough.

"You're not coming in," Harris whispered, determined, if she objected, to abandon the endeavour and risk the assassin's escape, permanently galling as that would be.

"I'll keep watch. If anyone comes, I'll warn you by breaking a window. I won't have you trapped in there." She crouched and pointed to a brick in the second course above the foundation, two in from the corner. "The mortar is only mud. Loosen it with your penknife. The key's behind."

He had her keep watch from the garden shed, which was weathertight, and entreated her by all things precious to take no chances. Leaving her the brick and knife, he crept down the outer stairs to the kitchen door. He tried it before inserting the key. The door yielded freely. Harris held it closed but for a wide crack. The cellar-damp odours flowed out, replacing in his nostrils the smells of the wet garden.

Until this moment, it had seemed only a rather vulgar

hypothesis that Crane would seek refuge in his murdered father-in-law's villa. The open door was the first sign someone was indeed here.

Harris glanced back towards Theresa's shed. It was comforting to see no trace of her, but detestably foolish to compromise her by looking. He would not look again.

In Crane's place, Harris would have remained in the kitchen and ready to leave, not dragged himself upstairs. He would be watching the outside door. Anyone standing in the opening would make an easy target, even for a poor shot. Harris widened the crack an inch. He opened the door just enough to slip through, dropping to a crouch once inside. No gun went off, the only sound the scrape of boots—Harris's own—on the brick floor. He removed them.

At the far, south end of the kitchen, the door stood open to the servant's room, and through its windows fell some glimmer from the gas lamps on Front Street. The long kitchen table stood out in silhouette. Otherwise, Harris must rely on memory for the location of the furnishings—sink and then wood stove to his right, dish dresser and churn to his left. He crept down the left wall towards the light, but never in front of it.

This was lunacy. Crane and death could be waiting anywhere. Fired from within the room, the cone-shaped lumps of lead would tunnel right through a body, in and out, two wounds per ball. Pain, Harris had heard, was more acute at the wound of exit. A dozen wounds without reloading.

Harris considered looking for a weapon of his own, one of those sharp or heavy objects in which kitchens abound. He concluded, however, that it would be awkward to carry and more so to use, unaccustomed as he was to taproom brawls.

It took him a stealthy half-minute more to reach Sibyl's room, into which the street lamps let him see unseen. Crane was not there. Harris began to think the basement held no one but himself. From within the house he had heard no sound he did not cause, no step or breath, no rub of fabric, no click of a pistol's being cocked.

He entered the housekeeper's cell and lit a match with his teeth. The room was unchanged from three months before, though since reading of what had passed here, he saw it through different eyes. The bedstead seemed higher and narrower, the place beneath it where Theresa had cowered more exposed. The dust lay undisturbed. No wounded man had bled here since.

He searched without result the basement storage areas. Then he climbed the stairs, fourteen of them, none of which creaked. Nor did the plank floors. He recalled Theresa's complaining of how quietly Sibyl had moved around.

Up here, curtains darkened even the front rooms. Harris lit a kerosene lamp, which he took care to hold well away from his body. Let the light be the target. Finding nothing, he began to wonder if the unlocked kitchen door might not have resulted from carelessness and have dated from an earlier visit of Crane's.

One storey remained to inspect. Harris doused his light and ascended the wide, spiralling staircase. Again the wooden treads—twenty-two this time—fitted so well that they uttered not a squeak beneath his stockinged feet. At the top he paused. Again from the house there flooded back to his ears nothing but absolute, sepulchral silence. And then something creaked. Not a floorboard—a bed-rope. The sound came from the right and in front, the southwest bedroom, William Sheridan's. Crane was lying on Sheridan's deathbed.

Assuming Crane were conscious, Harris could advance little further without disclosing his own presence. Nothing more was heard from the room for some minutes. Harris began to doubt. Might it have been a rat? Then the ropes creaked again, as under a man's shifting weight. Nothing so far suggested the room held more than one person, but a man with a revolver was worth six with muskets. Harris edged forward through the upstairs hall.

Hung from the right or north side to open inwards, the bedroom door stood ajar, so he saw the tall windows before he saw the bed. All the curtains were open. The sky had cleared somewhat, at least to the south, and at the docks the one steamer he had noted from the train still blazed with lights.

That would be Crane's ship, Harris realized, still being searched for her owner.

Her owner was here. Why would a man pursued, a man in pain, have climbed those thirty-six steps? Perhaps Crane wanted something special of Sheridan's he had never managed to make for himself, but almost certainly too he wanted to view something special he *had* made, his iron-hulled, screw-driven *Triumph*, the fastest ship on the lake, the product of his genius that had been meant to save him from his persecutors—and now could not.

Harris set down the extinguished lamp. In the hall stood a *prie-dieu* chair, which he lifted by the legs. It was a heavy brute of a thing, but he managed with its tall, ornately-carved back safely and quietly to push the bedroom door open wider.

"Who's there?" The voice—Crane's voice—was tight and startled, but still commanding.

Harris considered posing as the carriage driver, to gain access to the room, but was no mimic or any good with accents. He would be seen through at once.

"It's Isaac, Henry. That gun you have is more ticklish to use than you would think. Throw it out here. Uncocked."

"Stay out or I'll shoot."

Harris wanted to stay out, for he was afraid. Feeling himself on the brink of a new life, he particularly did not want a bullet to prevent it. At the same time, the new life could not begin with Crane at large.

"You won't get away now," said Harris. "You've been discovered."

"I'll shoot you anyway." Crane muttered something about its being a pleasure.

Then came the dry, mechanical noise of the sear locking into the tumbler as the hammer was drawn back. Back it would stay, poised to detonate the cap and to send the projectile flying, poised only until Crane applied pressure enough to the trigger to release this particular sear. How good a sense of that would he have?

Harris waited till the apprehensive trembling in his jaw and arms subsided. The chair was too heavy for more delay. Stepping forward into the doorway, he hurled the piece of furniture on top of the bed, under which he immediately dived. The air cracked open with an enormous sound and filled with the smell of burned powder. The bullet had presumably passed over Harris's head. Heaving the chair off him to his left, Crane fired a second shot. From the sound of floorboards splintering, he must have shot straight down through the mattress and ropes, but Harris was already rolling out the other side.

Now Harris was close enough to seize Crane's right arm before Crane could again cock the six-shooter. While Harris had thought to leap on top of Crane, pinning him to the bed, at close quarters Crane appeared too massive for that, so instead he seized Crane's gun arm in both hands. Crane's wrist felt thick and hard. Harris swung it so Crane's knuckles cracked against the bedpost. Crane cried out, but maintained his grip. The bed-ropes creaked. Crane's left fist slammed into the side of Harris's head. Blinded and dazed, Harris stepped back without releasing the wrist, pulling for all he was worth, hauling Crane clear off the bed.

Crane's bulk hit the carpet with a moan. The moan trailed into sobs, unfit to be heard from a man's throat and at the same time supplicating. It seemed Crane did indeed have a wound, which the fall had made smart.

"Give it up, Henry," Harris panted, recovering his sight but still tender from the head blow, still dragging Crane across the carpet to keep out of his left arm's reach. He was crushing Crane's right thumb so it could not move the pistol hammer. "Let go of the gun."

Crane persisted in whimpering, still grasping the weapon that was quite useless to him. The gunpowder stench was clearing. Into its place seeped the warm odour of blood. Harris lost patience.

Bleed to death if you like, he thought, but quick! I'm not giving an accomplice time to rescue you.

Harris bit Crane's hand, breaking a tooth and—mercifully—Crane's grip.

"What other weapons have you?" Harris asked sternly, to disguise his relief at scooping up the Colt.

It was more than a foot long, but lighter than he might have expected, perhaps under three pounds. Harris had never fired a revolver and did not much look forward to firing this one, which it was too dark for him even to inspect properly. He cocked it.

While breathing noisily, Crane had stopped crying. He lay supine, feet together, right arm outflung, below the more westerly of the two south windows on the checkerboard of watery moonlight that now fell through its panes. He was dressed for business, except that his shirt was outside his trousers and bore a dark stain.

"Well?" said Harris. He considered whether the greater risk lay in personally searching or not searching Crane's clothes.

"No others," Crane replied, catching his breath. "You've more go than I thought, Isaac."

"I want your hands accounted for, Henry. We'll say behind your head—*both* hands."

Crane complied. "When I first met you," he said, "downstairs here at Sheridan's table, I thought you would do well enough by the standards of—where was it? Holland Landing?—but you would never make a fortune."

The house remained connected to the gas main, as Harris discovered when he lit a pair of sconces to either side of the hearth. Crane's complexion was grey. For all the control he exerted over his voice, horror lurked behind his hazel eyes. His face strained away from the region between his legs. The blood on his shirt placed the wound in the lower part of the range Vandervoort had indicated, about the groin or just below.

"You could make one, though," Crane continued. "A fortune, that is. Choose your projects and backers well, and a man with your perseverance could make history."

"Now comes the bribe," said Harris. It was annoying how his tongue kept returning to the fresh stump of that lower incisor. "How much do you have?"

"Thirty-five hundred U.S. dollars, gold and notes. Consider, for example, steam generators of electrical current, for those submarine telegraph cables of the future."

It was the third piece of investment advice Harris had received today, though the only one to come with funds attached.

"Would you have the strength to reach New York state?" he asked. "The *Triumph* will not sail."

"I'm bandaged well enough to hold together over plank roads." Crane's voice gathered its old persuasiveness. "You'll let me go then and say nothing."

"I've already lit lights. The police will have seen them and be on their way." Harris realized he was exaggerating.

Crane tried his offer twice more and gave it up.

"You're a fool after all," he sighed, his small mouth taking an aggrieved, self-pitying turn. He seemed in less actual pain than before. Apparently his bandage was preventing further loss of blood.

Harris looked down at Crane with a distaste that no number of steamship keels or miles of track laid down could mitigate. A man of such talents should have seen further, done better.

"You don't want to pay for my silence, Henry, you who hate blackmail and blackmailers. Didn't you kill Harvey Ingram?"

"He killed himself," Crane replied. "Never did a case of liquor do such good, and I only wish I had sent it three years ago, when his extortionate demands began."

"Don't get up!" said Harris sharply.

Crane subsided. "The floor is cold and hard. Let me lie on the bed."

Harris might have acquiesced had the bedstead been anyone else's. It was a warm cherrywood, wide and high-posted in the style of the twenties—the time of William and Emily's marriage. Emily and William. For each upon this bed death had come too early. Harris noticed that the light, netted summer canopy had not been replaced, although the season was long past. Just beyond, on a wall parallel to the bed, the lively watercolour portrait of Theresa's mother hung above a maple and cherrywood chest of drawers.

A sense of fitness apart, moving Crane onto the bed would be risky. It might precipitate another struggle or more bleeding. Now that Crane was his prisoner, Harris felt responsible for keeping him alive—and was curious as well. There were questions only Crane could answer. Harris spread a brown checked blanket over Crane where he lay and slid a pillow cautiously beneath his head.

"Why did you kill Sheridan?" he demanded, standing over him.

"Some people cannot be reasoned with," said Crane in disgust. "You. William Sheridan. I gave him every chance to return MacFarlane's scrap of paper, but he had his 'principles'. I never intended to harm him. That's not my way. Everything I've achieved has been through finding grounds of mutual advantage, but his great snowy head shaking so righteously among the snowy pillows finished by making me angry."

Having seen Crane's temper, Harris could believe the murder had not been premeditated. It appalled him no less.

"Did you even know what that scrap of paper was?" he asked.

"Sheridan said it implicated MacFarlane in the cholera epidemic that killed my father... What does it matter? That's twenty-four years ago. My father left his wife and boys a sound enough hardware concern, which I more or less ran from the time I was twelve. I'm grateful, but there's nothing I can do for him now."

It sounded to Harris as if any gratitude Crane felt was towards the epidemic, for starting him in business so young.

"What did MacFarlane pay you, Henry?"

"*There* is cause for regret, if you like. What he did for me was to buy my share of Conquest Iron Works. I had invested too heavily in them, and it looked as though they would never get their foundry up."

"Conquest?" said Harris, surprised to hear this name from Crane's lips. Then he recalled what he had read in August of MacFarlane's involvement with the project. "Bricks and mortar are all in place, and they will be casting rails in a month or less. Could you not have held on?"

"Isaac, I had too much to hold on to it all, and that bloodsucker Ingram on top. So George has a great bargain at my expense."

"And Theresa?" said Harris. "Have you no regrets about her?"

"Many." Crane covered a cough with his fist. "For one, I wish I had looked under the bed."

The October night was cold and dank, the chamber dusty from neglect.

"Keep your hands behind your head," Harris insisted. "Go on."

He began to wonder if Crane had anyone to wait for after all. Or perhaps the light had scared the accomplice off. Traffic could be heard on Front Street, but still Theresa had not signalled any penetration of the house itself.

Crane, both hands behind his balding head, stared at the ceiling. His face looked dry and grey as ash, and deep vertical lines marked the region between his brows. He went on. Maybe the sound of his own flat voice soothed his fear, or perhaps he egotistically believed he could impress the other man with his worldly philosophy and his unwonted candour.

Harris stood between the two windows, the revolver in his hand and one eye on the door. Crane's confession amazed him. He needed to hear it.

"I thought," said Crane, "my position required a wife to ornament it."

"You had a wife."

Crane took no notice. "I soon learned, however, that educated women are not to my taste."

"You made Theresa believe you once loved her."

Crane shrugged or winced. It was hard to say which.

"Then when she disappeared," Harris continued, "you did not want her found."

"Frankly, no. Her sudden departure suggested she knew what had happened to her father, and I could never have made her see that these men of principle have no place in an era of progress and expansion. Just look at today's politicians. Young

John A. Macdonald has a far more convenient conscience than old Robert Baldwin or the late William Sheridan, and the generation after Macdonald's will have more convenient consciences still—and less sentimental baggage. Commerce and industry will flourish. There will be no white knights like you to call them to account."

"So—a tidy suffocation in the name of progress." Harris pulled his tongue away from the broken tooth and Crane back from the impenetrable future to his own dark past. "What does not seem in character, Henry, is the dismemberment of cadavers, and I wonder you had the stomach for it."

"Sibyl, you mean." Crane became wistful. "I found I did not. That Sunday afternoon, once I had the arm off, I knew I could not follow my original plan..."

"Which was to reduce her to pieces too small to be recognized."

"I couldn't do it. So—I packed the poor woman in ice. Tuesday night I contrived to burn her, a more thorough measure in any case."

"By then you had questioned me about Theresa," Harris said. He remembered the Tuesday—July 15—and the feel of the new upholstery in the gently rocking brougham, the desolating sound of the word *disappeared.*

"I could endure Theresa's death," Crane continued, "but not her turning to you, a former suitor. You satisfied me that she had not. Then, however, I was afraid I had set on a bloodhound. Since I had Sibyl's arm off, it seemed I might save it from the flames and use it to stop your searching for Theresa. A mistake..." Crane reached under the blanket.

"Let's see your hands, Henry. Both hands."

Harris's composure was more willed than felt. He was squinting past the revolver's drawn-back hammer over the cylinder, and down the barrel at a brown square of blanket eight inches below Crane's chin. Harris's right index finger curled around the trigger for the first time, just touching it. He had never before aimed a gun at a man.

"Fortunately," Crane gasped, "one becomes less squeamish. Shoot if you like, Isaac. It's all one."

Harris was Crane's keeper, and did not shoot. Crane was fumbling with something around his waist, another gun it might be, and still Harris did not tighten his trigger finger. He crouched and with his left hand pulled away the blanket.

There was no weapon. Crane had his trousers pushed down to his knees and was tearing linen dressings from his left thigh near the groin.

"Steady there," Harris stammered. "What—?"

"Opening—the—wounds." Crane sounded at this moment to be in the most exquisite and terrifying pain. Fresh blood pumped up darkly from the artery, soaking bandages, trousers, underclothing, and the rose-patterned carpet—and the chamber reeked of slaughter. "That's better," Crane panted.

From the bed, Harris seized another pillow to press down over the well of blood, but Crane would not let him. He would have to be clubbed insensible first. Harris uncocked the Colt and, grasping the barrel, raised the butt like a hammer above Crane's head.

"No, Isaac. Can't face a public hanging, not after having—the fall is too great..."

Harris hesitated. For murder confessed and unrepented, Crane owed his life—but he was not asking for his life. Did he owe society a spectacle as well?

Crane breathed laboriously. "Ever seen a man hanged, Isaac?" he asked.

Harris had. Perhaps one was enough.

The quantity of blood was frightful. While strength remained, Crane actually rubbed and worked the leg to keep blood flowing. The smell alone should have been enough to drive Harris from the room. He crouched instead beside Crane's pillow.

Outside in the moonlight the *Triumph* lay quietly at her berth, her twin black funnels empty and cooling.

Crane's fringe of hair was cut too short to be disordered by his struggle. His neckcloth remained tightly knotted. The fear had not left his face, but he was mastering it. His mouth worked dryly. While his thirst must be extreme, he knew there was no water and asked for none.

"Strange, Isaac," he said with effort. "In the end—I don't regret marrying Susan, even—" He paused for breath. "Even though marriage brought on all my troubles... She wanted it. I was happy in her arms—and not much since..."

His voice trailed off, and Harris was alone in the room. Henry Crane had made his mess and moved on, this time out of reach of bloodhounds.

The contest was over. So deadly earnest had it been, in nowise like a game, and yet Harris was reminded of his talk of chess with Vandervoort. Harris had cornered and overpowered the enemy. He had won, even though it was not his hand that had removed Crane from the board. Well, no one could say this victory had been bloodless.

Lurid in the gaslight, the viscous lake radiated out from the severed vessel over the carpet a yard and more, carried only by its own slow momentum now the pressure was gone. Harris surprised himself by not feeling nauseated. Anxious thoughts of Theresa in her garden shed crowded in on him—but before he properly knew how to think, glass splintered in the back bedroom next door.

She must have thrown the brick or a stone to warn him. Harris rose and stepped to the door.

"Henry?" a female voice called from deep inside the house. "Henry, what are those lights? Answer me." The voice was closer, clearer, not Theresa's, but possibly familiar. A woman's running steps sounded on the stairs.

Harris decided against using the revolver, which he stuck inside his belt. Waiting against the wall to the south of the door, he pinned the woman's arms from behind as she rushed in. A heavy, hooded cloak hid her face. Young and sturdy, she kicked fiercely until the sight of Crane lying in his blood stunned her into stillness.

"What have you done to him?" she cried.

"He has died of his wounds, miss." Harris might have known

Crane's accomplice would be a serving girl he had made fond of him. "Are you armed? Show me your empty hands, and I'll let go."

"He can't be dead, not after I bound him up and found him a carriage." She started to struggle again.

But Theresa was in the room. The kindled expression of sympathy in her face told Harris she knew this woman, whose shoulder she solicitously touched.

"Stop it, Miss Webster," she said. "Quiet now."

Miss Webster was quiet. Theresa loosened the girl's cloak and took the girl's hands in her own. Upon releasing her, Harris saw it was the seamstress he had let in front of him at William Sheridan's funeral—Vandervoort's quondam informant—Marion Webster.

"Oh, Mrs. Crane, he's not dead, is he?" In all simplicity, Miss Webster appealed to the woman she believed her rival.

"If you'll remain calm," said Theresa, "we shall see. Won't you sit down?"

"Theresa," said Harris, "you need not look. John Vandervoort will soon be here."

He had to speak, but knew her answer in advance. She was battle-hardened. No less than the Crimean nurses, she could look on scenes once thought unfit for woman's eyes. She had come through the wars. Now she must see the peace.

Harris righted the *prie-dieu* chair, still firm enough in the joints for all its rough treatment—although a bullet hole through the seat admittedly made it less than inviting. In any case, Marion Webster ignored it.

"See to Henry, missus," she insisted, advancing a step. "Do be quick about it. You have to save him."

She clasped her hands to her round cheeks and pressed her long, full lips quiveringly together. Plainly, she wanted to run to Crane, but was also scared.

Crane lay where Harris had dragged him, under the further window, equidistant from the bed and the hearth. Theresa went to him. Kneeling on a dry patch of carpet by his head, she held two fingers to a blood vessel in his neck. She had to feel his stillness. It amazed Harris how slight, even in her quilted mantle, Theresa appeared next to Crane.

She had to hear his silence too. In another moment, with steady hands, she undid his tie and shirt—her every movement quick, gentle, cool, precise. She removed her bonnet and set it behind her. A gasp escaped Marion Webster, whether at the state of Theresa's hair or at the directness with which Theresa laid her ear to Crane's chest. Theresa listened in three different places, about five seconds each time, then sat up.

"Yes, Miss Webster," she said. "He is dead."

The seamstress slumped down without regard to the chair, which Harris slid under her.

"And how are you, Theresa?" he said. "Have you any hurt?"

"Not so much as a scratch." She rose and came to him, her eyes bright upon him. "And you, Isaac? I can't tell what happened here. Are you injured?"

"A little bruised, perhaps. Nothing more. That was a fine throw you made."

"Wasn't it?" Tenderly her fingers brushed the side of his face Crane had struck.

After so long and uncertain a voyage, he touched the verge of bliss at last, although the taste of blood lay thick still in his throat. Then, over Theresa's shoulder, he caught Marion Webster looking up at them, her round face miserable with grief.

"Did he mention me?" she said. "Before he—you know, Mr. Harris—at the end? Mrs. Crane here didn't love him at all, so she won't mind. I practically carried him up here. Just tell me what he said about Marion Webster." Her voice kept getting louder, as if she feared they were receding from her into their own private realm. "He could be quite romantic, you know."

* * *

Before midnight, Vandervoort did see the light in Sheridan's window. He stifled an oath on entering the room and put a tin flask to his lips. After the most cursory examination of the mutilated carcass, he flung open a window and shouted down into the street for a constable to stand guard at the scene and for anyone to call off the volunteer searchers. The prisoner was dead.

One effect of this roaring was to scare away the cabman Crane's accomplice had posted in the back lane. Honest use might otherwise have been made of his vehicle, although it wasn't a long walk to Police Station No. 1. Theresa accompanied Marion Webster, Harris and the red-haired inspector following just behind.

Crane's escape had cost Vandervoort any chance of early promotion—he said, draining his flask—so he was not persisting in a course of stubborn and fruitless temperance. One day Toronto would have a well-ordered police force, one day soon. It could be done. Look at Montreal.

Harris was still too steeped in blood to look so far.

"You'll be wanting this," he said. He pulled the Colt Navy revolver from his belt and by the street lamps read the serial number—40099. "It's the one you took from Ingram, John. I don't suppose it was locked up."

"I told Morgan. I told Devlin."

The inspector explained that Crane had that day been brought in from the Berkeley Street Gaol to City Hall in anticipation of his appearance at the Sheridan inquest. Guard duty fell to Devlin and Morgan.

"Of the two," Harris said, "Morgan struck me as being slightly less muddled. Did he fire the fatal shot?"

"No," said Vandervoort. "Crane may have killed him by accident, if not in blind panic. Morgan took a bribe and turned his back."

"And carried forbidden letters too, I suppose, to the *Triumph* captain and this Miss Webster."

"She's a poor simpleton if I saw one," said the policeman, dropping his voice. "Crane would not have stayed two minutes with her if he had made it out of the country, but he wanted an accomplice here in case things went awry, as they did. I've made some use of the piece myself. I'll keep her clear of the Penitentiary if I can."

"He certainly won her loyalty." Harris marvelled at such universal persuasiveness. "So Devlin," he added hopefully, "refused Crane's bribe."

The name Devlin brought to mind a wharf rat never quite dressed, his angular face never completely shaved, his limp black hair never absolutely combed, his whining demands never totally met, his knowing look never remotely justified. Yet Devlin and his carbine had held out.

"Wrong again," laughed Vandervoort. "Devlin took Crane's money and shot him anyway. As you say, the boy is muddled."

Despite the lateness of the hour, eight or ten of the civilian volunteers who had helped search the docks were gathered outside City Hall to commiserate on Crane's demise. What a cheat! What a sell! They had rolled on Crane's rails or helped lay them. They had sailed his steamers for pay or paid to sail in them. They had looked forward to seeing the mighty brought low and were now to be most cruelly denied a public figure's public indictment for murder. Was Crane really dead or being spirited away by powerful friends? Rich men never swing. Show him to us then. When can we see him with our own eyes?

Harris and Vandervoort fended off their questions while making a path for Theresa and Marion Webster. They had reached the City Hall portico at last when out of its shadows into the lamplight stepped an Indian woman in a green taffeta dress.

"Inspector Vandervoort," she said without haste or hesitation, "I am Mrs. Henry Crane. When may I have my husband's body?"

The onlookers fell silent. They could not have known she was there in the dark doorway where beggars sat.

She did not stare while being stared at. Her strong, deep voice made Harris think she dropped her eyes from politeness rather than timidity. A long, straight nose dominated her copper-coloured face. Her shawl had fallen back off her wavy black hair, and she showed no sign of chill in her unseasonably flimsy gown. Her age appeared to fall between Theresa's and Crane's, late twenties.

Here then at last, thought Harris with quickened pulse, was the individual on whose strength of character so much had turned. She must have arrived from the Northwest this very night, expecting to find her errant husband alive—and must have heard otherwise from those clamouring to see his head on a pole. What now were her intentions? A hard-eyed Métis man in buckskin and ragged beard stood at her side, clutching a buffalo rifle, ready to second her will. To her reasonable demand, Vandervoort was responding most sluggishly.

"Well, John?" Harris prompted.

"*Your* body?" said the policeman at last. "That's as the coroner in his wisdom finds. You'll wait a week at least."

The buffalo hunter bristled at this tone.

Susan Crane perceived Vandervoort was tipsy and ignored him. Instead she addressed Marion Webster, who was gaping as if she beheld a chimera.

"Are you this Theresa who got my leavings?"

One bystander guffawed. The seamstress quailed and shook her head.

"Mrs. Crane," said Harris, "the lady in question deserves your sympathy sooner than your contempt."

Theresa now stepped forward and spoke with feeling. "I am the unfortunate woman your husband pretended to marry, and I can only wish you had made known your prior claim."

"A close race, these redskins," said Vandervoort. "Stand back there!" he admonished the volunteers, who were getting something of a show after all.

"Did you agree to keep your marriage secret?" Harris asked above the rattle.

"Secret?" the widow scoffed. "It was in the book and witnessed. I've always used his name."

The name Crane, Harris reflected, sounded Ojibway enough and would excite no suspicion. Possibly she thought that the white man kept only one book.

"He offered money to close my mouth," she continued, "but I said, 'Provide for your wife or don't. It's beneath me to make mischief in the South.'"

"Why talk to them now?" snapped her companion, speaking for the first time. "Let's go."

"Mrs. Crane," said Theresa, "I'm sorry you've come so far to hear hard news. Will you take my hand?"

"You're skinny for Henry's taste." Susan Crane glanced again at the ampler Miss Webster, who was still too terrified to speak, then took Theresa's hand. "He was sober and fine-looking, and he fancied me, but he only married for a moment's comfort. I soon saw that no knot holds weak rope."

"But you did come here," Theresa insisted, "expecting to see him again."

"Word of his trials reached the Red River. Is it true he killed your father?"

Theresa's throat caught. "And my father's housekeeper."

"And a constable," added Vandervoort, properly regretful. Morgan had been more use to him than most.

"No!" Marion Webster found her voice. "I don't believe it. It's all lies and mistakes—"

But the spectators' denunciations drowned the young seamstress out.

"—a proper seraglio, I tell you."

"—ran roughshod over everyone."

"—almost got away with it too."

"—five good pennies I'd pay to look on his worthless hide."

"—a *prize* specimen, that husband of yours."

Now a shiver seemed to pass over the Indian woman, if not of cold then of revulsion against this alien place. She might have pointed out that when she knew Henry Crane he was no murderer, no bigamist.

"I still want to bury him," was all she said.

"We'll help if we can," offered Harris and read in Theresa's eyes that he had spoken her thoughts as well.

The shortness of that night saved him from dreams of Crane

floating in his red lake. Head had barely touched pillows when a hotel servant arrived with shaving water and the news that Miss Sheridan had already left her room.

Harris found her in the breakfast parlour with black coffee before her. The dead black of her dress made her face pale, softening none of its tiredness, and still she glowed with purpose through her mourning weeds, straining towards nine o'clock and the convening of the inquest on her Papa.

"I've had no chance to mark his passing," she pointed out. "It seems a poor ceremony, this tribunal, but Papa would not have thought so. I'm sure he would have had some reminder for me of the Magna Carta pedigree of the coroner's court."

Harris smiled assent and said little.

The prospect of Theresa's accusing Crane to his face of her father's murder had until now overshadowed all other facets of the inquest, which this morning—with Crane absent—appeared in a quite different light. What loomed largest now was the imminent opening of that ornate coffin. The jurors must be sworn in the presence of William Sheridan's remains, whose condition after sixteen weeks Harris could not guess. The hermetic cast-iron casket must have retarded putrefaction—but by how much?

"Will I be required to see Papa?" Theresa suddenly asked.

"No."

"I'd rather remember him chuckling over his mail," she said.

She and Harris were soon breakfasted and walking back west past Sheridan's villa along Front Street. Autumn temperatures kept pedestrians up to a military gait. Septimus Murdock, short of breath as always, was heaving himself along eastward at an even brisker rate, dragging a well-scrubbed boy of six or seven by the hand.

"Hallo, Septimus," called Harris with pleasure. "How are you?"

"Isaac!" exclaimed his old associate. "I've been reading of your exploits in the papers. Bravo. Miss Sheridan I know of course by sight, but won't you introduce us?"

Harris did so. He believed he had mentioned to Theresa his highly industrious accountant and successor. Privately, Harris thought Murdock's new responsibilities must suit him, for the man seemed so much more at ease.

Murdock proclaimed himself delighted at Theresa's safe return.

"Like all my co-religionists," he said, "I greatly admired your late father and sincerely feel your loss. For compassion, for integrity, we'll never see his like."

Harris felt this to be so. However young, the country was old enough to have an irreplaceable past as well as a beckoning future.

"Tributes such as yours are solid comfort," Theresa answered. "And is this intelligent-looking gentleman your son?"

Shyly flattered, the boy dropped his satchel in confusion.

"One of many, I thank God, but the aptest scholar. I must get him off to the cathedral school." Murdock's goateed chin quivered as if he were about to say something quite bold. "I do believe he'll live to see a new harmony between Christian and Christian."

Here was a change, thought Harris. He wondered what could be the cause.

"I pray so," Theresa assented.

"Yes," Murdock continued, "Orange Grand Master Gowan himself has made some most conciliatory statements, and at today's ceremony, both Catholic and Protestant bands are to play. Call on me at the bank, Isaac, soon."

"Gladly," said Harris. "Which ceremony is that?"

"Why, to mark the early completion of Conquest Iron Works!" Murdock gestured towards a new brick chimney towering incongruously above the Front Street villas. "Think of it this afternoon when you hear the horns bray—Roman and Orange brass sounding as one. Come along, Decimus! Ah, Miss Sheridan, if only your father had lived..."

"If only," Theresa said dryly when their haste in opposite directions had carried Murdock out of earshot.

Harris thought to himself how Conquest's erratic fortunes came into that hypothesis. Newbiggins's venture had made Murdock a cashier, liberated Harris to be a full-time detective, and to some extent tempted Crane to become a murderer.

Sword's Hotel lay just ahead on the right. The older villas like William Sheridan's were set back behind gardens, but in the forties the experiment had been made towards York Street of building a row of four attached houses flush with the sidewalk. They did not sell. After ten years' service as Knox Presbyterian College, they had just been renovated and—with the addition of a new wing behind—opened to paying guests. By contrast to the more commercial American Hotel, Sword's was styling itself the choice of parliamentarians. It was into Sword's modern ballroom that Reform statesman William Francis Sheridan's disinterred casket was carried on the morning of Saturday, November 1, to be opened in the course of the inquest and in the presence of the jury.

Theresa arrived to find the spectators' seats already largely occupied by her father's constituents and admirers. The constable had not yet called them to order. A spontaneous and sympathetic hush nonetheless fell upon them as, with Harris at her side, she approached the coffin. It rested on low trestles and had been brushed clean of mud except in the deepest recesses of the abundant scrollwork. Theresa rested her hand upon the box's metal lid, so lately weighted down with earth.

"Here I am," she murmured.

Harris could imagine no words more consoling in the voice of her who had disappeared and was returned. For him, this would always be the memorable moment of a proceeding whose formal results could only be confirmatory, and which Friday's events had drained of any urgency.

Later, when the lid was lifted and the jurors sworn, they considerately uttered no gasps or exclamations, nor let any sign of the cadaver's condition appear in their faces. It transpired that Theresa's testimony would not be heard until after Professor Bernard Lamb had performed his post-mortem examination. This delay seemed for the best. Another week would give her time to recover from recent shocks before publicly relating Sibyl's death.

The inquest adjourned for the day before noon. Theresa looked in the assembly for Dr. Hillyard, but was told her Papa's old friend had been excused from appearing on the grounds of ill health and had again betaken himself to the West Indies.

Jasper Small had also been unexpectedly absent. He greeted Theresa and Harris at the door with inexplicit apologies and an invitation to lunch. He wore a new suit and bowler hat. He ordered Sword's best wine. Plainly his dishevelled state on meeting the train last night had reflected his anxiety alone and not his current fortunes. Had he a new client? After recounting as much of Crane's end as sorted with appetite and digestion, Harris resumed his inquisitor's rôle.

"The Garrison was not required after all, Jasper, but since when have you been on such intimate terms with the Attorney General as to approach him on the subject?"

"In truth, it's my senior partner who has the influence there," said the lawyer with his enigmatic smile. He then answered his own riddle by adding, "Lionel Leonard Matheson."

Harris put down his fork.

"Is he not Henry's lawyer?" asked Theresa in surprise.

"He was," Small gently corrected. "It seems my prosecution of the bigamy case impressed the old fox. When he lost, Henry discharged him—and Matheson felt at liberty to approach me."

"I know him socially," said Harris, "and believe he's honest, but he's a Conservative. Won't that mean quite a change in your work?"

"A John A. Macdonald Conservative, nothing like the hidebound old Tories that Willie Sheridan spent his life battering and educating." Not seeing what he wanted in their eyes, Small looked into his wine glass. He didn't see it there either. "The fact is," he admitted, "I'm no good on my own."

"You did the right thing then," said Theresa. "Now will you represent Henry's widow?"

Small brightened immediately. By not dying on the scaffold

or under sentence of death, Henry had improved Susan Crane's claim on his estate and saved his remains from perhaps being offered to medical students.

"She should thank you, Isaac, for letting him bleed," said the lawyer. "I can't imagine how you bore it—but then I've never been on a deer hunt."

"It wasn't the least like a deer hunt," Harris affirmed. "And I'm not sure I did do right to let him bleed in William Sheridan's bedroom."

"A fitting enough place," said Theresa. "Besides, it's All Saints Day. The ghosts are gone."

"Really, Theresa?" said Small. "I didn't know you held these quaint beliefs."

"Perhaps I don't," she rejoined with a smile, "but neither do I believe it was up to Isaac whether Henry lived or died. You disarmed him, Isaac. You prevented his escape. What was most required you did. Tell us, though, could you also have performed a ligature of the femoral artery? No? From what I saw, nothing less would have stopped the bleeding."

Harris felt steadied. Less and less seemed to stand between him and the new life with Theresa. He would need employment, of course, but nothing exalted. Last time, in waiting to be made cashier before he contemplated marriage, he had waited too long.

As the three friends were leaving the hotel, Theresa spied a patroness of the new Toronto General Hospital, with whom she stopped to a exchange a word.

"Before I forget," said Small, handing Harris an envelope, "this is from York Foundry. I believe you are being offered a position."

Here was a happy opportunity, thought Harris, though—with Conquest poised to cast its first rail—far from a sinecure. He perused and pocketed the letter.

"Your atheism distresses certain of the directors, but for some reason they do not consider your departure from the Provincial Bank a sign of unsteadiness."

Harris inferred that York Foundry had got wind of his futile attempt to protect their confidences from Newbiggins. Murdock had perhaps said something. Not feeling at liberty to resolve Small's puzzlement, Harris covered a smile by asking whether the lawyer had taken quite all his old clients to Matheson.

"Not quite. I haven't seen Esther myself since returning from Montreal, but my personal affairs are still rather untidy."

"Spare me the particulars," Harris entreated.

"Between the two of us, I believe I now share a mistress with the inspector of police." An amorous glint came into Small's grey eyes. "It's intolerable, but that thieving young tigress Nan Hogan has me between her paws."

Theresa's return mercifully redirected conversation to the imminent probate of her father's will. When Small left for his new office on King Street East, she rather less felicitously suggested stopping in to see what the villa she was inheriting would need to make it habitable.

New carpeting and floor in the bedroom, Harris grumbled to himself. It seemed soon to him, barely twelve hours since the removal of Crane's body—far too soon to be again pushing open the kitchen door and climbing the fourteen noiseless steps to the main floor. He insisted they not go higher.

In the front parlour, Theresa began pulling dust sheets from the furniture, starting with the pianoforte and a modern easy chair. The sight of the chair, ornately carved and heavily fringed, seemed to make her tremble. Into it she sank, covering her lowered face with her hands. Her inclined neck looked terrifyingly delicate with its lovely dark mole to the left of the nape. She wept softly at first. Presently she cried in strong, keening wails that shivered Harris to the core.

He touched her shoulder, then knelt before her and caught her in his arms as she, falling forward, threw hers about him. She cried more quietly, but for a very long time. She was at home. No one could see or hear. She was far from Harris, even as she pressed her moist cheek to his shirt front, far inside one of many private griefs. Part of her had disappeared again. He knew helplessly that, even though she gave herself to him, there would always be these times when she went from him, and he would be left wondering whether to search or wait.

"Was it your father's favourite chair?" he asked at last.

"No." Theresa finished crying and cleared her throat. "I can't explain. The chair has no closer connection to him than does anything else."

With these words, her arms tightened around Harris. Her tears flowed again. Through her plain wool bodice he felt her rib cage heave. His knees were numb with kneeling, as must hers have been, yet neither could bear to move.

Eventually, through the curtained south windows, march music drifted from the Esplanade.

"What's that?" Theresa asked in something like her normal voice.

"Conquest Iron Works," said Harris. "Your new neighbours."

"I had forgotten." She tore off her black bonnet and tried to push the hair off her forehead. "I detest factories and steam engines," she said, "don't you?"

Harris hesitated. He meant to fight Conquest's fire with York's, to match forge with forge, to bring ore from Lake Superior and build the new iron age. Despite specific misgivings, of an aesthetic nature mostly, he believed in industry. He believed in employment opportunities, a shrinking world, affordable goods widely distributed. One could not detest the entire tenor of one's age—but then he knew that behind her words Theresa had something much more specific in mind, the career of industrialist Henry Crane.

"How do they make us better or healthier?" she insisted.

"We were bad enough before steam," said Harris. "Look at MacFarlane and his cholera brig."

Theresa squirmed a little. "To think he'll be knighted!"

Harris regretted not having asked Crane about the future Sir George, whose confidence on board the train subsequent events had so conveniently justified. Crane was gone now, Hillyard indisposed, and MacFarlane's title would have to be borne with.

"Perhaps," said Harris, "the fundamental evil is haste. Henry could not wait for Conquest's fortunes to improve, and George could not wait for the quarantine."

"You were *too* patient in the old days, Isaac." Theresa disengaged herself altogether from his embrace, the more thoroughly to look him over. "I like you better now."

The marching bands had reached the new iron works and fallen silent. Now they struck up an infectious Offenbach polka.

The music on top of Theresa's gratifying avowal restored feeling to Harris's legs. On an impulse, he rose and extended his arms to Theresa where she sat, her skirt a wide black pool on the green and yellow carpet. Its sylvan pattern of twisting branches and curling leaves throbbed with delicious life.

"Do you mean for us to dance?" she asked in amazement.

Harris smiled and tried to catch her hands.

"Well, say it!" she insisted, a challenging sparkle in her large, green eyes. "Don't leave me in any doubt about your intentions."

"Wicked, I assure you. Come here."

"I haven't for years. I don't think I can."

"You can." Harris would leave her in no doubt. "Theresa, I'm asking you for this dance…and all the rest."

He led her to the unobstructed centre of the room. Side by side, they hopped and stepped forward, then back, to French music played by Toronto Protestants and Catholics for a Yankee venture. Behind drawn curtains the half light was theirs alone. Harris counted out the time.

"One—*two*—three—four."

"Like this!" Theresa cried, finding her way. She swayed into the music with a supple grace unknown among the polka dancers at the Peninsula Hotel. "Tell me, Isaac," she said. "Would you have looked inside Etta Lansing's shack if I had not called out?"

"Etta Lansing and her great scimitar of a knife were protecting *something* in there. I couldn't have left without finding out what." In a sense, he had not found Theresa at all, but had allowed her to find him—and knowing she had wanted to find him felt damned good. "Face to face now," he said. "I step back with you pursuing, then reverse."

"The music has stopped," she pointed out.

"No matter."

When they stopped at last, it was to kiss. Her fingers encircled the back of his neck. His cradled her slender black waist. Each returned the eager pressure of the other's body through all the petticoats and skirts, the trousers and drawers, the plackets and flies.

If the bands had started up again, they didn't hear.

Author's Note

Characters appearing in these pages are fictitious, and none should be identified with any actual person, living or dead. Streets and places, on the other hand, are depicted as faithfully as possible. Their names reflect 1850s usage; some have changed over the decades since.

Acknowledgements

A novel in a new voice can never have too many friends. It is a great pleasure to acknowledge here some of the people without whom *Death in the Age of Steam* might never have reached your hands. Invaluable early encouragement and advice came from Carol Jackson, Bonnie Laing, Robert Ward and Greg Ioannou. Through the Humber School for Writers Correspondence Programme, I had the great good fortune to develop the manuscript with Paul Quarrington, and to profit from his wise and sympathetic coaching. Parts of the novel were also supportively critiqued by George Fetherling and Austin Clarke. Both were made accessible by the University of Toronto's School of Continuing Studies, and both gave more than duty required. The opportunity to work with these three authors has been an honour.

I'd like to say a special thank you to two technical experts. Professor Roger Hall of the University of Western Ontario helped me with the historical details of pre-Confederation Canada, while Patricia Cooper vetted the manuscript with the keen eye of a horse owner. Both prevented me from committing many errors, and neither can be blamed for those—few, I hope—that remain. I know I made no mistake in entrusting this novel to my agent, Tina Tsallas of Great Titles Incorporated, for she introduced it and me to RendezVous Press. Working with publisher Sylvia McConnell and editor Allister Thompson has been a joy. Finally, I would like to thank my family, who never once told me I was wasting my time by writing—or even thought it.

Photo by Brett Newsome

Mel Bradshaw was born in Toronto, Ontario, and took his B.A. in English and philosophy at the University of Toronto. He continued studying philosophy—mostly ethics and aesthetics—at New College, Oxford.

Between degrees, he spent two years forgetting winter in Southeast Asia. Under the auspices of Canadian University Service Overseas, he taught English in northern Thailand and did odd jobs in Jakarta, Indonesia. He has also travelled to Zambia, Iceland, Poland, and points between. He now lives in his native town, devoting as much time as possible to reading and writing.